AND THE

She felt his breath fan her face as he bent to her lips. She couldn't believe he was kissing her—not this gorgeous creature with the fierce eyes. And she couldn't believe she was letting him, after the way he had insulted her. So how could she sit here and let him touch her like this?

Yet she couldn't move. She felt as if she had risen out of her body and was watching him kiss someone else, for she was so tense she couldn't allow herself to enjoy the touch of him. And all the while, she longed to forget her doubts and wrap her arms around his shoulders, plunge her hands into his glossy raven hair, and crush him to her. Deep down she had an unfathomable hunger for this man, a hunger that denied all logic.

"Author Patricia Simpson . . . a masterful storyteller."
—*Romantic Times*

Also by Patricia Simpson

Whisper of Midnight
The Legacy

Available from HarperPaperbacks

RAVEN IN AMBER

PATRICIA SIMPSON

HarperPaperbacks
A Division of HarperCollinsPublishers

This is a work of fiction. The characters, incidents, and dialogues are products of the author's imagination and are not to be construed as real. Any resemblance to actual events or persons, living or dead, is entirely coincidental.

HarperPaperbacks   *A Division of* HarperCollins*Publishers*
                    10 East 53rd Street, New York, N.Y. 10022

Cover photography by Herman Estevez

First printing: July 1993

Printed in the United States of America

HarperPaperbacks, HarperMonogram, and colophon are trademarks of HarperCollins*Publishers*

10 9 8 7 6 5 4 3 2 1

To Ol-Ha-The
Whose fierce beauty inspired this book.

PROLOGUE

Charleston, 1972

Ten-year-old Camille Avery walked across the attic floor, sneezing and calling for her grandmother's cat. She knew Solomon was up here somewhere. She had seen him dash into the dusty old room moments ago.

"So-lo-mon," she called, trying to keep the annoyance out of her voice. She knew that if the cat sensed the slightest threat in her voice, he wouldn't come to her. And he must. His life depended upon it. Her father, who sat in the car outside, had warned her that he wouldn't wait forever. As far as he was concerned, the damned cat deserved to be left behind if it couldn't cooperate like a decent animal.

"Ah-*chew!*"

Camille rubbed her nose and searched the shadowed corners of the attic, sneezing from the dust that kicked up with every step she took. It was odd to see Grandmother

Avery's attic empty. The huge space under the roof had always been stuffed with trunks and boxes full of family memorabilia. But Grandmother was dead now, the house was going to be put on the market, and all her belongings had been sold at an auction or given away to members of the family. Camille glanced around, thinking about her grandmother's funeral. She wished she hadn't seen Grandmother's face all stiff like that. A creepy feeling stole across the skin on Camille's shoulders and neck, and she wished that her older sisters had come back into the house with her. But neither Marissa nor Christine liked the cat enough to look for him.

"So-lo-mon. Come here, kitty-kitty."

If Solomon didn't show up in a few minutes, he would be doomed to spend the rest of his life in his dead mistress's empty house. That would really be creepy.

Camille heard the cat meow. The sound came from the chimney at one end of the attic. Though that part of the attic was bathed in shadow, she walked bravely over to the brick column and inspected the wall behind it. The wall was covered with mildew and cracks and rotting shelves, part of the old section of the house that had been built over two hundred years ago, according to the stories Grandmother Avery had told her. Camille held her breath and looked up, trying to see into the gloom where the wall met the rafters. She could hear the cat meowing, but she couldn't see him. She sidled closer, straining to locate him.

Then her foot came down on a loose board, flipping up a small piece of the flooring and scaring her witless. With a yelp she jumped backward, flushing first with fright and then at her own silly behavior. Something glowed near the tip of her shoe. At first she thought of cat eyes, of Solomon's green-gold eyes and how they glowed in the dark.

But Solomon couldn't be under the floorboards. He just wouldn't fit.

Intrigued, Camille hunkered down, craning her neck to see into the space. There, half-hidden by the floorboards, was a small chunk of yellow-gold rock, or something that looked like a rock. Could it be gold? A buried treasure? A thousand possibilities sprang to mind as Camille pulled out the rock, ignoring the cobwebs that clung to her hand.

The rock was attached to a leather thong, which she used to hold the necklace up to the faint light in the attic. She knew from her science class at school that the rock wasn't gold. It was amber, fossilized resin formed thousands of years ago. Awestruck, Camille grasped the chunk of amber in her fist while the leather thong draped over her fingers. The amber was heavy in her palms and smooth, the kind of smoothness that made her want to stroke it. How beautiful it was. How ancient. She could feel its age and its worth. And locked inside the amber, as if floating in the gem, was a black feather.

Who had hidden the necklace beneath the floor? And when? The necklace might have been there for a few years or a few hundred years. If she hadn't seen it glowing, she might not have even noticed it. Glowing? She frowned. How could the amber have glowed? It must have been a trick of light, some kind of reflection. Yet there were no windows near the chimney. A chill bristled the hairs on her neck. Then she felt something soft and warm rub the backs of her legs. Startled, she looked down.

"Solomon!" she gasped. "You silly cat!" She scooped him up before he could run away again, then slipped the amber necklace into the pocket of her skirt. She wanted to show her sisters what she had found. They'd never believe it.

Camille hurried down the stairs and shut the front door

behind her. Her father's Monte Carlo idled in the driveway while her sisters argued about who was going to sit up front with their dad. For a moment Camille watched their senseless, endless bickering. Then she decided she wouldn't tell Marissa and Christine about the necklace after all. They wouldn't understand. They never understood the things she talked about. And they might laugh. She hated it when they laughed at her.

1

Crescent Bay, Washington—
Nineteen Years Later

Camille Avery stood at the crossroad and wondered what madness had compelled her to come to Crescent Bay. She didn't like to travel, yet here she was—two thousand miles from her home in Charleston, South Carolina. She had taken a leave of absence from her job and had contracted to illustrate a book on the Nakalt Indians even though she had sold only a few major pieces of her work and still thought of herself as an amateur artist. Madness—that's what it was. Stark, raving early-onset midlife-crisis madness. Camille clenched her teeth. She was only twenty-nine, her teaching career well on track, her financial future seemingly secure. Why, then, hadn't it been enough for her? Why this compulsion to escape to the far reaches of the continent?

Twenty minutes ago a Greyhound bus had dropped her at the edge of the Nakalt Indian Reservation, where her friend Barbara had promised to meet her. But Barbara was nowhere in sight. For twenty minutes Camille had waited alongside the lonely highway without seeing a single sign of life. There was no light, no phone, no evidence of civilization other than the decrepit bus shelter behind her. And night was falling like a shroud upon the trees.

Impatiently Camille glanced down the gravel road that bisected the highway, wondering how far she was from the actual town of Crescent Bay. Normally she wouldn't care if she had to wait a few minutes, but it was getting late and a storm was blowing out of the north, sending frosty gusts and pellets of rain against her face and hands. She was woefully underdressed for such weather.

A gust of wind blasted her trench coat flat against her legs and whipped her short hair into a platinum flag. She clapped a hand to the side of her head and squinted at her watch. Four-ten. She was out of patience and starting to doubt that anyone would come for her at all. The January afternoon was gloomy and spooky, the forest around her full of swaying cedars and trembling alders. Dead leaves cartwheeled across the deserted highway and impaled themselves on brambles in the ditch. Camille blew on her fists, wondering where Barbara could be. What if she had been confused over her arrival time? Camille had often teased her friend about her absentminded ways. But could Barbara have forgotten her entirely?

After another minute, Camille decided to quit waiting and do something productive. She hoisted her heavy suitcases off the ground and set off down the gravel road, humming to keep her mind off the darkening sky and the cutting handles of her bags. As if her song had summoned forth the great god of precipitation, snow started to blow out of the sky.

"Ducky," she muttered, glaring at the flakes swirling around her. "Just ducky."

A half hour later she saw the first buildings of the reservation—two one-story houses badly in need of paint, and a tavern called the Sand Bar. Light poured from the windows of the bar while country-western music twanged over the wind. A glowing red *R*, the neon logo of the Rainier Brewery, hung crookedly in the window by the door. Camille set down her bags and rolled her aching shoulders as she surveyed the tavern. She disliked going into restaurants alone, but not half as much as entering a tavern out in the middle of nowhere without a companion. Either she had to stand outdoors and freeze or go inside and use the phone to call Barbara. Going in was the lesser of two evils at this point.

Camille picked up her bags and trudged to the tavern door, her tired arms and shoulders crying for mercy. She pushed open the door and walked in, and the sour smell of smoke and beer hit her full force. For a moment she just stood there, reeling from the smell and adjusting to the light and noise. Then she noticed all eyes had turned to stare, all male eyes—black and dark brown—as the Nakalt fishermen and sawmill workers surveyed her with suspicion.

She raised her chin. Because of her hair, she had been the object of stares ever since she could remember. She had hoped the snow might disguise her unusual white-blond hair, but from the looks directed at her, her hair shone through like a searchlight. Like a light bulb. Like a Q-Tip. She had been called all those names and many more. Each cruel label from her childhood still branded her memory.

"Hey!" a man shouted from the nearby pool table. "Look what the wind blew in!"

Camille ignored him and trudged to the bar, doing her best to hang on to her bags without bumping anyone.

A man tipped back his chair, preventing passage, and looked up at her. He smiled. His two upper front teeth were missing, and his hair was shaggy and unkempt. He wore an old plaid shirt, open down the front, and a tattered, grimy T-shirt. Camille pulled up short.

"Pardon me," she said.

"In a hurry, miss?"

"Yes, as a matter of fact."

"Relax. I'll buy you a drink."

"Thanks, some other time, perhaps."

"Some other time!" His companion elbowed him in the ribs. "Listen to that, would you! Some other time!"

Camille stared down at the chair blocking her path, hoping the man would recognize her intention to pass, but he just laughed.

"Ben, leave her alone," the bartender called, dragging a towel around the bottom of a glass pitcher.

Camille shot the bartender a glance of gratitude as Ben reluctantly tipped his chair upright. She could still hear him chuckling as she squeezed up to the bar.

"Thanks," she said to the bartender, smiling wanly.

He didn't smile back. In fact, he didn't look her in the eye. Camille felt a twinge of unease.

"Want a drink?" he asked.

"No thanks. Is there a phone I could use?"

With a nod of his head, he indicated the pay phone on the wall by the rest rooms. To get to it, Camille would have to walk the length of the bar, go past the pool table, and skirt the jukebox, offering herself at close range to every man in the place. But she had no choice. She had to call Barbara.

She left her bags at the foot of the bar and straightened her shoulders. Then, focusing her eyes on a distant plane, she ran the gauntlet, without actually seeing the face of a single man or making eye contact. Even though there were a few lewd comments and wolf whistles, she didn't quicken her pace. But by the time she got to the phone and rummaged in her purse for change, her hands were shaking.

She nearly dropped the quarter before she got it into the round slot, and then she plugged her free ear with her index finger so she could hear over the din of the music.

Barbara's phone rang and rang. Camille clenched her teeth and let it ring nine more times. Where was Barb? She was already late by at least an hour. How long could it possibly take to drive from the cabin to the bus stop? Certainly not this long.

Camille sighed. She'd just have to take a cab. She looked down but couldn't see a phone book, only the empty black plastic binder. Exasperated, she clanged the receiver into the cradle and turned. This time fewer men paid attention to her as she returned to the end of the bar. The bartender glanced at her with a dour look in his bloodshot eyes.

"Is there a taxi around here?" Camille asked.

The man next to her snorted in answer.

"I guess not," Camille murmured more to herself than anyone else as she turned toward the door, wondering what options she had in this remote place. Other than Barbara, she didn't know a soul here. She had no map and no idea how far Barbara's cabin was from the tavern. What was she going to do? A wave of panic swept through her, tightening her throat, but she refused to give in to it. She suddenly realized how her teaching position at an exclusive girls' school outside Charleston had isolated her. She wasn't accustomed to dealing with the outside world, public transportation or the lack of it, or groups of men. Living at the Lewis Academy had sheltered her from threatening situations but at the same time had taken a toll on her independence.

Camille set her jaw. She could handle being thrust back into the world like this. She was capable and logical. As long as she didn't give in to panic, she'd be fine. Barbara's absence was a minor inconvenience and nothing more.

"Car trouble?" the bartender asked.

Camille turned back to face him. "No. Someone was supposed to meet me at the bus stop and didn't show up."

"Where're you headed?" the bartender asked.

"To Barbara Stanton's. Out on Crescent Bay Drive."

"That'd be by the Makinna Lodge," Ben put in, smiling. "Have a drink and I'll drive you, lady. I just ain't ready to leave yet."

She forced a polite smile. "Thank you, no." She bent down to get her bags, worrying that Ben or some other man might make a more insistent offer. "I think I'll wait for her outside. I'm sure she'll show up any minute."

"I wouldn't hang around out there, if I was you," warned the man near her elbow. Camille glanced at him.

"Things is out there. Things in the dark." His eyes looked bleary, his speech was slurred. He was half-drunk, hardly a man to take seriously.

"I'm not afraid of the dark," Camille answered, sounding more brave than she felt.

"You should be." The drunk squinted at her and then hunched back over his beer.

Feeling more uneasy than she had when she'd entered the tavern, Camille walked to the door. A stocky man with long hair in a ponytail opened it for her, giving her a warning look that silently echoed the comments of the drunk at the bar.

"Thanks," she said, and staggered through the small parking lot to the gravel road. She sucked in the clean air and forced herself to hurry, wanting to leave the Sand Bar Tavern as far behind her as possible in case someone decided to follow her and cause trouble.

She hustled past the two houses and around a bend in the road, stepping into a puddle full of chilled water that soaked one shoe and nylon stocking. Barbara, in her forgetful way, had failed to mention that Camille should have brought a down parka and boots. Camille continued on, throwing glances over her shoulder to make sure she wasn't being followed. The road twisted through a grove of cedar that blocked the wind but also the light. Camille could see nothing but black shapes on either side of her. The hairs on the back of her neck rose and she quickened her steps, breathing raggedly with the effort of lugging her bags at a half run.

Suddenly a black shape swooped down at her, cawing so loudly and frightening her so thoroughly that she shrieked and dropped her suitcases, shielding her head with her forearms. The bird swooped again, flapping its huge wings close enough to her face that she felt a draft. Camille lost her grip on her panic and screamed.

The bird swooped again. Camille caught a glimpse of its body. The bird was at least two feet long, with a wing span of three feet or more. What kind of bird was it? And why was it attacking her? Screaming, Camille flailed her arms to keep the bird away and stumbled through the grove.

She broke clear of the cedars, skittered around a bend in the road, and ran headlong into a young man. He grabbed her to keep her from falling backward and then held her away from him, staring at her as if she were crazy.

"What's the matter?" he questioned. "What's going on?"

"That bird!" Camille sputtered, pointing behind her. "That bird attacked me!"

"What bird?"

Camille broke away and whirled to look behind her. No bird was in sight. She couldn't believe it had vanished so quickly. But there *had* been a bird. Even though the youth couldn't see it, she knew it had been there, for she wasn't the type of person to succumb to wild imaginings. Unable to explain the bird's disappearance, Camille slowly turned back to the young man.

"There was a bird in those woods back there," she insisted. "It flew down at me."

"I don't see any bird." He craned his neck to look past her.

"It was there. It was huge!"

"Well, it's gone now."

Camille glanced at him. He was taller than her by a head, even though he was not more than fifteen or sixteen years old.

"I heard you screaming," he went on. "I thought someone was being killed or something."

"No, it was just that bird. . . ." Camille's voice trailed off as she ran a hand through her hair, pushing back her bangs, damp from the run. She was shaking and unnerved and trying hard not to let it show.

"What are you doing out here, anyway?" he asked.

"It's a long story." She retied the loose belt of her trench coat. "I was supposed to meet someone, but she never showed. And I was walking to her cabin when that bird attacked me back there."

The youth raised his black eyebrows at the mention of the bird again. But he quickly hid his expression of disbelief and blew on his cupped hands. She felt no threat from the shaggy-haired boy. He was taller than she was, but his face was open and innocent, with kind, dark eyes.

"Do you want me to walk you to where you're going?" he offered, hunching his shoulders inside his jean jacket. He looked as cold as she felt.

"Would you?" She smiled in relief.

"Sure. I'm just killing time out here anyway."

"I'm not really sure where my friend's cabin is, though."

"Who's your friend?"

"Barbara Stanton. Someone told me her place was near the Makinna Lodge."

"Oh, yeah, Barbara's. You must be her friend from Charleston."

"Yes!" She smiled again, relieved to finally meet someone who could help her. "Barbara was supposed to have picked me up at the bus stop, but she didn't make it."

"You walked all the way from the main road?" he asked, incredulous.

"Yes."

"Barbara's cabin is about four miles from here. But my uncle Kit can give you a ride."

"I'd appreciate it. I'm Camille Avery," she said, offering her hand.

He took hers, suddenly shy. "I'm Adam Makinna."

"Of the Makinna Lodge?"

"Yeah."

"I'm so glad to meet you." Camille squeezed his hand. "I can't tell you how much!"

Adam Makinna took her around another few bends in the road until they came upon the outskirts of a small town dotted with lights. One of the first houses they came to, a brown ranch with a bare front yard and a black Jeep Cherokee parked in the driveway, belonged to George Makinna, Adam's great-grandfather. In the deepening dusk, the colors grayed and blended like a murky watercolor. Adam led Camille up the walk and ushered her inside, cautioning her to be quiet.

Camille stepped into the house, and the warmth from the fireplace met her chilled face like a soothing blanket. She sighed and glanced around, noticing that four old men sat on the floor in front of the fire, their legs folded beneath them, their eyes closed. One of them had both palms raised as he chanted in a monotone and swayed forward and backward. His arms were the emaciated limbs of the truly ancient, more like weathered wood than flesh and bone.

The interior of the house lay in shadow, with only the light of the fire to illuminate the long room. Camille could see the outline of another man standing near the far wall, his arms crossed, his head at such an angle that she was certain he was looking at her, the only one in the room to take notice of her arrival. The even voice of the old man droned on.

Adam closed the door quietly and held a finger to his lips when Camille turned to ask what was going on. Was she a witness to a Nakalt ritual? Barbara's manuscript about the Nakalt had mentioned many different ceremonies, some never seen by outsiders or even most members of the tribe. Camille watched in awe, wishing she had a sketch pad. She'd just have to remember the scene so she could draw it later to use in the book she was illustrating for Barbara.

The chant droned on, but Camille didn't mind. She was thankful to be in a warm room. Her feet were blocks of ice, her hands were numb with cold, and the tips of her ears burned. Gradually she thawed as the chant continued. Then she noticed how warm the amber amulet felt against her skin. Surprised, she put her hand to her chest, wondering what was happening.

She wore the necklace always, nestled between her breasts and out of view. It was her personal talisman, and she never showed it to anyone, not even Barbara, afraid that showing it to the world would lessen its magic. But in the nineteen years she'd worn the necklace, she'd never felt it grow warm like this. Never once had it caused her fear or surprise—not until she had come to this strange place.

If the amber got any warmer, it would burn her skin. But she couldn't very well pluck it out of her shirt, not in front of a roomful of strangers. She shut her eyes, wondering how hot the amulet would get and how long she could last without asking to be shown the bathroom.

Not a second too soon, the chanting stopped. The heat of the amulet tapered off. Camille breathed a sigh of relief, wondering what was happening to her. For a woman who didn't let her imagination get the better of her, she was certainly having a weird evening—first the huge bird and now the strangeness of the amber.

She opened her eyes and was shocked to see the old men scrambling to their feet at the sight of her. One of the men stepped forward, his eyes ablaze with anger.

"What is the meaning of this?" he demanded. His face was covered with liver spots and wrinkles.

Camille gaped at him and then realized he had directed the question to Adam, who stood behind her. She stepped aside.

"I'm sorry, sir, I didn't—"

"You didn't what, boy!"

"I didn't—" Adam looked at Camille and then at the

man standing in the shadows across the room, as if searching for the right words. "Hell, I didn't—"

"No profanity, Adam Makinna."

"Yes, sir." Adam hung his head.

The old man surveyed Camille coldly. His lower jaw protruded over his upper, like a bulldog. "You had no right to interrupt our ceremony."

"I'm sorry," Camille said. "I didn't know."

"You profane our sacred prayers."

"I had no idea. I'm truly sorry—"

"Let her be, Charlie," said the man at the far wall. He sauntered across the floor. "She is obviously contrite."

"But this is an outrage!" The old man's chest heaved with anger. "A woman—a white woman—has witnessed the resurrection prayer!"

"I know, Charlie. But what can one woman matter? You and Old Man must have chanted that resurrection prayer every night for a hundred years. One off night isn't going to matter."

Camille glanced up at the man speaking such sensible words but couldn't make out his features in the shadows of the dimly lit room. She caught glimpses as he spoke, of a face comprised of sharp angles, narrow nose, and flaring jawline. But she couldn't tell how old a man he was or whether his face reflected the authority she could hear in his deep voice.

"Don't be flip with me, Kitsap Makinna," Charlie retorted. "You may choose not to practice the old ways, but your grandfather and I know better than to anger the spirits."

"Don't you think the spirits would countenance an honest mistake?" Kit asked, laying a hand on Charlie's shoulder and bestowing a smile on him. Camille caught a glimpse of his smile in the firelight, a smile that could melt a woman's heart in an instant—not the heart of a sensible woman like herself, certainly, but one of those other females easily swayed by masculine charm. Then Kit leveled his gaze upon his nephew. "It was an honest mistake, wasn't it, Adam?"

"I was just trying to help Miss Avery. I told her you'd give her a lift, Uncle Kit, that's all."

"I didn't mean to cause any trouble," Camille interjected. The dark gaze landed on her then, and she felt herself flush. "I—" Additional excuses died on her lips. Flustered, she broke eye contact, glancing at the old man who had chanted. He was staring at the far wall, his black eyes glowing in the darkness beneath heavy lids. Even though she knew he wasn't looking at her, Camille sensed he was listening intently, tuned to something deep inside her. She wasn't wanted here. And she didn't want to linger another minute.

"I'll go," she said breathlessly, turning. "I'm sorry to have interrupted." She reached for the handle on the front door and pulled it open.

"Wait a minute," Kit called after her.

Camille fled from the house, Adam at her heels and Kit striding to catch up as he pulled on his coat.

"Miss Avery!" he called. His voice was deep and commanding, but Camille ignored him and kept walking toward the town. There were no sidewalks, and she sloshed through mud and standing water without bothering to go around the wet areas. She had to get far away from the house and those ancient listening ears. She had to get to something familiar, a place where she could collapse and regain her composure.

Kit and Adam caught up with her.

"Miss Avery—" Kit reached for her arm, but she shook him off.

"Please leave me alone," she said, staring straight ahead. "I'll take care of myself."

"Don't let Charlie get to you."

She took a deep breath, battling the urge to break into tears. It wasn't just Charlie that had got to her, it was everything on the reservation, especially that old man with the emaciated arms and knowing eyes. "Please, I need to be alone!"

"She needs a ride to Barbara Stanton's cabin, Uncle Kit," Adam said. "I told her you'd take her."

"Sure. We're going out there anyway. What do you say, Miss Avery?"

Camille stopped, weary and worried. "I don't want to cause any more trouble."

"You're no trouble." Adam cocked his head to see the expression on her lowered face. "It was my fault. I shouldn't have taken you in there."

"An understatement, Adam." Kit urged Camille to turn around and retrace her steps to his Jeep. Camille pulled away from the hand that cupped her elbow, but he seemed to take little notice of her reaction to his touch. She walked alongside the two Nakalt men, listening more to the rumble of Kit's voice than to the words he was saying to his nephew.

"If your father were alive, he'd whip the tar out of you, Adam."

"I thought they'd be done with the ritual when I got back."

"Well, they weren't. And you never should have brought a woman into the house, not even if she was Mother Teresa."

"But why are you so mad, Uncle Kit? What's it to you? You don't believe in all that mumbo-jumbo, do you?"

"Even if I don't, I still respect the elders. I observe their rules and respect their wishes. You'd be wise to do the same. You're a Makinna, Adam, a descendent of great chiefs. You must keep that in mind in everything you do."

"My dad said those days were over. No one cares about the old chiefs anymore. I know you don't."

"I care, Adam. I just don't expect an ancient one to turn up and solve everybody's problems."

They reached the car, and Kit strode to the other side of the Jeep. Adam let Camille sit up front while he settled into the back. Camille sank onto the bucket seat, thankful to be off her feet after nearly two hours of walking and standing, not to mention her long bus ride from Seattle. She sighed, aware that Kit was studying her as he started the car. She closed her eyes and leaned her head against the seat cushion, trying to force the tenseness out of her neck.

"Don't you have any belongings?" Kit asked as he backed out of the driveway.

Camille slowly opened her eyes as the realization struck her. She had forgotten all about the suitcases she had dropped in the road during the bird attack. With her luck, someone had probably driven over her bags and ruined her clothes, not to mention her drawing equipment. Where had her mind gone? Since her first step onto the Nakalt Reservation, she had entered a topsy-turvy world over which she had no control. She felt as if someone had blindfolded her, spun her around, and sent her stumbling in the dark. She had never liked the game of blindman's buff. And she liked the Nakalt version even less.

Camille glared out the window. If her clothing and supplies were ruined, she would take it as a sign and go back to Charleston where she belonged.

2

"Come on, Doc," Donald Two Hand complained, leaning on his shovel. "We're not going to find the gold in the dark. Let's call it a day and get out of here."

Oscar Duarte straightened, took off his hat, and wiped his forehead with the sleeve of his coat. Was it that late? He glanced out to sea where the Strait of Juan de Fuca met the Pacific Ocean. A faint sheen still showed at the horizon, but a purple curtain slowly sank upon the band of light, and a cold wind blew out of the north around the edge of Vancouver Island, heralding a wicked storm. Oscar was afraid of water, especially the sea, and didn't relish crossing back to the mainland during a squall. But surely another half hour of digging wouldn't hurt.

Oscar looked back at the Nakalt man leaning on the shovel at the other side of the pit. Two Hand was a stout man with an incredible set of shoulders, the kind of man who was so obviously capable of defending himself that no one ever challenged him. But no matter how many times Oscar tried to convince Two Hand that he needn't fear the Island of the Dead, he was never successful in keeping the man here after nightfall. Sometimes he wondered if Two Hand used superstition as a way to dodge the labor of digging all these holes. As far as Oscar was concerned, the Nakalt were a good-for-nothing, misdirected people with a real lack of a decent work ethic. He wouldn't be surprised if Two Hand was only pretending to be frightened of the spirits rumored to haunt this place. Oscar had never seen anything strange or unusual in all the weeks he had spent on the island looking for buried treasure.

His only real fear was to be discovered again by a Nakalt who was not as easily bought as Two Hand had been. That fool David Makinna had almost ruined everything and had taken up much valuable time.

At the rate they were going, they'd never find the gold, especially not with the way Two Hand worked. But Oscar didn't dare trust anyone else to help dig. Gold was a powerful presence, much more dangerous than any of Two Hand's restless spirits. Gold could induce a man to do things he normally wouldn't dream of doing; Oscar knew that well enough. And he hadn't come this far for nothing. Oscar replaced his hat on his thinning brown hair.

"A few more shovelfuls, Two Hand. I feel lucky."

"Oh, yeah?" Donald retorted. "I keep telling you, Doc. There's only one kind of luck around here—*bad* luck."

"Look—" Oscar waved an arc in the air with his left hand and then his right. "No spirits on the left, no spirits on the right. I don't see a thing."

"Don't talk like that." Donald glanced nervously over his shoulder. "Besides, some spirits you can't see."

"Oh? Which ones?"

"The dead." He dropped his shovel. "Come on, Doc.

Let's go. I'm serious. Besides, there's a storm coming and we don't want to get caught in it."

Oscar looked at his watch. "Listen, Two Hand. It's only seven-thirty. We could work for another half hour."

"No way, man. Not this guy." Donald backed away and reached down for the coat he had tossed on a clump of dried grass. "It's getting too dark."

"You're a coward, Two Hand."

"Oh, yeah?" He jabbed his arms into the sleeves of his jacket. "Well, I'm not a dried up old fish like you, Duarte. I've got some years ahead of me. And I plan to live to enjoy them."

"If we don't find this gold, my good fellow, neither of us is going to enjoy the remainder of our lives, be they short or long."

Oscar scooped another shovelful of dirt out of the hole, ignoring the shooting pains in his back as he tossed the dirt aside. Two Hand paced the edge of the hole, anxious to leave. Oscar threw another load to the side and another.

"For God's sake, Doc. Give it up!" Two Hand bounced in agitation. "Something's going on. Look at the ground!" He pointed to a spot ten feet behind Oscar.

Oscar turned and glanced down, watching the sod tremble and part slightly to expose fresh sandy loam.

"Spirits, Doc!"

Oscar chuckled. "Moles, you idiot!"

Oscar could tell that his explanation hadn't sunk in by the way Two Hand watched the ground with fear in his eyes. Exasperated, he tossed his shovel into the pit. Another half hour wasted. Another day and still no sign of the gold he knew was buried somewhere on this island. More time lost because of a superstitious fool. An idiotic, superstitious fool.

"Come on, Doc!" Two Hand turned and dashed toward the beach, stumbling in his haste to get off the island.

Oscar followed at a stately pace, unafraid and unwilling to rush. Besides, each day of digging wore him out and made every muscle—every bone—in his body ache all night. He wasn't a young man. He was sixty-seven years old, his days of excavating long since past. He was surviving these weeks on a diet of painkillers and little else. But it would all be worth the trouble. Once he found the Spanish gold buried on the island, his suffering would be forgotten. And he was going to find the gold, even if it killed him.

Mak-ee-nah felt the bone-crushing weight again, on his back, his shoulders, his head and limbs. The weight was so heavy he could barely take a breath. What had happened? Where was he? Back in his body again? After two hundred years trapped as a bird-spirit and spending his days and nights as a raven, he had entered his human body again. Why? His human body lay crushed under a layer of mud, buried forever atop five chests of Spanish doubloons. What good would it do him to become a man again only to die in the earth?

Mak-ee-nah gasped for breath in the close space. Perhaps it was his time to die. Perhaps it was time for him to ascend to the Land Above at last. Yet in two hundred years, nothing had changed. He hadn't redeemed himself for his lack of judgment in trusting the Spanish sea captain. His warriors hadn't avenged the slaughter of the Nakalt people at the hands of the Spanish sailors. Why should he be admitted to the Land Above now? He had promised his people he would return to them. He had promised to take care of them. But he had made the mistake of trusting Juan Carlos del Cordega, just as he had trusted the British. The

*British had taken him around the world as a visiting digni-
tary, touting him as a Native American nobleman and
showing him every courtesy and every court. The Spanish,
on the other hand, had stripped him of his finest clothes,
taken his valuables, bludgeoned him, and left him for dead.*

*But he hadn't died. He had been buried alive by a mud
slide, and by some grand scheme of the all-knowing, all-
seeing Ah-welth, he had been transformed into a raven-
spirit and trapped on Earth as a bird for eternity. Or so he
had thought.*

*Mak-ee-nah scrabbled at the mud with his fingers. He
had been reaching up when the mud slide entombed him
two hundred years ago. If he could only dig his way out,
clear a space for air, he might not perish. His appetite for
life was keen, his raven totem strong. He would not give up
and die without trying to help himself. He breathed, trying
not to panic, scraping with his nails, moving his head in the
wet earth in an effort to make more room for his face. The
idea of dying like this, drowning in the earth, seized him
with terror.*

*Then he heard the howls. Even in his tomb below the
surface, he could hear the howling coming closer. He could
hear the tempo of pounding feet on the turf, the snarling
and panting. The wolf-people had come to the island!*

*Mak-ee-nah closed his eyes. "O my brothers," he mur-
mured. "Come to me. Help me, my brothers, my warriors."*

*He could hear them above his head, sniffing at the earth,
padding in smaller and smaller circles.*

*"Dig in the earth, my brothers," Mak-ee-nah called, his
breath hot and stifling. The mud felt cool on his cheek as he
leaned against the clammy soil, suddenly light-headed.*

*"Help me from this grave," he gasped. He tried to scrape
with his fingers, but his hands felt heavy, his mind lethar-
gic.*

*Then he heard the wolves above him, growling and dig-
ging. He tried to hang on, to endure the weight on his chest,
clinging to the slender hope that the wolves would reach
him in time.*

*"Dig, my brothers," he murmured, closing his eyes. Ah-
welth had chosen this time to resurrect him. This was his
chance to redeem himself. He saw that clearly now. And in
redeeming himself, he might help his brothers find their
own redemption as well. Ah-welth had chosen him and
only him to return to his human form. But his warriors, the
ten valiant men who had died defending their families, had
remained wolf-people. He would not fail them this time.*

Camille's suitcases were found intact along the road. She
didn't know whether to be relieved or not because at this
point she was uncertain about staying on the reservation.
But Kitsap Makinna threw her bags into the back of his
Jeep and took off toward the cabin, unaware of her reluc-
tance to continue the journey.

They pulled to a stop in front of Barbara's cabin, and
before Kit had even cut the engine, Camille jumped out,
anxious to find out what had kept Barbara from meeting
her. Seeing the dark cabin ahead, she felt unease curl in
the pit of her stomach. Barbara was the type of person who
put a candle in the window for visitors, had their favorite
cake in the oven or a special handmade gift waiting on the
table. It wasn't like her to await a visitor without leaving the
outside light shining as a welcoming beacon. Wherever
Barbara was, she was not at home.

Pulling her trench coat tightly around her, Camille hurried to the front door, her wet shoes and stockings chafing
her insteps. She ignored the pain. Behind her the other
two doors of the Jeep slammed shut, the sound muffled by

the wind. By the time they had driven through town, past the imposing Makinna Lodge, and out to the bluff above the Strait of Juan de Fuca, the gale had picked up, blowing down branches and buffeting the Jeep. Now, on the very edge of the bluff, the wind blew even harder. Camille approached the door and stopped in her tracks.

The front door of the cabin was ajar.

"What's wrong?" Kit asked, coming up behind her.

"The door's open." Cautiously she poked her head into the cabin and felt the wall for a light switch. She found it on the left, but when she flicked the switch, nothing happened.

"The lights are out," she said over her shoulder. She was suddenly grateful that Kit and Adam had insisted upon accompanying her to the door instead of merely dropping her off at the driveway.

"The storm must have knocked out the power," Kit replied. "Adam, run back and get the flashlight out of the glove box, would you?"

"Sure." Adam loped back to the Jeep.

"We have power outages all the time out here," Kit explained, but his reassuring words had a hollow ring to them. "Why don't you let me go in first, Miss Avery."

Before she could protest his taking charge, she was brushed aside as Kit stepped into the cabin. She heard his sharp intake of breath and followed.

"Someone has broken in," he said just as Adam ran up with the flashlight.

"Jesus!" Adam exclaimed, flashing the light around the one-room cabin. The room was a jumble of papers, broken dishes, upside-down drawers, tossed pillows, tilted couch cushions, and mounds of clothes torn out of chests and taken off hangers.

Camille gasped in dismay.

"Adam, give me the light," Kit said quietly. He trained it on the nearest heap of debris and inspected it. Then, while Camille and Adam stood near the door, Kit slowly made his way around the room, poking into piles and shining the beam of light into each dark corner and cupboard.

Kit returned to her side, shaking his head. "No sign of your friend, Miss Avery."

Camille felt another rush of panic. She stumbled to the couch near the cold fireplace and picked up a cushion. Keeping her hands busy would let her think, enable her to take the next step toward composure and put this disaster in logical order. Surely there must be a reasonable explanation for all of this.

What if something bad had happened to Barbara? Barbara was the single person in the world she considered family, the only person with whom she shared the kind of friendship that never grew stale, never faded with time. She and Barbara went all the way back to the first days of college, when they had come together from two opposite poles, opposite worlds, and opposite philosophies. Yet their differences had forged a friendship that had spanned over ten years and still remained strong. Her relationship with her own sisters had never been as deep and sustaining as her friendship with Barbara Stanton, an absentminded anthropologist who foreswore anything that wasn't purple, a woman who could name every civilization that had existed on earth yet could not remember her own phone number, a person who could weave wonders with the written word but who alienated most people with her eccentric mannerisms, and one of the most creative intellects Camille had ever encountered.

"Miss Avery!"

She jerked to attention, realizing that Kit Makinna had

called her name more than once. She forced herself to
return to her trademark coolness.

"Yes?"

"Don't move anything else. The police will want to see
the place untouched."

"You're right, they will." Camille glanced around the
room, dismayed. She should have thought of that first. Her
failure to think logically upset her, made the panic rise in
her throat. If she didn't start sorting things out, she was
going to collapse into a blubbering mess. Once logic fled,
she had nothing to go on—never having been one to trust
instincts or hunches—and she would have a panic attack to
end all panic attacks. Already she could feel the familiar
tightening in her chest.

"It's all right, Miss Avery." Kit put his hand on her
shoulder, just as he had touched Charlie after the resurrection ceremony, as if laying hands upon her would calm
her, too. His hand was slender and tanned, his touch light
but reassuring, rather like the way a priest might comfort
a frightened member of his flock. Little did he know that
the contact caused the flutter in her chest to flare up, not
fade. Did he touch everyone he encountered in this manner? Well, she didn't like it. She had never liked being
touched by people she hardly knew and thought of it as an
unwelcome invasion of her personal space. She stepped
away from his hand, determined to work through her panic
without his help. She didn't need the shallow comfort of a
stranger.

For a moment she felt his scrutiny and knew without
seeing his face that his manner toward her had chilled considerably. She hadn't meant to offend him, but then again
he shouldn't have been so forward. She held out her hand
for the flashlight.

"May I?" She laced her words with businesslike crispness. He gave her the light and then folded his arms over his chest.

"I should call the police right now and report Barbara's disappearance."

She glanced around. "The phone must be here somewhere."

Adam stepped forward. "Why don't you come back to the lodge with us, Miss Avery? You can call from there."

"I couldn't, Adam. You've gone above and beyond the call of duty for me as it is."

"But you can't stay here."

"Adam's right." Kit's terse voice came out of the darkness. "Whoever did this might come back."

"Did Barbara have enemies on the reservation?" Camille asked, still hesitant to look at Kit's face, not that she could see much of it in the darkness.

"I didn't know her. I just arrived here myself. Do you know, Adam?"

"Only Old Man."

"Who's Old Man?" Camille asked.

"My grandfather," Kit explained. "George Makinna." He turned to Adam. "Why did Old Man dislike Barbara Stanton?"

"The usual. She was an outsider."

"Ah." Kit apparently understood. Camille didn't, but she was too distracted to ask.

"Well?" Adam inquired. "Are you coming back to the lodge with us?"

"I suppose it's the sensible thing to do at this point," Camille replied. "But I don't want to put you out."

"You won't." Adam took her arm as his uncle had done earlier that evening, only his touch was hesitant, as if he had never tried it before and wasn't certain if Camille would comply. At least the hesitancy proved it was an honest gesture. "We insist. Don't we, Uncle Kit?"

"The lady seems to know her own mind. Let her decide." Kit walked to the door of the cabin.

Camille scowled. She had certainly set him off. And she didn't want to make it any worse by drawing away from Adam or refusing his help, not after he had been so obliging to her.

"Okay, Adam. I'll take you up on the offer. But I want to look around outside first."

She led the way out of the cabin to where Kit stood on the flagstones, his arms once again folded over his chest.

"Coming?" he asked.

"I'm going to take a pass around the cabin first."

"Have at it, then"—he waved the air with a flip of his right hand—"Miss Avery."

Camille stomped away in disgust. She'd deal with his bruised male ego some other time. Right now she had to concentrate on Barbara.

Later, when they drove up to the lodge, they found the power out there, too. Kit pulled up in back and set the brake as Camille hopped out. She could hear the sea from the small parking lot in back but couldn't see the water, as the lodge was set above the beach and surrounded by twisting madrona trees.

Kit unlocked the door and held it for Adam, who carried one of Camille's bags into the huge great room that served as a lounge area on one end and a lobby on the other. A large golden lab ran up to Kit and Adam, twisting in delight to see them. Then it sniffed Camille, and she patted its big head.

"That's Sandy," Adam said with a smile. "Uncle Kit's dog."

"Aren't you a beauty," she remarked, stroking the dog's velvety ears. Sandy yapped playfully and wagged her tail.

Then Camille strolled into the main room, forgetting her wet clothing as she looked at the cedar ceiling, two stories above, supported by huge round beams. Each corner of the room boasted a post at least three feet wide carved with faces of wolves and ravens, the colors muted because of the lack of lighting. The wall that housed the six-foot fireplace was decorated with an array of animals and fantasy creatures, in the fashion of the heraldic screens Camille had read about in Barbara's manuscript. Spare pieces of furniture—mostly cedar benches with scattered cushions in red, white, and black, and carved chests that served as end tables—surrounded the sunken area before the fire. The room was impressive and peaceful, the first peaceful scene she had encountered that evening. A fire crackled in the grate, and Camille longed to stretch before the hearth and warm her feet. Instead she turned to Kit and saw him turn away at the same time. Had he been watching her? She felt a strange pricking sensation along the back of her neck.

At that moment, the phone rang. Kit reached over the reservation counter and grabbed the receiver. Camille listened idly, hoping he wouldn't be too long. She wished someone would offer her a cup of coffee or some dinner. She was tired, hungry, and cold and could use a warm bath.

Kit's voice rumbled in the background as Adam walked to the fire and piled on three more logs. She heard the receiver clatter back to its cradle.

"That was Frank," Kit said. "There's trouble with the backup generator at the hatchery. I've got to go."

Adam trotted across the floor. "That generator is on its last legs, Uncle Kit."

"You've had trouble with it before?"

"Yeah. Dad was always tinkering with it."

"Maybe you'd better come with me and show me what he did to it."

Camille realized they were about to abandon her.

"Make yourself at home, Miss Avery," Kit called over his shoulder as he pulled open the door. "We'll be back as soon as we can."

They were gone before she could mouth a single request. She heard the Jeep roar off down the lane behind the lodge. Sighing, Camille locked the door and turned back to the lobby. The dog sat near the registration desk, gazing at her in expectation.

"I guess it's you and me, old girl."

Sandy thumped her tail and lolled out her tongue. Camille had to smile. The goofy, honest dog grin raised her spirits, giving her the impetus she needed to continue her duties of this long night.

She found the telephone number for the police on a decal stuck to the phone receiver. She punched in the number, looking down at the dog while she waited for someone to answer. A dispatcher informed her that the chief of police and his officers weren't available at the moment, due to the storm, but promised to have someone call her as soon as possible. Camille hung up. She'd have to stay in the lobby in case the police called back.

Make herself at home. Sure. She wasn't the type to wander around the house of a stranger, poking into places she didn't belong. She wouldn't want someone doing that in her house. With Sandy at her heels, she explored the perimeter of the room, searching for a candy machine or a beverage dispenser. All she found was a magazine rack and a set of rest rooms with worn vinyl floors.

Camille filled a thin paper cup and took a drink. Water in uncoated paper cups always tasted like pencil shavings to her. She poured out the rest and threw the cup in the trash. Then she washed her hands and glanced at her reflection in the mirror. Even in the dark rest room she could tell she looked like a wraith, with her hair blown into points. Grimacing, she smoothed it down with her comb and then left the rest room.

She walked to the fireplace. At least she could get warm. She sat down on the bench nearest the fire and pulled off her shoes. She set them on the hearthstones, side by side. Then she put her feet out in front of her, soles toward the flame. She wiggled her toes and leaned back on the cushions. That felt much better. The dog curled up on the floor beside her, giving Camille a sense of security that had escaped her the entire day. She patted Sandy's head and closed her eyes.

3

"Miss Avery."

Camille stirred at the sound. She opened one eye and peered up in the direction of the voice. A dark shape, all shoulders and unruly hair, loomed over the bench where she had fallen asleep in front of the fire, and she squinted to see who it was in the dim light of the lodge. A faint odor of cedar mixed with the fresh smell of the sea drifted down toward her, enticing her to breathe in the fragrance of the man. She breathed and lifted her head off the pile of cushions. Then the man shifted and, with the movement, presented his face to the flickering light of the fire.

Camille stared at him, sleep vanishing in an instant as she looked into the eyes of Kitsap Makinna, into the face of the most handsome man she had ever seen. She had caught glimpses of his features throughout the evening but hadn't received the full impact of his looks until now, when the firelight danced across his face.

She'd heard the phrase *tall, dark, and handsome*—and had seen some tall, dark, and handsome men—but such a mundane label would never be attached to the man standing over her. His was not the fine-boned prettiness of a male model or the rugged good looks of a quarterback, but a stark beauty she had never encountered before, as if the fierce spirit of a proud, wary bird of prey—an eagle or a hawk—were trapped in the black-eyed, raven-haired creature standing above her.

"You plan to sleep here all night?" Kit demanded, breaking the spell.

She realized with a hot flush of embarrassment that she was gaping at him.

"No." Camille struggled to her feet, trying to hide her face by brushing out the wrinkles of her coat. She didn't often let her composure slip like this in the presence of a man, and her lapse not only embarrassed her, but angered her as well. And Kit, with his curt behavior, did nothing to improve the state of her emotions.

"I was waiting for the police to call back," she answered, flashing him a glance as she put on her shoes. "Besides, I didn't know where I should sleep."

"I thought I told you to make yourself at home." His black eyes glittered at her, and his left lid blinked almost imperceptibly, which again reminded her of an eagle.

And there he went again, telling her what to do. She straightened and pulled her coat around her, trying not to be curt in return. She should be grateful for this man's help. Instead she felt a swelling antagonism, which increased each time he dictated to her.

"The bench was perfectly fine," she said, raising her chin.

Once more he surveyed her, and it was hard to tell if he approved of her appearance or damned her for falling short of some unfathomable Nakalt requirement for the behavior of women. Surely such a handsome man should have the lazy-lidded eyes of a charmer, but Kit's eyes were hard-edged and dark with intensity, as if he would sooner come to blows with someone than talk to them. His full upper lip curled slightly on the right side as he appraised her face and her short blond hair. Then his glance slid off her with a slow blink of dismissal. He turned.

"Follow me."

He walked to the front desk, where both of her suitcases sat on the floor. Sandy walked with him and sniffed the edges of the cases. Kit easily picked up Camille's bags and pulled a flashlight out of his jacket pocket, snapping it on to illuminate the dark stairway.

"I can take one of those," Camille put in, holding out a hand.

"I've got them."

He told the dog to stay and then strode to the stairs.

Camille fell in step behind him, trying not to examine his tall figure as he climbed the stairs ahead of her and led the way down a central hallway. He had the easy walk of a man comfortable with the size and condition of his body. He wore a dark blue jacket and jeans and a pair of black rubber boots that on another man might seem shabby. But Kitsap's natural grace lent his casual clothing a certain rugged flair.

He pushed open a door with his elbow and motioned her inside. Camille walked past him, trying to ignore the intoxicating fragrance that wafted from him. Really, she should get hold of herself. He was just a man, after all.

"There's a bathroom over there." He indicated the door with the beam of the flashlight. "A closet for your clothes there. Couch. Table and chairs."

Camille glanced around the small suite, what she could

see of it in near total darkness, anyway, and was pleasantly surprised to find it clean and uncluttered, built entirely of rustic cedar planks.

"And the, uh . . ." She paused, wondering why the mention of a bedroom should put a knot in her tongue. "The, uh, bedroom?"

"In here." Kit strode across the floor and opened another door, shining the light on a double bed made of hand-lathed wood spread with a coverlet patterned in the style of the northwest coastal Indians. A fireplace had been built between the two rooms, to provide heat for both parlor and bedroom.

"I'll build a fire," he said. "It's too cold to sleep up here."

While he bent to the task, Camille walked over to the bed, running her hand over the nubby texture of the spread, fascinated by the reds, whites, and blacks of the bird design.

"Raven?" she asked over her shoulder.

She saw the imperceptible blink pass across his eye again.

"Yes. You know a bit about our culture, I see."

"A bit. I've always been fascinated by Native American art." She forgot to be angry and smiled.

Then she turned to make a comment concerning her excitement about starting the illustrations for Barbara's book but caught Kit watching her with such a dark expression on his face that the words died on her lips. She paused, taken aback, and he rose quickly to his feet.

"That'll warm up the room," he said, brushing his hands together and not quite meeting her glance.

"Thanks, Mr. Makinna."

"The name's Kit."

"Kit." She held out her hand, trying to hide her unease. "Mine's Camille."

He looked into her eyes and then shook her hand with a brief but very firm handclasp. "Well, I've got to get some sleep. Breakfast's at seven."

"Good."

He seemed surprised, as if he had thought the mention of the hour might annoy her. She was pleased to have caught him off guard.

She smiled. "I like to get an early start on the day."

"Seven will come soon enough," he replied. "Good night."

"Good night. And thanks for all your help."

"No problem."

She watched him stride out of the bedroom and cross the parlor and realized she had held her breath until the moment he closed the door behind him. Camille dipped her hand into the top of her blouse, drawing out the amulet she had found in her grandmother's attic. The amber felt warm again, and she wondered why. Perhaps the anger she felt toward Kitsap Makinna had raised her body temperature, which in turn had heated the amber. Still dressed in her trench coat, she sat on the elevated hearth of the fireplace, holding the amulet in her hand. Was it just firelight flickering through the amber, or was the necklace glowing? She cupped it in her hands and gazed down at the golden disk, letting it warm her cold fingers, glad of its smooth familiarity in this strange and shadow-filled place. Until she found Barbara, she would have to depend on the amulet to ground her to reality.

In the morning the first thing Camille did was dial Barbara's number on the old rotary phone near her bed. The phone buzzed a busy signal again, probably because it was off the hook, buried under a pile of debris in the cabin. Next she called the police, having memorized the number from the night before. The dispatcher again promised to have an officer call her at the first availability. Camille put down the phone, wondering what would happen if someone was in real danger. How long would it take for the authorities to respond?

Feeling helpless and frustrated, she took a quick shower and dressed in the pale light of dawn, hoping she applied her makeup correctly. The power was still out, and she had trouble seeing her reflection in the small bathroom mirror.

Afterward she walked down to the lobby, following the fragrance of bacon and eggs. Her stomach rumbled noisily, reminding her that she hadn't eaten since lunch the previous day. Shadows bathed the wide stairway down to the lobby, and she kept her hand on the rail to guide her steps. Off to the side of the great room where she had fallen asleep on the bench the night before, she found a small dining room that overlooked the beach and a magnificent view of the strait and the band of Vancouver Island, just coming to life with the first hint of dawn.

Camille strolled to the window, her hands behind her back, watching gulls soar and dive over the placid water at the base of the bluff. Lemon-colored light filtered onto the beach and the rocks below, spreading westward to the clouded lavender sky. Camille sucked in her breath, stunned by the spectacular vista.

"Beautiful, isn't it?" a deep, dry voice said behind her.

Camille whirled, surprised that someone had come into the room without her hearing. Kit stood in the doorway, holding a cup of coffee, Sandy at his feet, her tail thumping a greeting. He was dressed in jeans again and a hand-knitted sweater in a brown-and-gray pattern that set off the width of his shoulders. In the morning light his hair shone blue black and was thick and full, brushed casually off his forehead and ears. He wasn't an overly tall man—not more than five feet ten—but had the exquisite proportions possessed only by smaller, more tightly knit men.

Something surged in her chest as she stared at him, and she had to struggle against a choking sensation in order to respond to his comment. She was acting like a complete idiot in front of this man, and her lack of control annoyed her.

"Gorgeous," she replied, yet even her words made her blush. She meant to comment on the scenery, not the man standing before her, but she wasn't certain how he would interpret what she had just said, since she was gaping at him and not the beach.

He smiled, but not widely enough to show his teeth. Then, as if he had caught himself, he looked over his shoulder.

"Hattie, how about breakfast for Miss Avery?"

"Okay, boss," a woman's voice sang from the adjoining room.

"And a cup of coffee." His Adam's apple bobbed in his throat as he spoke, and his jawline jutted out from the taut skin of his neck near his ear. Camille stood by the window, uncertain which view was more magnificent—dawn lighting up the Pacific Ocean or the sharp profile of Kitsap Makinna, the finest physical example of a Nakalt man she had seen so far, or any man for that matter. Then he moved from the doorway to allow the passage of a short woman who bustled out of the kitchen carrying a plate of bacon and eggs and a coffeepot.

"Good morning," Hattie greeted her, smiling merrily. She was a short woman with a round wrinkled face, silver hair, and a torso like a barrel. Camille guessed she was probably in her seventies, but the energy and kindness sparkling in her impish eyes made her appear much younger. "Did you sleep well? Kit tells me you had an exciting night last night."

"I slept very well. Thank you." Camille pulled out her chair and sat down as Kitsap set his empty cup on the table.

"Did either of you hear anything about Barbara Stanton yet?" she inquired.

"No," Kit replied.

Hattie shook her head as she slid the plate in front of Camille. Then she poured coffee in the cup near Camille's wrist. "Do you take cream or sugar?" she asked.

"Neither, thank you. Just black." Camille looked up at Hattie gratefully. "This looks wonderful."

"Had to make it campfire style in the fireplace," Hattie replied, glowing at the compliment, "what with the power being out."

Camille watched Kit pull his blue jacket off the back of one of the chairs. Hattie looked up at the movement and held the coffeepot poised above Camille's cup.

"And where do you think you're going?" she demanded.

"To the hatchery." Kit thrust his arms into the sleeves of his coat and pulled it over his shoulders.

"But what about Lydia?"

"What about her?"

"Lydia told you she was coming back this morning with all the supplies. She'll want to start right away."

"Then she can start. She knows what has to be done just as much as I do." Kit frowned, and Camille looked down at her plate of scrambled eggs, wondering who Lydia was.

"But, Kit, what about Miss Avery?"

"She can take care of herself." He zipped his jacket. "No offense, Miss Avery, but I've got a generator to fix."

"Don't worry about me." She sipped her coffee, glancing up at him. His gaze locked with hers for a cool moment, and then he gave his zipper an extra tug at his chest and looked away.

"If Old Man needs me, Hattie, I'll be at the oyster hatchery until noon and then at the main building for the rest of the day."

Hattie made a disapproving noise in answer.

"If the doctor calls, transfer him to the hatchery office. Don't let him talk to Old Man first. You know how he is."

Hattie put a hand on her hip and pursed her lips, waiting for Kit to finish his string of instructions.

"And if the power company makes it out, send them my way first, would you?"

"Is that all, boss?"

Kit pinched her cheek. "That's it."

Hattie pinched him back, although she had to stand on tiptoe to reach his face. "You're a fool, Kitsap Makinna, leaving to fix that generator and feed fish when you could be showing off the countryside to this beautiful young lady."

Camille blushed and was thankful that Kit didn't turn to look at her. He seemed embarrassed for a moment, too, but quickly recovered, remarking stiffly that the fish were hungry. Then he walked out of the dining room, calling for Sandy to come with him.

Camille gazed after his retreating form. Though no one had ever called her beautiful before and she would never consider herself overly attractive, she felt a strange new hunger twisting in her heart. A few times during college she had fancied herself in love, but she'd never experienced this sudden and painful wrenching feeling with any of the men she'd known. After college she'd had only a smattering of dates, due to her odd life-style living on campus at an all-girl school lorded over by aging deans. Since college she had managed to insulate her heart from the ravages of romance Barbara had suffered and now at twenty-nine counted herself lucky for escaping youth unscathed, attributing her survival to her practical nature.

But there was something about Kitsap Makinna that drew her eyes and compelled her to stare after him, which wasn't like her at all. She wasn't the kind of woman who responded to a man simply because of his drop-dead looks, and she had never been attracted to men full of arrogance and conceit. Kit had all the qualities of the kind of man she usually avoided. Yet the challenge in those black eyes of his touched her on a level so deep she couldn't even put a word to the emotion flaring inside. She only knew it felt like hunger—and not for the cold scrambled eggs on her plate.

"That man!" Hattie made a clucking sound. "Didn't even wait for his breakfast—in too much of a hurry to clear out, I expect."

"He seems to be busy," Camille ventured as Hattie sat down and poured herself a cup of coffee.

"He's got something on his mind, something bothering him. I can tell that just by looking at him."

"Have you known Mr. Makinna long?"

"All his life. Ever since he was a little boy. He was a rascal, that one." She smiled at the memory, and her eyes sparkled. "Although not half as much as his brother, David."

"That would be Adam's father."

Hattie nodded. "David ran the hatchery and dabbled at fixing this lodge, but he drowned several weeks ago." She sipped her coffee thoughtfully. "They found him floating out in the bay. A tragedy. A real tragedy."

Camille chewed her bacon, remembering Kit's comment about just getting back to the reservation. "Is that why Mr. Makinna is here?"

"Yes. And it's a good thing, too. He's so good for Adam. If Kit hadn't come back to take care of what needed to be done, Adam would have fallen to pieces. And Lydia, too."

"Who's Lydia?"

"David's widow. Not Adam's mother, though. Adam's mother died a long time ago. Lydia married David about four years back. She always wanted Kit, but Kit left the reservation and never came back. He got himself a good education and a fancy degree, you know."

"He has a lot going for him, it seems."

"Yep." Hattie nodded. "Drives the girls crazy around here, knowing he's spoken for."

"Oh?" Camille's voice came out higher than she expected.

"Now that he's back, everybody expects he and Lydia will eventually tie the knot. In the old days, a man often married the widow of his brother, you know." She stared off into space. "It'll be nice to see that happen with Kit and Lydia, after all these years." Then Hattie glanced back at Camille. "You'll meet her soon. She's gone to Port Angeles to pick up supplies for the remodeling. But she should be back this morning."

"What's being remodeled?"

"The lodge." Hattie indicated the dining room with a sweep of her pudgy hand. "Kit's promised to stay and help her redo the place so Lydia will have a way to make a living now that David's gone."

Camille looked down and finished the remaining scrambled eggs, trying to convince herself that she didn't care one way or another about Lydia or about the matrimonial intricacies of the Makinna family. She heard Hattie pour herself more coffee.

"Did you know Barbara Stanton?" she asked.

"I talked to her once or twice."

"If you don't mind my asking"—Camille pushed away her plate—"when was the last time you saw her?"

Hattie pursed her lips. "Let me see now. I saw Barbara at the store. She was looking for cherry pie filling."

Camille smiled. Cherry pie was her favorite dessert. Barbara must have planned to bake a treat for her.

"When was that, Hattie?"

"That was Saturday. Yes, Saturday morning."

"You haven't seen her since?"

Hattie shook her head. "She spent a lot of time in that cabin writing. Didn't see her out much lately, you know."

Today was Friday. Surely someone had seen Barbara since Saturday. Camille counted backward to the last time she had talked to Barbara on the phone. That must have been Saturday, too. The other times since then she had gotten a busy signal. She stood up. She was going to call the police again. And if they couldn't make it to the phone, she was going to walk to the station and sit there until someone helped her.

When Camille called the police a few minutes later, she finally reached Donald Two Hand, chief of police, who apologized for his department's slow response and promised to send someone to the cabin to look it over. He'd already put out a missing person bulletin and would search the reservation for signs of Barbara. That was all he could do. Two Hand explained to Camille that since Barbara was a white woman, his department really didn't have any jurisdiction over crimes committed against her. The county sheriff would have to handle that, and the sheriff was not known for expedience when it came to problems on the reservation. He suggested that Camille stay at the Makinna Lodge for the time being until they had a chance to look for clues on the cabin property. He assured Camille that the Makinnas were a fine family and would be happy to help her in any way. And certainly Barbara Stanton would show up soon. It was a well-known fact that Barbara took long walks on the beach. Maybe she got held up somewhere by the storm.

Camille hung up the phone. Now what? She couldn't just sit around and do nothing. She decided to search the area on her own.

The beach search proved futile. Camille climbed up the trail along the face of the bluff, panting as she ascended the blocks of cedar that served as crude stairs. At the top she paused to catch her breath and glanced around, glimpsing the blinding white peak of Mt. Baker shining in the January sunshine to the east. Heartened by the striking view, she swung back into action, trying not to feel too despondent over the fact that she had found no trace of Barbara. She tried to tell herself that just because she hadn't found anything didn't mean that no clues existed as to Barbara's whereabouts. Perhaps the police had discovered something.

She walked the path back to the lodge and noticed a red pickup in the parking lot. The bed was full of rolls of flooring material, Sheetrock, gallons of paint, and adhesives. The vehicle must belong to Lydia Makinna. Camille glanced at the lodge, wondering if she wanted to go in just yet. She couldn't hang around outside without looking conspicuous. So she walked to the back entrance and was just about to reach for the door when Adam popped out of the lodge.

Camille glanced at him in surprise, since it was Friday and a boy his age should be in school. But before she had time to say anything, a woman shouted at him from inside the lodge.

"Adam Makinna, you be more careful. You dinged the corner on that last piece of Sheetrock."

Adam rolled his eyes as he jumped down the stairs and loped past Camille.

"Need some help, Adam?" she asked, following him to the truck.

"Yeah. I need to get that witch off my back. Do this, do that." He copied the tone of the woman's voice and screwed up his features.

"Isn't there school today?" Camille inquired, taking an end of the Sheetrock that he slid toward the tailgate.

"Yeah, but Lydia needed me to help. I'm not missing much, anyway."

Camille let his explanation slide and backed up toward the door, struggling with the Sheetrock. She looked over her shoulder, gauging the distance to the lodge. This Sheetrock was heavier than she had anticipated.

"Wait a minute." She lowered the white panel to the ground. "Let's do this sensibly."

Adam put down his end. "What do you mean?"

"Why not back the truck up to the porch there? That way I don't have to walk backward up the stairs or across the drive, either."

Adam followed her gaze. "Yeah. That makes sense. I'll back up the truck if you hold that Sheetrock for a second."

"Sure."

Adam jumped in the truck and carefully backed it to the porch while Camille gave him hand signals until he was perfectly positioned for unloading.

As he turned off the engine, a woman opened the door and leaned out. "Adam, what in the hell are you doing?" Then her glance landed on Camille and she closed her mouth and stepped all the way outside. The screen door banged behind her.

Camille watched her, knowing this person had to be Lydia. She was a tall woman, almost as tall as Kit, with generous hips and full breasts. She was on the verge of being overweight, but the loose skirt and blouse she wore artfully disguised her plump figure, and her attractive face and skin showed evidence of great care in her makeup. The most striking feature of Lydia Makinna, however, was her hair. It fell to her knees in a long ebony cloud, shot with a white streak an inch wide that originated on one side of her widow's peak. Camille thought the hairstyle was a bit impractical, but a woman who displayed it in all its glory, unpinned, was obviously proud of her hair and its unusual coloring. So this was Lydia Makinna, the woman destined for Kit. They would make an undeniably striking couple.

"Hello, I'm Camille Avery." She smiled in greeting, unable to step forward to offer her hand since she was busy propping up the Sheetrock.

Lydia walked to the edge of the porch and crossed her arms over her round breasts. Rings glittered on her hands.

"I'm Lydia Makinna. How do you do?"

Camille had to admit that Lydia had a real presence, accentuated by her unusual height, but also by the pride with which she spoke. Camille found herself feeling shorter than ever.

"I thought if Adam backed up the truck, we could save a few steps."

"How ingenious of you. Adam is perfectly capable of carrying everything in, though, Miss Avery."

"I don't mind helping."

"Suit yourself."

Camille watched Lydia look down at the ground as if to check for damage sustained by the porch or the yard in moving the truck. Then she turned and swayed across the porch to the back door. Camille let out a breath as she disappeared into the lodge. Lydia had a presence all right. Something akin to the North Pole.

Adam caught her staring and chuckled.

"Warm and nurturing, isn't she?" he remarked wryly, hoisting the Sheetrock off the ground.

Camille tried not to encourage his criticism by smiling.

They set to work unloading the truck and had everything into the lodge after a quarter of an hour. Camille worked quickly and quietly, with a fierce determination that made up for her diminutive size. By the time the last can of paint was stacked in the lobby hallway near the rest rooms, she felt a sheen of perspiration on her skin. She pushed back her damp bangs as Adam motioned for her to follow him into the kitchen.

Lydia sat at a table near a window, drinking a diet soda and looking at a magazine. Her hands were long and elegant with beautifully manicured red nails. She didn't acknowledge their presence in the kitchen until Adam opened the refrigerator.

"Adam, you shut that refrigerator right now."

Adam froze.

"How many times do I have to tell you to keep out of the kitchen when you're filthy dirty?"

Camille looked down at her own clothes, dusty white from the Sheetrock.

"I just wanted a cold drink," he protested, slamming the door.

"Hattie, get Adam and Miss Avery a soda," Lydia directed from her seat. "Then you go down and get that uncle of yours, Adam. I don't know why he went down to the hatchery when he knew I was coming back."

"The generator was busted."

"Oh, that generator." Lydia snapped the pages of the magazine, displaying her displeasure. "So important."

"It is, Lydia. We could have another storm and no backup power. The filtration system and pumps wouldn't work."

"Don't you sass me, Adam Makinna." She turned and glared at him, her dark brown eyes cold and glittering.

Camille popped the ring off the soda Hattie gave her. She had heard kids sass their parents, and Adam was far from being impertinent. She felt sorry for him, having to live with such censure, and decided right then and there to take him under her wing.

"It's warm in here, Adam," Camille remarked, fanning herself with her hand. "Let's go outside, shall we?"

"Sure."

"Excuse us, Mrs. Makinna." She bestowed a frosty smile upon Lydia and left the kitchen, glad to get away from the woman. They strolled the length of the porch, which wrapped around three sides of the lodge, widening at the front to form a deck, strategically positioned to afford a breathtaking view of the strait and the open ocean.

They sipped their drinks and gazed in silence at the clay beach below the bluff and the steel blue water for a few minutes until someone pulled into the parking lot.

"Maybe that's your uncle now," Camille said.

Adam leaned over the deck railing to get a better view of the side of the house. He sighed. "Great."

"Who is it?"

"The truant officer."

4

That evening, Camille took a place at the dinner table just as Kit breezed into the lodge, accompanied by his grandfather, George Makinna, and his big golden dog. Her appetite vanished when she saw the old man with the glowing eyes shuffling across the great room toward the table where she sat. He wore a western-cut plaid shirt and brown knit pants and a pair of old-fashioned glasses—the kind with clear rims on the bottom and dark frames at the top—but the glasses didn't shield her from his subtle scrutiny. Though he was old, he still had a thick head of hair gone completely white, and his straight hairline and the shape of his face reminded her of Kit. Just like his grandson, George Makinna must have been a handsome man in his day, but over the years his body had shriveled around his features, so that his nose, cheekbones, and ears protruded from his skull.

He shuffled to the chair at the head of the table, opposite Lydia.

"Lydia," he said, nodding toward her.

Camille glanced at Lydia, whose face stretched in a gracious but forced smile.

"Old Man," she acknowledged stiffly. "Please join us."

At Lydia's cool invitation, Kit laid his hand on Old Man's shoulder in the gesture already familiar to Camille. "I thought Old Man might like some of Hattie's home cooking," he said, pulling out the chair for his grandfather. "All he had in his kitchen was peanut butter."

Old Man lowered himself on the chair. "I like peanut butter."

"Well, you can't live on it, Old Man."

Lydia watched Kit, her eyes opaque with anger—the only outward sign that she was upset—as Kit took a seat next to Adam and opposite Camille. Her fingertips drummed on her water glass. Camille knew that Lydia was angry at Kit for having spent the day at the hatchery, and he had apparently compounded his transgression by showing up with Old Man. Judging from the look in Lydia's eyes, Kit was in for a taste of her wrath.

Before Lydia could speak, however, Hattie carried a plate of pork chops into the room.

"Hattie . . ." Kit took the plate from her. "Come and sit down."

"We don't do that anymore," Hattie replied, glancing at Lydia.

Lydia's fingers stopped drumming.

"Why not?" Kit asked, looking from Hattie to Lydia.

"I didn't think it seemly that the cook appear at the dinner table, especially when we have lodgers."

"But Hattie's a member of the family."

"Not really."

"She's been with the Makinna family longer than you have."

Kit's words hit home, spreading a deep flush of anger over Lydia's already pink face.

"Since when did time have anything to do with status?" she inquired coldly. "I married a Makinna. Hattie's a Johnson, completely unrelated."

"If you count only blood ties, Lydia. But friendship has nothing to do with pedigree." Kit turned back to Hattie. "Come on, Hattie, sit down." Kit motioned to the spot next to Camille. Hattie shrugged, got another place setting, and pulled out the chair.

Lydia flushed even deeper when she saw her objections being overruled. "Do you think you can just barge in here and start changing the way we do things?"

"It seems to me that you're the one changing family tradition, Lydia."

Camille heard Adam sputter, and she glanced at him to find him fighting back a grin. Uncomfortable with the family problems displayed at the table, she looked down and spooned mashed potatoes on her plate with measured strokes, as if all her concentration were centered on the simple act.

"And what about you, Old Man?" Kit continued, cutting his meat. "How long have you been living on your own?"

Lydia looked up from her plate, ready to defend her position again. "He wanted to leave."

Kit turned to his grandfather. "Is that right, Old Man?"

"Yes." Old Man took the mashed potato bowl from Adam. "It was time for me to go."

"Why, for crying out loud? You've lived in the lodge all your life."

"It was no longer home to my spirit."

Kit glanced back down the table to Lydia. She dabbed her lips and stared back.

"Was his presence also not seemly to lodgers?" Kit demanded.

"It was his decision, not mine, Kitsap."

"I don't like strangers in my home," Old Man put in. His hand trembled as he lifted his fork.

Camille glanced at her plate, unsure whether he referred to lodgers such as herself or to Lydia, who apparently shared no affection with the old man. She tried to concentrate on her meal, which—though simply prepared without sauces or garnishes—was as good as, if not better than, the food prepared by professional chefs at the exclusive school for young women where she taught mathematics. But try as she might, she couldn't distract herself, nor could she shake the feeling that Old Man was staring at her. Finally she looked up.

Old Man was pushing his peas into his mashed potatoes and not even paying attention to her. Still, her senses were taut with the feeling that he was surveying her again, perhaps on a deeper level. She hoped he would be able to see past the jumble of unresolved questions in her heart and find the innermost place that she had always kept simple and honest, hoping that honesty could substitute for faith.

"Besides," Old Man added, lifting the potatoes and peas with his fork, "why should you care, Kitsap? What goes on here doesn't concern you anymore."

"How do you know?"

"If you were truly concerned, then you would stay."

Camille saw Kit's lips tighten as he reached for his water.

"Just because I choose to live off the reservation doesn't mean I don't care."

Old Man shook his head. "Your Nakalt heart is gone, Kitsap. And when you say such things about caring, I cannot hear you."

Old Man continued to eat without looking at his grandson. Kit watched him, exasperated, while a heavy silence fell over the dinner table.

Lydia traced the rim of her water glass with a manicured nail. Camille felt as if she were an unwelcome intruder and wished she had never come down for dinner.

"Have you heard anything about that poor Barbara Stanton?" Hattie asked Kit, trying to break the oppressive mood.

"No." He turned to Camille. "Did the police ever call?"

"I called them. Donald Two Hand promised to look at the cabin soon. He suggested that I stay here until they investigate, if that's all right." She looked from Kit to Lydia to Old Man, not certain who was in command. "I'm happy to pay."

"Nonsense," Kit retorted.

"Since we're catching up on the community bulletin board," Lydia drawled as she helped herself to more salad, "there's another item that needs to be addressed. Adam?"

Adam slumped on his chair.

"Adam!" Lydia repeated tersely. "Tell your uncle who came to the lodge today."

"Who?" Kit inquired.

Adam scowled. His face was a narrow version of Kit's, with the faintest shadow of facial hair above his lip. He hugged his arms as if to defend himself from attack.

"Who?" Kit said again.

"The truant officer."

"You skipped school?"

"Yeah!" Adam retorted hotly. "To help Lydia unload the truck."

"Unload the truck?" Lydia exclaimed. "What about last Friday and the Friday before that? The truant officer says you've been skipping nearly every week."

"So?" Adam stared at the wall behind Camille.

"So you're going to flunk, Adam."

He shrugged. "So what."

"You want to end up like your good-for—" She broke off, suddenly catching herself with venom on her tongue.

"Say it!" Adam jumped to his feet, knocking his chair backward. He glared at Lydia, his hands balled into fists. "You want to say it! So go ahead!"

"Adam—" Lydia glanced apologetically at Camille as if to make up for her stepson's outburst.

But Adam would not be chastised into submission. He threw down his napkin so hard that his spoon flipped upon the table. "Say it, Lydia! My good-for-nothing father—"

"I will not have that tone of voice in my house, Adam Makinna!"

"Who cares!" Adam retorted. "I don't want to live here anyway."

"You won't if you drop out of school."

"So?" He leaned toward her. "You're no snow maiden, Lydia. You're a witch! And my father didn't drink until he married you!"

"Adam!" Kit admonished, reaching for him.

Adam wrenched away and stumbled out of the dining room with Kit at his heels. For a moment Lydia stared after him, the color high on her wide cheekbones. Then she rose in her calm, majestic fashion.

"Excuse me," Lydia declared. She dropped her napkin to the table and stalked to the stairway, obviously overcome by Adam's accusation and behavior.

Camille heard the lobby door slam over the tinkle of Sandy's collar tabs as the dog padded to Camille's chair and sat down near her. Camille reached out and stroked the dog, wishing she could leave as well. She had no desire to sit at the dinner table with Old Man. But if everyone got up and left Kit's grandfather all by himself, it would be the height of rudeness. Then Hattie rose, clucking, and set about clearing the table, totally abandoning her.

Camille looked up to find Old Man gazing at her.

"The boy is going through a difficult time," he remarked. "The loss of his father is hard for him."

"It is for anyone."

Old Man nodded and put his napkin on the table. "So you're Barbara Stanton's friend?"

"Yes."

"I don't like Miss Stanton."

"I'm sorry to hear that."

"She studies us, takes many notes, records our stories and recollections. But she doesn't hear a word of it here"—he touched his chest with a gnarled hand—"where it counts."

"Barbara is well respected for her anthropological works."

"Science, bah!" He waved her off. "Miss Stanton sees us as objects to study, not as people. We are as numbers to her."

"I always thought Barbara was particularly perceptive."

Old Man shook his head. "Oh, she is smart. I'll give her that. But she is removed. Miss Stanton thinks she is better than us. She may not want to be better, but it has been ingrained in her from birth. Does she come from a rich family?"

Camille nodded in silence, surprised by Old Man's observations. He had seen through Barbara's carefully packaged persona to her true character, a character she tried so hard to camouflage. Barbara wanted nothing more than to forget she came from a privileged background, but she had been stamped with the indelible mark of the wealthy.

"On the other hand, your family is not rich, is it, Miss Avery?"

"No." She swallowed, wondering what he thought of her. It couldn't be good, not the way he studied her without smiling. Yet she had never tried to hide her background or pretended to be someone other than herself. The one thing she could say about herself was that she tried to be honest.

Old Man sat back on his chair and cupped his gnarled hands over his stomach.

"You are much different from your friend."

Different. Did that mean he approved of her? Or did he simply dislike her in a different way? Camille continued to pet Sandy, thankful to busy herself with the dog because she didn't know what else to say to Old Man. Sandy put her head on Camille's thigh and wagged her tail, and Camille looked down at her. Certainly the dog was easier to get along with than any of the Makinnas. Another silence settled between them while Hattie bustled about, taking the dishes from the table.

"Why have you come here, Miss Avery?" he asked after a long pause.

"To do illustrations for Barbara's book."

He gazed at the wall, as if weighing the truth in her words.

"Your heart is different from Miss Stanton's."

"Oh?"

"Its voice is powerful but has no language."

Camille stared at him. She had felt her heart today as she had never felt it before, hard and tight and choking her. Whenever the thought of Kit made her heart surge inside her, she fought it down and tried to ignore it. Even now she felt the sudden swell and couldn't make a reply to

Old Man's words. At her silence, Old Man crossed his hands over his belt.

"Perhaps your heart speaks a tongue you don't understand, Miss Avery."

"Perhaps," she replied. How could he see people so clearly? She had blocked the feelings in her heart for as long as she could remember. The only time she let her emotions loose was when she drew or painted. She could control a pencil, a piece of chalk, or a brush, but she had no control over pain that people could inflict upon an unguarded heart, like the pain inflicted on a fat girl with pale hair who looked nothing like her beautiful brunette sisters. Long ago she had stopped listening to the comparisons. Long ago she had locked her heart away where it was immune to both pain and hope, and only let it out when she was alone, working and safe.

"You will learn the language here," Old Man added, nodding toward her.

"Perhaps." Her heart surged again, and she looked down at the dog, trying not to give in to the painful ache inside. If she lost control and started listening to her heart's insistent clamor, she could be in big trouble. Like an unruly child denied recess, she was quickly nearing the end of her emotional tether.

Late that evening, Camille slipped from her room. Though she was tired from the long day, she couldn't sleep, and worry about Barbara kept her awake imagining the worst. She tied the sash of her navy blue velour robe and slipped down the stairs to the lobby, thinking that a few minutes in the moonlight on the deck would distract her and calm her fears. She flowed through the shadows of the great room and quietly opened the side door near the dining area.

The air was crisp but still. A nearly full moon hung above the trees, scattering silver glitter on the edge of the deck and the water below. Stars flickered in the deep indigo above, and not a sound broke the calm except for the soft sigh of water at the base of the bluff. She walked to the rail and leaned against it, marveling at the sudden peace she felt.

The waves that rolled across the shale and clay made a strange noise, as if chanting *home, home, home* over and over again. Was the sea telling her to go back to Charleston? Camille listened again, trying to open herself to the true nature of the sound, but she felt no threat whatsoever in the song of the waves. Could the chant be part of the language her heart had to learn? *Home, home, home.* The sound was more lullaby than warning, as if it were telling her she belonged here. But surely she could never call this reservation home.

Camille drew in a deep breath of the cedar-laced air and raised her face to the moonlight. She had to smile at her own foolishness. What had gotten into her? One day at Crescent Bay and she was imagining she could hear the ocean talking to her. Promising herself to keep a tight rein on her imagination, she sank onto a wood deck chair that sat in the shadows near the side of the lodge. Then she pulled her knees to her chin, intending to sit there and enjoy the beauty of the night until she got too cold.

A few minutes later the quiet was shattered by the sound of a vehicle pulling up out back. Camille remained on her chair, hoping that whoever had come to the lodge would not disturb her peaceful vigil. But soon she heard the clump of boots on the wood deck, and Kit strode around the corner of the lodge. He didn't notice Camille in the shadows and strolled to the edge of the deck. For a moment he stared at the moon, and then he sighed and leaned on the rail. His wide shoulders slumped and his head lowered to his clasped hands while moonlight streamed over his black hair and highlighted the nape of his neck above the collar of his shirt and sweater. The sight of his neck bent at such an angle made him appear tender, vulnerable.

Camille knew she should make a sound or call out a greeting to him instead of violating his moment of privacy. But she couldn't bear to lose this chance to study him openly. His legs were so straight and trim, his hips so lean, that the sight of them made her heart surge into her throat again. She clutched her knees even more tightly. She couldn't imagine why Old Man had accused Kit of not caring. He seemed to be concerned about everyone around him.

Even now he was slumped over his hands, distraught about something or someone, probably Adam. She ached to slide her hands over his shoulders and give him comfort. Yet even speaking to him now would be awkward, since she hadn't acknowledged his presence right off.

Then the lobby door opened and closed. Kit looked aside to see who approached, then turned back to his contemplative stance as Lydia strolled across the deck to him. She was also dressed in a thick robe.

"You didn't find him?" she asked.

"No."

"He's probably at his friend Bobby's house."

"Does he do this often?"

"Only when he's really upset. Kit—" She reached for his arm, but Kit stood up straight to avoid her touch.

"You think dredging up his father's problems is going to improve Adam's behavior?"

"I was simply speaking the truth. David was a drunk. And Adam has got to face that."

"He doesn't need you to tell him the truth, Lydia. He knows." Kit turned away from her and crossed his arms over his chest. Camille heard Lydia heave a deep sigh of anguish.

"Kit, what I said at the table tonight about Hattie—"

"Forget it."

"I just don't want to argue with you, Kit. I've been waiting so long for you to come—"

"Drop it."

"Oh, Kit—"

She reached for him. Camille swallowed as she watched Lydia wrap her arms around Kit and lay her head on the back of his shoulders, just as Camille herself longed to embrace him.

"Kit," she whispered. "I only married David to be closer to you."

"Don't, Lydia." Kit lifted her hands and stepped away. "My brother hasn't even been dead a month."

"I know. It's just that I've been through a lot lately. I could use a shoulder to cry on."

"Is that all you want?" Kit asked, leaning on the rail again. He braced his boot on the bottom railing. "Just a shoulder?"

"Yes. We've both suffered a loss, Kit. We could comfort each other, you know."

Lydia touched his hair, and Camille felt a shaft of jealousy sear through her. She nearly jumped out of the chair. She should have jumped—should have dashed for the door—but she kept her arms locked around her knees, rigid with jealousy and hypnotized by the vicarious sensations she was feeling through Lydia.

"Kit—" Before Kit could edge away, Lydia moved her

hips against his back and Camille saw her hand slide around Kit's thigh. Camille bit the side of her lip, wondering what it would be like to touch Kit in that way. She flushed at the thought, unaccustomed to wondering such things about a man. Though the air was cold, she suddenly felt very warm beneath her robe. Her breathing nearly stopped as she watched Lydia nuzzle his thick, raven-colored hair.

With an oath, Kit broke away and turned. For one horrifying moment he faced Camille and their gazes locked— his in heated surprise, hers in flushed chagrin. Then he strode across the deck to the stairs and stormed to the edge of the bluff, disappearing down the trail that led to the beach. Camille watched him, still holding her breath, wondering what she would do when Lydia turned around and caught sight of her.

5

"You!" Lydia exclaimed. "What are you doing here?"

Camille let go of her knees and sat up straight as Lydia approached.

"How long have you been sitting there?"

"A few minutes." She rose to her feet. "I didn't want to interrupt."

"I'll bet." Lydia swept her with a scathing glance. "Do you always spy on people?"

"I didn't mean to."

Lydia stared down at her, and her eyes took on a new and glittering quality of distrust. "Or were you out here to meet Kit?"

"No. I just came out for some air." She drew herself up as tall as she could, admonishing herself for defending her behavior with such lame excuses. She had deliberately watched everything between Kit and Lydia. She felt the tips of her ears burning with shame.

Lydia put her weight on one hip and her hand on the other. "Listen, Camille, because I'm only going to tell you this once. Stay away from Kit."

"What?"

"Don't play innocent with me. There isn't a woman on this earth who can look at Kitsap Makinna without wanting him. I can see it in your eyes as plain as day."

Camille blinked, surprised.

"But Kit doesn't need any more trouble in his life. Especially women trouble. I've waited six long years for him to come back to me. And if you get in my way or do anything to hurt him—so help me, I'll make you sorry you ever stepped foot on this reservation!"

"I have no intention of—"

"Kit is mine." Lydia jabbed her finger in the air just above Camille's robe lapels. "And don't forget it!"

Lydia stalked to the door and slammed it behind her while Camille gaped after her in hot indignation. Who did Lydia think she was? And how dare she assume that Camille lusted after Kit? She hadn't given the slightest outward indication of her attraction toward him, no matter what Lydia said. There was a big difference between appreciating male beauty and lusting after someone.

With a sharp tug, Camille tightened the belt of her robe and resolved to put all thoughts of Kit and Lydia behind her. The sooner she left the lodge, the better it would be for everyone.

Camille heaved a sigh, fighting down the hard ball of resentment that Lydia's words had produced in her stomach. Her attempt at finding peace had been shattered, and now she'd never get to sleep. She clenched her teeth, glanced toward the water one more time before going back into the lodge, and paused when she saw someone appear at the top of the bluff. Was that Kit coming back?

A tall figure stood on the edge of the bluff, facing the lodge. But something wasn't quite right. Camille strained to make out the details of the figure as he walked closer. He was tall like Kit and had dark hair. But the man wasn't wearing a stitch of clothing.

Camille's hand involuntarily went to her throat as she stared. For some odd reason her amulet felt warm again. She reached inside her robe and held the amulet in her palm as she studied the approaching figure. What was going on? Why would Kit come back to the lodge without his clothes? He didn't seem like the kind of man to parade in the nude, especially after the way he had reacted to Lydia's advances. She stared at the naked man, whose magnificent shoulders moved in silhouette in the moonlight. He even walked with Kit's easygoing grace, his dark hair blowing back from his face as he padded toward the lodge.

Maybe she was wrong about him. Maybe this was Kit's way of coming on to women—shockingly naked. Well, she wasn't interested in exhibitionism. She had never appreciated outlandish behavior, and she wasn't about to start now. Kit could keep his striptease act to himself or perform for Lydia, whom she was sure would love the show. For an exhibitionist, however, Kit wore an odd expression, neither smug nor seductive, but noble and open, as if he were unaware of his nakedness.

Disgusted and disappointed in Kit—and somewhat confused—Camille relaxed her grip on the burning amulet, dropped it against her thick robe, and stumbled to the door. She went inside it without looking back and rushed to her room. She leaned against her door and vowed this would be the last night she spent in the Makinna Lodge. First thing tomorrow she'd pack her bags and leave. She heard wolves howl in the distance and hugged her arms at the eerie, haunting wail.

The next morning Camille walked down to breakfast, wishing she were in her own apartment where she wouldn't have to face the prospect of eating with strangers. She felt crabby and tired and had no desire to make conversation, especially with Kit. Since his wanton display of the previous evening, he had fallen considerably in her estimation. Perhaps he was still asleep or had already left for the day, and she wouldn't have to look at him.

Unfortunately he stood in the dining room, gazing out the window and drinking coffee. Camille paused at the entrance to the room and squared her shoulders, determined to face him and tell him what she thought of his disgusting behavior.

"Up so early?" she inquired.

He turned at her entrance. "The early bird catches the worm, Miss Avery."

"What—no sniffles?"

His dark brows came together in confusion.

What an actor. Camille swept forward and poured herself a cup of coffee from the machine on the sideboard. She could feel his gaze on her back. She took her time with the coffee, hoping he would realize from her tone that she had not appreciated his show last night.

"Good morning, Miss Avery," Hattie called from the kitchen.

"Good morning, Hattie." Camille forced a pleasantness she didn't feel into her voice.

At the sideboard she took a sip of coffee, holding the cup to her lips with both hands. She glanced at Kit. He wore a white sweatshirt with a white shirt beneath it. The light color accentuated the deep tan of his skin and the sootiness of his hair. She couldn't believe that she could still admire his appearance after his cheap show and her vow to squelch all physical response to him. Camille tore her gaze away from his face and glanced out the window.

"Are you going to let me in on the joke?" he asked, no humor in his voice.

"It's no joke." She shot him a glare. "And I didn't think you were amusing last night, either."

"Last night?"

"Come on, you know what I'm talking about, Makinna."

"No, I don't." He stepped toward her, his brows still knitted. "Enlighten me."

"I'm talking about last night and your parade on the bluff."

"My parade?"

She stared at Kit, challenging him to admit to what he'd done, but he continued with his blank expression of innocence. Exasperated, Camille brushed past him, intending to find a seat at the table, but he touched her arm as if to grab her. As soon as he reached out, however, he retracted his hand, apparently remembering her earlier aversion to being touched. His movement was enough to stop her, but she didn't turn to face him, standing stiff and silent.

"Cut to the chase, Miss Avery."

"All right. I'm talking about you wandering around without any clothes on."

"No clothes?" He stared at her.

"And if you think I'm like other women, you've got a big surprise coming."

"What are you talking about?"

Slowly she turned, her rage mounting. She was more angry now at his refusal to admit to his licentious behavior than at the behavior itself. "Perhaps you think you can parade around in the nude and catch my fancy, Mr. Makinna. But I'm not turned on by that kind of thing."

"Lady, you must be crazy—"

"I know what I saw, and I didn't like it." Now she was the one being dishonest, for she hadn't disliked the sight of Kit's naked figure. Quite the contrary. She just couldn't admit it to him.

Disgusted with herself and Kit, Camille put her mug on the table and rushed to the doorway of the dining room. She had to get out of the lodge, away from Kitsap Makinna. She'd leave money on the bed upstairs, pack her bags, and get out before she ever had to look him in the eye again. Even though he called to her, she ignored him and hurried up the stairs. She heard his footsteps echoing behind her.

Kit stopped in her doorway and stood on the threshold as she gathered her belongings.

"What are you doing?"

"I'm leaving."

"And going where?"

"To Barbara Stanton's cabin, where I should have stayed in the first place."

She was so upset, she threw her clothes into her suitcase without folding or stacking them.

"At seven o'clock in the morning?"

"Yes!" She slammed shut the suitcase and pulled it off the chair.

"What if the police haven't had time to investigate?"

"They've had their chance." She snatched her trench coat off a hook and stuffed her arms in the sleeves. She grabbed her purse and pulled out her wallet, counting out money to cover her stay at the lodge, all the while highly conscious of Kit's surveillance.

"You must have been dreaming."

She glared at him and resumed counting. "I know dream from reality."

"Whoever you saw wasn't me."

"Really? I saw you on the deck last night. I saw you run off. Then, when Lydia went into the lodge, you returned, hoping to impress or shock me. It didn't work."

"I didn't return to the lodge until after midnight."

"Sure." She picked up her suitcases. "Now if you will excuse me, Mr. Makinna, I'll be on my way."

"I'll take those for you."

"Thank you, but I can manage." She swept past him and struggled down the stairs with her heavy load. He didn't follow her this time, for which she was glad.

The morning air was damp and cold, with a mist shrouding the mountains on the peninsula. Camille lugged her bags around the side of the deck toward the bluff, figuring that her route would be shorter along the beach than if she took the winding lane from the Makinna Lodge to Barbara's cabin. As she hurried across the deck, she saw again the image in her mind's eye of the naked man with the magnificent shoulders walking toward her, his long hair blowing in the breeze. Long hair? Camille paused at the top of the stairs leading to the ground. Until that moment she hadn't remembered the detail of the naked man's shoulder-length hair. Now the vision hung in her thoughts as bright as day, confounding her. The naked man had had long hair. Kit's hair was stylishly short.

Something didn't figure. Camille shook her head in denial and stomped down the stairs. The man had looked exactly like Kit. It had to have been Kit. There was no other explanation.

◆ ◆ ◆

For a half hour she walked toward Barbara's cabin, her shoulders and arms aching from her heavy bags. Her feet were soaked from stumbling through pockets of water left by the outgoing tide. Ordinarily she wouldn't be so clumsy, but she was saddled by her suitcases and badgered by a large, noisy raven who continually glided past her head, so close at times that she was almost afraid it would hit her. She remembered the huge bird she had seen in the cedar grove on her arrival at Crescent Bay. Surely this wasn't the same bird that had dive-bombed her the other night.

She tramped down the beach, determined to put her illogical fears behind her, knowing the reservation had wrapped her in a strange mood. Miserable and cold, she walked on until she knew she was close to the cabin and then searched until she found a faint trail up the clay bank. Brambles tore at her socks and sleeves. She gritted her teeth and pressed on, reaching the top of the bank out of breath and out of sorts. Not until she got to the top did she notice that smoke was curling out of the chimney, mingling with the low-lying mist of early morning.

Barbara was back! Instantly Camille forgot her misery, and nearly shouted out loud as she staggered to the door. She pushed it open, Barbara's name on her lips, but her voice faded when she saw a tousled head rise from the couch.

"Miss Avery?"

"Adam!" She set her suitcases on the floor. "Your uncle has been looking everywhere for you."

"Who cares." He sat up, elbows on knees, combing the hair off his forehead with his long, thin fingers.

Camille watched him for a moment. "You should call your uncle and tell him where you are, Adam. He's worried about you."

"If I call him, he'll tell me to come back. And I don't want to. I've had it with Lydia."

Camille sat down beside him. "She's worried about you, too."

"No, she isn't. She's just worried that I'll make her look bad. My dad never lived up to her expectations, either."

"She has high standards."

Adam snorted in disgust. "Lydia has what Old Man calls delusions of grandeur. And I'm sick of her."

Camille surveyed the one-room cabin, still a scattered mess. Had Donald Two Hand and his men looked it over for clues yet? She couldn't wait any longer for them to do their jobs. She wasn't about to go back to the Makinna lodge, either.

"I'll tell you what, Adam. I'm going to call the tribal police to see if they've checked out the cabin. If they have, we can clean up the kitchen area and make some breakfast."

He glanced up in surprise, as if he had expected to be forced to return to the lodge, and then a smile slowly unfolded on his face.

"And"—Camille held up her hand—"if you promise to call your uncle to tell him where you are."

His smile faded, but at Camille's stern expression he finally nodded in assent.

"Okay, okay."

She found the phone and was fortunate enough to reach Donald Two Hand immediately. No, he hadn't heard any news about Miss Stanton. And yes, he and his men had searched the cabin and found no clues as to the identity of the thief. She could move in at her earliest convenience.

Camille hung up the phone, wryly thanking Two Hand under her breath for his promptness while she wondered if he would ever have updated her on the status of the investigation.

She handed the receiver to Adam, the smile still on her lips. While Adam punched in the number for the lodge, Camille inspected the kitchen, formulating a plan of attack. She could hear Adam's voice in the background, and from what she could tell, at least Kit wasn't scolding him harshly for running off. Camille picked up all the unbroken dishes and piled them by the sink to be washed. Then she found a broom and dustpan on the back porch and swept the broken pieces of stoneware into a pile. The canned goods and boxes of foodstuffs she arranged on the cupboard shelves, wondering why the thief had seen fit to ransack the kitchen. What could he have been after that Barbara would have put in the cupboard? Money? Anyone who knew Barbara was aware that she never used anything but plastic for financial transactions.

Adam set to work without having to be instructed. The thief had even dumped the trash. Adam righted the wastebasket and used the dustpan to scoop the trash into it. Then he found a clean towel hanging from the refrigerator door handle and dried dishes while Camille washed them. They worked quietly at first, shoulder to shoulder, until Camille broke the silence.

"So what test are you avoiding on Fridays?"

Adam's hand stopped rubbing the plate he was drying, but almost immediately he caught himself and returned to his task. "Test?" he repeated vaguely, feigning confusion.

"Yes. Friday is a test day. Any teacher knows that."

"You're a teacher?" Genuine horror tinged his words.

Camille shot him a sidelong glance and a smile. "Yes. I teach math."

Adam shook his head.

"I'm a good teacher. My girls always do well on national tests."

"Your girls? What about the boys?"

"I teach at an all-girl prep school."

He turned and stared at her. "That sounds awful."

"It's okay." She wrung out the dishcloth to wipe the counter. She didn't mention that her career at the Lewis Academy had become a predictable, boring existence spent teaching debutantes who cared more for designer labels than trigonometry. Though she was proud of her students' test scores, she wasn't completely satisfied with her job. And that was part of her reason for agreeing to do the book and coming to the reservation. She had to discover if working outside the academy could satisfy her.

The rest of the reasons for coming here were harder to define. For months she had been aware of an intense need to leave her present life, and she'd chalked it up to the early onset of midlife crisis. Deep in her heart she knew it was something much more but refused to think about it until she found a better explanation. Perhaps after her stay on the reservation she would feel more certain of her direction.

Camille forced herself not to think about that aspect of her life and cleaned the Formica, rinsing the cloth another time. "How is the school here on the reservation?"

"It's all right. But our teachers don't give a damn. They don't think we're going anywhere. And I guess they're right."

Camille frowned at his words and pulled the plug to empty the sink. "Life is what you make it, Adam."

"I've heard that song before."

"Look at your uncle. He's got a good education."

"Uncle Kit's the exception around here."

"You can be, too."

Adam stacked plates and cups in an upper cupboard. Then he folded the towel and set it on the counter.

"So what subject are you avoiding?"

He curled his lip. "Geometry."

She chuckled. "You say it like it's a disease!"

"It is. I hate it. All those triangles, those points, bisecting, dissecting—I just can't stand it."

Camille smiled and opened the refrigerator. "Barbara has eggs in here and some cheese. Shall I make an omelet?"

"Sure."

"I'm not nearly as good a cook as Hattie. I just want to warn you."

"It'll be fine." He smiled, obviously relieved that the subject had changed. "Do you want me to start on the living room area while you make breakfast?"

"That'd be great."

At the breakfast table Camille opened one of her puzzle magazines, asking Adam if he could help her with a particularly nasty section that had her stumped. She explained how to do the puzzle, using logic and deduction to eliminate some elements and connect others.

"You actually enjoy doing these?" Adam asked.

"Yes. I often eat alone, and I like to have something to occupy myself."

Adam chewed his food as he surveyed the puzzle, which looked more like a jumble of information than a logical progression. Before he knew it, though, he was bent over the table as deeply involved as Camille in trying to find a solution. They spent the entire meal huddled over the magazine, and then as they cleared the table, Adam suddenly shouted.

"I got it!" He rushed over to the magazine. "Look, if the red car belongs to the brick house, that means the Swede eats ham sandwiches!"

Camille looked over his shoulder, surveying the results of his deduction. "Yes! And if the Swede eats ham sandwiches, that makes the German drive the black sports car. It works!"

"Yeah!" Adam turned and beamed at her.

"You got it, Adam! Good job."

His grin was infectious, and Camille smiled as she washed the dishes. Adam continued to clean the cabin, humming under his breath.

Adam left before dinner, promising to apologize to his stepmother and uncle for running off. Camille watched him go, knowing she would miss his easy company and his help. Together they had set the cabin to rights, and later he had built a fire that crackled on the hearth, keeping the chill of the late rainy afternoon at bay. After Adam had disappeared down the trail toward the beach, Camille rubbed the backs of her arms as she walked to the fire.

Whoever had ransacked the cabin had stolen Barbara's portable computer. The police hadn't known it existed, since the thief had taken her boxes of disks and all cords and cases. Barbara had loved her laptop computer and had praised it many times. It probably contained the latest version of the manuscript, too. All that was left was a box that held a printout. Adam had picked up every page off the floor and painstakingly put it in order earlier that afternoon. Camille reached for the stationery box and carried it to the couch by the fire. In the event the computer and backup disks were never recovered, this manuscript would be extremely valuable—irreplaceable, actually—the only record of Barbara's endless hours of writing. She would have to make certain that nothing happened to it.

Camille slid the box under the end table and then retrieved her address book from her purse. She was going to call Barbara's parents and see if they'd heard from their daughter. She punched in the long-distance number, and while she waited for the connection to be made she stared at the ceiling.

"Barbara," she said out loud, "where *are* you?"

6

"*Makinna, looks like* you got company."

Kit looked up from the desk at the hatchery office, where he had been studying results from last year's report. From his seat near the window he could see Lydia sauntering across the parking lot toward the hatchery building. He sighed and ran a hand through his hair while he glanced toward the other Nakalt tribal member who worked at the hatchery. Frank Hall was a short, squat man with a square head accentuated by his flattop haircut and his wide mouth. Kit remembered him from his youth as one of the best swimmers on the reservation. Now, at nearly fifty, Frank was overweight and out of shape, but he still had a twinkle in his eye and a ready smile.

Frank tapped a pencil on the edge of his desk and grinned at Kit. "Saturday night and the snow maidens are frisky," he teased.

Kit shook his head and waved off Frank's remark, returning to his file folder of disappointing figures. He couldn't believe how run-down the hatchery had become in six years. Rusted machinery and trash littered the dike all the way to the pens in the pond. And even the numerous pens for raising fish had dwindled to a forty-by-hundred-foot area of fingerlings. As a teenager Kit had helped build the aquaculture pond, a huge expanse of nearly eight hundred acres surrounded by an earthen dike, the pride of the Nakalt Indian Reservation and quite a technological feat for its time. But now only a fraction of the pond was used for raising salmon. The rest lay abandoned and silent, too shallow to maintain the proper temperature for raising young salmon—a costly and unforseen problem.

A tight feeling gripped Kit around his chest, a feeling that had lodged there the day he had come to look at the generator. In fact, the tightness had never left and had only increased with each new revelation that the aquaculture project was slowly failing. Judging by the trends in the folder he held in his hands, soon there would be no salmon to hatch and none to return.

"You don't stand a chance with that woman coming after you, Makinna. You know that, don't you?"

"She's persistent, I'll give her that."

"Persistent, hell. She's obsessed."

"Maybe." Kit closed the folder and opened the lower drawer of the metal desk, returning the folder to its proper place as Lydia swept into the office.

"It's the Snow Maiden!" Frank exclaimed, jumping to his feet as if in salute.

Lydia disdained his sarcastic comment by ignoring him and directed her attention to Kit. "Quitting time, Kit."

"Is it?" He turned his left arm and looked at his wristwatch. Five o'clock. Where had the time gone?

"I thought we could zip over to Port Angeles and make a night of it."

Frank whistled and wiggled his eyebrows. Kit shot him a black glance and closed the desk drawer.

"Lydia, I've got a lot to do."

"No, you don't." She sat on the edge of the desk, her curvaceous hip tilted upward as if beckoning to him. "You don't need to be here."

"But who—"

"You don't have to take over where David left off."

"Oh, don't he?" Frank interjected, leaning forward with a leer. "You'd like nothing better, Lydia, admit it."

"Not to you, Frank Hall. Why don't you go on home."

"This sounds more interesting—"

"Go on," Kit interrupted. "Go home, Frank. I'll close up."

Frank grinned at Kit and then winked. "Fine with me." He grabbed his coat off the coat tree by his desk. "See you later."

Kit forced his expression to remain blank, even though he loathed Frank's insinuations—in fact, everybody's insinuations—that he and Lydia were a matched set. His brother wasn't buried a month, and already matchmaking had begun. The tight feeling around his chest clamped harder. Tribal expectations and Lydia's pursuit had been among the reasons he had left the reservation so long ago.

Another reason had been Ann Gregory, a chain-smoking, fast-driving blonde who had seduced him when he was seventeen years old. He'd wound up living with her and dropping out of high school, wasting two years of his life. She had taught him what women wanted of a man, and for a while her insatiable appetite had been enough to keep him interested. But Kit had soon tired of her dissolute habits and lack of ambition and gotten on with his life.

He stood up as if to slough off the memory. Women. He wasn't about to allow Lydia to wheedle her way into his life. He wished more women were like Camille Avery—standoffish, skittish, and reserved. Yet Lydia would never possess any of those qualities. No two women were as dissimilar as Camille Avery and Lydia. Lydia flaunted her sexuality like a billboard with neon lettering and lights. Camille Avery was wound so tight that a real caress might set her spinning into hysterics. She certainly hadn't appreciated his touch, that was obvious. Yet it was refreshing to meet a woman who didn't automatically come on to him. He kept a smile from pulling at the corners of his mouth at the thought of her and leaned back on his seat, pushing up the sleeves of his sweatshirt.

"Lydia, you go on without me. I've got too much to do."

"Oh, come on, Kit. It's Saturday night. We could both use a couple of drinks and some good music."

"Do you know how long it's been since David's death? Less than three weeks."

"So?"

"So try a little respect for the dead."

"I was thinking of the living." She touched his hand. "You, for instance. Always working so hard—"

"You don't have to worry about me." He withdrew his hand. "I can take care of myself."

She tossed her hair back as Kit surveyed her, wondering what he had to say to this woman to get through to her that he wasn't interested in her. She returned his stare, her eyes full of smoldering lights. Her lip twitched slightly.

"I don't think you know what you need, Kit."

"And you do?"

"Yes." She slipped her silken hair over her left shoulder. "But you've never given me a chance to show you what a real Nakalt woman can do for a man."

"Lydia—"

"Your white women didn't satisfy you, did they?"

Kit's hands tightened around the arms of his chair. He was quickly losing patience with Lydia, who seemed to think his private life was up for discussion and that his sexual encounters had occurred only with white women. He had always been attracted to blondes, it was true—a propensity he had battled for years—but his relationships had been with a variety of women, not just white women.

"Admit it, Kit. They just weren't enough, were they?"

Kit opened a drawer, trying to ignore her as she leaned over the desk, planting both hands on the blotter so that her generous breasts loomed at eye level. He looked down.

"It takes a Nakalt woman to bring a Nakalt man real satisfaction, Kit. Haven't you found that out yet?"

"One woman's the same as the other when it comes right down to it."

"Not true, Kitsap. You know that isn't true."

Kit spread his hand over a folder, flicking the corner of it, refusing to look at her.

"You've got a secret way of doing things, Kitsap Makinna, handed down by your grandfather to your father and to you. David knew the secret, but I'm sure you're the expert in the family. You always did everything well."

Kit was silent. Talking with Lydia about the intimate bonding between a man and a woman robbed the act of its sanctity.

"Did you share the secret with your white women?"

Kit hadn't, but Lydia didn't need to know about his sexual activities. He looked at her face. "Drop it, Lydia."

"Why?" Her eyes flashed at him, full of arousal. "Does the truth disturb you?"

"No. This subject disturbs me. My brother is dead. He

was your husband, for crying out loud. Didn't you care about him at all?"

"I did at first. But he wasn't you, Kitsap. He could never be you."

"You shouldn't have expected him to be."

Her face flushed and her full lips compressed into a tight line. For the first time Kit noticed the puffiness under her chin and the lines around her mouth. Lydia wasn't a young maiden anymore. She was a thirty-three-year-old woman whose weight had crept over the line of pleasingly plump. In a few more years at the same rate, her looks and figure would disintegrate into middle age.

She rose from the desk and squared her shoulders. "I'm not going to wait around for you to come to me, Kit, not like in the old days when I had to play the part of the shy, retiring maiden. I'm not a maiden anymore, and I'm tired of waiting for you to make the first move."

"Has it ever occurred to you that I'm never going to make a move?"

"But why? Can't you see that we belong together?"

"No. And I will not discuss it with David still warm in the grave."

She raised her chin. "David's death has nothing to do with my feelings for you. I've always wanted you, Kit."

"I can't help that. And if you don't drop it, I'll hit the road so fast it'll make your head swim."

"You wouldn't leave Adam right now, would you?"

"He can go with me."

"What about Old Man? What about the lodge?"

Kit rose to his feet. Lydia slid her hands from the desk without taking her gaze off his face. They faced each other across the expanse of the desktop. "Lydia, listen to me. I am not going to be part of your life. The sooner you realize that, the better off you'll be."

She blinked, finally realizing that he meant to refuse her again. Her manicured hand fumbled for the strap of her purse, the only outward sign of her insecurity.

"Go dancing, if that's what you want, Lydia. Find a man who will appreciate you."

"Who? Somebody else? I'm the Snow Maiden, god-dammit—not some slut looking for action! I am destined to be yours! Yours!" She sucked in a breath, her large breasts rising up. "And don't you forget it, you bastard!" She whirled and marched to the door, turning before she went out.

"You think you're too good for me, don't you! You've always thought so! Well, someday you're going to want somebody the way I want you. And I hope she kicks you in the balls!"

She stomped out of the building.

Kit sighed and rubbed his hand over his mouth and jaw. How many times would Lydia play this scene before she gave up? Would she ever give up? Was her conviction that she was the legendary Snow Maiden and he the prophesied chief so strong that she would sacrifice her pride? Her blind faith was aggravating as hell, but sad in a way, too, for she couldn't see that her persistence only drove him farther and farther away. He shook his head and returned to his work.

Her ears still buzzing from the hours she had spent on the phone, Camille sat at the table, one leg crossed under her. She concentrated on her drawing, trying to remember every detail of the ritual she had witnessed at Old Man's house. She hoped if she kept her hands busy, she might blot her worry for Barbara from her thoughts. But as she inked over her pencil lines, her mind went over the phone conversations she had had earlier that evening regarding her missing friend.

None of the phone calls she had placed had eased her worry or given her anything to go on. Barbara's parents were on a cruise in the Mediterranean and couldn't be reached. Their housekeeper was certain that Barbara hadn't called for a couple of weeks. None of Barbara's friends from San Francisco had heard from her either. After receiving no help from those closest to Barbara, Camille had called anyone even remotely connected to her, only to get the same results. It was as if Barbara had dropped off the face of the earth. It wasn't unusual for her not to call or send a note, but the silence concerned Camille. How could Barbara just disappear? Something must have happened to her.

Sick with worry, Camille took her only other recourse and called the county sheriff's office. There she got such vague advice about working with the tribal police that she knew the county sheriff would do nothing, just as Two Hand had predicted. By the time she got off the phone she was surrounded by darkness, with only the fire and the lamp on her table for light. When a wolf howl pierced the silence, she looked up from the phone in surprise. The wolf was not far from the cabin.

Camille shuddered and then walked to the fire and piled on another log. A burst of orange sparks flew upward, startling her. She squatted and held her hands out to the heat. In her small apartment at the Lewis Academy, she had no fireplace, nor had she ever lived in a house with one. She hadn't realized until coming to the reservation how comforting a fire could be, especially when she was faced with the realization that she was utterly alone.

The wolf howled again and was answered by another. Camille sat back on her haunches and listened, trying to judge from which direction the noise was coming—probably along the lane from the Makinna Lodge. Slowly she rose to her feet. Funny, but she thought she remembered Barbara remarking that there were no wolves on the Olympic Peninsula anymore. They'd been shot and trapped into oblivion. If any wolves did exist in the area, they probably kept to the high slopes of the Olympic Mountains. Why would they come so close to civilization?

Camille returned to her chair, still warm from the heat of her body, and in an effort to get her mind off the wolf, she studied the image she had drawn of Old Man chanting. Even though she had not worked from a photograph, she thought she had done a fair job of capturing his likeness. But Old Man's face blurred as the wolf howled again, singing mournfully into the night. The hairs on the back of her neck and arms prickled, and she glanced toward the door. Either her ears were playing tricks on her or the wolves were getting closer every minute.

Another howl sent her to her feet. She crossed the room to the kitchen sink and looked out the window. Even though she was slightly unnerved by the sound of the animals, she wanted to get a glimpse of them, never having seen a wolf in the wild. But at nine-thirty the night was pitch black and she couldn't see a thing except for the dark towers of trees in the side yard. For good measure, she tugged the chintz curtains closed so no one could see into the cabin. When she turned around, she noticed her amulet lay warm against her skin.

The wolf cried again, and Camille realized that it had moved to the front of the cabin. She grabbed the broom for use as a weapon, although she wasn't sure about its effectiveness against a wolf. But there wasn't any other weapon in the cabin.

On each side of the door was a long narrow window made of textured gold glass. She could see only distorted images through the bumpy glass, and nothing in the distinct shape of a wolf. In fact, all she could make out was a tall image, much taller than any wolf. Perhaps she was looking at a tree, but she couldn't remember a tree of that height so near the path to the front door.

Camille's curiosity was piqued. Her amulet glowed with heat until she had to pull it out of her shirt again. She gripped the broom handle tightly and turned the lock on the door, opening it a crack.

There on the path stood the same naked man she had seen on the bluff, surrounded by ten pacing wolves, their eyes glowing an eerie greenish blue in the darkness as they circled around the legs of the man, their tongues lolling between their teeth. Camille gaped at the huge, long-legged creatures, which were much larger in real life than they had appeared to be on television. They had big ruffs around their necks and great bushy tails. Then she saw the man step toward her.

"Leave me alone," she yelled, certain of his identity even though she still couldn't explain the change in his hair. "I know it's you, Kit." But Kit didn't heed her warning. He took another step forward, the wolves at his heels. She focused her attention on his upper torso, too embarrassed to glance at the rest of his naked anatomy.

"Come any closer and I'll call the police!"

"Wait," the man said, holding up his hand.

Camille slammed the door and locked it. Then she ran to the back porch to make certain that the rear entry was secure. She turned around and glanced at the front door. Kit could easily kick it in and have his way with her, if that was his intention. At this point she wasn't certain what he did want. Perhaps he just enjoyed shocking her. Camille gripped the broom in both hands, brandishing it like a baseball bat, ready to whack him over the head the moment he came through the door.

7

Camille waited for Kit to kick down the door, but he never made a move. In fact, he didn't even call out to her. She waited for a full ten minutes, wondering why he wasn't trying to get in, until her amulet cooled, until the broom felt like a lead weight in her hands. Finally she let it droop to the floor. Kit must have wanted to scare her and nothing more. She frowned, wishing he'd freeze in the cold.

She had a nagging sensation that she was being watched, but she wouldn't chance opening the front door again to see if Kit had gone. He might be standing on the porch waiting for her curiosity to overcome her good sense again. Camille glanced around the room. All the curtains were closed. There was no way he could see her, unless he knew of a chink between the logs or a crack in the window trim of which she was unaware.

Had Kit harassed Barbara? Was that why she had run

away? Had he done something to frighten her off the premises? Camille walked to the couch and sat down with the broom across her knees. Why would a man such as Kit have to pester women when he could have any woman he chose just by crooking his finger at her? Maybe he had a psychological aberration that compelled him to frighten people. Maybe he had a hangup about white women and derived a twisted pleasure out of victimizing them. Camille reached for the phone and called the police. She wasn't going to let Kit hassle her.

Donald Two Hand promised to come out immediately. Camille sat back to wait for him—trying not to worry that he might show up tomorrow or later, for that matter—and didn't relax until she heard the sound of a car pulling up in the drive.

"Miss Avery?" a gruff voice called from the other side of the front door. "It's the police."

Camille jumped to her feet and hurried to the door, opening it wide. "Come in." She looked past the powerful shape of Donald Two Hand but could see no evidence of Kit or his wolves.

Donald Two Hand stepped into the cabin and glanced around as he hooked his thumbs in his utility belt. He wasn't a tall man, but he had a powerful chest and arms so muscular that the sleeves of his uniform stretched over his biceps. He was one of the ugliest men she had ever seen, with ruddy, pitted skin that looked like the hide of a strawberry. His eyes were set above wide round cheekbones and appeared small and cold in the shadow of his prominent brow. But he had the air of a man who meant business, and his powerful presence reassured her.

"You say you saw a prowler?"

"Yes." She shut the door. "I think it was Kitsap Makinna. He was standing out there naked."

Donald Two Hand blinked and then looked her over as if there must be a reason she was spouting nonsense. Camille stood straight, her spine stiff.

"What's that again?"

"The man was Mr. Makinna. He might have been wearing a wig."

"What kind of wig?"

"A black one, shoulder length. And he had a bunch of wolves with him. About ten, I'd say."

Donald Two Hand pursed his lips as if to dislodge something from between his front teeth and studied the opposite wall. His gaze drifted to the couch, to the manuscript box on the floor beside it, and then to the drawing on the table. At his silence, Camille suddenly realized how farfetched the description might sound to someone who had not seen Kit and his animals.

"You say he was naked?"

"Yes."

"What was he doing?"

"Well, he was just standing out there at first. And then he started walking toward me."

"Did he say anything?"

"No. But after I told him I was going to call the police, he said 'Wait.' "

"And then what did he do?"

"I don't know. I slammed the door and called you."

Two Hand ambled back to the door. "I'll look around."

"Thanks."

She waited on the doorstep as Two Hand tramped around the damp grass, shining his flashlight into the bushes and trees. For a few minutes he disappeared around the back of the cabin and then returned to the front door.

"I don't see anything out here, Miss Avery."

"He must have gone home."

She ushered him back into the cabin, where he switched off the flashlight and scratched his head.

"You sure it was Kit Makinna?"

"I couldn't swear, but it certainly looked like him."

"That would be awful strange behavior for Kit Makinna—to be exposing himself to women. And you say the prowler had a bunch of wolves?"

"Yes."

"Not dogs."

"No. Wolves."

Two Hand shook his head. "There haven't been wolves around here for years."

"What are you saying, that I fabricated the incident?"

"No." Two Hand squinted and glanced at her. "Not exactly. You haven't been drinking, have you, Miss Avery?"

"Of course not!"

"It's not that I don't believe you, Miss—"

"You *don't* believe me! You think I made it up!"

"Now I didn't say that—"

"Why would I make something like this up?"

"I don't know, Miss Avery. But I can't see Kit Makinna walking around in his birthday suit with a bunch of wolves."

"But it's—"

"With what happened to your friend, I'd suggest going back to the Makinna Lodge. At least for the night."

"No." The last place she wanted to go was back to the lodge and Kitsap Makinna. "I don't want to go back there."

"I don't think it's good idea for you to stay here."

Camille sighed in exasperation. "Are you going to file a report on this?" she asked, angry that he doubted her.

"Yeah, I'll file a report." He walked to the door. "In the meantime, why don't you let me give you a lift to the lodge?"

"No thanks." She shook her head. "I'd rather stay here."

"What if the naked guy comes back?"

"I'll take a picture as proof."

Two Hand didn't smile. "You're on your own, then, Miss Avery."

"Fine. Thanks for coming."

He shut the door behind him. Camille listened to his car pull away, and then she locked up. She was too upset to be frightened and almost wished the naked man would return so she could call Two Hand back and have him see the man for himself.

She trudged to the sofa and propped the broom up on the arm of the couch, keeping it close by in case Makinna decided to come back for an encore.

No more wolves howled that night, and the naked man didn't reappear, but she never left the couch and spent the night sitting up, ready to defend herself.

Kit yawned and stretched as he glanced at the hall near the rest rooms. The supplies that Camille and Adam had unloaded from the truck were stacked neatly against the wall. On top of the stack were five gallon buckets of off white paint, the color Lydia had chosen for the bathrooms and most of the other rooms as well. Sunday morning was the one day out of the week when he liked to sit around and read the paper and take his dog for a walk. But this Sunday he'd have to forgo such pleasures. If he didn't start on the lodge soon, he wouldn't get done with the project until summer, and he had no desire to be on the reservation that long. He pushed up the sleeves of the raggy gray sweatshirt he had found in a box of David's clothing and lifted a bucket just as the lobby door swung open.

"Good morning, Old Man," he called as his grandfather shuffled into the lodge.

"Good morning." Old Man shoved back the hood of his parka, which dripped with rain. Underneath it he wore a red ball cap with a fish appliqué sewn on the front.

"What are you doing up and about on a miserable day like today?"

"I'm headed for the cabin."

"Barbara Stanton's cabin?"

"Yep. Come with me, Kitsap."

"Why are you going there?"

"I want to talk to Miss Avery."

"Why?"

"I had a dream about her last night."

"You and your dreams." Kit shook his head. His grandfather and the other elders were always having dreams, and as far as he knew, nothing had come of their visions. Old Man's crony, Charlie Adams, had dreamed of Lydia as the Snow Maiden when she was just a little girl, and that dream had caused Kit nothing but trouble. With a screwdriver he pried off the lid of the pail and set it aside.

"Laugh all you want, Kitsap. Someday you'll realize that spirits can talk to you in your dreams."

"I'm not laughing, Old Man." Kit stood up and wiped his palms on his thighs. "I'm just being skeptical."

"Skeptics never dream spirit dreams."

"Maybe they don't." He searched through the supplies for a paint stirrer. Old Man hobbled up behind him.

"I dreamed of the wolf last night. He came to me and spoke."

"What did he say, Old Man?"

"*Queece*. Snow."

"What's so significant about the word *snow*?"

"Maybe it has something to do with the Snow Maiden."

"For crying out loud, not that again!"

Kit rifled through a box of brushes and rollers, his movements sharp with annoyance. He was so upset, he couldn't even see what his hands touched.

"But first there was a strange vision, Kit."

"I don't want to hear, Old Man!" He found the small piece of wood used to stir the paint and turned back to the bucket, glancing at his grandfather in hopes that his harsh words hadn't offended the old man. He didn't wish to be cruel, but he was out of patience with dreams and prophecy. He'd had enough years ago. And though he'd run away from the reservation for just that reason, nobody seemed to recognize the fact that he didn't want to play the game—not then and not now.

Old Man gazed at him with dismay etched in the lines around his mouth. He adjusted his glasses on his nose with a trembling hand. At the movement, Kit was struck anew by the age of his grandfather, a hundred-year-old man who was kept alive by his dreams and rituals. A hot shaft of shame coursed through him.

He sighed. "All right, Old Man. What was the first part of the dream?"

"Why should I tell you?" Old Man stared out of the window. "You will not hear, anyway."

"Just tell me, for crying out loud. I'm listening."

"But will you believe?"

"I'll believe." He ran a hand through his hair and tried

to smooth the angry edge from his voice. "Would you just tell me?"

"I will tell you if you promise to come with me to Miss Avery's cabin."

Camille Avery's cabin was the last place Kit wanted to visit. The woman had a crazy misconception about him, and nothing he said seemed capable of changing her mind. The fact bothered him, and he didn't know why. Most of the time he didn't pay much attention to what people thought of him, so why should he make an exception for her? Besides that, it would be better for him to steer clear of her because he'd found himself worrying about her off and on since he had first met her. And God knew he didn't need anything else to worry about now.

"You will not come, then, Kitsap?"

"All right. I'll come. You shouldn't be walking around in the rain anyway."

"There is nothing wrong with rain. It cleanses the earth."

"It'll give an old man like you a good case of pneumonia."

"Ha. I haven't been sick in years. It's you young people who drive everywhere that get sick, breathing all those fumes."

Kit replaced the lid on the paint bucket and pressed it down with the heel of his shoe. Then he lugged the bucket to the side of the hall, out of the way.

"Okay, Old Man. Now tell me the dream."

George Makinna licked his lips. "I saw Miss Avery in my dream. She was standing near the river out near the bridge and she was brushing something off her arms."

"What's so strange about that?"

"She was brushing off something white, Kitsap. Snow."

Kit felt a chill race down the backs of his arms and shoot

across his scalp. But he only chuckled wryly. "So, maybe she didn't want to get wet."

Old Man frowned. "You laugh. But it is not funny. She was brushing snow off her sleeves. This was a Snow Maiden dream, brought to me by a wolf spirit, who spoke to me of the word *snow* to explain the dream."

"What does it mean, though? That Camille Avery is the Snow Maiden?"

"I'm not certain how to interpret the dream yet."

"But how could a white woman be the Snow Maiden?"

"It is a strange idea to consider, isn't it?"

Kit's smile faded quickly. "There must be an explanation, another interpretation."

"I don't know." Old Man headed for the door. "The Snow Maiden in the legend was the daughter of the North Wind. And what is the color of the wind, Kitsap? I don't know."

Kit didn't know, either, and followed in silence.

At the door Old Man turned, slipped his hand into the pocket of his parka, and drew out a long black feather.

"This was on my doorstep when I woke up." He cradled it in his wrinkled, arthritic hands as if it were a precious heirloom.

"A raven feather?"

"Yes. A sign."

Kit grabbed his parka from a knob near the entry and then held the door open for his grandfather. Old Man shuffled onto the back porch as he carefully replaced the feather.

"Charlie was mistaken about Lydia being the Snow Maiden. I don't want to make the same mistake. So I need to be very certain this time. Very certain."

"Yeah," Kit agreed, zipping his coat. "Don't say anything to Miss Avery, okay, Old Man? I've had enough trouble with Lydia about this."

Oscar Duarte swore under his breath when he heard the doorbell ring. He had been enjoying his second cup of coffee and didn't wish to be disturbed on a Sunday morning, especially if it was some idiotic youngster selling candy bars to raise money for a sports club, as so often happened when he was trying to relax. He walked to the door, planning to look through the fish-eye lens. If a uniformed child stood on his stoop, he wouldn't answer.

He put his eye to the lens and was almost pleased to see Donald Two Hand standing there, his back facing the lens.

Oscar opened the door.

"Hi, Doc," Two Hand said, stepping inside while Oscar quickly shut the door behind him.

"I thought I told you never to come to the house."

"Well, I got the book. Thought you might like to have it first thing." Two Hand held out a computer manual that he had bought from a bookstore in Port Angeles.

"Good." Duarte reached for the book. He scanned the cover. *Macintosh Reference Guide.* Perhaps now he could find his way around Barbara Stanton's portable computer. He wasn't accustomed to using such a new contraption, and he had to admit that he was stumped. Barbara had claimed to keep a journal, but so far they hadn't been able to find one. He had heard of people using their computers to balance checkbooks, remind them of appointments, and perform other personal organizational tasks. Perhaps the missing journal wasn't missing after all but was somewhere in the files of the portable computer. Now all he had to do was learn how to get into the files, which would be easy once he had a manual.

Oscar glanced at Two Hand, who stood in the foyer gawking at Oscar's house, which was decorated with artifacts of digs he had worked on since he was a college student. The walls were covered with everything from African masks to framed tapestries. Oscar frowned, primarily because Two Hand had violated an agreement never to visit him at his home, but also for his gawking. What would Two Hand know about the objects? Not in a million years would he appreciate the hours of sweat and tedium represented on the walls he gaped at with such idle curiosity. What Two Hand was staring at was more than forty years of Oscar's life, forty years of unappreciated slave labor that had gone unrecognized by the scientific community. He had never discovered anything out of the ordinary, never made a headline. But that would change. Once he found the Spanish gold, his life would change forever.

"Nice place," Two Hand commented in a gross understatement.

"Thanks." Oscar tucked the book under his arm. "Have you talked to the Avery woman?"

"Yeah. She doesn't suspect a thing. Thinks Kit Makinna is harassing her."

"Kit Makinna?"

"Yeah. She's a hysterical type. Thinks Kit is running around showing his dick."

"You can't be serious!"

"I am." Two Hand shook his head and chuckled. "She doesn't suspect a thing. And if we need to, we can scare her off. Should be easy."

"Well, I don't think that will be necessary, now that I've got this." He tapped the book with his free hand. "We'll soon find out if Miss Barbara Stanton wrote anything down that would implicate us."

Two Hand stuck his thumbs in his belt. "Those computers make me jumpy."

"Leave it to me. I'll call you."

"Good." Two Hand craned his neck as if looking for the source of the delicious coffee smell wafting from the kitchen.

"I'll call you, Two Hand."

"Oh. Yeah. Fine." He nodded and lumbered out to the stoop. "You digging tomorrow, Doc?"

"Yes. You'd better be there."

"I'll be there. Don't you worry."

"And if you show up here again, the deal is off."

"Oh, yeah?" Two Hand narrowed his small eyes. "You need me more than I need you, Doc, and don't you forget it."

8

"*This Miss Avery* worries you," Old Man remarked as he and Kit walked up the beach toward Barbara Stanton's cabin.

Kit shot a glance at his grandfather, but the old man wasn't looking at him. He felt slightly relieved that he wasn't being scrutinized by his grandfather's piercing eyes. "I never said that."

"Some things you do not have to say, Kitsap."

Kit frowned and watched Sandy range far ahead, charging clusters of seagulls and ravens, enjoying her freedom. He might have enjoyed the walk along the shore, too, had it not been for the sudden turn in the conversation. He didn't want to think about Camille Avery, much less talk about her.

"When I was a young man such as you . . ." Old Man continued, reaching down for an agate that had washed up on the sand. He held the stone up to the light and looked through it, then put it in the pocket of his parka. "I had woman trouble, too."

"I don't have any trouble."

"Bah! Women give themselves to you too easily, don't they?"

"I guess." Kit bent down to pick up a rock and tried to ignore the knot in his gut. He had no wish to discuss his love life with Old Man any more than he wished to talk about it with Lydia. And there was some part of him that didn't want to admit to anyone how long he'd gone without female companionship. He skipped the stone across the water and smiled ruefully. Lydia thought he was a womanizer, falling for every blonde white woman who crossed his path. That might have been true when he was in his late teens and early twenties. But now at thirty-four, he rarely even dated. He hadn't the time or the inclination to enter into any more meaningless relationships. And deep in his heart he had always felt that he should marry a Nakalt woman to remain true to his heritage.

"Do you know the way to end your problem with women?"

"Yeah," Kit replied, laughing dryly as he tossed another rock. "Quit seeing them."

"Marriage."

Kit stopped a toss in midair.

"I can find you a good woman, Kitsap."

Kit's arm came down in a swoop. "No thanks, Old Man."

"You are wasting the best years of your life. You should have a wife and a family."

He knew he should. But how could he tell his grandfather that he had never found a Nakalt woman who remotely interested him? Yet a woman like Camille Avery, with her platinum hair and vulnerable hazel eyes, had at-

tracted him the moment he had seen her across a shadowed room. He wasn't certain anymore whether his pref-
erence for blondes was part of a need to distance himself
from his people and their damned prophecy or if he really
was attracted to women like Camille. And if he couldn't
decide for himself, how would he ever explain it to his
grandfather?

"There are many beautiful young women on the reservation, Kitsap. Any one of them would make a good wife
for you. Have you seen Frank Hall's daughter?"

"No. And don't arrange anything, Old Man. I have
enough to do around here."

"And there is Lydia."

"Lydia is not an option." Kit sighed. "Enough marriage
talk, Old Man, all right?"

Thankfully, Old Man let the subject drop and walked
along quietly. Kit took a deep breath of the pungent sea air
and squinted in the sunshine that suddenly broke through
the rain clouds. Being on the secluded beach with only his
grandfather and his dog filled him with an ache of satisfaction made more poignant by the fact that such satisfaction
would be short-lived. Soon he would return to Seattle to
his fisheries job, his desk and tie, the endless meetings, and
bumper-to-bumper traffic. The prospect did not appeal to
him.

"Who's that?" Old Man asked, breaking into his
thoughts.

Kit looked up the beach toward the cabin, where he saw
a small figure wading out in the water.

"Some fool," Kit replied. The water of the strait was
deceptively placid on the surface but dangerous beneath,
full of strong currents and treacherous undertows. One
slip on the clay shoals and even an innocent foray like wad-

ing could wind up in tragedy. Besides that, who in his right mind would go wading in the middle of winter?

"I'll go on ahead," Kit remarked to his grandfather. "And get that kid out of the water."

Old Man nodded, and Kit broke into a run. His footfalls were steady and sure on the rocky beach, and he was heartened to find that he hadn't lost his agility after years of being off the reservation. It took a practiced eye to spot the best place to leap and a great deal of balance, all of which had to be learned over time. Kit leapt from rock to rock, vaulting tidal pools, and felt like a boy again.

He arrived at the place where the wader stood in the water and stopped short when he recognized the nearly white hair sticking out from under the hood of a gray sweatshirt. Camille Avery. She was up to her thighs in the water. Damn that woman—she had been nothing but trouble since her arrival at the reservation.

"Avery!" he shouted. Her back was turned to him, and she didn't respond. He cupped his hands around his mouth and yelled louder. "Avery!"

She turned and glanced his way. He motioned for her to come to shore, but she shook her head and waded out even farther, until she was up to her waist. She was reaching for something ahead of her. What in the hell was she doing?

Suddenly she lunged forward, lost her footing, and plunged into the water. Without thinking, Kit ripped off his parka and tore into the water, splashing through the shallows and then knifing into the waves, closing the gap between them with powerful strokes. The sea was icy cold, and he gasped from the chill as he broke the surface. He could see Camille thrashing in the water five feet away. With one more stroke he reached her, grabbed for her, and pulled her toward shore.

The current was strong, and Camille twisted and

kicked, impeding his progress. By the time he reached the shallows, he was winded and his breath came in great heaves. He struggled to his feet, dragging Camille with him.

"What do you think you're doing?" she shouted, her hair streaming in her face. She yanked her arm from his grip and glared at him.

"What do you think *you're* doing?" he yelled back. "You could have drowned out there!"

"What?" She wiped her face with her hand.

"Undertow!" Kit shouted. "Only a fool would be out here!" He flashed a glance over her body, her curves outlined by her sodden pants. Until that moment he had never realized how petite she was. Her slender thighs weren't much larger than the tops of his arms. His glance swept upward, and he was almost disappointed that the bulky sweatshirt concealed the rest of her. Then Kit noticed she held something under her left arm—a brown-and-white herring gull, oddly contorted by a plastic ring from a set of pop or beer cans. The plastic had trapped its neck and one leg, crippling the bird.

She hadn't been wading, she'd been trying to rescue a bird. He felt like a damned fool. His glance met her accusing eyes, and he quickly looked away.

"Come on," he said. "I'll give you a hand. It's freezing."

"I was doing just fine before you jumped on me," she said through gritted teeth, although she did allow him to guide her by the arm.

"I thought you were being pulled under."

"You could have asked first."

"Sorry. From what I could see, I thought you were in trouble."

Camille slipped on the greasy clay bottom, and Kit clutched her elbow to keep her on her feet.

"See? It's dangerous around here," he remarked. "You shouldn't try any more rescues without a canoe or a boat."

They reached the beach, and Camille immediately wrenched away from his grasp. Old Man stood waiting for them, and Sandy barked at the bird until Kit had to grab her collar to restrain her.

"Bring the bird to me," Old Man instructed, shoving his hand in the pocket of his knit pants. He drew out a pocketknife and fumbled to open the blade, but his hands didn't tremble at all when he gently cut the first ring of plastic.

"There you are, my sister," he crooned to the wary gull. Camille held the bird steady while he cut the rest of the bonds, even though Kit could tell she was as frozen to the bone as he was. He studied her in grudging admiration as she ignored her comfort to save a bird.

Old Man slipped the plastic from the bird, and it shook its head, its entire body shuddering from the unbelievable release.

"Should I let it go now?" Camille asked Old Man. He nodded, and she carefully put the bird on a nearby rock. It limped away, flapped its wings, and took off. Camille watched it go, shading her eyes from the sun, while Kit watched her shapely lips curve into a small smile of wonder and joy. Then she grinned, her teeth chattering, and looked over her shoulder at his grandfather. Kit was struck by the innocence and honesty of that pure smile and the look of utter happiness on her pale face. Something inside him twisted and ached at the sight of her.

Then his grandfather gave a small nod of approval to Camille. That nearly imperceptible nod was the greatest praise he ever bestowed, especially upon someone who was not a Nakalt. Kit felt a fierce pride for Camille well up inside him, confusing the hell out of him. Why should he take any pride in her actions?

Suddenly a huge raven swooped down from a spruce tree near the cabin, splintering the beauty of the moment with a raucous caw. It flapped so closely to Camille that she had to stumble backward to avoid being hit.

Kit grabbed her to keep her from falling on the rocks.

"Thanks," she gasped, staring after the bird. "Do all the ravens around here dive-bomb people?"

"No. He probably thought we had something to feed him." Kit saw his grandfather put his hand in the pocket of his parka, most likely to touch the feather he had put there earlier that morning. Kit frowned. To his grandfather, life was one sign after another, hung together like some kind of spiritual poem, and he could probably attach mystical significance to the appearance of the bird. But Kit was too cold to hear Old Man's theories about dive-bombing ravens. "Come on," he said, his voice terse with impatience. "Let's get out of these clothes before we freeze to death."

Old Man built up the fire while Kit and Camille slipped out of their wet clothes. In the small bathroom at the back of the cabin, Camille changed into a dry pair of jeans, a T-shirt, and a thick navy sweater. She ran a comb through her hair and glanced at her face in the mirror. The cold water had drained all the color from her cheeks, which only heightened the contrasting effect of her dark brows and large hazel eyes. She grimaced at her eyebrows, hating them more than ever. Then, still shivering, she pulled on a pair of thick socks and grabbed the pile of her damp garments.

She slipped out of the bedroom and saw Kit standing near the fire, wrapped in a gray wool blanket. The hair at the back of his head was as black and glossy as the feathers of the huge raven on the beach.

"Would you care for some coffee?" she asked.

Old Man nodded, and Kit remarked that coffee would be great.

She started the automatic coffee maker and then walked back to the fire.

"How about if I throw your clothes in the dryer?" she asked.

"You don't have to do that," Kit countered.

"Well, I don't have anything you can wear on the way back. And I'm not letting you have my blanket." She reached down for Kit's clothes, which lay on the floor near the hearth. "It won't be any trouble."

"All right. Thanks."

Camille walked to the back porch, threw both Kit's and her clothes in the dryer, and set the timer for a half hour. Then she served coffee, insisting that Old Man take the chair by the fire. The hot coffee was a welcome addition to dry clothing, and Camille gratefully wrapped her frozen fingers around her mug. Kit had to bare an arm in order to hold his cup, and Camille had to force herself not to stare at his tan shoulder and upper arm, both well developed. A fleeting image of his arm atop the sheets of a woman's bed—her bed, if she wanted to be honest about it—skittered through her mind before she turned off the thought, amazed at herself.

Suddenly Kit sneezed, nearly spilling his coffee. He set his mug on the mantelpiece and sneezed again. "You picked a damn fine time of the year to be rescuing waterfowl, Avery. We'll probably both wind up with pneumonia."

"A quick winter dip never hurt anyone," she retorted, put off by his criticism. "Besides, I didn't ask you to save me. I'm an excellent swimmer."

"Swimmer or not, don't go out there again."

Camille glared at him. Who did he think he was—her father? If he had been less curt, she might have thanked him, but his critical comments and preachy attitude riled her and squelched any thoughts of gratitude.

"Kitsap is right," Old Man put in. "There is danger all around us, Miss Avery, especially to those who don't know the reservation or the sea."

Camille decided to ignore Kit and concentrate on Old Man, who wasn't nearly as aggravating. "Do you suppose Barbara had an accident on the beach?"

"She may have." Old Man sipped his coffee, laced with lots of milk and sugar. "She was known to take long walks up to North Beach."

"Where is that?"

"The farthest tip of the peninsula," Kit answered, "where the Pacific Ocean meets the strait. It's a long walk, about five miles or so, right, Old Man?"

"Yes. At least."

"Has anyone looked for Barbara up there?"

Old Man shrugged.

"Could you draw me a map? I'll hike there myself."

"It is a hard trip, Miss Avery. Kitsap can take you by boat."

Camille glanced at Kit, and he didn't have time to hide his expression of protest. She felt a mild sense of deflation but countered it with good sense. After all, why would she want to spend an afternoon in a canoe with him? He'd probably give her all kind of directives, from how to sit to what clothing to wear.

She forced a smile. "Mr. Makinna is a busy man. I don't want to put him out."

"My grandson needs to go to North Beach. He needs to reacquaint himself with the land. Perhaps he will find his Nakalt heart on North Beach."

Kit turned to the fire, preventing Camille from reading his expression, but by the look of his stiff stance, he didn't agree with his grandfather's words.

"Do not walk alone up there, Miss Avery. It is a dangerous trail. And do not go out at night. There are spirits abroad that can bring you harm."

Kit turned slightly. "Old Man, don't frighten her with nonsense."

"Nonsense? It is no nonsense." Old Man set down his cup and leveled his glittering gaze upon her. "We old ones know of things that modern science will never be able to explain."

"Like what?" Camille inquired, intensely curious.

"In time you may be told, Miss Avery, when you are ready to accept it. Here." He touched his chest above his heart.

Kit shook his head as he stared at the fire. The dryer timer buzzed, and Camille rose. She walked to the porch and opened the dryer door, pulling out the jumble of clothes, her jeans wrapped around Kit's, her socks clinging to his briefs. The sight of their clothes intertwined made a flush creep up her neck. Quickly she pulled the garments apart, leaving her clothes on the dryer and folding Kit's into neat bundles.

He accepted his folded clothes with a smile of thanks and ducked into the bathroom to change. Old Man shuffled into the kitchen with his mug and put it on the counter. Camille followed him.

"May I ask a favor of you, Mr. Makinna?"

"Yes?"

"It's about Barbara's book. I'm supposed to do the drawings for it, but without Barbara here I don't know where to go for subject matter."

"There is the museum in town."

"Good. I'll go there."

"There is also the lodge, which has authentic corner posts and a collection of basketry that rivals that of the museum."

"Really? I didn't see it when I was there."

"Lydia has it stored in the attic during her remodeling."

"Do you think she'd let me see it and take a few photographs?"

"Lydia is unpredictable."

"Oh." Camille couldn't hide the disappointment in her voice.

"However, I will speak to her." Old Man pulled on his parka. "You come to dinner at the lodge tonight and I will show you what you need for your drawings."

"Would you?" She beamed. "That would be great, Mr. Makinna."

He nodded at her as Kit strode out of the bathroom, fully dressed, the blanket over his arm.

"Thanks," he said, handing her the cover. "Nothing like warm clothes after a swim."

"I have invited Miss Avery to dinner," Old Man commented. "At the lodge."

"Oh?" Kit glanced at him in surprise as if his grandfather weren't the kind to entertain strangers.

"You will come here and pick her up at seven so she won't have to walk in the dark."

"All right." Kit shrugged into his coat. "As long as I don't have to go swimming again."

"You didn't have to this time," Camille retorted, her temper flaring at his sarcasm.

She shut the door after they left and wondered if Kit would show up with or without clothing the next time she saw him.

♦ ♦ ♦

Camille spent the rest of the day reading Barbara's manuscript so she would have questions to ask Old Man in case he was willing to talk at dinner. Some of the manuscript she had already seen, since Barbara had sent her the first half of the book while she was still at the Lewis Academy. The second half, however, was completely new to Camille and full of interesting stories and details about Nakalt artifacts and customs.

One of the items mentioned was an amulet made of amber that encased a raven feather, supposedly an unusual and rare item. The amulet was no longer in existence, having been lost two centuries ago. But many Nakalt elders held a firm belief that the amulet would be delivered to the tribe when a legendary chief came back to his people.

Camille pulled out the disk of amber she wore on a thong around her neck and rested it on her palm. If the Nakalt amulet was rare, her necklace must be extremely valuable. She had never had it appraised, never had an expert look at it. Something inside her had cautioned her against having the necklace displayed to others—an irrational feeling, surely, but one so strong that she had never doubted it.

It was strange that she should possess an amulet that fit the description of the lost Nakalt talisman. But how could hers possibly be connected to the Nakalt amber? She had found hers in an attic in Charleston, South Carolina. How could the Nakalt necklace show up on the eastern seaboard? And who could have stolen the Nakalt amber in the 1700s? She doubted the Nakalt had even made contact with the outside world at that early date. Maybe it had been lost in an accident at sea, swallowed forever by the waves. She'd have to ask Old Man if he knew anything more about the necklace. Perhaps she'd even mention her amulet to him. If there was one person on the reservation she trusted implicitly, it was Old Man.

She slipped the amulet under her sweater just as someone knocked on her door.

9

Camille opened the door to find a thin, brown-haired man standing on the porch. He was dressed in a corduroy sport coat and slacks and a gold turtleneck.

"Miss Avery?" he asked, holding out his hand. "I'm Oscar Duarte."

The name meant nothing to Camille, and she hesitated before she extended her hand.

"I know your friend, Barbara Stanton."

"Oh. How do you do." She shook his hand. He clasped hers by gently squeezing the ends of her fingers in a handshake meant for women. Camille disliked the limp gesture.

"I hear she's missing."

"Yes." Camille stepped back, allowing him to enter the cabin. "We don't have any clues to her whereabouts. Do you know anything?"

"Alas, no." He passed through the doorway and looked

around in a brisk fashion. Camille had the sneaking suspicion that his brisk survey didn't miss a single detail.

"When was the last time you saw her?"

Oscar put a hand to his chin. He had long, bony fingers with clean, perfectly groomed nails. "Oh, I don't really know, exactly. Let's see. A few weeks ago, I suppose, at the Sand Bar Tavern."

"What was she doing there?"

"She was having a drink with David Makinna. I happened to stop by and saw her."

Why would Barbara have met David Makinna? And did the meeting have anything to do with David's death? Camille glanced at the far wall. If David had looked anything like Kit, it wouldn't be hard to guess why Barbara might want to spend a bit of time with him, although David was a married man and Barbara usually didn't mess around with married men. She had probably been gathering information for her book.

"Makinna had an eye for the ladies," Oscar put in with a little smile.

"Oh?" Camille didn't like his smug expression and decided she didn't like the man, either.

"I've heard that Miss Stanton kept a journal."

Camille shrugged, suddenly reluctant to tell Oscar Duarte anything about Barbara.

"I've been thinking," he continued, "if someone could find her journal, the authorities might be able to figure out what happened to her."

"I don't know where it would be—"

"Well, keep your eyes peeled for it. It might be our only hope for discovering where she is or what happened to her."

"It's odd, she never mentioned you to me, Mr. Duarte."

"Didn't she?" he said, smiling. "I'm crushed!"

"What was your relationship to her?"

"Well, I'm considered the resident authority on the Nakalt. I've done excavations up and down the coast here. Barbara—Miss Stanton, that is—often came to me for help. If you'd like, I could help you with the illustrations for the book."

"That's very kind of you, Mr. Duarte. Perhaps I'll contact you."

"I have a card." He reached into the pocket of his sports coat. "Here. Call me anytime."

"You're very considerate. Thank you."

"And if you hear anything about Barbara, do call me. I'm worried about her."

"I will."

She headed for the door just as Kit's Jeep pulled into the drive. Oscar hesitated on the porch, scowling at Kit as he climbed out of his truck. Camille noticed, however, that the scowl eased into a polite smile as Kit approached.

"Ready to go, Avery?" Kit asked.

"Yes."

Oscar held out his hand to Kit. "Oscar Duarte. And you are—"

"Kit Makinna."

"David's brother?"

"Yes."

"Why haven't we ever run into each other?"

Kit surveyed Oscar for a brief moment, and by his expression Camille could tell he held the same intuitive distrust of the man that she did.

"I've been away."

"Well, I'm sorry about your brother. We were all shocked and saddened by the news."

"Thank you."

Oscar turned to Camille. "Well, I must be off, Miss Avery. Don't hesitate to call me if you hear anything."

Camille nodded and forced a smile. She and Kit stood on the porch until Oscar got into his Volvo station wagon and pulled out of the drive.

"What did he want?" Kit asked.

"He was inquiring about Barbara."

Kit watched Oscar's car disappear down the lane while Camille walked into the cabin to get her trench coat. She returned and looked up to find Kit studying her. For a moment their gazes locked, his guarded and glittering, while her heart hammered against her chest, clamoring to be heard. Camille fought back the rush inside her and stepped forward.

"Ready?" she said, her voice cracking. She forced her glance to remain steady.

"Yeah. Let's go."

She followed him to the car, anxious to get to the lodge and talk with his grandfather.

Old Man had made good on his promise. He had convinced Lydia to unpack the baskets so that Camille could take photographs of them after dinner. Camille smiled as she slung the strap of her camera case over her shoulder and walked down the stairs, happy to have taken some excellent shots of the Makinna basket collection. Kit had kept his distance all evening, however, preferring to let the others help her. She was glad in a way, because his presence always set her on edge, and he would have been a distraction while she was taking pictures.

She stopped on the stairs to wait for Old Man, who came down behind her, and caught sight of Kit sitting near the fire. He was poring over a fat file folder cradled in his lap, his elbow perched on his knee and his hand immersed in his glossy hair. A bottle of beer sat on a carved box next to his seat. She watched him sip from it without taking his eyes off his reading.

She couldn't figure him out. What had she done to annoy him? Ever since that afternoon his attitude toward her had become cooler than ever, and throughout dinner he had hardly spoken a word to her.

Old Man reached the bottom stair. "Well, Miss Avery, did you get something to work with?"

"Yes. Thank you so much." She smiled at him. "You've been a great help."

At the sound of Camille's voice, Sandy barked and wagged her tail, knocking a flurry of Kit's papers to the floor.

"Dammit!" he exclaimed, and reached down. Camille hurried across the floor to help, but when she knelt down to gather the papers, she was nosed on the neck and shoulder by the dog.

"Sandy!" Kit admonished. "Cut it out!"

"It's all right," Camille put in, chuckling.

Kit scowled as he accepted the papers from her and leafed through them. "Oh, great. No page numbers—"

Camille straightened as Kit reordered the pages. He hadn't thanked her, hadn't even acknowledged her presence, and his foul temper perplexed her. What was the matter with him? She stood looking at him, wondering if she should leave before she made him any angrier.

Camille had wanted to ask Old Man about the necklace without Lydia being present, and this was the first moment since her arrival that Lydia hadn't hovered about monitoring her every move. She decided to ignore Kit's irritable behavior and take advantage of the opportunity to talk to Old Man.

She turned and watched Old Man lower himself to the bench near the fire.

"Before I go, could I ask you one more thing, Mr. Makinna?"

"Of course."

Camille stepped toward him and placed her camera on a nearby table. "I've been reading in Barbara's manuscript about an amber necklace that once belonged to the Nakalt."

Old Man nodded his head slowly. "It is true. We once possessed such a necklace."

"What happened to it?"

"It was stolen."

"Stolen?" Camille sank to the other end of the bench. "By whom?"

"By Spanish soldiers."

Spanish soldiers? Camille thought of the Spanish heritage of Charleston, South Carolina, the city in which she had lived and had found the necklace nineteen years ago. Could the Spanish soldiers who stole the necklace have taken it back to Charleston? The necklace might have been hidden in the floorboards of the house her grandparents owned, forgotten for decades until the time Camille stumbled across it.

Could the necklace she wore belong to the Nakalt? It would be too coincidental. Yet if the necklace did belong to the Nakalt and she told them she had it, how would they feel about her afterward? Her family had owned property in Charleston for hundreds of years. What if her ancestors had been responsible for the theft? Would the Nakalt condemn her for the part her family had played in history?

"You stare at the fire, Miss Avery," Old Man remarked, "but you are not watching the flames."

Camille jerked out of her thoughts. "I was just thinking

about the soldiers. How did they get hold of the necklace? And when?"

"Late in the seventeen hundreds." He placed one gnarled hand on top of the other. "To possess the amber, they murdered a great chief and slaughtered many of the people."

"Why?"

"Because the necklace was powerful. Yet the Spaniards were unaware of a most important aspect of the necklace."

"And what was that?"

"To take the amber in violence brings terrible misfortune upon the thief. Even death."

"So the Spaniards died?"

"We don't know. We only know that the amulet was never returned to us. But someday it will be ours again, and the Nakalt will be strong. That is our belief."

Camille sat in silence, wondering whether or not to say anything about the amber that lay against her skin. Before she could decide, Old Man murmured a phrase in another tongue, which Camille hoped he would translate. As if he read her mind, he repeated the words in English.

"When the great chief returns with the Snow Maiden, then will the amber return. That is the prophecy."

Out of the corner of her eye she saw Kit look up and shake his head.

"So a chief will bring back the necklace?" Camille asked, a tremor in her voice.

"That is our belief."

How did she fit into the prophecy? She certainly wasn't a chief. Perhaps her necklace wasn't the Nakalt amber after all.

"It was thought that Kitsap was to fulfill the prophecy," Old Man continued, glancing at his grandson. "But he has never accepted it as truth."

Disgusted, Kit put his folder aside. "Just because I ended up with a certain set of genes doesn't make the prophecy come true, Old Man."

"Bah!" Old Man waved him off. "More science talk!"

"What do you mean?" Camille asked. "What do genes have to do with the prophecy?"

"Kitsap is the living image of one of our great chiefs, Miss Avery. You can see the portrait of this chief in the museum."

"You mean to say that Mr. Makinna looks like another man?"

"Yes," Kit put in. "But when family resemblance occurs in the Makinna clan, it suddenly becomes a phenomenon."

Old Man ignored Kit's sarcastic remark. "What troubles you, Miss Avery? You seem upset."

"It's just that—" She broke off.

"Go on, Miss Avery," Old Man urged, pushing up his glasses. The flames reflecting on the lenses gave his eyes an otherworldly expression.

"It's just that I owe your grandson an apology."

Kit crossed his arms. "For what?"

"For accusing you of running around naked."

Old Man stood up. "What?"

"The other night when I stayed here, I saw a naked man and thought he was Mr. Makinna here. He looked just like him, except for the long hair. And he was totally naked."

"Naked?"

"Yes. I saw him again last night at the cabin, too." She turned back to Kit. "I must have seen the chief instead of you." Although what a chief would be doing prancing around in the buff was beyond her. "I'm sorry I jumped to conclusions, Mr. Makinna."

Instead of accepting her apology with a smile, Kit

frowned. "I know it wasn't me, Miss Avery," he replied. "But it couldn't have been the chief, either."

"Why not?"

"Because he's been dead for two centuries."

Camille stared at him. Then she heard Old Man wheeze and turned to glance at him.

"Are you all right?" she asked, seeing the stricken expression on his face.

He nodded, coughing, as Kit strode to his side. "Are you sure you're okay, Old Man?"

"Yes." He wheezed again as Kit helped him sit on the bench. Camille stood by, worried that she had upset the old man. He was so thin and fragile.

"What did I tell you, Kitsap?" he sputtered. "My dream—"

"Don't talk, Old Man. Just take it easy."

"But she can see him!"

"Who?"

"Mak-ee-nah! His spirit."

"Oh, for crying out loud!"

"He has appeared to her. The great chief returns!"

"Listen to what you're saying, Old Man." Kit laid his hand upon his grandfather's forearm. "It's absurd."

"Why?"

"Why?" Kit gestured toward Camille with his long, slender hand. "Why would a great chief appear to her? She's a—"

Kit broke off, and Camille felt herself flush with indignation.

"What are you saying, Kitsap?"

"I'm saying that she's a white woman. Why would Mak-ee-nah show himself to a white woman? It doesn't make sense."

Camille felt her cheeks grow hotter. "What's wrong

with being a white woman?" she said, her voice husky with anger.

"Nothing. I just don't think a white woman belongs in the Nakalt prophecy, that's all."

"I saw what I saw."

"Yes, well, there's probably a good explanation that doesn't include spirits and prophecy."

"You think you have all the answers, don't you?" Camille retorted. "You think I'm just a hysterical woman, don't you?"

Kit scowled. She scowled back.

"I think it's time I said good night." She picked up her camera case. "Thank you, Mr. Makinna, for your help."

"Miss Avery—" He reached out.

"Good night." She turned on her heel and hurried for the door.

"Kit, go with her," Old Man said.

Camille threw on her coat, hoping Kit wouldn't follow her because he felt obligated to do his grandfather's bidding. She would rather face the so-called spirits in the night than be accompanied by a bad-tempered male chauvinist.

As she opened the door, she saw Kit rise to his feet. She quickened her step, going around the house on the trail that led to the beach. She felt safer walking that route rather than the dark, twisting lane through the cedars, and she only hoped Kit would take the wrong path if he decided to come after her.

She hurried to the edge of the bluff, her camera case banging against the side of her hip, then descended the plank stairs.

"Avery!" Kit called out in the darkness.

She didn't answer him and hoped that he hadn't seen her before she disappeared down the face of the bluff. He couldn't even call her by her first name or make use of the title *Miss*. When he used just her last name, it sounded as if he were calling to a fishing buddy. She didn't like it.

Camille stumbled onto the beach, which was much darker than she had imagined. No moon shone to penetrate the inky blackness of the water that merged with the blackness of the rocks and sand. She'd be lucky if she didn't trip over a piece of driftwood and break her leg.

Behind her she heard Kit on the stairs. He hadn't been fooled into thinking she'd taken the road. In scrambling across the rocks, Camille turned her ankle, but she hobbled on in an attempt to outdistance him.

"Avery!" he called again.

Ooh, she hated the sound of her name like that. She wouldn't answer him.

"Dammit, wait up!" he yelled.

She broke into a trot, squinting at the ground to try to make out the dark shapes in front of her.

"Hold it!" he shouted, nearer than he had been the last time.

She kept to her course, determined to shake him, but could hear his footsteps and then his breath as he ran up behind her. He caught hold of her arm.

"Stop, dammit!"

"Let go of me!" She wrenched free.

"Why didn't you listen to me, dammit!"

"Why should I? All you're doing is swearing at me." She took off, stomping across the damp compressed clay.

"It's high tide, Avery!"

"So what!"

He didn't reply, and she couldn't hear him following her. Maybe he'd given up and decided to go back when he realized she wasn't going to concede to his demands. He must think that all women would do whatever he said—

and perhaps most women would—but she wasn't about to join their ranks.

She hurried down the beach until she saw the twinkle of the cabin's porch light, then smiled to herself. She hadn't needed that bossy Kitsap Makinna's help after all.

Then she noticed the tide pool in the shadows. It stretched from the huge rocks at the water's edge all the way to the steep bank, making the beach impassable in front of the cabin. With a deep flush of chagrin, Camille realized that Kit had tried to warn her about the water and she had cut him off. To get to the cabin, she'd have to scale the overgrown bank or return halfway down the beach. She stopped and tried to decide what to do.

Kit appeared on a trail along the top of the bank, shining a flashlight at her. She looked away, hoping he hadn't seen the crestfallen expression on her face.

"Go back," he yelled. "There's a trail by the big madrona tree."

The big madrona tree was a hundred yards back. She wasn't about to retrace her steps that far in the dark. She'd try her hand at scaling the bank first.

Camille studied the silhouette of the bank and caught a glimpse of something glowing and green in the shadows behind Kit. She narrowed her eyes, focusing on the point. Now she saw four points of green, then six. The wolves were moving in the forest behind Kit. She stumbled closer, about to call to Kit to be careful, but the green eyes disappeared. What was happening to her? Had the wolves really been there? Or was she simply seeing things?

She wasn't about to give Kit any more reason to call her crazy and decided to hold her tongue. As she trotted forward, she stubbed her toe on a rock but limped toward the bank undaunted.

"Go back!" Kit warned.

"I can do it," Camille retorted. She ducked under the twisted vine maples and guarded her face with her sleeve as she pushed through brambles. Fortunately the brambles soon gave way to a patch of bushes that were only just above her knees.

"Go back, Avery!" Kit called from above.

"No way!" She gritted her teeth and grabbed for a bunch of the plants to help pull her up the slope. A few more feet and she'd reach the top. Her foot slipped in the wet clay soil, and she clutched another handful of the plants as she scrambled for a foothold. Something started to tingle on her palms and fingers. Then she felt herself sliding backward as the ground gave way beneath her and the plants were pulled out of the soil. She cried out, her hands and knees burning.

Suddenly Kit's hand grabbed her right wrist. He dragged her up the bank on her back, nearly wrenching her arm out of the socket. By the time he set her on her feet, her skin was on fire and it was all she could do to keep from breaking into tears.

"Nettles," Kit declared, his voice thick with exasperation. He aimed the flashlight at the ground and pulled up some smaller plants that grew near the edge of the bank.

"Nettles?" Camille repeated. She held her throbbing palms in front of her face.

"A stinging plant." He rose. "Here, let me put this on your hands."

He pinned the flashlight between his arm and his chest and then rubbed the crushed leaves of the smaller plant on her fiery skin. The moist pulp dulled the burning sensation somewhat. Camille gritted her teeth and refused to admit to the pain.

"Smarts, doesn't it?" Kit asked, rubbing her other hand.

"A little." She watched his slender fingers as he ministered to her. He actually had a gentle touch when he wasn't grabbing at her. His head bent close to hers and she regarded him briefly, letting her gaze dwell on his hair.

"This is the best antidote for nettle sting." He glanced up and she lowered her eyes. "Feel any better?"

"Yes. But it's on my legs, too."

"We'll have to get that at the cabin. Come on." He took her wrist and guided her quickly down the path. She let him pull her along, thankful that she didn't have to look where she was going and could concentrate on maintaining her control. The skin on her knees felt as if someone had poured acid on her flesh.

"Your key?" Kit asked when they got to the door.

She fumbled in her pocket with her tender hands and held out the ring.

Kit opened the door and turned on the lights. "Take off your skirt and nylons," he said matter-of-factly.

She didn't argue. She tossed her soiled trench coat over a chair and unzipped her skirt, letting it slip to the floor, and peeled off her hose. As she stepped out of the pile of fabric, she looked down and saw blotches of red on her knees and thighs. She should have been embarrassed to undress in Kit's presence, but her legs burned right through her modesty.

Kit directed her to the couch and then knelt beside her, rubbing the leaves on her legs. Camille closed her eyes and braced one arm on the seat of the couch and the other on the back. She had never felt anything like this. It was worse than any bee sting.

"How are you doing?" Kit asked.

"Better." She breathed through her nose so she could keep her teeth clenched.

"I told you not to climb up that bank."

At his reproof, Camille opened her eyes and glared at

him. "I thank you for your help, Mr. Makinna, but I don't need a lecture."

"You know"—he sat back on his heels—"you're about the most bullheaded woman I've ever come across."

"Well, you're about the bossiest man I've ever met."

"Bossy?" The left corner of his mouth curved up in a slow smile of amusement. "I'm not bossy."

"Yes, you are. You've been telling me what to do from the moment I got here."

"For your own good."

"How do you know what's good for me or not?" Indignant, she sat up straight, her burning skin forgotten. "You don't even know me."

"That's right. I don't." His quiet smile faded into a straight line that accentuated a small muscle on the right side of his mouth. His skin was a shade darker at the corners of his mouth and beneath his lower lip where the rise of his strong chin curved inward. Camille flushed at the thought of kissing him in those shadowed places.

She thought he was going to rise to his feet and leave with an oath as he had left Lydia on the deck. Instead he reached out and cornered her by putting one hand on the arm of the couch and one on the back. Wide-eyed, Camille stared at him, hypnotized by the black eyes that never wavered from her face.

And then he leaned closer. She felt his breath fan her face as he bent to her lips and closed his eyes. In shock, she stared at his sooty lashes, much thicker and fuller than her own, and stiffened as his warm mouth pressed into hers. She couldn't believe he was kissing her—not this gorgeous creature with the fierce eyes. And she couldn't believe she was letting him kiss her after the way he had insulted her. She was still not convinced he was innocent of exposing himself to her, either. So how could she sit here and let him touch her like this?

Yet she couldn't move. She felt as if she had risen out of her body and was watching him kiss someone else, for she was so tense she couldn't allow herself to enjoy the touch of him. And all the while he kissed her, she longed to forget her doubts and wrap her arms around his shoulders, slide her hands into his glossy raven hair, pull him into her, and kiss the curve of his jaw where it angled toward his ear. Deep down she had an unfathomable hunger for this man that denied all logic.

But she couldn't allow her hunger to show. He was a stranger to her, and she wasn't about to relinquish her self-control to a man she hardly knew. So she did nothing but press backward into the couch, stunned and rigid, her eyes still open and confused.

Kit drew back and sat on his heels. His eyes smoldered at her, and two crimson patches appeared on the sharp planes under his cheekbones.

"You don't like me, do you, Miss Avery?"

"I . . ." She hesitated in her reply. If she told the truth—that she was wildly attracted to him—she'd sound like an idiot. Yet if she told a lie, she might damage his ego and lose the chance to get to know him better. She struggled inwardly—frantic when she realized that logic had no place in the matters of the heart—and tried to decide what to say as Kit rose.

"You don't have to make excuses," he said, his voice husky with emotion.

Camille stared at him. She hadn't meant to offend him. "Kit—"

He turned away and she scrambled to her feet, forgetting that she was dressed only in panties and a sweater.

"It's not that—"

"Forget it," he replied. "Good night."

She watched him walk to the door, wishing she could find the words to explain the situation without revealing her infatuation for him. But time ran out before she could marshal her thoughts into words. Kit left the cabin, leaving her frustrated and ashamed of her lack of honesty.

10

After Kit left, Camille tossed in bed, caught in a nightmare about Barbara drowning in the sea. She could hear Barbara calling her name over and over again, but she couldn't reach Barbara to save her. She couldn't drag her legs through the water fast enough, and all the while she ran in slow motion, she could barely breathe because of a terrible stench that lay over the water.

"Klootz-mah!"

She woke up with a start, jerking to a sitting position, and at first couldn't remember where she was. Then she recalled she was in a one-room cabin on the Nakalt Indian Reservation. Yet why was it so foggy? And what was that smell? She coughed and rubbed her burning eyes.

"Klootz-mah!"

All of a sudden she came fully awake and realized the cabin was full of smoke.

She gasped, pressing her nose into the crook of her

elbow, and jumped out of bed while the amulet banged against her breast. The necklace was so hot that she gasped again and grabbed it with her free hand. She stumbled over the floor, barely able to make out the door across the room. Without taking time to find her shoes or coat, she rushed to the door—and then remembered the manuscript. She couldn't leave without Barbara's book.

The manuscript still lay in the box near the end of the couch. Camille dashed toward it, kicking her toe against the leg of the end table. The fireplace was a wall of roaring heat almost too hot to approach, and the hot air lifted the hair on her head as she bent down for the box.

"Klootz-mah!"

Who was that out there calling to her? It was the same voice that had called her name over and over during her dream, but the voice belonged to a man, not Barbara.

Camille located the warm cardboard box and pulled it toward her. Then she ran for the door, coughing and choking, the skin on her face and hands hot and tight. She flung open the door and rushed into the cool air—straight into the arms of the naked man.

Camille screamed, flinging up her arms in self-defense and completely forgetting about the manuscript box. It fell to the ground, splitting on impact, scattering pages across the yard while a breeze swirled more of them out of the pile. Camille looked down in horror as she saw the valuable document fluttering away.

She forgot her fear of the naked man. She didn't even notice the wolves trotting around her, their heads hung low as they surveyed her. All she could think about was losing Barbara's work. With a cry of dismay, she dropped to her knees and snatched up the nearest papers.

"Please!" she implored of the naked man standing above her. "Help me!"

She scrambled across the grass, the manuscript box in one hand, picking up the papers. Out of the corner of her eye she saw the naked man bend over and attempt to grab one of the pages, but he was too clumsy to catch it before it blew away. Camille clenched her teeth as she chased two pages into the rhododendrons. Behind her she could hear the crackle of the cabin fire, but she had to let it wait until she'd recovered most of the book.

Within seconds she had gathered all the papers in sight and stuffed them into the ruined box. Then she turned to the naked man, expecting him to have recovered some of the pages, but he held out his palms and shrugged.

"I cannot touch your papers," he remarked.

She glanced at him, puzzled by his strange excuse, and for the first time saw him up close. Her initial impression had been correct—he bore a strong resemblance to Kit. No wonder she had been confused. Yet she saw a few differences between the two men as the firelight flared across his sculpted features. Kit appeared somewhat fierce in his beauty. This man's face was both fierce and foreign, with lines tattooed across his right cheek and a small ring in his left nostril. His hair, shoulder length and loose, wafted around his face in the breeze. His bare shoulders dwarfed her own, and his chest was sculpted like the armor of a Roman centurion. She stopped herself from looking any lower and raised her glance while a blush warmed her already scorched face.

He was smiling at her, the same shattering smile she had seen Kit bestow on Charlie Adams.

"Wh-who are you?" she stammered.

"I am Mak-ee-nah." The wolves trotted to him, prowling around his legs. One sat near his feet, cocked its head, and regarded Camille with what seemed like human curiosity.

She stared in alarm at the huge creatures.

"My brothers will not hurt you, *klootz-mah.*"

"*Klootz-mah,*" she repeated. "You were the one calling to me, weren't you? You woke me up. You saved my life."

"I could see the fire."

"Why didn't you pound on the door?"

"I cannot touch it."

"Why?"

"It is not of my world." He brushed away a strand of hair that blew across his mouth. Firelight flickered across his forearm, which was braided with sinew and muscle.

Camille wanted to know more about this man and find out why he appeared to her. But she had to call the fire department before the cabin was engulfed in flames. At the moment, the fire seemed to be contained in the chimney, but she didn't know if it would spread to the rest of the house soon. Unfortunately the nearest phone was at the lodge. She would have to run there in her flannel nightshirt and bare feet.

"I've got to get help," she said, glancing around for a safe place to put the manuscript box. She found a dry spot under a cedar tree and put a heavy rock on the top of the box to keep the lid pinned down.

"You go with warriors," Mak-ee-nah said behind her. He turned and addressed the wolves in a strange tongue. Two of them trotted to Camille's side. She looked up in surprise.

"They will protect you, *klootz-mah.*"

"They're tame?" she questioned.

He smiled as if her question highly amused him. "No. They are wild. But they are your brothers, too. Now go."

She took off at a run, her feet freezing and tender. Fortunately the lane was mostly free of rocks and muddy, which cushioned her steps. A wolf loped on each side of her, and she found it hard to believe that she was running with two wild animals. They didn't seem to think the run was out of the ordinary and loped with determination, neither looking back at her nor wandering off the trail.

She did her utmost to keep up with their steady pace and arrived at the lodge gasping for breath. The trip had taken less time than she had guessed—not more than ten minutes—but her feet were aching. She stumbled up the stairs and pounded on the lobby door. While she awaited a response, she looked over her shoulder and saw the wolves sitting at the edge of the clearing, their glowing eyes the only evidence of their presence.

Adam appeared. "Camille!" he croaked, opening the door.

"The cabin's on fire! Call the fire department!"

Adam ran to the reservation desk and picked up the phone while Camille braced her hands on her thighs and tried to catch her breath. Just as Adam hung up the phone, Camille saw Kit stride across the great room toward her, and she straightened slowly.

All he wore was his wristwatch and a pair of jeans, zipped but not buttoned and slung low on his hips. The waistband opened to a V, revealing the slight shadow of dark hair that feathered downward from his navel. His hair was tousled and his feet were bare, but Camille found his just awakened appearance tremendously appealing. The sight of him was also the final proof that Kit and Mak-ee-nah were not one and the same.

"What's going on?" he asked.

"The cabin's on fire," she replied.

"You called the fire department?"

"Yes. They're on the way."

For someone who had just awakened, Kit's thinking

seemed clear. "Adam," he instructed, "get Miss Avery some clothes. I'll be right back."

He turned and ran up the stairs, coming back in a few minutes fully dressed. Camille jumped to her feet as Kit snatched his parka from the hook.

"I want to come," she exclaimed.

"No." Kit threw a glance her way, a cold glance that stuck her deep inside. "Stay here."

"But—"

He didn't wait for her reply but ran out to his Jeep and pulled out of the drive as sirens wailed in the night.

Camille dressed in a pair of Adam's long underwear, wool socks, rubber boots, and a parka that was three sizes too large. She knew she must look ridiculous but disregarded her appearance and insisted that Adam drive her to the cabin. She wanted to see what happened and retrieve Barbara's manuscript. While they hurried to the vehicle Camille saw the wolves take off into the forest.

The pickup rumbled to a stop out of the way of the fire truck, and Camille jumped out. She could see two firemen on the roof spraying the chimney and more on the ground. Kit stood on the lawn, his legs apart, his arms crossed over his chest, talking to the lieutenant in charge of the volunteers. Guilt washed over Camille. In one day she had managed to insult Kit and destroy Makinna property. She crossed the grass, hoping he would accept an apology, because she had no wish to suffer that cold look from him again.

She drew up alongside him, but he didn't even turn to look at her. She half expected a reproach or a lecture. Instead he was darkly silent, and his silence was worse than anything he could have said to her.

Camille stood beside him, wondering what to say, her

hands stuffed in the pockets of the parka, when Adam trotted up.

"Is it bad, Uncle Kit?" he asked.

"No." Kit stared at the cabin. "Just a chimney fire which burned through to some of the logs."

"More smoke damage than anything," said the lieutenant. "You were lucky you didn't die from smoke inhalation, young lady."

Camille nodded, feeling she would rather die than endure Kit's dark disapproval. She couldn't bear it.

"What woke you up?" Adam asked.

"A dream." Camille hunched her shoulders against the cold and glanced around the clearing, wondering where Mak-ee-nah had gone. "A dream about Barbara."

"Well, you're lucky," the lieutenant commented, rubbing his nose. "But you won't be able to spend the rest of the night here. The place is a mess. You got a bed for her at the lodge, Makinna?"

"Yeah," Kit replied without taking his gaze off the cabin.

Camille swallowed. She had to do something, say something to clear up the misunderstanding between them. Hesitantly she reached for his arm.

"Kit, I'm—"

She broke off as he swung around so that her hand slid off his sleeve. His rejection stung her, and she realized how he must have felt each time she had shaken off his hand.

"Adam, you can take Miss Avery back, can't you?"

"Sure, Uncle Kit."

"Thanks for coming out so fast, Bob," Kit remarked to the lieutenant, slapping a hand on his upper arm as he walked past him.

"You bet," he replied with a smile.

Camille wilted. Kit hadn't looked at her once.

Camille hardly slept the rest of the night. She woke up early and pulled on her borrowed clothing, hoping to catch Kit at the breakfast table before anyone else appeared. She had to set things right between them, no matter how foolish she sounded, no matter how illogical her feelings for him seemed. She splashed water on her face and hair and wished she had a toothbrush and a comb. She ran her fingers through her hair and pinched her cheeks, hoping some color would show up on her pale face. Her hands hurt at the movement. They were still sore and red from the nettle stings. Then she headed downstairs, determined to face Kit.

He wasn't there. Hattie informed her that he had already gone, and in a foul mood, too. Camille accepted a cup of coffee but soon left for the cabin to set the place to rights and shoulder the responsibility for the smoke damage.

She opened the door to the cabin and was met with a sooty mess, dripping with water. From the looks of it, the cabin would have to be cleaned from floor to ceiling. She sighed and stepped in, already planning how she would go about the job. She put down the manuscript box she had rescued last night and took off her parka.

Then she set to work, stripping the blankets and linen from the bed, the curtains at the windows, and the pillows from the couch. She piled them next to the washer, along with her clothes, which all reeked of smoke. Then, while she did load after load of laundry, she mopped up the water on the wood floor and started on the kitchen area. She clumped around in the heavy rubber boots and baggy long underwear and wondered why she had ever come to the reservation in the first place. It seemed so long ago that she had stepped off the bus, and her reasons for being here had been lost in confusion and mystery. Though the cleaning job ahead of her was gargantuan, she almost looked forward to a task in which she could lose herself. She could handle cleaning. What she couldn't handle were the questions about Barbara's disappearance and the sudden way her relationship to Kit had veered into hard feelings.

About ten o'clock she heard a vehicle pull up outside. She looked out the window and saw Adam, Lydia, and Hattie getting out of the truck, which was loaded with ladders, buckets, and jugs of cleaning liquid. Before they had crossed the lawn, Camille saw Kit's Jeep rumble to a stop, followed by a van painted with the logo of a chimney sweep.

Her heart rose and then sank. She could use the help, but she had no desire to put herself further in debt to the Makinna family. They had given her a place to stay on two occasions, and treated her with kindness. In return, she had nearly burned down their cabin. How would she ever be able to make amends?

Grandly, Lydia swept across the porch. "I hear I missed all the excitement last night." She looked around the blackened walls and then leveled her glance on Camille. "How did you manage to do this?"

"I'm not quite sure."

Lydia clucked her tongue and shook her head, obviously enjoying the chance to gloat over Camille's foolishness.

"It was a chimney fire," Adam put it. "It wasn't her fault."

"When I want your opinion, Adam Makinna, I'll ask for

it. Now go get that ladder." She pointed toward the door. "And don't dawdle."

Adam shot a surly glare in her direction before he walked away.

"I'll help you," Camille said, anxious to get away from Lydia. She caught up with Adam and touched his arm.

"Adam, you shouldn't be here helping when you ought to be in school." She purposely kept her voice down so Lydia couldn't hear.

"There isn't school today," Adam answered. "It's a holiday. Presidents' Day."

"Good. I didn't want you getting in trouble on my account."

"Yeah. I get in enough on my own."

Adam reached down and picked up an end of the paint-spattered aluminum ladder. Camille lifted the other. Together they carried it to the end of the cabin near the back porch where Lydia planned to start the cleaning process. Already she was issuing orders to everyone. Camille made certain the ladder was secure, while she listened to Lydia's curt instructions and realized that she had lost control of her own cleaning project.

After a while Kit came in to assess the fire damage to the logs near the chimney. Lydia stood at his elbow, pointing at the wall and offering her comments while Camille finished scrubbing a wall on the other side of the fireplace. She marched up the ladder to wipe off the beams, her anger increasing with every step. The way Lydia went on, she made it sound as if Camille had practically ruined the entire cabin. Kit didn't say a word, just stood there looking up at the wall, his hands in the back pockets of his jeans.

Camille clenched her teeth as she got to the top of the ladder and steadied herself by holding on to the beam. Kit would probably never speak to her again, not after Lydia's tirade. Scowling, Camille looked down at the beam, and her heart flopped. Lying on the varnished timber was a book. She picked it up, scanned the cover, and opened it to the first page, her heart starting to pound even before the words hit her consciousness. She had found Barbara's journal. Unwilling to share the discovery with the Makinnas, she slipped it under her sweater and quietly got down from the ladder.

Later that evening Camille and Adam drove to the lodge with pizza and beer, which Camille had bought as a thank-you for the Makinnas. Everyone had decided to eat pizza at the lodge and watch a movie, taking it easy after the strenuous day of cleaning. Camille stared at the dark lane overhung with alders and wished she could spend the evening at the cabin and not the lodge. She was dying to read Barbara's journal, which she had tucked out of sight before anyone had noticed what she had found. She was also not anxious to confront Kit. He had left with the chimney sweep early in the afternoon and hadn't returned for the rest of the day. There was no telling what kind of mood he was in.

Adam broke into her thoughts.

"I was wondering, Miss Avery, if I could ask you something."

She glanced at him. His tone wasn't usually so hesitant. "Sure, Adam."

"It's a favor, actually."

"After today, I owe you a favor. A big one."

He smiled, turning down the lane toward the lodge, but his smile was brief and unsure. "I've been thinking a lot lately, about school and all."

She nodded, hoping he would open up to her.

"What you said about Uncle Kit and choices—well, I'd kinda like to be like Uncle Kit."

"He's a good man."

"Yeah. I'd like to go to college like he did."

"That's a good start."

"But if I flunk out, I won't be going anywhere. So . . . well, I was hoping you could help me with my geometry."

"Your geometry?"

"I can understand the way you explain things," he went on in a rush. "You know the way you explained your puzzle magazine? Well, I could get it after you told me how to organize my thinking." He gripped the wheel tightly while something closed around Camille's heart. None of her students at the Lewis Academy had ever given her a higher compliment. "My teacher doesn't explain stuff the way you do."

"I'd be happy to help you, Adam."

"How about tonight? I've got a test this Friday, and I thought if I could get some help before then—"

"I'll turn you into a geometry ace." She grinned. "In no time."

"Great!" He grinned back at her, and her heart soared.

In another moment they arrived at the lodge, and Camille's good mood disappeared as soon as she saw Kit's Jeep parked outside. Adam must have read her expression.

"What's wrong?" he asked, turning off the engine.

"Your uncle's here. Maybe I shouldn't stay."

"Why?"

"He's pretty upset with me for the fire, among other things."

"He's not mad at you."

"You must not have seen his face last night or today."

"Don't take it personally, Miss Avery." Adam pulled the key out of the ignition. "Uncle Kit's upset about everything around here. My dad drank a lot the last few years. He, uh, he didn't take care of stuff like he should have, and Uncle Kit's finding that out wherever he goes."

"I was the one who nearly destroyed the cabin, though."

Adam shook his head. "My dad should have had the cabin chimney cleaned a year ago, that's what Uncle Kit said."

"Still, I don't think your uncle approves of me."

"Well, Old Man likes you. And if Old Man likes you, he'll get everyone else to like you, too. Now come on, I'm starved!"

He jumped out of the truck and pulled the white pizza boxes off the seat. Camille grabbed the carton of beer and followed him into the house, not nearly as confident of Old Man's powers of persuasion.

Lydia started the movie when Camille and Adam arrived with the pizza, and everyone sat in the family room off the kitchen, a private area that Camille hadn't seen before. Camille took her plate to a chair and paused momentarily when Kit looked up from a recliner at the side of the room. He immediately switched his gaze to the television, however, and Camille sank to the chair.

She couldn't eat. Most everyone else had hearty appetites and an avid interest in the comedy on the screen. But she could enjoy neither the movie nor the meal. And from the glances she snatched of Kit, he didn't seem to be enjoying himself, either. After he finished his pizza, he rose and walked out of the room, taking his half-finished beer with him. Camille heard him put his dish down in the kitchen.

Soon afterward she rose. Lydia glanced up at her.

"What's the matter?" she asked. "Don't like the pizza?"

"I need to get a drink of water," she lied.

"Hattie, get Miss Avery a drink."

"That's all right. I can help myself, if you don't mind."

"Suit yourself." Lydia turned back to the movie, and Camille strolled out to the kitchen, her stomach knotted and her head aching. She stacked her plate on Kit's and glanced out toward the lobby. She could see Kit sitting by the fire, his feet upon the hearth and Sandy at his side. He raised the bottle of beer to his lips.

She had to talk to him. Knowing she would feel more comfortable with something in her hands, Camille found a glass in the cupboard and filled it with water. Then, squaring her shoulders, she walked toward Kit. Sandy looked at her and wagged her tail. Surely Kit knew she was approaching, but he didn't look her way and continued to study the fire.

Camille lowered to the bench across from him and gulped a mouthful of water, unsure how to start or what to say.

"I'm sorry," she blurted.

Kit took a swig of his beer. "Sorry for what?"

"For causing you all that trouble. For practically burning down the cabin."

"My brother should have taken care of it. It wasn't your fault."

Camille swallowed, wanting to set everything right between them, including the time he had kissed her. "I'm also sorry for what happened earlier—between us."

"Forget it, Avery." He took another swig.

She watched him, helplessly lost for words. She could explain a math problem. She could lecture to a group of teenagers without batting an eyelash. But she had no experience with revealing her feelings. She didn't even have enough guts to tell him how she hated it when he called her Avery. And his harsh gaze did nothing to encourage her.

"I just wanted to tell you that it was okay. What you did to me, I mean."

He turned and stared at her in surprise.

"I didn't mind it."

"You didn't *mind* it?" His tone was incredulous, and she thought she might have insulted him again.

"What I mean is, I—"

"You were stiff as a board."

"I'm not accustomed to"—her glance darted from his face to the fire and back again—"well, you surprised me, that's all. I don't generally kiss a man I've known for only three days. And I just didn't know what to think."

"Kissing doesn't require a whole lot of thinking, Avery."

"Maybe not for you."

Kit narrowed his eyes and took another sip of his beer.

Camille stood up. "What I wanted to say is that I hope you didn't get the wrong impression. I don't dislike you. And I hope we can be friends."

"Friends?" Kit looked up at her. "I've never had a woman for a friend."

"There's always a first for everything."

For a moment, he regarded her, and then his lips twitched into a small smile. Relief flooded through her.

"Friends, then?" She held out her hand, and he got slowly to his feet and took it in his. His skin was warm, his handshake strong and lingering. Camille let her hand remain in his, deciding not to pull back this time until he made the first move.

At that moment Lydia appeared in the doorway and stopped when she saw Kit's hand around Camille's. Camille resisted the impulse to pull away. She felt Kit's grip tighten as if to keep her close to him.

"Did you get your drink, Miss Avery?" Lydia asked.

"Yes, I did." She held up her glass in salute.

Lydia looked at Kit. "Aren't you going to watch the movie, Kit?"

"I don't seem to be in the mood."

"It's really funny."

"Some other time." He turned his back to her.

"Well, if nobody's going to watch it, maybe I should just turn it off." Lydia flipped her hair over her shoulder, obviously angry that she was having no effect on either of them.

"I'm coming back," Camille put in, stepping away from Kit, but his fingers tightened around hers.

"Hold on a minute," he said softly. The confidential tone sent a shiver racing down her back.

"In a second or two," she added for Lydia's sake.

Lydia smiled coolly and returned to the kitchen. When she had gone Kit slowly released Camille's hand, and she looked at him expectantly.

"Listen, Avery." He shifted his weight onto his right foot. "I'm sorry for getting your dander up last night."

"You mean when you called me a white woman?"

"Exactly. Sometimes when my grandfather gets going with his prophecies and predictions, I lose my head and say things I regret."

She was amazed to hear him apologizing and let him continue uninterrupted.

"His damn prophecies altered my life forever. Don't let him alter yours. He can be very convincing."

"But what or who have I been seeing at night, then?"

"I don't know. But use your head. You're a sensible woman. Does seeing a two-hundred-year-old spirit seem plausible to you?"

"Not exactly, but I touched him, talked to him—"

"I don't know how to explain that. Just take everything

Old Man says with a grain of salt. That's my advice to you."

"But what if there really is an amber necklace?"

"I'd hate to see it surface. My grandfather and the other elders pin all their hopes on the Nakalt prophecy. If that necklace showed up and failed to deliver, it would break their hearts. Break their spirits."

Camille's hand shook as she sipped her water. She hadn't thought about that aspect of the necklace.

"I'm going out," Kit said, picking up his empty beer bottle. "Do you want a ride home?"

His offer surprised her. "Thanks, but no. I promised to help Adam with his homework."

Kit nodded and gazed at her for a moment as if he were reluctant to leave. His glance focused on her short blond hair, and Camille found it hard not to put her hand to her head as if to brush off his scrutiny. Did he think her hair looked unattractive? Why had he ever kissed her in the first place? And would she ever have enough guts to ask him?

"Well, good night, Avery." He picked up his empty beer bottle.

"Good night."

She watched him walk away, more uncertain than ever if she should tell Old Man about her necklace.

11

Kit set the brake on his Jeep and slipped out. The spongy earth beneath his feet allowed the sound to go unnoticed. He closed the door without slamming it so he would not disturb the creatures of the night. Then, taking a trail that only someone who knew it was there could find, he ducked into the forest. Though it was dark, he didn't use a flashlight but let his ears and feet lead him to his goal, sensing with his spirit what his eyes failed to see.

After a thirty-minute walk he came to a small waterfall about ten feet high. On the bank at the base of the waterfall was a big flat rock. He knew it well, for it was there he had spent the three days of his vision quest when he was thirteen years old.

Kit found the rock and sat down, crossing his legs at the ankles. He breathed in and let the sweet air of the forest fill him, cleansing him inside. Then he let out a long sigh to pour out his troubled thoughts—thoughts of the lodge, of

Adam and Lydia, of the reservation, and of Camille Avery.
Then he breathed in again, repeating the process until he
felt purged and calm.

Soon all he heard was the roar of the water, filling up his
ears and soul.

For the last six years he hadn't thought much about his
vision quest, having classified it as cultural flotsam in his
non-Indian world, but he could remember the quest as if
he had experienced it only yesterday. And now he felt the
need to look at it again, to escape the reminders that
placed him in the modern world, and to sit in the forest
where he could be a primal man alone with the One
Above.

When Kit was thirteen, there weren't many youths
going on vision quests. A quest required rigorous training
and discipline that few were willing to undertake. But Old
Man insisted that Kit follow the ancient ways, not only
because he was a descendent of chiefs, but because he was
destined to fulfill a prophecy. Every day for years, Kit
plunged into the cold waters of Puget Sound as part of his
ritual cleansing. He fasted, prayed, limited his intake of
certain foods, and spent long hours learning the old ways
from his grandfather.

By the time he was thirteen, his voice began to change
and his shoulders widened. His grandfather deemed it was
time for Kit to undertake his quest. With nothing but a
knife, he was sent into the hills. He walked most of the first
day, waiting for a sign to stop. Weary and hungry, he saw a
raven dive earthward, took that as a sign, and followed the
bird to the waterfall.

There he stayed without eating or sleeping. The raven
stayed with him, cawing, diving at him, and making a gen-
eral nuisance of himself during Kit's prayers. Though Kit
grew irritated at the raven's loud squawking, he had to

admit that the bird's noisy company was better than being totally alone out in the wilderness.

On the third day Kit had a vision both vivid and puzzling. In his vision, he saw a raven dive out of the sky, directly at him, and then plunge into his chest beak first. Kit jumped to his feet, screaming with fright, as the raven buried himself in his chest. Yet no blood spurted out of the wound, and the raven simply fell apart into a pile of feathers and fluff. Amazed and shaking, Kit reached down and picked up the beak, which lay among the feathers. He shook it in his closed hands, like a rattle, and the beak spoke to him, saying, "Two is one. One is two. Two is three."

Confused, Kit sat down and waited for an animal spirit to come to him and interpret his dream. He waited until dusk, worrying that an animal might not show up at all. He didn't want to spend another night on the mountain, but if he didn't see an animal, he would have to remain by the waterfall. Just as he was about to settle in for another long vigil in the dark, he looked up at a spruce tree by the edge of the stream and saw an owl.

Kit froze in a crouched position. Many of the Nakalt elders still believed that the dead traveled the earth in the form of owls. To see an owl was not a good omen. Kit stared at the huge golden eyes, which stared back at him, and as he maintained eye contact, he stealthily reached for the handle of his knife. If the owl should turn into a dead person and try to make off with him, he'd put up a good fight. At the same time he slid the knife from its sheath, he heard a wolf howl upstream. The noise startled the owl and it took off, soaring over the clearing and down the path of the stream, disappearing into the twilight and cedar.

Kit swallowed in relief and rose on trembling legs. Thanks to the wolf, he was safe from the dead. He would remember to offer his gratitude to the wolf spirit in his prayers. But for now his vision quest was over, and he must return to the lodge of his grandfather. He picked his way down the mountain and, in his delirium from lack of food and sleep, felt as if he floated all the way home.

"Two is one. One is two. Two is three." The phrase still made no sense to him, even now that he was a grown man. His grandfather had suggested many interpretations, but none had ever satisfied Kit. He looked around the clearing, wishing he could see more than dark shapes and shadows, wondering if his sacred spot had changed over the years. After twenty-one years he had changed significantly—he was no longer a youth frightened of owls. He now knew there was no need to waste time worrying about fantastic spirit creatures when the world held plenty of real dangers. At the thought of reality, Kit felt the spell of his spirit place dissipate and knew it was time to leave. He rose to his feet, promising to return when he could see his sacred spot in the daylight.

Just before eleven, Camille finished helping Adam with his geometry. Adam drove her back to the cabin and walked her to the door. She could tell he wanted to come in and talk, but since he had to go to school the next morning, Camille thought it best to dissuade him from coming in with her. He took the hint and left in his good-natured way. She watched him walk to the truck, realizing that in a few short days she had grown fond of him. She was certain that the feeling was mutual.

The phone rang as she was making herself a cup of tea. Lydia was on the other end, wanting to know if Adam had left.

"Yes, just now. Shall I try to get him?"

"No," Lydia replied. "I wanted to make sure he didn't hang around too long. You know how young men are."

Camille didn't know what she was getting at. "What do you mean?"

Lydia sighed in exasperation. "Don't play innocent with me. You know as well as I do that Adam shouldn't be spending so much time with you."

"Why not?" Camille straightened, indignant, even though Lydia couldn't see her.

"He might want to follow in his uncle's footsteps."

"He does. He told me so."

Lydia paused. "He did?"

"Yes."

"Well, I hope you had the decency to set him straight."

"Decency?" Now Camille was really puzzled. What did decency have to do with going to college?

"Don't play the dumb blonde with me, Camille," Lydia threatened. "It won't work. I know how women like you operate. And I won't have you ruining Adam like Kit was ruined."

"Ruined?" Camille questioned incredulously. Lydia's insinuation struck her like a blow. How could the woman think she had a sexual interest in Adam? The thought was ridiculous, twisted. He was only sixteen years old, almost half her age. Just a boy. She slumped against the wall, barely able to breathe, unable to speak, wondering what kind of mind came up with such accusations.

"Surprised, huh? Thought you had me fooled, didn't you?" Lydia's voice grated in her ear.

"I am teaching him geometry," Camille answered, working hard to keep her voice level. Her hand shook. "And that's all."

"Sure. Sure you are."

"He's just a kid, Lydia."

"And you're a starving old maid from an all girls' school, panting after every male that crosses your path."

Camille slammed down the phone, unwilling to listen to any more of Lydia's venom. She was still shaking when she got Barbara's journal and carried it to the couch. She flipped the pages to the end of the journal, forcing herself to close off her mind to Lydia's accusations.

She sat down and read the last entry, which left off abruptly on Friday—the day before Barbara had disappeared. The only clue to her disappearance was a curious comment about North Beach and something unusual she had seen on the bluff. Frustrated, Camille thumbed through previous entries but found no other mention of North Beach. She closed the journal, squeezing the covers together, wondering why her friend had to be indefinite the one time it really mattered. The rest of the journal was full of details about the Nakalt and various tribal members, with lengthy descriptions of the flora and fauna on the reservation. But the entry about North Beach was sketchy at best. What had Barbara seen? Why was it suspicious?

Worrying, Camille prepared for bed and slipped under the covers, even though she knew she would never get to sleep with Barbara's enigma and Lydia's accusations eating at her. She switched on the light and reached for Barbara's journal, settling in for a long bout of reading. It would take hours for her frazzled nerves to calm down.

Later, she tried to sleep, but Lydia's words kept burning through her thoughts. *Old maid.* She had never considered herself an old maid. Did others see her that way? She twisted and turned, wondering what had happened to Kit to ruin him. She buried her face in her pillow, squeezing the sides with her arms, wishing she could bury her face in Kit's chest instead. She could still remember the low tone of his voice, the touch of his hand, and her heart surged into her throat, pressing the breath out of her. She flopped on her back and looked at the shadowed beams above, seeing an image of Adam's laughing innocent face and then Old Man's stoic visage. All three men had become important to her in such a short span of time. Yet all of them put her in a panic in one way or another. She flung her forearm over her eyes, blocking out the images, afraid she would go crazy from the indecision and hunger that ate at her. What would her students think of logical, well-organized Miss Avery now?

She pulled the blankets around her ears and closed her eyes, and was just about to drift off when the howl of a wolf brought her out of her slumber.

Mak-ee-nah was coming. She was certain of it. Already her necklace was growing warm. She sat up. Her amulet had warmed at the appearance of the naked man on the bluff and last night during the fire when Mak-ee-nah had come to the cabin and saved her life. Was the amulet somehow connected to Mak-ee-nah?

Wide awake and trembling with anticipation, Camille jumped out of bed and dressed hastily, donning Adam's castoff parka she had borrowed the previous night. She strode to the door, remembering Kit's words about being sensible, and was determined to find out just who and what Mak-ee-nah was—man or spirit—and perhaps obtain some kind of proof to show Kit and Old Man.

She recalled Mak-ee-nah's claim of not being able to touch the cabin door and decided that it might be wise to remain close to the entryway as a safety precaution, in case he decided to harm her. Frightened but curious, she ventured outside. Mak-ee-nah stood on the path, the wolves hovering behind him, and when he saw her he raised his right hand in greeting.

"Klootz-mah," he called.

"Good evening," she replied. She was careful to keep her gaze above his waist.

He walked forward, but she remained on the porch, maintaining a boundary between them.

"You are safe? Well?" he asked, inspecting her from head to toe.

"Yes. It was just a chimney fire."

He nodded. His face was open and intelligent, his expression much less guarded than Kit's. Perhaps Mak-ee-nah hadn't been "ruined" as Kit had.

"I wanted to thank you for saving my life last night, Mak-ee-nah. I could have died in there."

"I do not want you dead, *klootz-mah.*"

"I'm glad of that. But I'm curious about how you show up like this. These wolves—"

"They are my warriors."

"I've been told you are a chief of the Nakalt."

"Yes." He clenched his jaw and looked toward the sea. "Long ago."

"I've been told you are a spirit."

"Now I am a man." He looked back at her, his expression no longer open. "And you ask many questions."

"I don't mean to pry. But you could be a Nakalt man trying to trick me, for all I know."

"In your heart you know who I am, *klootz-mah.*"

"But you were supposed to have died—"

"I have been raised from the dead."

"You have?" Camille stepped backward, fear coursing through her, and wondered if she should run into the house and bolt the door.

"Do not be afraid," Mak-ee-nah put in. "I mean no harm to you."

"But how can you—how did you—"

"*Ah-welth* has raised me up."

"Who is *Ah-welth?*"

"Our Father."

"But if you've been dead all this time, how can you be alive now?"

"*Ah-welth* is powerful. He can do anything." Mak-ee-nah held out his arms. "He gives me the human being body I had when I walked this earth long ago."

Camille tried not to survey his human being body too closely while Mak-ee-nah continued to speak.

"For many years *Ah-welth* has kept me from entering the Land Above. I have been waiting in darkness."

"Why?"

"Long ago I made a mistake. My warriors died. My people died. I live in shame with such a blood debt on my hands."

"For two hundred years?"

He nodded solemnly. "And the years are as stones tied to my spirit."

She gazed at him, her fear welling into compassion, and ventured back to the edge of the porch. "But can't you do anything about it?"

"Yes, now that the amber has returned."

"The amber?" Camille choked.

"Yes." He pointed at her chest. "You have it."

"How do you know?"

"It calls to me. It is mine."

Camille swallowed and clutched the necklace, which burned her skin through two thick layers of clothing.

"You must give it to me, *klootz-mah.*"

"What will you do with it?"

"I will right a wrong done to my people. I will give back their strength."

"How?"

"By giving the amulet to the rightful chief."

Camille hung back, unsure what to think. Was Mak-ee-nah telling her the truth? From what she'd been told, she knew the amulet was a powerful talisman. What if she relinquished it and it fell into the hands of the wrong person? She hesitated, unable to make a decision on the spur of the moment.

"Come," he urged. "I cannot take it from you, *klootz-mah.*"

"I know that. And I'm not going to give it to you just yet, either."

"You do not trust me?"

"No."

"So." He narrowed his eyes at her and then smiled. "It is good not to trust too much."

"I have to speak to one of the elders before I do anything. Could I bring him out here to meet you tomorrow night?"

"He will not be able to see me."

"Why?"

"Only you can see me." He motioned toward her chest again. "You wear the amulet."

"Oh." Camille frowned and looked at the ground. Proving Mak-ee-nah's existence was going to be harder than she thought.

"You think me ugly, *klootz-mah?*" he asked, breaking into her thoughts.

She looked up, surprised. "No."

"Why do you not look at me?" He held his arms wide, as if inviting her inspection.

"Well—because you're naked!"

"Naked?"

"You don't have any clothes on."

"You would look at me covered? Then you could not see me."

Camille blushed at his challenge. Her glance darted down his sculpted chest to his abdomen, down his slender hips to his uncircumcised organ, farther down to his long, muscular legs. He looked every inch like the famous statue of *David* by Michelangelo. She flushed at the sight of him and at the expression of amusement that covered his handsome face when she raised her gaze to meet his.

"Not ugly?" he asked, smiling.

"Not at all."

He nodded as if pleased with himself and her.

"But aren't you cold, Mak-ee-nah?"

"No. My body is strong. It was always strong."

Camille didn't doubt him on that point.

"Didn't you wear clothes in the days when you were a chief?"

"Sometimes. But my clothing was taken from me."

"Would you like a blanket?"

"It is not of my world. I could not touch it."

Camille tilted her head. "Then how could you have touched *me* the other night?"

"You are part of my world, *klootz-mah*. You have been and always will be."

"What is that supposed to mean?"

He smiled. "We are like the salmon-people. We are born, we die, we return, over and over. Since I can touch you, you must have been of my world at one time."

What was he talking about? Reincarnation? Camille stared at him, incredulous, but at the same time half believing him. She could hear Kit's voice reminding her to take everything Old Man said with a grain of salt. What about the things Mak-ee-nah was telling her? His words were infinitely more incredible. But how could she explain his appearance otherwise?

"I confound you?" he asked.

"Yes!"

He grinned.

Something in his open expression compelled her to grin back.

"If my lack of clothing displeases you, *klootz-mah,* I can show you a place which has garments that I can put upon my body."

"Where?"

"In a strange carriage. One I cannot touch. But come, I will show you."

He turned but realized she wasn't following. "Are you frightened to go with me?" he asked, twisting to look at her.

"Yes."

"If I had wished to harm you, *klootz-mah,* I could have done so already."

He spoke the truth. Besides, if he took the amulet from her through an act of violence, he would suffer the consequences. She decided to trust the protection of the amulet and go with him.

They walked together through the forest on a trail that wound near the edge of the bluff. Camille continued with her barrage of questions, discovering that Mak-ee-nah had spent six years as a traveling dignitary, sailing to England with the British and touring the Continent as a guest of many royal houses. It was easy to see why he had been so honored. He was a delightful conversationalist, with a philosophical bent and a natural wisdom to lend weight to his ideas. His grasp of the English language was remarkable, and of course his physical appearance bordered on the extraordinary, as Kit's did.

He did not possess Kit's cutting sarcasm or his bitterness. And he was quick to smile and chuckle, a trait that soon endeared him to Camille. Sometimes the trail forced them to walk single file. When that happened, Camille dropped behind Mak-ee-nah, which gave her an opportunity to survey his figure. Because he treated his nudity as if it were natural, Camille found herself treating it in a similar fashion. She let her gaze travel the rippling wedge of his back and over the roll of his lean, powerful buttocks as he walked, appreciating his fine physique without feeling the least bit guilty. And all the time she drank in the vision of his nakedness, she might have been looking at Kit, for she knew he and Mak-ee-nah were similar enough to be twins. The thought made her pulse race.

They continued to walk for another half hour until they reached a clearing on the bluff above the ocean. In the clearing was parked a blue pickup with a canopy on the back.

"There is the carriage," Mak-ee-nah said, pointing toward the vehicle.

"That's a truck," Camille replied.

"Look in the back."

"But it doesn't belong to us."

"The items in the back do not belong to the owner of the truck. Go look, *klootz-mah*."

"Why do you call me that? What does it mean?"

"It means woman."

"My name is Camille."

"Ca-meel." He tested the name on his tongue.

"It means flower. Like the Camellia."

"Ca-meel. It is good. Now, go look."

Camille approached the truck with Mak-ee-nah at her heels. She turned the handle of the canopy and was surprised to find it unlocked. Relieved that she wouldn't have to vandalize the truck any further, she lifted the door and looked in.

The truck bed was stacked with boxes filled with baskets, clothing, weapons, and bone and stone implements. Many of the objects were still covered with mud and debris, as if they had been recently unearthed. Camille turned to Mak-ee-nah.

"What are these?"

"They are the possessions of my people."

"Someone is stealing them!"

Mak-ee-nah nodded gravely.

"Who? Have you seen who?"

"No."

"Well, I can find out who owns this truck."

"How will you do that?"

Camille backed up and pointed at the license plate. "See that plate with the designs on it? From those letters and numbers, we can find out who owns this truck."

"Ah. It is a strange family crest. Ugly."

"It isn't supposed to be a work of art, just a way of keeping track of vehicles." She paused for a moment and memorized the number. She would call the police in the morning.

That done, she turned to Mak-ee-nah. "Which objects belong to you?"

"The cloak. The black one. See it? And the yellow one." He pointed at various items while Camille climbed up on the tailgate and stepped into the truck. One by one she handed the requested items to Mak-ee-nah. Carefully he stowed them in a wooden box carved with the design of a bear.

"I will clean these," he explained. "Then I will wear them so you can look at me."

She smiled, wondering now if she might not prefer his nudity after all. He had such a beautiful body, and she had become comfortable with seeing it thoroughly displayed.

"Next time you see me, Ca-meel, you will be happy with my look, so happy that you will give me the amulet."

She chuckled, not admitting that she was awed already. "Shall we go back now?"

"Wait." Mak-ee-nah glanced at the wolves, whose ears were all trained toward the break in the trees where an old road met the clearing. Mak-ee-nah held up his hand, cautioning her not to speak, as he listened intently.

"Someone is coming," he murmured.

Camille stared into the darkness, seeing and hearing nothing.

"Take the box and hide yourself," he instructed.

"What about you?" she asked.

"I cannot be seen."

The box was heavier than she anticipated, and she puffed as she carried it behind a huge cedar stump and set it on the spongy earth. She crouched behind the stump, watching the road, as the wolves fanned out and disappeared into the mist. Only Mak-ee-nah stood in the clearing, waiting, his hair blowing softly around his shoulders in the breeze off the sea.

Soon Camille heard the sound of a car. A Volvo station wagon rolled into the clearing and stopped. The door opened and a man got out and yawned.

It was then that Camille noticed she had forgotten to shut the canopy door.

12

At the same instant, Oscar Duarte noticed the open door, too. He hurried to the back of the pickup and poked his head inside the canopy while Camille watched, wondering what he would do. Mak-ee-nah stood to the side, arms crossed over his chest.

Duarte slammed the canopy door and locked it with short, angry movements. Then he glanced over his shoulder as if to locate the thief. Camille held her breath, certain that he would catch sight of Mak-ee-nah, who stood only a few feet away. But what Mak-ee-nah had told her was evidently true—he seemed to be invisible to everyone but her.

Camille breathed a small sigh of relief and watched Duarte march to the cab of the pickup. He flung open the door and leaned in, straightening a moment later to shine a flashlight on the clearing. The beam streamed across the dried weeds toward her. Camille froze in her squatting position behind the stump. Though her parka and jeans were made of dark material, her light hair was uncovered, and she had no way to conceal it. What if Duarte should catch sight of her? What would he do? Even in the dark Camille could tell he was extremely upset.

Duarte tramped around the clearing, checking the ground for tracks, which he could locate easily in the damp earth. Mak-ee-nah trailed to the side, fascinated by the flashlight and seemingly unaware of the imminent danger Camille was in. She pressed closer to the stump, her heart pounding, knowing that within moments she would be revealed by the beam of Duarte's powerful light. She didn't know whether to stay or run, certain that he would hear her if she decided to take off through the underbrush.

Fortunately for her, Mak-ee-nah had a plan. He spoke to his wolves in his strange tongue full of clacks and ooh-sounds, relaying a secret message to his warriors. Camille heard a menacing growl behind her and nearly jumped to her feet in alarm. Yet in a split second she realized the growl was meant for Duarte and not her, and was thankful she had had enough sense to stay crouched.

Duarte flashed the beam in the direction of the growl, illuminating the glowing eyes and gaping jaws of a huge wolf.

"My God!" he gasped, staggering backward. The wolf stepped out of the shadows, forcing Duarte to retreat. He stumbled and caught himself. In no real hurry, the wolf stalked forward.

"Shoo! Back!" Duarte yelled, his voice cracking in fright.

Mak-ee-nah nearly doubled over in laughter as he observed Duarte's ignoble retreat.

"Get back!" Duarte slammed into the side of his Volvo

and fumbled with the door handle behind him, never taking his eyes off the animal.

The wolf growled again and loped toward him.

Duarte yelped and wrenched open the door, toppling backward into the car and dropping his flashlight in his haste. The beam soared heavenward, toward a lightening sky.

Engine screaming, tires spinning, the Volvo roared out of the clearing, tearing up clumps of sod as Duarte raced away and disappeared down the darkened lane.

Camille remained hidden until she was sure he wasn't going to return. Then she rose and walked across the clearing to join Mak-ee-nah, who knelt by the flashlight, inspecting it from all angles.

"Nice work, Mak-ee-nah," Camille remarked as she trotted up to him.

"Fear is a powerful weapon," he replied.

"It is indeed."

Mak-ee-nah rose. "This lantern. How does it work? Where is its flame? Does it use train oil?"

"No. It uses a battery."

"Batt-er-ee."

She reached down, opened the case, and let the large cell slide onto her hand.

"Current flows from this battery to a wire in the light bulb. See?" She pointed to the light bulb. "It heats up the wire inside until it glows and gives off light. It works on the principle of electricity."

"Ee-leck-trissty." He smiled. *"Klushish!"*

"Klushish?"

"Very good! I like this."

"It's called a flashlight."

"Ah. Flash-light."

Camille replaced the battery and shined the light into Mak-ee-nah's face. He gasped and covered his eyes.

"It is like sun on water!"

She laughed and aimed it at the truck, sobering quickly. "I'm going to alert the authorities about Duarte's stealing."

"We will stop the thievery practiced against my people. From now on, there will be no more taking."

"Why don't you get your box and we'll go back."

"You must return alone, Ca-meel."

"Why?"

Mak-ee-nah looked up at the sky. "The sun is coming and I must go."

"Why?"

"I am a man only at night."

"What?"

"I must go, Ca-meel."

"But I don't know my way—"

"My brothers will take you back." He padded toward the wolves, who sat in a ring at the edge of the clearing, and instructed them in his native tongue. Looking at him, she frowned. What was he—some kind of Nakalt vampire? Why couldn't he go abroad in daylight? What would happen to him if he did?

Mak-ee-nah turned and held up his hand. "Remember. Next time you see me you will give me the amulet, *klootz-mah.*"

"Maybe."

He smiled and crossed his arms over his broad chest. "Good-bye, Ca-meel."

"Wait! Where are—"

One of the wolves howled, startling her, and she looked away for an instant. Then she heard a strange flapping noise and whirled around to see a large black bird flying toward the beach. A chill raced down her back. Had Mak-ee-nah transformed into the black bird? Was the bird a raven—the same raven that had been harassing her?

She glanced back at the wolves sitting just five feet away. Only two remained. One of them, a big wolf with a notched ear, had escorted her to the lodge the night before.

"That wasn't Mak-ee-nah," she commented aloud, as if he could understand. "Was it?" He cocked his head at her words and panted. Unafraid of the animal, Camille studied the wolf's bright, intelligent eyes. But no matter how intelligent the wolf was, he would never be able to answer her questions.

She glanced at the forest trail. Without Mak-ee-nah for company, it would be a long walk back to the cabin. "Well, come on, boys," she said with a sigh. The wolves rose and trotted out ahead, leading the way home. She followed them, thinking about the scene that would erupt when Kit and Old Man found out about the artifact theft. They would be outraged.

Oscar pounded on the door of Donald Two Hand's mobile home. None of the lights were on, a sign that Two Hand was probably still asleep, but Oscar didn't care. He was too upset. He pounded again and then glared impatiently at his watch. Five o'clock. Where was the bastard?

Oscar glanced over his shoulder at the shrubbery surrounding Two Hand's unkempt lot, half expecting to see the huge wolf running toward him. Where had the animal come from? There weren't supposed to be any wolves left on the peninsula. Could development and clear-cutting be forcing them out of the wilderness? He wanted a rational explanation for what he had seen—needed one, in fact—

for he refused to fall prey to Indian lore the way Two Hand did.

He raised his hand to pound again just as the door was pulled open.

"What in the hell?" Two Hand grumbled, running a hand over his thatchy hair.

"Two Hand, someone's found my pickup at the trail head. Vandalized it!"

"Doc?" Two Hand squinted. "Is that you?"

"Of course it's me!"

"Christ." Two Hand opened the screen door. "What in the hell time is it?"

"Five A.M." Oscar stepped into the messy living room, strewn with newspapers and empty beer cans. Two Hand found a pack of cigarettes, fumbled one out, and stuck it in his mouth. He was dressed in a pair of black uniform pants and a dingy T-shirt, both of which looked as if he had snatched them out of a pile in the corner. Oscar stood by the door, unwilling to venture onto the dirty rug, much less breathe the stale ashtray air.

"Five A.M.?" Two Hand lit his cigarette and breathed in, squinting at Oscar. "Why in the name of hell are you here?"

"Somebody broke into my pickup, I told you."

"So?"

"They found the artifacts. They took some of them!"

"Did you see anyone?"

"No."

Two Hand waved him off. "Probably just some kids messing around, Doc. Who else would go all the way out there?"

"What if somebody puts two and two together? What if whoever broke in wasn't a kid?"

"Doc, you're just working yourself up again." Two

Hand exhaled a cloud of smoke. "If someone makes a report, I'll handle it. Don't worry."

Oscar scowled. He didn't have Two Hand's confidence.

"You feeling okay, Doc? You look like you seen a ghost."

"I saw something all right. A wolf. It chased me to my car."

"A wolf?"

"Yes."

"Not a dog."

"I know a wolf when I see one. And there aren't supposed to be any around here, or at least that's what I've been told."

"There aren't. But it's funny you should mention it, Doc." He took a drag on his cigarette. "That Avery woman said she saw some wolves, too. I didn't believe her."

"Well, you'd better believe me. I know a wolf from a German shepherd. I suggest you take out some dogs and do some tracking."

"I'll handle my job, Doc. You handle yours."

"Yes, well, I'm considering holding off for a while."

"What?"

"I don't like this. I'm going to move the truck and hold off working."

"You can't do that, Doc. I've got those investors coming. Besides, you're already way behind schedule."

"I didn't anticipate the difficulty we'd have locating the site of the fort."

"Fort or no fort, Doc, you only have a few more days."

"Then get your shoes on. We can move the truck and get out to the island before it's light."

"I haven't even had breakfast."

"Do you want to find the gold or not?" Oscar said. "I'll be in the car."

◆ ◆ ◆

Camille yawned as she opened the door of the lodge. After her return to the cabin she'd gotten very little sleep and had woken up at nine-thirty, anxious to report the artifact theft to the authorities. Donald Two Hand hadn't been available to answer the phone, so she had left the information with one of his officers. Then she had dressed and walked to the lodge, hoping Kit might take her to North Beach. Even if he was too busy to take her anywhere, she still wanted to tell him about the artifact theft and talk to him about the necklace and Mak-ee-nah and whether or not she should mention the necklace to Old Man. She surmised that Mak-ee-nah would visit the cabin again tonight and wanted to make a decision about giving him the necklace. The amber amulet was not an appropriate subject for a phone conversation. Besides, talking with Kit face to face gave her the opportunity to see him, something she desired more and more as the days flew by.

"Hello," Camille called out, wondering if anyone was around. Hattie came out of the kitchen to the reservation desk.

"Hi, Camille," she greeted.

"Good morning, Hattie. Is Kit around?"

"He is, but he's busy," Lydia replied, strolling into the lobby from the dining area. Her long hair was pulled back, and a scarf was tied over her head. She held a paintbrush in one rubber-gloved hand. Her eyes were flat, her mouth cold and unsmiling. "What do you need?"

Camille felt her cheerfulness at seeing Hattie fade as she turned to Lydia. The last time she'd talked to Lydia, she'd hung up on the woman, and she still found it hard to be civil. "I'd like to talk to Kit for a minute."

"Well, I'm afraid you can't. Like I said, he's busy."

Camille stepped forward, unwilling to take Lydia's word for it, but Lydia shifted her weight in a subtle movement that blocked her path.

"I said he's busy."

Out of the corner of her eye, Camille saw Hattie duck into the kitchen, probably unwilling to witness a cat fight. Camille didn't doubt that Lydia ached to scrap over Kit, probably convinced that her sheer size could easily dominate her petite opponent. What Lydia didn't know, however, was that Camille didn't back down easily once she made up her mind to fight. Camille flushed with the realization that she was considering herself a contender for Kit's attention.

"I don't want to bother him, Lydia, but I have a couple of questions."

"Don't you think you've taken up enough of our time?" She refused to budge. "We've got other things to do than constantly cater to your needs."

Camille raised her chin and was about to reply when Kit breezed around the corner, coming to a stop at Lydia's side. Hattie—bless her soul—hovered behind him.

"Miss Avery—"

"I told her you were too busy, Kitsap," Lydia informed him, "but she wouldn't listen."

"Is something up?" Kit asked.

"Yes, but I'd like to speak to you alone." Camille forced herself to meet Lydia's frosty stare with one of her own.

Lydia turned toward Kit. "If you don't get that tile in today, Kit, it won't have time to set."

"I know that."

"I'll only take a minute," Camille put in.

"Well, come over to the fire, then." He motioned toward the great room. "Want a cup of coffee?"

"Kitsap . . ." Lydia sputtered, enraged.

"Go ahead and finish painting, Lydia." Kitsap smiled at her. "I'll be back on the job in no time."

Lydia shot Camille an I'll-get-you-later look and walked off, her long braid slapping her hips.

Camille removed her parka and sank to a bench near the fire while Kit brought two mugs of coffee to the table at her elbow, and sat down across from her.

"I'm sorry to have interrupted," she began.

"I needed a break anyway. I've been up since dawn, tiling the bathrooms."

"Tiling? Maybe I could work a trade with you, then."

"What do you mean?"

"I've done two tiling projects—a bathroom and a kitchen counter. Both of them them turned out great."

"You looking for a job?" He sipped his coffee, a smile dancing in his black eyes.

"Yes, if I could get you to take me to North Beach today or tomorrow."

"What's the rush?"

"Last night when I was reading Barbara's journal, I came across an entry about North Beach. She saw something suspicious going on there."

"Like what?"

"She didn't say. But it might have had something to do with her disappearance because it was the last entry in her journal. Maybe we could find some kind of clues out there. And even if we don't, I could get some shots of the totem poles your grandfather mentioned."

"I'd like to take you there, but I should get the tile done."

"I could help."

Kit looked her up and down as if judging her skill. She straightened, trying to appear as tall as possible by throwing back her shoulders. Her breasts thrust outward, and

Kit's glance dropped at the movement. For a moment he stared, and she felt a hot, anxious stab twist inside. When he slowly raised his eyes and met hers, his gaze was full of smoldering lights, his mouth a grim line.

"You want to install tile?" he asked, his voice husky.

"If Lydia won't throw me out."

"Lydia doesn't own the lodge." Never once did Kit break his gaze. Camille felt as if she were falling into the black depths of his eyes.

"Who does?" Her voice was just as husky as his.

"Old Man."

He leaned back on the bench, a half smile on his lips as he continued to gaze at her. The old sweatshirt he wore draped across the muscles of his shoulders and outlined the twin planes of his well-developed chest. Camille dragged her coffee cup to her lips and took a sip, barely registering the hot liquid she swallowed. Having seen plenty of Mak-ee-nah's naked figure, she could imagine what Kit's lean body would look like without his sweatshirt and jeans. She had the wildest urge to cover his relaxed body with her own and smother him with kisses, to feel his body mold into hers, to know the pleasure of her breasts pressed against his chest, her lips pressed into his.

"What's the matter, Avery?" he asked softly. "Do I have something on my face?"

She caught herself gaping and blinked. "You do have grout on your cheek," she replied.

"Where?" He brushed his skin.

"You missed it. There." She pointed to just under his cheekbone, but he missed it again.

"Did I get it?"

"No. Here." She leaned across the table and rubbed two fingers over his cheek before she could talk herself out of touching him. His skin was warm and smooth, and it was all she could do to keep from running her hand the rest of the way up the side of his face and into his hair. His eyes still smoldered at her as she sat back.

"Thanks."

"There's a few more things I wanted to talk to you about, Kit."

"What's that?"

"The naked man came again last night."

Kit's eyes immediately flashed back to their usual hardness.

"He spoke to me."

"What does this guy look like?"

"I've told you—he looks just like you!" She leaned forward. "But he has tattoos on his cheek and a ring in his nose. His hair is down to here." She grazed her shoulder with her right hand. "He calls himself Mak-ee-nah and says he's been raised from the dead."

"I'll bet." Kit snorted derisively. "Has he tried anything with you? Did he hurt you?"

"No. He took me to a place where he'd found a truck filled with stolen Nakalt artifacts. And guess who showed up?"

Kit raised his eyebrows.

"Oscar Duarte."

"Duarte?" Kit drank his coffee, his brows knitting over the sharp bridge of his nose.

"And if it hadn't been for Mak-ee-nah, Oscar Duarte would have found me hiding."

"What did this Mak-ee-nah do?"

"He sent a wolf after Duarte. Scared him silly."

"Did you tell the police about the truck?"

"Yes."

"I can't believe it! Duarte's stealing artifacts?"

She nodded.

"Bastard! I wonder how long that's been going on."

"His truck bed was full of them."

Kit squeezed his hands around his coffee cup. "Wait until Old Man hears about this."

"There's more, though, Kit." Camille leaned forward. "I know that Mak-ee-nah is who he says he is. He's no ordinary man pretending to be someone else."

"What makes you say that?"

"Because he was standing right in front of Duarte, and Duarte couldn't even see him."

Kit stared at her in disbelief.

"He couldn't!" she repeated, not knowing what else she could say to convince him.

"How could you see him if Duarte couldn't?"

"I have the—" She broke off, suddenly unsure whether she should divulge the secret of the amulet.

"You have what? X-ray vision?"

Camille shook her head while Kit leaned toward her, his forearms on his thighs.

"Listen, Avery, are you sure you weren't dreaming all this?"

"Yes, I'm sure. I even got the license number of the truck."

"You'll have to admit it's pretty farfetched."

"I know. But it's true. You have to believe me."

"But why would this Mak-ee-nah character show himself to you?"

"Because." Camille sighed and bit her lip. She looked at the floor, debating the points in favor of and against telling Kit about the amber. Yet she had to tell someone. She couldn't face Mak-ee-nah again without knowing what to do about the necklace.

"Because?" Kit repeated doubtfully.

"Because of this." Sighing in resignation, she put her

hand into the neckline of her sweater and pulled at the thong of the amulet. Gently she drew it upward until she clasped the amber with her other hand and drew the thong over her head. Then, with trembling hands, she held it out for him to see.

"For crying out loud," he whispered.

"It's the Nakalt amber with the raven feather inside, isn't it, Kit?"

"I'll be damned—"

"It's Mak-ee-nah's. He knew I had it."

"Does anyone else?" His stare bored into her.

She shook her head. "But Mak-ee-nah wants it back."

"Christ." Kit stood up and leaned over her hands, staring at the necklace but not touching it.

"I found it in my grandmother's attic when I was a little girl."

"You've had it all this time?"

Camille nodded. "At first I didn't know it was connected to your legends. Then when I learned about your famous amulet, I was afraid to show anyone, for fear they would lay the blame at my feet."

"What blame?"

"For what has happened to the Nakalt over the years. For their suffering." Distraught, she clenched her fingers around the smooth amber, and Kit sank to his knees before her. She raised her eyes to his and implored him to understand her, fighting back tears that had suddenly sprung up in her eyes.

Kit reached out and cupped the side of her face. "Hey," he murmured, drawing his thumb across her cheek in a gentle caress. "You're not responsible for that, Camille."

She gazed at him, her eyes burning, wanting to believe him, loving the sound of her name on his lips.

"What should I do, Kit?" Her words were thick as she

tried to ignore the exquisite feeling of his hand on her face. "Every time Mak-ee-nah comes to me, the amber starts to warm. I know it belongs to him, but I also know the amulet is very powerful. Should I give it to him? Will something happen to the Nakalt if I do?"

"I don't know, Camille. I'm out of my league on this one."

"I wanted to tell your grandfather, but when you mentioned the necklace not meeting his expectations—"

"I know I did say that." Kit's hand drew away, and he sat back on his heels. "But maybe Old Man should hear about this."

"Mak-ee-nah will be back tonight. I know he will."

"Okay." Kit stood up. "I'll tell you what. I'll come to the cabin tonight and wait for this Mak-ee-nah character to show."

"But you won't be able to see him."

"What about the wolves you claim come with him?"

"Well, yes, you could see them."

"Good. I just need some proof before I take this to Old Man. I don't want to get him going for nothing."

She nodded.

"Put that necklace back in your sweater for now and don't tell anyone else you have it."

"Okay."

He reached for her hand and helped her up from the chair. She let him help her, glad that he was finally in on the secret of the amber, and felt as if a weight had been lifted from her shoulders.

But noticing she was still upset, he flicked her under the chin. "Hey." He smiled his world-weary half grin at her. "You still want that tiling job?"

"Sure."

"After we finish up here, we'll see about North Beach and your friend Barbara."

"It's a deal." She tried to smile back.

Kit patted her lightly on the shoulder and then led the way toward the dining room.

13

As promised, Kit showed up on her doorstep that night, hoping to get a glimpse of Mak-ee-nah's wolves. Camille fussed around in the kitchen making tea while Kit sat on her couch in front of the fire. It had been a long time since a man had sat on her sofa, and certainly never one as fine as Kit. Gazing at him, she felt as if she had momentarily trapped a rare wild animal for observation. She dropped a teabag into the cup and looked over at his black head as he studied the drawings she had made of the ritual and the Makinna basket collection.

"Feeling anything yet?" he asked, glancing up as she carried the tea to the couch.

If he only knew. She hid a smile and gave him a cup. "Not yet."

"Your drawings are quite good. This one of my grandfather is remarkable."

"Thanks."

"I thought Adam said you were a math teacher."

"I am."

"You should be teaching art."

"I'd like to teach both someday." She sat down on the other end of the couch and tucked her legs beneath her. Kit regarded the movement and let his gaze slide up her legs. She felt as if he'd touched her, and her heart thumped wildly.

"Or you could start a tiling business."

"Jack of all trades, master of none. That's me." She smiled and flexed her fingers, hoping she had got the last of the grout cleaned from her nails. Unlike Lydia, she never could work with a pair of rubber gloves on her hands.

"Could have fooled me, Avery. You did a full day's work in about half the time. And a good job, too."

She winked. "Organization is the key to all things, Mr. Makinna."

He smiled and gazed at her, his eyes full of warmth. She gazed back, comfortable with him for the first time since they had met. She had enjoyed working with Kit. He was as meticulous as she was, a man of concentration and few words. And though they hadn't said much to each other the entire afternoon, the shared task had formed a bond of respect between them and a sense of a job well done through team effort. Kit had capped the day by taking her and his grandfather out for dinner at a local cafe, much to Lydia's annoyance.

"What will you do when you finish the lodge, Kit?"

"I don't know." He put his arm on the back of the couch, and his hand nearly touched her shoulder. He picked at the pile of the upholstery. "Go back to Seattle, I guess."

"What kind of work do you do?"

"I work for a company that develops innovative techniques for fisheries."

"A new slant on an old Nakalt tradition?"

"You might say that." His eyes glittered. "I don't get away from my desk and tie as much as I'd like, though. That's the price I've paid for success."

"You think that's bad—in my job I'm stuck with hundreds of teenage girls out in the middle of nowhere."

He laughed, and Camille could tell by the tight, dry sound of it that Kit didn't laugh often—not like Mak-ee-nah, whose rich laughter was well oiled and well used.

"How long are you going to be here, Avery?"

"I don't know." After all that had happened to her on the reservation, it seemed as if she'd never lived anywhere else. "I had planned to stay a month, but with Barbara gone, I'm not sure. Until she shows up, I'd like to stick around."

"Is your school on some kind of winter break?"

"No. I took a leave of absence. And I've got to prove to the deans that this book Barbara and I are working on will be a critical success so they can feel good about giving me the time off. They're such witches."

Kit smiled again. "I'm using up my vacation allotment to remodel the lodge. That's my idea of a good time."

Camille got to her feet and held out her hand. "Any more tea?"

"No thanks." He gave the cup to her. "Adam tells me you're good at puzzles."

"I enjoy trying to figure things out. Why?"

"I've got one for you."

"Oh?"

"But I don't know the answer."

"Well, I can give it a try. What is it?"

"It's a saying. 'Two is one. One is two. Two is three.' Does that make any sense to you?"

Camille looked down at the cups in her hand. "It sounds similar to the riddle of the Sphinx. Do you remember that from Greek mythology?"

"Not really. I've never been interested in mythology."

"The Greek character Oedipus was posed a question by the Sphinx. The riddle went, 'What goes on four legs in the morning, on two at noon, and on three in the evening?' Oedipus answered 'Man.' "

"Man crawls at birth," Kit put in, seeing the solution, "walks upright when an adult"—he paused as his logic faltered—"but what about the third leg in the evening?"

"Old people use canes."

"Right!" He smiled. "That's good."

"But that really doesn't help us much with your riddle." Camille returned to the couch and stood in front of it. "Two is one, one is two . . ." She bit her lip, concentrating. "Could it have something to do with marriage? You know how it's said that two shall be as one?"

"What about the 'two is three' part?"

"Could it relate to having children?"

Kit frowned. "Then what does 'one is two' mean? Divorce?"

"I don't know—" She broke off. "I'll have to think about this one for a while, Kit."

Camille strolled to the kitchen counter and put down the cups while she thought over the words of the puzzle. When she returned, she found Kit putting another log on the fire. And as she stood watching him, she felt the necklace grow a shade warmer.

"Kit—"

He looked over his shoulder at her.

"He's coming."

Camille clutched the amber as the howl of a wolf drifted over the sound of the crackling fire. Kit rose slowly and crossed the floor to Camille.

"You won't be able to see him, Kit. But he'll be able to see you and hear you."

"I'll believe this when I see it," he replied.

"He'll be here soon. Feel the amber."

Kit put two fingers on the necklace and pulled back in surprise. "It's hot."

She nodded. "That's the way it always gets when Mak-ee-nah shows up. Come on." She headed for the door and switched on the porch light, Kit at her heels. He opened the door for her and practically ran into her when Camille paused, shocked at the sight of Mak-ee-nah in his finery.

He looked magnificent. The black sea otter robe was wrapped around his powerful frame, belted at the waist with a colorful cloth sash. He had painted his face with some kind of glittering substance and pulled up his hair into a twist decorated with a spruce bow and sprinkled with the white down of an eagle. His earlobes glinted with copper and shells, the jewelry complementing his fierce masculinity instead of detracting from it. In one hand he held a war club, in the other a huge fish on a stick.

"So?" he said, holding out both hands and smiling broadly at her look of surprise. "Do you like to see me with clothes, Ca-meel?"

"You look magnificent."

"Ah!" He bestowed his flashing smile upon her as the wolf with the notched ear trotted forward, headed for Kit. Camille heard Kit suck in his breath as the animal approached, but he stood his ground. The huge wolf sniffed Kit's shoe and then the side of his leg while Kit watched in alarm and fascination.

"Who is the man?" Mak-ee-nah asked, coming closer.

"Kitsap Makinna, a friend of mine."

Mak-ee-nah strode up to the very edge of the porch and studied Kit's face, leaning side to side to get a good look at him.

"He is much like me," Mak-ee-nah commented.

"Amazingly similar, don't you think?"

"He is not afraid of my warrior."

"No. He isn't a coward."

"He is as his name—brave."

"Kitsap means brave?"

"Yes." Mak-ee-nah stepped back. "What is he doing here?"

"He came to see if you are real."

Mak-ee-nah chuckled. "He is as a blind man but for my brothers, the wolf-people—unless you give me the amulet, Ca-meel. Then he would see me as you see me."

"I haven't made up my mind about that yet."

"You will know soon." He turned to her. "You are his woman?"

Camille blushed, glad that Kit couldn't hear that particular question. "No."

"Then"—Mak-ee-nah held up the stick—"this *pow-ee* is for you, Ca-meel."

"Halibut?" she asked, recognizing the shape of the fish. "I love halibut!"

"Cook it and I will stay. My hunger for things has returned in great force since I have become a man. And I have eaten nothing but mussels this evening."

She took the stick that skewered the heavy fish. "You want me to cook this now?"

He nodded. "There is no woman to cook for me but you, *klootz-mah*."

"It might take a while. I'll have to go in the cabin."

"I will wait on the beach. Call my name when you are finished."

Camille carried the fish into the cabin while Kit held the door. As soon as she had taken possession of the fish, he had been able to see it and marveled at the size.

"There's a fine fellow for you," Kit remarked, chuckling. "He wants you to cook the fish?"

"Yes. He says now that he's a man, his appetite is back."

"Just for food, I hope," Kit remarked.

Camille shot him a glance. The thought that Mak-ee-nah might have a sexual appetite hadn't entered her mind.

"Here . . ." Kit held out his hand for the fish. "Let me help you cut that."

Together they fixed a feast for Mak-ee-nah, hoping he would enjoy the foreign tastes of the modern world. Though Camille worried she would ruin the fish, Kit showed her how to broil the halibut to perfection. Camille made a salad, steamed some carrots and peas, and cooked a potato in the microwave. She salted nothing, remembering from Barbara's book that the Nakalt didn't use seasoning during the time in which Mak-ee-nah lived. But they did use oil in which to dip their food. Clarified butter would have to suffice. She melted some in a cup and put it on his platter.

"Do you think he'd like something to drink?" Camille asked.

"Just give him water or fruit juice. I don't want him getting tipsy and fawning all over you. Especially when I can't even see what he's doing."

Camille glanced at Kit, surprised by the genuine sound of jealousy in his voice. He busied himself with putting a knife and fork on Mak-ee-nah's plate and then handed it to her.

"He looks just like you," she teased. "Simply imagine yourself doing what you'd do."

His eyes flashed at her, but he made no reply, and his silent regard sent a frisson of pleasure through her.

Camille had made one mistake in fixing Mak-ee-nah's meal. She had forgotten that stoneware was not of his world. Neither was a fork and knife, or the vegetables, for that matter. Mak-ee-nah improvised by finding a large flat rock, upon which he placed the halibut steak. Once the physical limitations were solved, he ate his meal with gusto, offering to share many times, refusing to accept Camille's excuse that she had already eaten with Kit. Finally she did accept a bite of halibut, hoping to appease him, and found that Kit's recipe was indeed delicious.

"Klushish!" He put the rock on the ground beside the log on which he sat as regal as a king, licking his fingers. "Thank you, Ca-meel."

"You're welcome."

He patted his stomach. "The fish was good cooked in that way."

"Kitsap Makinna cooked it."

"A man cooked? Is he your slave?"

"No." Camille grinned at the thought.

"Does he live in the cabin with you?"

"He lives in the big lodge down the beach."

"He watches you as a hawk watches a rabbit."

"He is curious to know why I speak to thin air."

"His curiosity can end if you give the amulet to me, Ca-meel."

"I'm sorry, Mak-ee-nah. I believe the amulet belongs to you, but I must speak to an elder tomorrow before I give it to you."

He narrowed his eyes. "Each day is a wasted day for the Nakalt people."

"I realize that."

He stood up, and a few pieces of down wafted to the ground at his feet. "I will go now. See that the bones of the *pow-ee*-people are taken to the water."

His request surprised her. "All right."

"And tomorrow night you will eat with me."

Camille rose, hearing in his command a jealousy as plain as Kit's. Though he was imperious in his request, Camille smiled. "All right. It's a date."

"Date?" Mak-ee-nah glanced at her and then at Kit, obviously wanting to appear dominant in the presence of the other man.

"I agree to meet you here."

"Ah." Mak-ee-nah nodded. "And then you will give me the amulet?"

"Maybe."

"So." He smiled, measuring her with eyes that sparkled in amusement.

"Now do you believe?" Camille asked Kit as they went back into the cabin.

"I don't know what to believe!"

"You saw the wolves."

"Yes—" He broke off, uncertain.

"That in itself is unusual, don't you think?"

Kit nodded and strode to the kitchen area, as if to out-distance his thoughts.

Camille trailed behind, hiding a smile. "He asked if you were my slave."

"He did, did he?" Kit picked up the broiler pan and carried it to the sink.

"If I give the amulet to him, then you'll be able to see him."

"That's what he says. I wouldn't believe everything he tells you. It could be a trick." Kit turned on the water, filling the sink.

"Wasn't Mak-ee-nah a respected chief of the Nakalt?"

"As far as history relates it. But we don't know that much about how he operated. Obviously he has the ability to impress women."

"Why shouldn't I be impressed?" she retorted. "He's absolutely beautiful." The words slipped out before she realized that her comment could be taken as an opinion of Kit's appearance as well.

" 'Magnificent' was the word you used, I believe." Kit picked up a towel. "Here. Dry."

Camille lifted a glass from the drainer. "He's quite charismatic."

"And accustomed to having his way. Remember, Camille, if this Mak-ee-nah is who he claims to be, he is not an ordinary man. He's also not a modern man."

"What are you getting at?"

"He might expect things of you that a modern man wouldn't dare consider."

"Such as?"

"Let me put it this way. In his day, women were objects to be bought and sold." Kit stopped washing the dishes and looked at her. "And used."

"Mak-ee-nah doesn't strike me as the type to take advantage of women."

"Don't underestimate him."

Camille finished her task, the smile fading from her lips. At first she had thought Kit was simply jealous, and his reaction pleased her. But now his words sounded more like a warning, one that she decided she should take seriously.

After the dishes were done, Kit pulled on his coat and walked to the door. "I'll come by about eight tomorrow morning and pick you up," he said. "We'll talk to Old Man first thing and then head out to North Beach."

"Great!"

"Thanks for helping at the lodge."

"Thanks for cooking the *pow-ee*."

"Do you want me to take the bones down to the beach on my way out?"

"Would you mind?" she asked, and picked up the dish piled with the discarded remnants of the fish.

He smiled and opened the door as she held out the plate. He took it. "I'll be right back."

Kit walked to the edge of the bluff and let his eyes adjust to the dark before he descended the narrow path to the beach. All the way down he was careful not to spill the contents of the plate, remembering the tales his mother had told him when he was a boy. According to the old stories, if a person failed to return the bones of the fish to the sea, the fish spirit would go back to his lodge and no longer have a whole body. Whatever had been carelessly discarded would be missing on the human form of the fish-person when he returned to the Land Above.

Kit rinsed the plate in the sea and remained in a squatting position, his forearms resting on his thighs as he gazed across the silver water. He had listened to those tales, only half believing them, just as he lived his life now—half in the world of the white man and half in the ways of the reservation. Since he had seen evidence of Mak-ee-nah and his wolves, however, he suddenly felt his convictions sliding off their already crumbling foundations.

Scowling, he rose and shoved a hand into the front

pocket of his jeans. He had forgotten how peaceful the reservation could be, how utterly cut off from the rest of the world. Mak-ee-nah's appearance only made it seem more otherworldly. He could feel himself slipping under the spell of the place.

Kit turned back to the trail. What was coming over him? The reservation wasn't magical. For most of his people, it was a place of poverty, crime and hopelessness. How could he let Camille and her "spirit friend" make him lose his sense of reality? He returned to the cabin, intent on rising above his doubts.

Camille met him at the door and took the empty plate. Framed in the dark by the lighted doorway, she seemed more petite than ever. A wave of concern swept over him.

"Do you feel safe here?" he asked, pausing on the porch. "You could come back to the lodge."

"I'll be all right. Mak-ee-nah won't hurt me."

"Do you think he'll come back?"

"I'll be fine, regardless."

Kit glanced at his truck and then back at her. He didn't like the thought of her being out here alone. But the alternative was staying with her at the cabin. He doubted she would go for that, and he doubted that he would be able to keep his hands off her if he stayed any longer. "Well, good night, then. See you in the morning."

"Bye, Kit. Thanks."

Oscar had just taken a painkiller and slipped into a hot bath when the phone rang. Swearing, he stepped out of the water, wrapped a towel around his scrawny midriff, and cursed his way to the phone near his bed.

"Yes!" he snapped.

"Doc, it's me."

Donald Two Hand. The superstitious slacker. He should have known. Oscar rubbed the ache in the small of his back.

"What do you want, Two Hand?"

"You'll never guess who found your truck."

Oscar stopped rubbing. "Who?"

"That Avery woman."

Oscar hiked up his towel, surprised.

"She got the license plate number and everything."

"Shit."

Two Hand paused, and Oscar knew he was taking a long drag on his cigarette. "This might be harder than I thought, Doc," Two Hand continued.

"Why?"

"Because the Avery woman is the hysterical type. She's called about one thing or another every day since she got here. She won't be talked out of this one, you can bet on it."

"But what about the evidence? She won't have any evidence since we moved the truck."

"Yeah, but what about the artifacts she took? If she shows them to somebody and gets the elders riled up, there's no telling what might happen."

Oscar squinted in pain. With this news, he was going to need another painkiller. Maybe more than one. "There's no way we can be linked to the artifacts," he mused, more to himself than Two Hand. "Except for that damned journal."

"Yeah. That journal. Wherever it is."

"We've got to do something, Two Hand. I'm not going to let that little meddler ruin everything. Not when we're so close to finding the gold."

"I can probably hold her off for a few days. Make some excuses."

"Good. And by that time, I'll think of something."

14

Old Man took the news of the smuggling and Camille's possession of the amulet with a closed expression, almost as if he had expected to hear of it. Confounded, Camille watched him struggle to his feet and shuffle to the fireplace.

"Yet another violation," he said, poking the coals, "in a long list of violations."

"But isn't there anything that can be done?" Camille asked.

Old Man turned and surveyed her. "You have told the authorities. Now we must wait for them to act."

"Considering how they're handling Barbara Stanton's disappearance, I'm beginning to wonder how effective they are," Kit put in. "Isn't there something we can do?"

"Why should you care, Kitsap? The reservation is none of your concern anymore. When you are done with the lodge, you will be gone. What does it matter to you that Nakalt artifacts are being stolen?"

"Because the artifacts are part of the Nakalt heritage, part of our history. And they don't belong on the wall of some collector's house!"

"Ah." Old Man replaced the poker in its rack. "Such passion from a man whose heart is not with his people."

"It has nothing to do with my heart, Old Man. We're talking about justice here."

"Ah, justice." Sagely, Old Man nodded his head. "When you have lived as long as I have, Kitsap, you will know that justice is compromise for the Nakalt. True justice belongs only to the white man."

"How can you just stand there and take it?"

"I am old, Kitsap. I am tired. Years of Nakalt *justice* have stooped my shoulders." He sat down with a sigh and pushed up his glasses. "Fighting for justice is a battle for warriors, Kitsap, and there are so few left."

"Warriors are a thing of the past, Old Man."

"Don't be too sure. Camille has told of Mak-ee-nah's arrival, which will bring a new dawn to the Nakalt. You will see."

"I've heard that song before."

Old Man shrugged. "Doubt everything, Kitsap, and you will have nothing on which to build."

Kit strode to the window and looked out, stuffing his hands in the back pockets of his jeans. For a moment his grandfather studied him in silence.

"A white woman's heart can see more clearly than yours, Kitsap."

"Because she's been deluded by your prophecies."

"Because she has opened herself to possibilities."

"Right. The possibility of being disappointed when things don't materialize. No thanks." Kit turned, his face hard as stone. "I'm going to load the canoe. You coming, Camille?"

"Yes," she answered, rising, her heart heavy for Kit in his bitterness.

"You go ahead, Kitsap," Old Man put in. "Miss Avery will be out in a moment."

Camille glanced at Kit's grandfather, wondering why he wanted her to stay. He told her to wait and shuffled into the kitchen while Kit strode out the front door. From the living room window, she watched Kit tie his grandfather's canoe to the rack on top of his Jeep. He had intended to take David's powerboat up to North Beach but found out from his grandfather that David's launch was still impounded by the police. The trip would take more time if they took the canoe, but Old Man seemed to think the journey would be more peaceful and enjoyable in his hand-hewn craft, one of the last remaining cedar log canoes on the reservation. Camille wondered just how enjoyable the trip could be, seeing how agitated Kit had become. His movements were sharp with anger, his face stormy. If he didn't care about the reservation and the Na-kalt people, why did he get so upset about the things his grandfather said?

Old Man appeared at her elbow. "When you return from North Beach, I will be gone, Miss Avery."

"Oh?"

"I'm going to the forest to pray about the amulet and Mak-ee-nah. Don't give up the necklace until I return with an answer."

"I won't," she promised. "But how long will you be gone, Mr. Makinna?"

"A day, three days, maybe more. But here, Miss Avery." From his pants pocket he drew out a small bag of leather, not much larger than a coin purse, decorated with conical-shaped dentalium shells and the stylized body of a whale.

The top of the bag was cinched together with a leather tie. "This is for you," he said, holding it out.

Camille let the bag rest on her open palm. "What is it, Mr. Makinna?"

"Protection." He folded her fingers over it, insisting that she take it. "Put it in your pocket."

"All right." Camille felt foolish as she slipped the pouch into her parka pocket, but she didn't want to hurt Old Man's feelings, especially when the bag seemed so important to him.

He nodded.

"What's in it?" she asked.

"A little of this. A little of that."

"Well, thank you."

"It is for North Beach. But do not tell Kitsap. He gets angry about things he doesn't understand." He opened the door for her.

She paused on the doorstep. "Mr. Makinna, I think you're wrong about Kit's heart. I think he does care."

"Oh, I know he does, Miss Avery. But he is fighting within himself because he won't listen to his heart. I am trying to make him face that."

"Maybe he doesn't know the language of his heart, either. Like me."

"But you are willing to learn. And you are learning, aren't you?"

"Yes. I know I am."

"Your heart sings for my grandson, doesn't it?"

Camille blushed and looked out at the street, wondering how to answer his question. She didn't want to lie to Old Man but wasn't certain of the truth. Her heart had been doing crazy things to her these past few days, but did that mean she was falling in love with Kit? Or was she merely infatuated with his looks and caught up in the curious spell of the reservation?

"I'm not sure yet," she murmured.

She felt his hand pat her shoulder. "Soon you will know."

She turned, her ears still hot, and looked at him.

"I hope you find that which you seek, Miss Avery."

"And you, Mr. Makinna."

He smiled and his eyes twinkled. Camille gave him a second glance over her shoulder as she stepped outside. In all the time she had known Old Man, she had never seen his eyes twinkle.

Two hours later the canoe glided up to a wide shale beach, but the grating sound of the landing was overpowered by the thunder of surf just around the point on their right. Camille rested her paddle across the sides of the canoe and let Kit pull the boat up to the sand. Her shoulders burned, her arms trembled. She and Kit had been paddling for two hours, and she wasn't accustomed to such hard physical labor.

Kit's mood, on the other hand, seemed to have transformed with the activity. His face was flushed, his eyes were sparkling, and a smile hovered on his lips. Camille had a tough time keeping her gaze off him. He had also taken off his coat and rolled up the sleeves of his red-and-black wool shirt, revealing his strong forearms, which only made matters worse for her concentration.

She picked up her Polaroid camera for the totem-pole shots, climbed out of the canoe, and nearly fell over in the process. Her legs were cramped from kneeling for such an extended length of time, and she felt strange touching solid ground after hours of rocking on the water. Kit grinned at her over his shoulder.

"You all right?" he asked.

"Yes." She adjusted the strap of her camera case and glanced around. The scenery they had passed en route had been so stunning, she had taken two rolls of 35-mm film with her other camera, shooting rock arches, twisted, windswept trees, bald eagles soaring over the water, and intimate coves so pristine that she wondered if humans had ever set foot upon them.

Yet all those sights paled in comparison with North Beach. Above the wide stretch of sand was a gentle, sloping meadow, crowned by a stand of weathered totem poles shining silver in the sun. Behind them was a cliff, over which a small river cascaded into a green pool, which in turn emptied into the bay where they had landed. Camille stared, awestruck.

"Beautiful, isn't it," Kit commented, coming up behind her. "Every time I see this place I am amazed by its beauty."

"Like the Garden of Eden," Camille whispered. "No wonder Barbara liked to hike up here."

"This was the ancient winter home of the Nakalt."

"Why did they abandon it?"

"They were massacred here. The survivors were afraid to come back, afraid of the ghosts of the dead who were never properly buried."

"Such a shame."

"It is. Superstition and fear have limited my people for years."

Camille glanced at Kit. He had just said "my people." Was he beginning to accept his place among the Nakalt? Was he beginning to listen to the song in his heart? Apparently he was wondering the same thing, for she caught him gazing at her with a puzzled expression between his brows.

Then he shaded his eyes. "Let's split up, Avery. You take this side of the beach, I'll take that one. If you find anything, holler."

He turned away before she could respond. Camille watched him go, wondering if the song he heard might include her. She was certain he had been jealous of Makee-nah the night before, yet he had not made a move toward her after that first fiasco of a kiss. He seemed to be waging his own battle in regard to his feelings for her, and the fact that he was unsure of himself—a handsome man of the world like him—touched Camille deeply.

She would have liked to explore the beach with Kit but knew that each of them would probably be distracted by the other's company. So she set off toward the waterfall and the pool, searching every foot of ground for clues of Barbara or anything that could be considered suspicious.

Having found nothing after an hour or so, they met back at the canoe at lunchtime. Camille's stomach growled as she lifted the small cooler Hattie had sent with them. Inside were egg-salad sandwiches, apples, bean salad, and cupcakes. Kit poured coffee for both of them while Camille arranged food on the plates. Then they carried their lunches to a pile of huge rocks at the edge of the bay where the beach met the open sea. They each chose a different rock on which to sit and then ate, mostly in silence, while they gazed at the sparkling blue Pacific Ocean.

After lunch Camille convinced Kit to pose for her in front of the totem poles. Though he protested that he wasn't photogenic, she found him to be an excellent subject, with his dark hair, red shirt, and striking features contrasted against the silvered cedar. He explained some of the animal shapes of the poles and then walked down to the beach, leaving Camille to finish her shoot alone.

Later she sat with a tablet and sketched the bay while Kit combed the beach. Often she would look up and find him staring off across the water, the wind ruffling his hair. What was he thinking? She couldn't see his face from such a distance, but his proud stance emblazoned his image in her mind.

She continued with her drawing for more than an hour, lost in concentration, and all the while thinking about Kit's riddle. *Two is one, one is two, two is three.* She wished he knew what it meant, for she was annoyed that she couldn't figure it out and wanted to know the solution. Yet there was no book in which to look up the answer, no place to find a clue. Sighing, she kept drawing until Kit called her name. She glanced up and saw that he had climbed the rise above the large rocks where they had eaten lunch. He called her name again and motioned for her to come.

Had he found something to do with Barbara? She dropped her tablet and pencils to the ground and dashed across the beach, slipping in the sand. Then she trotted up the rise to where Kit stood, watching something in the water.

He turned as she puffed to a halt. "Orca!" he exclaimed, pointing toward the waves. "Killer whales."

The wind whipped his words away, but Camille followed the line of his finger.

"Oh, Kit!"

There in the water were five black-and-white killer whales, like glistening black jelly beans, rolling and diving, their tall dorsal fins slicing through the waves. Camille stumbled forward, astounded, never having seen orca in the wild.

Kit said something else, but Camille shook her head and pointed at her ear. He stepped behind her and, with his hand on her shoulder, leaned toward her so she could hear him over the wind.

"Orca are the largest members of the porpoise family."

"How big do they get?"

"About twenty-five feet."

"They're huge!" She looked back at him and grinned, highly aware of the close proximity of his mouth.

"They communicate with each other by whistling and squeaking," Kit went on. "They sometimes even cry out when they're in trouble."

"Just like humans."

"Yes. Just like humans."

Camille smiled at the wonder of seeing the killer whales, but also for the closeness she shared with Kit. She loved the sound of his voice and could hear the joy in it as he talked about the animals. She also loved the touch of his hand on her shoulder and hoped he would go on touching her. She couldn't imagine why she had ever shaken off his hand. She longed to sink back against his chest, longed to feel his arms wrap around her. She wished he would kiss her again so she could return it and show him how she really felt about him. But he never made a move, just kept rattling on about the orca, and she kept asking questions, afraid that once the zoological lesson was over, he would move away from her.

Just as she was learning to relax enough to enjoy being close to him, she felt Kit's grip tighten. Then his hand slid off her shoulder as she twisted to look at him, wondering at the sudden change in his demeanor. His entire body had gone stiff, and he was concentrating on something far out to sea.

"What is it?" Camille asked, stepping away from him.

"I don't know." He shaded his eyes and squinted. "I

thought I saw something glint out there. Something metallic."

Camille followed his stare, focusing on a small hump of an island. "Is that unusual?" she asked.

"For that island it is."

"Why?"

"It's tribal property. No one's supposed to be out there."

"Why not?"

"It's one of our sacred places, a burial ground called the Island of the Dead."

Camille hugged her arms. "With a name like that, who'd want to trespass there?"

"Good question." He continued to scan the island. "I could have sworn I saw something."

"Maybe it was just the sun reflecting on the water."

"Maybe. . . ." Kit sounded unconvinced.

"Do you suppose someone is getting those artifacts from the island?"

"There's a good possibility of it."

"Do you think Barbara saw the same thing? She might have had a pair of binoculars." A chill flew down Camille's back. "You don't suppose she found out about the artifacts and—" She broke off, unable to finish the sentence or complete the thought.

Kit glanced down at her. "If she stumbled upon a smuggling operation and threatened to broadcast the information, she might have run into trouble. Who else have you told, Camille?"

"Just Old Man and the police."

"Good." Kit returned his attention to the island.

Camille touched his arm. "Why don't we go out there?"

"It would be too far in the canoe, with just us rowing. We'd get caught in the dark. We can go tomorrow."

He remained watching, until Camille grew impatient and decided to return to her drawing. The spell between them had been broken, and she doubted she'd have another chance to share such closeness with Kit, at least not on North Beach. Disappointed, she wandered away, along the pile of boulders, keeping her eye on the orca, who were now cruising the small bay near the canoe.

Suddenly a rock dislodged from the weight of her foot and tipped, throwing her sideways. For a horrifying moment she fought for balance, her arms whirling like windmills, and then she teetered and plunged to the sandy beach below. With a thump she landed on her rear, miraculously hitting a patch of sand instead of the barnacle-encrusted boulder just inches away.

Kit appeared at the top of the bank and leaped down beside her. "Are you okay?" he asked.

"I think so." She leaned back, bracing herself on her extended arms, and grinned in embarrassment at her clumsiness.

He dropped to his knees beside her in the sand. "That could have been a nasty fall," he commented. "You're lucky."

"I'm accident prone, that's what I am."

He smiled. "Can't argue with that."

Camille glanced up to find him studying her, his eyes clouded and dark.

Her gaze locked with his as the humor of the situation dropped away and something serious and intense took its place, causing Camille's heart to bang against her ribs. This was her chance to kiss him, to tell him how she felt, but now that the chance had arrived, she was too nervous to say anything.

"Kit—" She broke off and attempted to sit up. She felt vulnerable sprawled on the sand in front of him.

He rose, pulling her to her feet, but kept her close by running his hands under her open parka to the back of her jeans, which in turn pressed her against him. She flushed at the intimacy of the position.

"Feel any better?" he asked hoarsely.

"Much," she murmured, wondering where to put her own hands. His male scent, mingled with the smell of cedar, emanated from his warm chest. She breathed in deeply, marveling at the chance occurrence that had thrown them together.

His hard eyes bored into hers as if challenging her to be the first to step away, and then his Adam's apple bobbed in a hard swallow, as if he were choking back his heart as well. Desire intensified his sharp features—his straight fine nose, his chiseled cheekbones, the shadowed ledge of his lower lip. Suddenly all Camille wanted to do—the single most important act in the universe—was to reach up and kiss that shadowed line.

She raised on her toes, and as her face tilted upward, his lowered and he bent down to capture her lips.

At the touch of his mouth on hers, something burst inside Camille. An inner wall of reserve broke apart, flooding her with a hot abandon she had never experienced. In that instant she knew she wanted Kit. She didn't want just his kiss, just his embrace—she wanted all of him.

She slid her hands up his chest, pressing against his mouth, wondering why she had waited so long to taste the burning sweetness of his lips. He was strong and hungry, as ravenous as she was, and his arms held her like steel bands, one at her waist and the other across her shoulders, while he savaged her lips, demanding that she open her mouth to him.

His tongue swept into her, shattering the rest of her reserve. Her hands roamed over his chest as if they had a mind of their own, and she let them go, sighing with pleasure at the width and the hardness of his torso. Then her fingers slid up the straining column of his neck and into his glossy hair, trapping his mouth to hers as hard as he clamped her frame to his.

Still it wasn't close enough. Kit's jaw slanted across hers, forcing her mouth so wide that she thought he might devour her. One of his hands clutched the back of her head. Camille felt herself melting into him as he pulled her against him so hard, he nearly lifted her off her feet. She molded against his contours in a wall of heat and need, shocked by her lack of control. She wanted to crawl all over him, smother him with kisses, feel every inch of him.

She had kissed other men, but always with a sense of detachment. With Kit, however, her world had shrunk to enclose only them, and she was aware of nothing but the sound of their labored breathing and the roar of desire in her ears. She knew what was happening between them was inevitable—like the roll of the seasons and the change in the tides—and she could neither control nor stop the course they had set.

She was aware that this was her first real kiss with Kit, an event that should be savored and cherished as a first step in their relationship, something to be done with a certain amount of reservation. But with Kit she couldn't stop at just one kiss, not when her entire body cried out for him. His ravenous mouth had already taken them far beyond the chasteness of a first kiss, anyway.

Neither of them could pretend for a moment that chasteness had anything to do with their intentions.

At last Kit broke from her mouth, only to murmur her name against her lips as he let her slide down his body. She felt every hard inch of him and closed her eyes against the resounding throb that burgeoned inside her.

"God," he breathed, his lips on her throat. She arched backward, reveling in the sensation of his kisses on her neck. To support her, he swept his long, slender hands under her sweater and T-shirt, fanning them across her back.

"Ah, God." He moaned. "No bra."

Camille gasped as his hand slid around to the front of her torso, moving upward to cover her breast. She had always thought her breasts were too small to make a bra necessary. But somehow they had swelled during Kit's kisses, and she could tell by the way he sighed that he liked what he had found. He squeezed her gently, cupping her, weighing her as she found his lips again.

"Take off the parka," he demanded, his voice gravelly with passion.

She shouldered out of the overlarge parka and let it fall, not caring where it landed. Kit's fingers were on her nipple, pinching it and rolling it, and Camille closed her eyes in ecstasy, transported by the unbearable flames his touch was lighting inside her.

"Kit—" Her voice came out in a whimper of shivering need, a voice she didn't even recognize as her own.

He dropped to his knees before her and pushed up her sweater. At first the cool air felt alien to her, until his warm mouth found her breast. She gasped in wonder at the things he was doing to her with his teeth and tongue. Trembling, she pulled up the rest of the folds—the amulet caught between her shirt and sweater—exposing both of her breasts to him, offering herself like a pagan altar, and almost crying out from the exquisite ache welling up in her chest. She caught a vision of a child suckling her just as Kit did, and the ache shifted even deeper.

"Kit," she said. "Oh . . . Kit—"

Weak in the knees, she sank to the sand, still holding her

shirt. Giddy with desire, she knelt against him as he hurriedly unbuttoned his shirt and threw it aside. It was too cold to disrobe entirely, but he yanked up his T-shirt.

"I've got to feel you," he whispered. "Skin to skin."

She looked down as he gathered her against his bare chest, which was so much darker than her own. But she wasn't prepared for the touch of her hard, cold nipples against his hot flesh and gasped in surprise. Kit seemed overwhelmed, too, for his head dropped to the small of her shoulder and he swayed against her with a moan. Camille clutched his back, closing her eyes at the heat between them and the surprising softness of his hair on her neck.

Then Kit found her lips and kissed her again, pulling her bottom lip, nipping the corners of her mouth.

Camille could feel his stomach rising and falling against hers and soon found herself matching the back-and-forth swaying motion he had initiated.

"Touch me," he murmured, his breath hot and moist in her ear. "Please. I'm going crazy."

His words sent a shimmer of heat down her legs. But she did as he requested and trailed her hands from his back and around his rib cage to his abdomen. He was trim, warm, hard as a rock, and she flushed with desire from just touching the ridges of muscle above his navel.

"Lower, Camille," he urged.

She broke from his lips and looked down, following the line of his zipper with her palm. She cupped his fullness and heard him sigh, and heard an echo of his sigh slip out of her own throat.

Feeling his hard length made her entire body break out in a sweat. But she knew she couldn't stop, couldn't turn back. She wanted Kit as she had never wanted a man, and no matter what happened afterward, she wanted him inside her.

With a shaking hand she unbuttoned his jeans and unzipped him, while Kit stroked her hair and cheek and held his breath.

"I didn't plan for this," he gasped.

"Nor I," she answered, drawing him out of his briefs. He was incredibly silken, incredibly firm. She took him in her hand, and his lean hips pulsed involuntarily. He let out a ragged sigh.

Camille's mouth went dry. It wasn't enough to hold him in her hand. It would never be enough until he was deep inside her, as deep as he could bury himself.

She couldn't believe she was unzipping her jeans, desperate to give herself to a man, desperate to have him take her—hard and demanding. She had never ripped off her own clothes, had never done anything with a man that was not in a bedroom after all the prerequisites had been fulfilled. Yet here she was, out in broad daylight, pulling down her own pants, not even getting them all the way off before Kit had pressed her backward onto the parka, his shaft straining against her panties.

Ruthlessly he pulled them aside, and with their legs tangled with each other and the legs of her jeans, he pushed into her. She was ready for him, moist and arching and breathless, crying out in pleasure as he thrust into her petite frame.

"Am I hurting you?" he asked, pushing deeper.

"No," she panted.

"You're so small. I should stop—"

"Don't. Oh, don't." She grabbed handfuls of his damp T-shirt and held on for dear life as he slid all the way inside. "Kit!"

"Ah, God!" he exclaimed, closing his eyes. For a moment he hung motionless above her, rigid and breathless.

Then he kissed her and put his thumb on her, kneading

in a circular motion that was soon driving her crazy with desire. She spread her legs wider, which allowed him even more room, and arched into his hand between every stroke.

Kit's body strained forward and her body bowed up, following his rhythm as she anticipated his moves. His face was dark with concentration, his eyes sealed with passion, while his mouth pressed kisses upon her lips and throat.

Soon his pace increased and he broke off kissing her. The change in tempo caught Camille up in a whirlpool of sensation, pulling her with it. She gasped Kit's name, wondering what he was doing to her. His hand left her then, and he rose up and plunged into her with a ferocity that sent her flying out of the whirlpool. Camille froze stiff as stone as an unbelievable spasm caught her in its grip. She forgot to move, forgot to breathe, forgot to think. All she could do was feel—and it was like no other sensation she had ever felt, as if the sun had exploded into a supernova inside her.

She sucked in snatches of air—unable to breathe fully—and grabbed his forearms as he released his seed in a burst so powerful and so sustaining that he cried out. Camille clutched his hips, pinning him against her while delicious warmth spread deep inside her. For a moment they hung together in suspended disbelief, part of the timeless cycle of earth and sky, of sand and sea, as they fused into one being and momentarily lost themselves to an exquisite otherworld.

Then, with a great sigh of release, Kit relaxed his elbows and let his weight sink onto her. He embraced her, slipping his arms under her shirt so he could touch the round contours of her bare breasts and caress her back. She could feel his hands and arms trembling.

"You're so small," he murmured. "Everywhere."

She held him tightly and looked up at the incredible blue of the sky. Being with Kit, joined with him here, was like a miracle to her, as if they were *in* the Garden of Eden and were the only two human beings alive. She pressed her mouth to the hard curve of his jaw below his ear and kissed the stretch of skin beneath it, and was so filled with completion and joy that she felt as if she would burst.

To relieve her of his weight, Kit rolled onto his back, still inside her, and embraced her, nuzzling her hair. She moved on top of him, heedless of the chill or her naked legs, wishing she could lie with him forever on this beautiful deserted beach. Then Kit suddenly stopped caressing her.

"What's this?" he asked, reaching out to the sand at the edge of her parka.

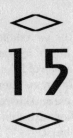

15

Kit held up the small leather bag, decorated in the unmistakable design of the Nakalt. He didn't have to look at it twice to know where it had come from and what was in it. His grandfather was up to his tricks again, trying to twist fate into his own notion of order by giving Camille a bag of charms. And what had been the purpose of the charms? To ensure that they would be thrown together as man and woman, seduced by nature and lust? A black wave of betrayal flooded over Kit at the realization that Camille hadn't made love to him because of any feelings she might harbor for him. She had been enchanted in some way, induced to surrender to him by the shamanic practices of an old man. He'd had it with his grandfather.

"Kit, what's wrong?" Camille asked, sitting up in alarm.

He slipped out of her and was overcome by another wave of desolation. She had felt so warm, so right, so wonderful—he should have known it wouldn't last.

"Kit!"

"Let me up," he said harshly.

"What's wrong? What have I done?"

Kit rose to his feet and glared at her, holding up the leather pouch. "My grandfather gave this to you, didn't he?"

"Yes, but—"

"Why?"

"To protect me." She scrambled to her feet and tried to grab it out of his hand, but he snatched it away.

"Protect you, like hell."

"Kit, what are you talking about? What's wrong?"

"Nothing. Get your clothes on."

"I will not." She stood her ground. "Not until you tell me what's bothering you."

"I said, get your clothes on!" He yanked his briefs and jeans over his legs, never once looking at her. Then he grabbed his shirt and shook out the sand, trying to keep from retching out of sheer disappointment. The bottom of his world had just fallen out. How could he have been so stupid as to believe she cared for him, that her embrace had meant something?

"What's happened?" she implored, her voice breaking behind him. "How can you act this way after we—after we were so—"

"So what, Avery? So driven?" He held up the small bag again. "That's what this pouch is all about, lady. To drive us together. To engage us in a mindless coupling."

"Is that what this was to you?" she gasped, her face blanching. "A mindless coupling?"

"Why not? With this little baby right here, any willing male would have done the job. Didn't Old Man tell you that?"

"I thought you didn't believe in any of your grandfather's hocus-pocus."

Her comment hit him like a fist to the solar plexus. He *had* believed in the power of the charms. Stunned, he could only stare at her, too angry and hurt to admit that he didn't know what he believed anymore. He balled the bag into his fist and forced his gaze to remain above thigh level, where her sweater concealed her beautiful breasts and where he couldn't see her sleek pale legs. The blank curtain of hurt on her white face, which grew paler by the moment, struck him to the core. He had intended to add the part about an assured pregnancy to the list of the bag's powers, but her stunned expression froze the words on his lips. Maybe she'd be fortunate enough to slip through that crack in the sidewalk of fate. As for himself, he refused to think about the alternate possibility—that of a child between them. It simply couldn't happen.

Kit turned away, hating himself for succumbing to her, hating his grandfather for trapping him again, hating the way he felt when he looked into her shattered eyes.

"You're saying that you—that you made love to me just because of that bag?"

"Yes." He glanced at her, his eyes fierce with wishing it weren't true.

"And that what I felt—" She broke off, turning her back to him. She leaned her palms on a boulder. He could see her shoulders shaking and knew that she was crying. He stared at her, rooted to the spot, betrayal and anguish like lead weights on his feet and hands.

"Forget it, Avery," he said, picking up her jeans and panties. "It's not such a big deal."

"Not a big deal?" She whirled to face him. "How can you say that?"

"I've found it pays not to think of sex as something other

than what it is." He tossed the clothes to her, and she caught them without taking her eyes off his face. "It's just sex. Two people chasing after an orgasm, hoping they won't reproduce along the way—and *so* natural."

His sarcasm wounded her. He could see her expression of stark disbelief before she looked down at her torn panties. Her hands shook as she stepped into them.

He wanted to reach out and help her, wanted to tell her that he was sorry. But his heart was a rock, his soul like ice. He knew he was being a bastard, but he couldn't stop himself. The years of giving himself to women, only to have his Indian blood come between him and happiness, had finally robbed him of the power to hold back the pain. The bag and his grandfather's meddling was the final straw.

He had been a pawn long enough. For years he had always been ready to believe a woman loved him and tried to love in return, only to find that his body was all they had been interested in. They hadn't wanted to get to know him or share his life. All they'd wanted was to touch his hair, feel his kiss, and take him to their beds, seeking out a new and different sexual experience with an "exotic male," as some of his lovers had classified him. A few of the women had actually asked him to speak his native tongue during lovemaking, saying what a turn-on it would be to go to bed with a real savage. Kit still flushed with anger at the thought. He had tried to approach women on more than a surface level, but none of them had returned his thoughtfulness in kind.

Was it because he had dated non-Indian women that he had never found happiness? Would it have been any different with a Nakalt woman? With Lydia?

And now there was Camille, another white woman, just like all the rest. He had seen her staring at him. Did she know that his looks were a curse to him, that he'd trade places with an ordinary-looking man any day, just to see if a woman's heart could be had through deed and character alone?

He watched her drag on her clothes, looking as miserable as he felt. When she was finished she glanced up, her hazel eyes opaque with hurt.

"You're wrong, Kit, you know. When two people care about each other, it is more than mere sex, far more. Why else would they call it making love?"

"I don't know, Avery. You tell me."

She stared at him. He knew her well enough to guess that she was grinding her teeth.

"You think I'm a bastard?"

She nodded.

"Do you think you're a bitch?"

She shook her head, her brows knitting together in confusion.

"Then answer me one question, Avery." He stuffed his plaid shirt into his pants. "Do you love me?"

She paused, obviously shocked at the question. He studied her face, looking for the lie he knew would be there somewhere.

"Come on, Avery, just answer the question."

"I—"

"Just answer yes or no!"

"I like you, Kit. You're a very attractive man. But—"

"That's it. That's all I needed to hear." He snatched the parka off the ground. "You're a hypocrite, Avery. Just like all the others."

"What do you mean?"

He threw the parka to her and took off toward the canoe, striding down the beach so quickly that she had to run to catch up with him.

"Dammit, Kit!" She grabbed his arm. "What do you mean?"

He turned and glared at her, and felt the hardness in his own eyes. "You have no business talking about making love. You don't know the meaning of the word." He pulled his arm free, but she stepped in front of him to stop him from walking away.

"Wait a minute! You expect me to know whether or not I love you after knowing you less than a week?"

"Yes. Otherwise what we had was just sex and nothing more."

"That's crazy!"

"It's not making love if you don't love the man you're with."

"What about you, then? I doubt you're deeply in love with me!"

"What I feel doesn't matter." He brushed past her and bent down, busying himself with tidying the canoe. "I'm not the one with illusions about men and women."

Camille stared at him. He could feel the intensity of her regard, but he didn't turn around—couldn't turn around—because he didn't trust his own eyes to remain dry.

After a moment, he heard her stride up the shale beach to get her drawing equipment and her other camera. He sighed and looked out to sea. Their beautiful day together had been ruined, leaving him raw and ragged inside. What if he were wrong about the bag of charms? What if she had surrendered to him because she cared for him? He'd never know the truth now, not the way he had handled the situation, throwing anger and accusations at her as if she were responsible for every woman who had said thanks but no thanks to him.

Kit tossed a rock and watched it skip over the surface of

the bay and then sink, as his heart plunged deeper into the blackness inside him.

They didn't exchange a single word on the two-hour trip back to the lodge. And when they beached, Camille hopped out of the canoe and hurried away, praying that he wouldn't follow her. Ten feet from the canoe, she burst into tears and walked on in the dusk, swiping at her wet cheeks and cursing herself for being a fool.

She wasn't the type of woman to let herself get carried away by anything, especially by a man, and to have made love with Kit with no thought to the future went against her nature. Yet she had never been so certain of anything in her life. And Kit had been more wonderful than she had dreamed possible. Why had that bag of charms fallen out of her pocket? It had ruined everything. If Kit hadn't found the bag, their day might have ended in glory instead of tears.

Night had fallen by the time Camille hiked up the bluff trail, and her amulet grew warmer with every step. She expected to see Mak-ee-nah any moment. Sure enough, there he stood on the edge of the bluff, waiting for her, the breeze blowing back his hair. She scowled, remembering that he had told her he would come to dinner and that she would eat with him. She'd had her fill of men for the day.

"Ca-meel," he called, but his smile faded when she drew closer.

"Hi," she mumbled, continuing across the grass to the cabin. He followed her.

"You are crying. What is wrong?"

"Nothing. I've just had a terrible day." She paused at the porch and looked back. "Would you mind if I called off our date? I don't feel up to it."

He studied her face. "Sometimes it is better to talk and get the trouble out of your heart."

"I don't feel like talking. Maybe later, Mak-ee-nah. All right?"

He nodded. "If you want to find me, I will be on the beach."

"Okay."

Camille rushed into the cabin, desperate to be alone, desperate to shower off the sweat and sand and all that remained of her afternoon with Kit. She peeled off her clothes as she walked to the bathroom and stepped into the spray of the shower, determined to wash away all memory of him. Yet as the water stung her skin, she remembered the smell of him—salt and cedar and man—and knew that she could never wash away the memory of his scent. She lathered her torso and remembered the way his mouth had felt upon her breasts. No amount of scrubbing would scour away the memory of the sensation that even now tightened her nipples in response.

She closed her eyes and put her face to the spray, as if to block out the visions that swirled around her. But she would never forget. Kit's image was still there, a brand in the darkness of her thoughts. Frustrated, she turned off the shower, dried quickly, and pulled on clean jeans and a sweater. She would gain nothing by being alone, not with Kit haunting her every moment. If she forced herself, she could join Mak-ee-nah on the beach. Surely he could distract her from her obsession with Kit.

Promising herself to leave just as soon as her hair dried, Camille sank onto the bed. She knew she should put away her drawing equipment or make something for dinner—anything to occupy her hands and mind—but she was too devastated to move. Before she knew it, she grabbed a pillow and hunched over it, crying as if her heart would break. She did love Kit. She loved him so much, she felt as if she'd crack in two out of sheer hopelessness. It was obvious that Kit didn't care for her. And after today she was sure there would never be a chance that he would come to care for her. It was a one-sided affair, the worst kind, and one she should get over as soon as possible. But how?

Emotionally and physically exhausted, she fell asleep.

Hours later, she woke up at the sound of a wolf howling. Mak-ee-nah must still be out there if the wolves were around. She turned on her side. An eerie blue light streamed in through the window by the sink. The moon must be full. Her stomach growled and she sat up, running her fingers through her hair, feeling oddly restless.

Midnight. She had slept for a good six hours. Camille rose and rubbed her arms, stiff from rowing. She should apologize to Mak-ee-nah for her abruptness earlier. He didn't deserve to be punished for Kit's heartlessness.

After brushing her teeth and hair, she slipped on her parka and stepped outside, bracing herself to meet the cold air. Then she walked across the silvery ground toward the edge of the bluff. Down below she saw the glow of a fire and smelled a delicious aroma floating on the breeze. Her stomach growled in response. Then she saw a figure move in silhouette against the fire and knew that Mak-ee-nah was still on the beach.

She walked down the trail, careful not to stumble in the darkness. Mak-ee-nah looked up as she approached and waved to her. She waved back and picked her way over the jumble of rocks to the spot where he sat staring at the flames, watching over two fish butterflied between sticks that had been lashed together. The smell wafting up from the fire made Camille's salivary glands surge into action.

"Hi," Camille said, holding her hands out to the fire.

"You are rested?" Mak-ee-nah asked, glancing at her.

"Yes. I'm sorry I was so short with you, earlier."

He looked confused. "You are still the same size, Ca-meel."

She smiled. "I mean angry, upset."

"Ah." He stood up and pulled the alder rack away from the fire.

"That smells good," she remarked, leaning closer.

"It is salmon. *So-har.*"

"*So-har.*" She tried the word on her tongue, and he shook his head, smiling. "It looks delicious."

"You are hungry?"

"Yes."

"Sit and I will give you some when it has cooled."

Camille found a flat rock free of barnacles on the top and sat down while Mak-ee-nah stirred the coals with a stick.

"You have come to give the amulet to me?" he asked.

"Not quite. George Makinna, an elder, has gone to the forest to pray about it. When he gets back, then I'll know what to do."

"You know what to do, Ca-meel, without anyone telling you. The amulet is mine."

She nodded. "Still, I'd like to wait. I promised him."

"But that is not why you were crying."

"No." Camille's gaze followed a shower of orange sparks that soared upward as a log collapsed upon itself. Mak-ee-nah threw a sidelong glance at her as if expecting more of an explanation but turned back to the fire when he realized she was not going to add anything to her response.

"Why are you not married?" he asked.

"I've never found a man I cared to spend my life with."

"Your father indulges you in this?"

"My father has nothing to do with my life."

"You do not seek his counsel? You do not live with him?"

"No." She felt a small sad smile lift one corner of her mouth. "We don't do things that way anymore. People live far away from their families. And if a man wants to marry a woman, he asks *her*, not her father."

"Ah!" Mak-ee-nah poked the fire again.

"Women even ask men to marry them sometimes."

Mak-ee-nah stared at her. "Truly?"

"Truly."

"And does she pay a husband price for that man?"

"Bride prices and dowries have been abolished, too."

"You are saying that a man can ask for a woman when he has no possessions to offer in return?"

"Yes. He can be poor or rich. It doesn't matter."

"The world has changed, Ca-meel."

"Yes, it has. And sometimes I think it might have been better when you were alive."

"I am alive now."

She blushed, hoping she hadn't offended him. "I meant when you once lived—in the eighteenth century."

"I would have liked to know you in those days, Ca-meel. I was a chief. A *tyee*. I had much to offer a woman then."

She blinked, realizing how he had altered the course of the conversation. Did he find her attractive? Did he look upon her as eligible wife material? The thought sent a warm sensation of pleasure through her.

"You have much to offer now, Mak-ee-nah," she replied, knowing well the value of a proud, confident, and intelligent man.

His glance darted over her face. Then, as if unsure of himself, he leaned toward the fish rack and released the cooling salmon.

"Here, *klootz-mah*," he said, cutting off a piece for her. "Eat."

Camille held out her hand to accept the slab of fish he gave her. The meat was succulent, cooked to perfection and flavored by the alder wood Mak-ee-nah had gathered along the beach. More ravenous than she had expected to be, she quickly devoured the fish, licking her fingertips in appreciation when she was finished.

"That was excellent!" she exclaimed. "You don't need a *klootz-mah* to cook for you, Mak-ee-nah."

He laughed and stuffed a chunk of the pink meat into his grinning mouth. His teeth were strong and white in the firelight, his face an everchanging study in angles and shadows. He pulled off a section of his portion and offered it to her, insisting on feeding her. She accepted the fish and glanced up to find his black eyes glittering in amusement as he pushed the fish into her mouth. Their gazes met and she felt a momentary shock, unsure for an instant whom she was looking at—Mak-ee-nah or Kit. The action of feeding her was primal, as was the glance that passed between them. The pads of his fingers and thumb brushed her lips and then were gone as he sat back, smiling. He remained looking at her, the laugh dancing in his eyes, and she felt the warmth of his gaze as he surveyed the line of her nose, the curve of her lips, and the wisps of hair that brushed her forehead. Camille stared back, mesmerized by his confidence and outright animal magnetism.

Then Mak-ee-nah ran his pink tongue over the fingers that had just touched her lips. A shaft of desire seared through her, and Camille sucked in a breath, overcome by his overt sensuality, so different from Kit's. She jumped to her feet, shocked by her reaction to him. Was she dreaming? How could she react this way? Was it that damn bag of charms again? It couldn't be—Kit had kept the bag.

Camille stumbled to the edge of the sea and hunkered down to wash her hands in the frigid water, trying to shock herself to her senses. She rose, wiping her wet hands on the legs of her jeans, and heard Mak-ee-nah come up behind her. He also bent down and washed his hands. Out of the corner of her eye, Camille could see him straighten. She was reluctant to look him squarely in the face, however, afraid that his undeniable charm might mesmerize her further.

"Thank you for the salmon," she said, staring at the dark hump of Vancouver Island across the strait.

"You are welcome, Ca-meel."

His voice sounded too close for comfort. Before she could move away, however, she felt his fingers in her hair. Camille froze, uncertain what she should do.

"Your hair is like moonlight," he murmured. "Why do you wear it like a boy's?"

"If I grow it long, I look like a witch."

"That I do not believe." He let the blond strands fall through his tanned fingers.

Camille's eyes fluttered closed at his touch, which was much lighter than she would have guessed. His fingertips slipped behind her ear, down the line of her jaw, and then lifted her chin.

"You are beautiful, *klootz-mah*," he murmured. "So pale."

She dared not look at him but could feel the intensity of his gaze on her profile. Vaguely she recalled Kit's warning about Mak-ee-nah's potential misuse of women. But there was nothing unpleasant in his touch or his manner. Still, she slowly eased away from his hand and turned her back to him, afraid of the roil of emotions his touch had churned up inside her.

"I should be getting back—"

"Do not go," he said softly as he stepped behind her. She felt his hands encompass the tops of her arms as he drew up against her back. He was a wall of warmth and strength.

Camille hesitated, knowing she should bolt away, but she was attracted to Mak-ee-nah just as much as she was drawn to Kit. His long, slender hands squeezed her shoulders as he urged her backward.

"When you are here with me, *klootz-mah*, I feel alive." His voice was hoarse and soft. "So alive I am in pain."

"Mak-ee-nah—"

"In my other life I could have asked for you. I could have demanded you." Mak-ee-nah lowered his head until his mouth pressed the hair just above her ear. "Yet in this life, I cannot even expect mortality." His voice was so full of anguish that Camille leaned against him, letting her head relax on his shoulder as her hand reached back to touch his where it grasped her arm.

He pushed his nose into her hair, and his breath was hot and moist on her scalp, sending shivers of delight and alarm down her back and legs. She shouldn't be with him, letting him hold her and stroke her like this, but he was so much like Kit in every way that she let him touch her, closing her eyes against the weakness of desire that assailed her.

Mak-ee-nah stroked the arc of her throat, sliding his fingertips up and over her chin and around the perimeter of her half-parted lips. The feather-light touch, more sensual than most men's kisses, made her sigh raggedly. Then he gently grasped her chin between his thumb and forefinger and urged her to turn her face toward him. She raised her head slightly and turned to look up at him, and he covered her mouth with his, tasting her with light, controlled kisses while his hands slipped down to cup her breasts.

His kiss deepened as he caressed her, and for a moment she thought of succumbing to him, of twisting in his arms so she could embrace his magnificent chest and plunge her hands into his luxurious ebony hair. But the jolt of longing in her breasts jerked her back to her senses, and she pulled away.

"I must go!" she exclaimed, stumbling back.

"Why?"

"I shouldn't be here with you."

"Why, Ca-meel?"

"I—I love someone else. And I would only be hurting you and myself if I stayed."

He strode up to her. "Whom do you love? The man who has made you cry?"

"Yes."

He stared at her, his eyes glittering. "The one who looks like me?"

"Yes."

Mak-ee-nah scowled and turned his head to look at the water. Camille watched his jaw clenching and unclenching, wondering what he could be thinking.

"What has he done to make you weep?"

"He—he said some things that made me realize that my love for him is not returned."

"Then you must forget this man."

"I know."

Mak-ee-nah faced her. "I will make you forget him. He will be but a dream to you."

"Just looking at you makes me think of him, Mak-ee-nah. When you touched me just now, I imagined—"

"Say no more, *klootz-mah,* or you will find that I am more mortal than you think." The wind blew his hair across his face, and he brushed it away with an impatient gesture. "Now go."

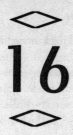

16

Camille rose early the next morning and left for Makinna Lodge. She was in love with Kit. Her heart sang for Kit, just as Old Man had guessed, and the song was clear and strong. Mak-ee-nah would never be able to make her forget Kit. Nothing would make her forget him. She knew for certain that the bag of charms had nothing to do with her reasons for making love with him on the beach. And it *had* been making love, for she had loved Kit the moment she had seen his face in the firelight of the lodge on the night she had arrived in Crescent Bay.

Her heart surged in her chest as she hurried along the lane, compelled to tell Kit that he was wrong about her and about his grandfather. No matter what Kit did—laugh, turn his back, or make light of her emotions—she intended to tell him what lay trapped and near to bursting in her heart.

Just as she gained the steps of the lodge, the door swung open and Adam ducked out.

"Hi, Camille," he said, swinging a backpack over his shoulder.

"Adam Makinna!" Lydia bellowed from inside.

Adam stopped in his tracks as the door burst open again.

"Get back here, you good-for-nothing—" Lydia broke off, seeing Camille standing down below.

"Good morning," Camille said coolly, wondering what Lydia would have said or done to Adam had she not been standing there.

"What do you want?"

"I'd like to talk to Kit."

"Kit isn't here." Lydia swung around to face Adam. "And you—get back in the house."

"I'm not going to."

"What do you mean, you're not going to?" She took a step closer. "I told you to."

"I have to go to class this morning."

"And what is your uncle supposed to do? Get this place ready by himself?"

"I've got a quiz, Lydia."

"You can take it some other day."

"Uncle Kit told me to go ahead."

"Well, Uncle Kit needs his head examined. Guests are due tomorrow and the lodge is in an uproar. We need every spare hand we can get."

"Then why don't you hire somebody?" Camille took a step up the stairs, too angry to keep silent any longer. "Adam isn't your handyman. He needs to go to school."

Lydia pivoted around, her eyes blazing. "You just stay out of this! What Adam does is none of your business."

"It most certainly is."

"Since when?"

"Since he's become my friend." She took the last stair

and came abreast of Lydia. "You have no right to make him skip school. And if you do, I'll call the truant officer."

"You wouldn't dare."

"Try me."

Lydia flipped her long hair over her shoulder. "I have six Japanese businessmen and their wives arriving tomorrow afternoon. If Adam doesn't stay and help, we'll be showing the guests into half-finished rooms."

"I'll help."

"You?" she said scathingly. "I never want to see your pasty face around here again."

With that, she turned and stormed into the lodge, leaving Camille and Adam standing on the deck, stunned.

Adam switched his pack to his other shoulder. "Don't mind her," he said.

"It's hard not to." Camille looked over her shoulder at him. "You'd better get while the getting is good."

"Yeah." He turned to go and then paused. "Could I stop by the cabin after dinner if I can get away? I've got that test Friday, and I still need some help."

"Sure, Adam."

He nodded toward the door. "Just go on in. Uncle Kit's working upstairs."

"I thought Lydia said he was gone."

"Oh, he's there. Just go on in."

"I'd better not, not while everyone's so busy. I'll—I'll come back some other time."

Adam glared at the closed door. "Why'd my father ever marry her?" he grumbled. "Didn't he know what she was like?"

"Maybe she was different with him. People can change."

"Not her. She's always been a witch."

Camille didn't doubt that, but she thought it prudent to

change the subject. "Adam, you'd better go. You'll be late."

"Yeah. Bye, Camille. And thanks."

"You're welcome."

She stepped off the deck and watched him stride away before she set off down the lane. Her heart twisted painfully at the thought that she'd have to wait to tell Kit of her love for him. How could she wait? And yet, how could she be so impulsive? It wasn't like her to blurt out her feelings without examining the consequences first. There was no way to tell how Kit would react to her confession of love. Judging by his behavior so far, he'd probably reject the idea that she loved him. He'd probably try to convince her that men and women were incapable of love, that all they really wanted from each other was sexual gratification. Was she prepared to argue that point with him? She hadn't won the making love/having sex argument. What made her think she'd do any better arguing about love with him?

Camille took another step toward the road. Perhaps it was better to wait until she could justify her feelings for Kit before she approached him. He wasn't the type of man to accept "I love you just because I do." Though she felt she would die if she didn't tell him immediately, she fought back her heart and returned to the cabin.

By the time Adam arrived after dinner, Camille had completed four more drawings for the book. She spent a few hours helping Adam with his geometry and a composition for his English class while a windstorm howled outside. Then she sat in silence across the table from him, inking in her drawings as he wrote his thesis. He worked quietly and steadily for a good two hours, talking only when Camille replenished their tea every so often. At eleven she looked up from her work to see him leaning on his hand, his eyes closed.

She smiled as she gazed at his young face, molded in the same handsome pattern of his uncle and Mak-ee-nah. In sleep, his appearance was innocent and soft, his youth doubly evident in comparison with the expressions of the two older men. All too soon his face would take on the lines of care and bitterness that marked Kit and gave character to the fierce Makinna eyes.

Did the Makinna strain stamp all male offspring with such striking looks? Would a child by Kit bear a likeness as strong as Adam's? If a son was born of Kit and a white woman, would the child still favor the Makinna half? Camille flushed at the thought. She had never considered becoming a man's wife, much less bearing his children, much less bearing the child of a Nakalt Indian. She was a fool to consider it anyway, because she knew Kit would scoff at the idea. He'd never ask her to marry him. He didn't even care for her.

Camille chided herself for slipping into such a strange fantasy and was reaching out to Adam, intending to awaken him, when someone knocked on the door.

She rose, walked to the door, and pulled it open, only to have the wind nearly rip it out of her hands.

"Whoa!" she gasped, grabbing the handle and looking at the man standing on the porch, his coat blasted against his torso. Kit pushed the hair out of his face.

"Is Adam still here?"

"Yes. Come on in before you get soaked."

Kit crossed over the threshold, slicking back his wet hair with his hand. He glanced at Adam, who was now slumped over his forearm.

"You call that studying?" he asked, his voice frosty.

"He just fell asleep. He's been working so hard."

Kit's gaze returned to her. "I came to get him so he wouldn't walk home in the storm. There's been some trees blown down, and I didn't want him to get hurt."

"Has anything been damaged?"

"Not yet. But the weather forecast calls for seventy-mile-per-hour winds tonight."

"What about Old Man?" Camille asked in concern. "He's out there somewhere."

"He'll probably be all right. But after I drop Adam off, I'm going to run out to some of the places Old Man might be, just in case."

"I hope he'll be okay. He's so old and frail."

"But he's wise to the ways of nature. Don't worry."

Just as the words left his lips, the lights flickered and went out, plunging the cabin into darkness.

"Great," Camille exclaimed. "Another power outage."

"Why don't you have a fire going?"

"I've been worried about starting one by myself since the chimney fire."

"For crying out loud." His voice was terse in the darkness behind her. "I had the chimney sweep come out here to solve that problem."

"I know, it's just that—"

"I'll start one for you."

"There's no wood in here. I'll get some from the wood-shed."

She felt her way to the door, pulled it open, and shuffled onto the porch. The night was pitch black, and the wind buffeted her as she plunged across the lawn to the wood-shed. Kit followed close behind and waited in the driving rain as she struggled with the rusty latch of the shed. Once opened, the door swung wide and she felt her way into the darkness of the small shed, an oasis of calm in the mael-strom of wind and rain. The close air was heavy with the smell of cedar, reminding her of the scent of Kit's skin. For a moment she paused, and Kit, unable to see that she had stopped, ran into her.

She stumbled forward, and his hands shot out to keep her from falling. For a moment they both teetered, struggling for balance, and Camille ended up pinned against him, her back to his chest, just as she had stood in Mak-ee-nah's arms the previous night.

The door of the woodshed slammed shut behind them, but Kit barely took notice of it.

"Sorry," he said, his voice husky.

"That's okay. I shouldn't have stopped so suddenly."

Kit didn't release her. No matter what she thought of him, she still felt wonderful in his arms. Out of pure selfish need he held her, while a pang of protectiveness flashed through him as he realized anew how petite she was. He had to bend over to embrace her so that he wouldn't lift her off the ground. She made a movement against the link of his arms, as if to step away, but he tightened his grip.

"Wait," he whispered, his mouth near her ear. What could he say to keep her there with him? What could he do that wouldn't drive her away? There was such a fine line when it came to truth and accountability—for both of them. And he had learned that his temper and his bitterness could easily push her away.

Yet he could no longer think. Once again his desire for Camille swept aside his reasoning. Even without the bag of charms he was driven by his hunger for her. Feeling like a ravenous animal, he buried his face in her hair and closed his eyes, sucking in the scent of her as he swelled with need.

He swept his hands up her torso and cupped her

breasts, running his thumbs across her nipples and finding them hard as pebbles. There was no denying her response to him, and he thrilled at the discovery that she wanted him, too.

"I've got to get the firewood," she murmured.

"The what?" His tongue felt thick, as thick as the hard swell in his groin, as thick as his thoughts.

"The firewood." Her head rolled back onto his chest, just below his chin.

He glanced down at her, and in a sudden flash of lightning outside the small window of the shed, he could see a wet gleam on her lower lip. He bent down to capture the gleam of light and pressed her against his loins until the ache was too intense to bear. She pulled away from his mouth with a gasp.

"Kit, I want to tell you something." She turned in his arms to speak to him, but he kissed her into silence, backing her up to a stack of wood. Her hands pressed against his coat, but he ignored them, too wild with desire to listen to anything or acknowledge her protest.

"Kit—"

"Don't talk," he said, pinning her hips between the wood and his body. For now he only wanted to feel her— the way her body molded into his, the way her breasts blossomed at his touch. He could forget who he was and where he was when he was with Camille. He wanted to forget everything now and plunge into the world where only the two of them existed, the world they had shared on North Beach. He hadn't been able to think of anything else since. Passing his finger over her lips as if to seal them, he whispered, "Don't say a word, my heart."

What had he just called her? Was it madness that let such words slip out? He hadn't wanted to speak endearments to her. He simply wanted to hold her, kiss her, keep her close. Yet at his words, she looked up at him and her hands slipped around his neck, warm where his skin was cold. He felt the soft bow of her surrender as she yielded to him, arching up to meet his mouth with hers. Her lips were lush, warm and full of promises that he dared not even think about. Instead he closed his eyes—blocking out the name he had called her—and crushed into her, moving against her in a rhythm her body instinctively knew.

He kissed her everywhere her pale flesh was exposed to the darkness—her cheeks, her throat, her neck, her ears and forehead—and she let out sweet little cries and sighs that made his blood race in jagged surges. Then he reached down between her legs and cupped her. Even through her jeans, he could feel the heat radiating from her. She moved against his hand, and he thought he would burst from wanting her. He slid his hands around her rump and lifted her, urging her to wrap her legs around him. Then he pressed even closer, moving her on top of him until he had to clench his teeth against the driving ache inside. As she kissed his throat, he reached for the button of her jeans and popped it open.

"Camille!"

Camille stiffened, and Kit's hand released her zipper.

Adam was calling her. Through the fog in his head, Kit could hear his nephew's voice shouting over the wind, as if he were far away.

"Miss A-very!"

"Damn!" Kit took a step backward. Camille let go of his neck and slid to the ground. Reluctantly he released her.

"Is that Adam calling?" she asked, her voice so slurred with passion that Kit wanted to embrace her all over again.

"Yeah. The kid's got great timing."

"He saving us from ourselves."

"Maybe I don't want to be saved." Kit bent to pick up an

armful of wood. "Do you?" He paused in the darkness, waiting for her answer.

"We've been foolish, Kit, messing around without protection. That's a sure way to get more than we bargained for."

He heard the rasp of her zipper as she fastened her jeans and snapped them. She hadn't answered his question. Women were good at not answering questions directly. But she was right. The next time he came to her, he'd make sure she wasn't in danger of getting pregnant, if it wasn't too late already.

"Miss Avery!" Adam drew closer.

"Here!" she called out, stacking wood in her arms. "In the woodshed."

The door opened. "You in here, Camille?"

"Yes, getting wood with your uncle."

"The lights went out."

"Yes, I know." Her voice was controlled now, and the darkness hid all evidence of what she and Kit had really been doing in the woodshed. Kit had to smile, knowing how flustered Camille would be if Adam could see her face.

Adam held open the door for them to pass through. "Some storm, huh, Uncle Kit?"

"Yeah." He liked his nephew. But this was one time he wished the kid were on the moon.

Kit built a fire while Camille put away her drawing equipment. When he achieved a blaze strong enough to suit him, he straightened and looked at Camille. Her hair was still tousled from the tryst in the woodshed, and her cheeks flushed each time she caught his eye. She was so beautiful, so delicate, so small, he felt another wave of protectiveness envelop him. He wanted to take care of this woman. He wanted to make sure she came to no harm, that she would be safe and happy. If he didn't know any better, he'd swear he was falling in love with her. He immediately discarded the idea, however, ascribing the way he felt to his protective nature and acknowledging that his physical response to her was nothing more than lust—glaring, raw, glorious lust.

"You ready to go, Adam?" he asked gruffly, turning to his nephew.

"Yeah. Thanks, Camille, for your help."

"You're going to do well on the test, Adam. You've got the basics down pat."

He nodded and stepped toward the door while Kit put his hand on the knob and looked back at Camille.

"Are you sure you're going to be all right here tonight?" he asked. "It could get cold if the power stays off all night."

"I'll be fine." Camille hugged her arms.

He wished he could stay with her, certain they would need no fire to warm them. But he had Adam and Old Man to attend to and shouldn't linger another minute.

"You're welcome to come to the lodge tonight," he offered.

"Thanks, but Lydia doesn't want me there."

"I told you, Lydia doesn't own the lodge."

"Yes, but she's the mistress of it. I wouldn't feel comfortable there."

"Are you sure?"

"Yes." She smiled, her hazel eyes glinting with warmth.

"Call if you need help."

"I will."

He opened the door. "Good night, then."

"You'll be careful out there looking for Old Man, won't you, Kit?"

"Yeah." His glance met hers, and between them hung a flicker of hunger and promise so strong that his loins tightened in response. He hated to leave, but he had no other recourse than to walk out the door. "Maybe I'll check on you later—to see if you're okay."

He watched her clasp her hands together as her eyelids fluttered. Had he misinterpreted her? Did the prospect of inviting him in later on that night make her nervous? She'd been delightfully responsive in the woodshed, but perhaps she'd had time to reconsider the implications.

"That would be—be good of you, Kit," she answered.

Good? *Good* of him? His intentions were anything but good. He didn't want to come back and check on her safety or make sure the fire wouldn't go out. He wanted to drag her to the bed, strip off her clothes, and do things to her that she probably hadn't even—

He flushed at his own thoughts and turned away. "So long, Avery."

She followed him out the door and stood in the wind and rain to watch them go. They ran across the grass to the Jeep and then hopped in. Kit honked good-bye as he circled around and headed down the lane. He didn't look back, unable to bear the vision of her standing there, a small, white-capped sprite against the inky curtain of night.

By morning the storm had blown east, leaving in its wake felled trees, fir branches littered across the ground, and a beach piled with new driftwood, kelp, and shells. Camille walked down the beach, awed by the havoc wreaked by the gale, and poked at dead sea pens and jellyfish that had washed ashore. The same huge raven kept abreast of her, busily picking at the cracked clam and mussel shells left behind by the gulls and then cawing as he soared to a new

perch. She watched him, wondering if the bird were Mak-
ee-nah in his daylight form.

Then far down the beach she heard a dog barking, and
her heart leapt at the thought that Kit and Sandy might be
walking along the shore as well. But the closer she got to
the dog, the more she realized that she was the only person
on the beach and that Sandy was out for a solitary morning
run.

The large golden dog loped up, tongue lolling and eyes
sparkling as she caught sight of Camille. Seeing that Sandy
was bent on jumping up to greet her, Camille caught her
by the scruff of her neck and urged her down, laughing at
the dog's exuberance.

"You silly thing!" she admonished happily, patting
Sandy's head and shoulders. "You're a wet mess. You think
I want you jumping all over me?"

Sandy barked and thumped her tail.

"Where's your master?" Camille asked, glancing
around again, wishing Kit were in pursuit. But she saw
nothing except logs, rocks, and sand.

Sandy barked again and lunged at the raven, who sat on
an overturned stump. The raven didn't fly away but stood
its ground and cawed sharply, flapping its wings at the dog,
which was enough of a display to discourage further attack.
Sandy's ears perked up in confusion because the bird
hadn't been frightened of her.

"I wouldn't mess with him, if I were you," Camille ad-
vised. "Come on, Sandy."

The dog loped off, nose to the ground, while Camille
continued her stroll. She planned to end up at the lodge
and try to talk to Kit if he wasn't too busy preparing for the
Japanese businessmen. After last night she was even more
determined to tell him how she felt. He had called her "my
heart." Those whispered words had sounded like a prayer

to her. Had he meant them? Or had he merely said them in the throes of desire? Did he call every woman he kissed "my heart" as some men called women "honey"? More than anything, she longed for the words to be true and significant. Kit was "her heart" as no man had ever been, and she wanted the same to be true for him.

Yet he hadn't come back to the cabin as he had proposed last night. Had something prevented his return, or had he reconsidered and decided not to bother with her? If he only wanted to slake his thirst for a woman, perhaps the effort of driving back to the cabin was too much for him after a long night. Perhaps he had gone elsewhere. Camille refused to think any further about that possibility.

With her walking stick, she pushed aside a dead sea star that had turned bright orange in the morning sun. Sandy barked again, only this time the sound of it was sharper. Camille looked up at the noise and saw the raven gliding in a circle above the dog, who was now digging furiously in a pile of kelp. Camille strode forward, watching the curious behavior of the dog as she plunged her nose into the kelp fronds, snorted, and then continued to paw in the sand and gravel underneath.

"What is it, girl?" Camille called, jogging up to her.

The raven alighted on an overhanging snag and clacked its beak.

"What is it?" Camille questioned, looking at the bird as if it could understand her. But the bird only cocked its head and studied the dog.

Camille looked down. For a moment she thought her eyes were playing tricks on her. She thought she saw a hand among the glossy green kelp leaves.

Sandy dug, barking and snorting, spraying Camille's shins with pebbles as Camille reached out with her stick and pushed the seaweed aside, wondering how the fresh kelp could produce such a stench.

"Dear God—" Camille cried, staggering away. She pressed the back of her hand to her mouth as she stared down in horror, momentarily frozen with shock. Then she turned and retched, overcome by the sight at her feet. After the wave of nausea passed, she stood up slowly and brushed her bangs off her clammy forehead. She felt faint with disgust, dazed with horrified disbelief. But she couldn't just stand there. She had to get help. And she couldn't let the dog do any more damage.

"Sandy!" she gasped without looking back. "Come on, girl! Come!"

Camille was thankful that Sandy obeyed her. Urging the dog to stay with her, she stumbled down the beach, headed for Makinna Lodge and help.

17

Camille burst into the lobby of the lodge, surprising Lydia, who came out of the dining room carrying a huge arrangement of yellow chrysanthemums.

"Where's Kit?" Camille demanded, breathless.

Lydia ignored the question as she placed the vase on the registration desk. "I told you to stay away from here."

"Tell me where he is, Lydia, or I'll find him myself."

"Don't you dare threaten me," Lydia retorted. She skirted the desk and headed for the kitchen.

Camille sighed in exasperation. "May I use your phone, at least?"

She took Lydia's silence as an affirmative answer and picked up the phone to dial the police. As she held for Donald Two Hand, she saw Kit come down the stairs. He was dressed in a black shirt and black jeans that heightened the contrast between his rich dark skin and his white teeth. "Hi," he said, trotting down to her. "I thought I heard your voice."

"Kit, you've got to come and see what Sandy found on the beach."

"You mean now?"

"Yes. But wait a minute—" She broke off to talk to Donald Two Hand.

Hearing Camille's urgent words to both Kit and Two Hand, Lydia appeared behind the registration desk. "What's going on?" she asked.

Without answering her, Camille finished the conversation and hung up the phone. Surprisingly, Donald Two Hand had just promised to come to the lodge right away.

"A body?" Kit asked.

"Yes!" Camille pushed back her bangs, trying to blot out the vision that had made her retch a few minutes ago.

"You can't be serious," Lydia put in. "Whose body?"

"I don't know. I couldn't look at it. It was too awful."

She felt Kit's hand on her shoulder and was grateful for his familiar gesture of support.

"All I saw was a hand and an arm. The rest was covered with kelp."

Lydia glanced at Kit as if to check whether he believed Camille. She noticed Kit's hand where he squeezed Camille's shoulder and his arm draped across her back. Cool hostility replaced the doubt in Lydia's eyes.

"Come on, Kit. Two Hand can catch up," Camille said.

Lydia trailed behind them. "Sure, go on, Kit. This is all we need today. Another interruption."

"I'll be right back," Kit said, opening the door.

"Sure. That's what you always say. You're spending more time with her than you are on the lodge."

Kit ignored her complaint and guided Camille outside. "Keep Sandy here," he instructed Lydia, "and tell Two Hand we're down on the beach."

"If you're not back in an hour—"

Kit turned. "Drop it, Lydia." His voice was terse and commanding, and Camille looked back to see Lydia stomp off in a huff.

"Let's go, Avery," he added, cupping her elbow.

For once she appreciated his take-charge personality.

Ten minutes later they arrived at the peculiar lump covered with kelp. Camille stood to the side while Kit used a stick to lift off the strands of seaweed wound around the body. She couldn't monitor his progress without being overcome by nausea, so she focused her attention on the beach in order to watch for Two Hand's arrival.

After a few minutes Kit turned to her. "Camille, why don't you go on back to the lodge? You don't need to see this."

"It's okay. I'll stay."

"It's pretty bad. No sense for both of us to be here."

"I want to stay."

Kit sighed. "Why?"

"To be with you." She dared not look around in case she caught a glimpse of the body.

"This isn't something we need to do together. Why don't you go on."

"Oh, there's Two Hand now," she put in, glad for the change of subject. She didn't want to leave and wondered why Kit wanted her to go. She didn't have time to ask before Two Hand came striding up to them, his florid face red with exertion.

"Morning, Miss Avery. Kit."

She nodded at him, and Kit turned at the waist, his fist to his nose in an effort to block the fetid odor.

"Well, let's have a look at it," Two Hand said, stepping up to Kit.

"It looks like a woman."

"Yeah."

A woman? Camille hugged her elbows against the dark shaft of fear that had shadowed her heart ever since she'd glimpsed the blue-white hand sticking out of the seaweed. The body couldn't possibly be Barbara. It just couldn't be. Was that why Kit had wanted her to leave? Did he suspect the same thing she did? Camille clenched her teeth and partially turned around. She had to know. Yet she couldn't bring herself to look at the body, partially decomposed from time spent in the water and being rolled for hours in the surf. She didn't know whether she could endure the sight.

Two Hand turned back to her. "You say Kit's dog found the body?"

"Yes. She was digging around in the kelp."

"Kind of made a mess of things."

"I got her away as soon as I realized what it was."

"Good thing, otherwise we'd have a hard time recovering the remains. I'm going to have to call the coroner, Kit, and get a crew out here."

"Do you suspect foul play?"

"It's hard to tell. The storm must have washed her ashore," Two Hand mused. "Wonder if it was a drowning?"

Camille couldn't stand another agonizing minute of not knowing if the body was Barbara's. She whirled around and stared down at the swollen white figure with the sandy brown hair and horribly blotched face. The moment she turned to look, Kit lunged for her and dragged her away.

"Camille, don't!" he said, pulling her toward the water.

Camille collapsed against him with a cry while his arms came around her in a crushing embrace as if he could purge her of the horrifying reality on the beach.

"Dammit!" he said, his nose in her hair. "I told you to go, Camille. Why didn't you go?"

"It's her!" Camille sobbed, clutching his shoulders. "Oh, Kit, it's Barbara!"

Kit took Camille back to the lodge and gave her a stiff drink. She refused to break down in Lydia's presence, calling upon some inner reserve to retain her composure. He admired her pluck and self-control and damned Lydia's heartless questions and comments when she discovered the particulars of the situation. Kit would have preferred to be alone with Camille, certain he could offer her the silent solace of his arms, but both Lydia and Hattie hovered around her, preventing any personal interaction. When he realized he wasn't being effective, Kit bowed out to check on Two Hand's progress, curious to find out why the coroner hadn't shown up. Surely he would have parked in the space behind the lodge. He left Camille with a promise to be back as soon as possible.

He found Two Hand on the beach, zipping up Barbara's remains in a body bag.

"I thought you were going to call for a crew," Kit remarked.

Two Hand straightened and wiped his hands on his pants. "Changed my mind. Everybody's so busy, what with those Japanese coming, that I thought I'd just take care of it."

"What about clues?" He wondered if Two Hand was following the correct procedures. "Did you look for clues?"

"Clues?" Two Hand snorted contemptuously. "After that storm last night, any clue that washed ashore with the body is long gone. Besides, this lady's been dead for a while."

"Camille thinks it's her friend, Barbara Stanton."

"Might be." Two Hand pursed his lips. "Have to wait for dental records to be checked, though, just to be sure."

"There was an entry in Barbara's journal about something going on at North Beach. Miss Avery and I were wondering if it might be connected to the theft of the artifacts, and that someone might have wanted to silence Barbara Stanton."

"You mean kill her?"

"Yeah."

"That could be." Two Hand adjusted his utility belt and cleared his throat. "You say Miss Avery has her friend's journal?"

"Yeah. That's how Camille knew something suspicious was going on."

"I should have a look at that journal. It could be important evidence if this turns into a murder instead of a drowning. Think you could get it from the Avery woman?"

"Probably. She wants to find out what's happened more than anyone."

"Meanwhile, I got to get this body over to the medical examiner. Want to give me a hand, Kit?"

Kit helped him carry the body up the beach to the squad car.

Two Hand opened the trunk, and they gently swung the body into the car. Then he closed the trunk and turned to Kit.

"I'd appreciate your cooperation, Kit, in keeping this quiet for a while."

"What do you mean?"

"Well, those Japanese guys are thinking of buying land for a fancy resort. If they get wind that some white chick has been found dead on the beach, I don't think they'll be too thrilled. You know how the Japanese are."

A tingle of apprehension raised the hairs on the back of

Kit's neck. "The Japanese are coming to look at Nakalt property?"

"Yeah, didn't you know?"

"No. I assumed they were coming to fish."

"Haven't you heard about them wanting to buy the island?"

"The island?" Kit stared at Two Hand in disbelief.

"Yeah. The old burial site. The Island of the Dead."

Kit stepped backward. "You can't be serious."

"Sure. They've offered us two and a half million for that rock heap."

"You're joking!"

"Naw. They want to build a fancy golf resort."

"I mean about selling the Island of the Dead. The tribe can't do that!"

"The elders decided to go ahead. We need the money. Have you seen the school?"

"Yes, but—"

"The hatchery's just about gone tits up. So we had to do something. The resort will create a whole new economy here."

"But to sell the island. It just can't happen! We've lost enough land as it is!"

"We don't use that island, though, Kit. Why not make some money off it?"

Kit stared at Two Hand, wondering how the man could be saying such things. Was he willing to give up a piece of Nakalt property and heritage? After the heartbreak of allotment, when so much land was taken by hard times and the white man, how could any reasonable member of the tribe consider sacrificing even a single inch of reservation soil? They'd had to fight for every scrap of land they had now and still battled for the right to fish their waters. Who knew how long they would retain that privilege? What did the Nakalt have other than their property and their prophecy? It was imperative that they keep the reservation land intact, even if their dreams of returning glory never materialized.

"Everyone voted in favor of it," Two Hand put in, obviously aware of Kit's stunned reaction. "Except for your grandfather, the crazy old coot."

"He's the only sane one among you!" Kit retorted.

"Yeah, well, if you wanted to have a say, Makinna, you should've stuck around."

"Apparently."

"You get on an awful big high horse for a guy who don't bother to keep in touch with his own people."

"I'm here now."

"Well, you're just a bit too late, aren't you?"

"We don't need money from outside. We've got the aquaculture center."

Two Hand snorted again. "Oh, yeah? That place went downhill fast."

"But if someone took charge of it and dredged the pond—"

"And who would that be? You? You don't want to stick around here. Nobody else is qualified to run the place. Your brother tried, but now he's dead. And hell, he wasn't much good these past few years anyway."

"You got any more good comments about my family?" Kit demanded, his voice terse again, his fists balled at his sides.

"No offense, Makinna," Two Hand replied. "I'm just telling you the facts. And if you can't handle them, why don't you go back where you came from?"

He pushed past Kit and opened his car door. "And like I said, keep quiet about finding the body. I don't want you blowing the deal."

"And if I do?"

"You won't be welcome here. Ever again. And that's a promise."

Kit watched him drive off while a burning feeling flared deep inside. Was he too late? Should he intervene? Was he really willing to get involved with the Nakalt affairs? If he weren't willing to stay on the reservation and attend to the problems, he shouldn't make any objections to the land sale or anything else the elders decided to do.

Kit ran a hand over his jaw, around his ear, and then up into his hair. Not only must he deal with foreign business-men who were due any minute, he had to ensure that Camille would weather the news of her friend's death and in addition make a decision about what he could do concern-ing the upcoming sale of land.

He hesitated outside the door of the lodge, momentar-ily overcome by the urge to jump in his Jeep and leave it all behind. He didn't need this. His life was complicated enough already. If he returned to Seattle, he could be back to his regular routine in five hours and forget about the reservation. He turned from the door, rubbing his jaw again, while a vision of Camille's stricken face loomed before him. He felt the hard dig of her fingers in his shoul-ders and remembered the way she had wept against his chest. She was hurting and alone. He couldn't just leave her when she was devastated by the death of Barbara Stan-ton. He'd never forgive himself if he walked away from her now, even though he wasn't sure what part she played in his life. Besides that, his grandfather was still not back from his trip to the mountains. He also felt a duty toward Adam. In all respects he was now the boy's father and should see that Adam learned the things his father had never taught him. He couldn't leave Adam at such an im-portant stage in his life when the boy entered manhood.

Sighing heavily, Kit pushed open the door of the lodge and went in.

Camille heard the door close and looked up, relieved to see Kit come into the lodge. Though Hattie had been kind to her, she didn't feel comfortable in anyone's presence but Kit's. She longed to sink against him and feel his arms wrap around her again, and she didn't know how long she could keep up the pretense of self-control. As Kit crossed the lobby toward her, she rose and put her glass of brandy on one of the boxes that served as an end table.

"Could you take me home, Kit?" she asked.

"Why don't you stay here?"

"I've got to go back and make some phone calls. People should know about Barbara."

"Aren't you going to wait until the medical examiner has a look at the body and makes certain it's her?"

"I know it is."

Hattie wrung her hands. "The poor girl. Drowning just like David."

"If it was a drowning," Camille remarked.

"Do you suppose there was some connection?" Hattie put in.

"Of course there was a connection." Lydia swept forward. "David was last seen on the beach with her. I say they were having an affair and something went wrong."

"You don't know that," Kit protested, turning toward her. He knew David had been a well-known womanizer in his day, but he wasn't going to let Lydia start an unfounded rumor about the possible indiscretion of his dead brother. David's reputation had enough stains upon it already.

Lydia, however, was not easily silenced. "David had the hots for her, the two-timing bastard."

"No, not David." Hattie shook her head in disbelief.

"Your precious David was seen talking to her at the

Sand Bar Tavern, too. Oscar Duarte saw them there. Do you think Miss Stanton was just doing her research? Don't be a foolish cow, Hattie Johnson."

"Lydia!" Kit admonished.

"You want me to drop the subject, Kit? Just like everything else? Well, I'm not about to. David was probably sleeping with Barbara Stanton. He always had an eye for other women, just like you!"

"Lydia!"

"And I don't want *her* staying here!" Lydia pointed at Camille. "You hear me, Miss Avery? I don't want you here. Ever since you and your friend got here, there's been nothing but trouble!"

"I'm leaving anyway," Camille retorted.

"No, you're not." Kit took her arm. "I don't want you going back to the cabin. You shouldn't be alone right now."

"I want to go, Kit. You can either give me a ride or I'll walk."

Lydia smiled in triumph. "Go ahead and walk, Miss Avery. Kit's got better things to do than baby-sit you all the time."

"I don't want you to go back, Camille. I don't think it's safe."

"I'm not staying here." She pulled her arm out of his grasp and took a step toward the door, hating Lydia and her jealous, accusing personality as she had never hated anyone. "Good-bye, Hattie."

"Good-bye, Miss Avery. You be careful, now."

"I will." Just as she stepped out on the porch, she saw three black cars pull into the parking lot.

"They're here!" Lydia exclaimed behind her. "Quick, Kit, go change."

"Camille—" He broke off, unsure what he should do— go with her to the cabin or attend to the guests.

She decided for him, wanting to be alone anyway. "I'll be fine, Kit. I'll see you later, maybe?"

"Yes."

She glanced over her shoulder and did her best to give him a brave smile. Then she ducked down the lane before the Japanese men and their wives could see her tears.

Camille spent the rest of the day making phone calls, trying to explain what had happened to Barbara. She would have thought the calls would get easier to make as the day wore on, but with each successive conversation a new wave of grief washed over her. She couldn't believe that she would never see her friend again, never talk to her, never tease her for her absentminded ways.

How had Barbara died? Camille couldn't even think about it. She didn't want to imagine her dearest friend experiencing a horrible death. To get her mind off Barbara's fate, Camille packed up Barbara's belongings and thoroughly cleaned the kitchen, knowing she could keep her misery at bay if she kept her hands busy.

She worked until sundown, until someone knocked on her door. Tired and cranky, she walked to the front of the cabin. Adam stood on the porch.

"Hi, Miss Avery."

"Adam!" She brightened and motioned him in, but he hung in the doorway, one arm tucked behind his back.

"I don't want to bother you, Miss Avery, but I heard about your friend, Barbara, and I just wanted to tell you how sorry I am." He held out a handful of flowers—pink and white carnations tied up with baby's breath.

Camille was overcome by his thoughtfulness. Tears welled up as she accepted the bouquet and raised it to her nose. She tried to sniff the fragrance of the carnations, but the lump in her throat prevented her from inhaling. Instead she glanced up at Adam. "Thank you, Adam. They're lovely."

"Do you like them?"

"I do. Carnations are my favorite."

She tried to smile, but her lips trembled uncontrollably. Adam, sensing her grief, shuffled his weight from one foot to the other.

"Won't you come in?" Camille said, motioning toward the fire again.

"No. I have to get back. Lydia, you know."

"Well." Camille wiped her cheek with her fingertips. "How was your test? Didn't you have that geometry test today?"

"Yeah, I did. That's another reason I wanted to come by." He reached into the back pocket of his jeans and produced a square of paper, which he unfolded and turned for her to inspect.

Camille took the paper and brought it close enough to see in the dim light. Before she could even focus on the score or the problems, Adam pointed at the top of the paper.

"See? Eighty-eight percent!"

"Adam, that's great!"

"Yeah. And look what my teacher wrote. Can you read that?"

Camille tilted the paper and studied the comments written in red pen: "Good job, Adam. Your work has improved!"

Camille looked up at him while pride squeezed out her grief. Adam had worked hard, and she was thrilled with his success. Even in the diffused light of dusk, she could see the glint of pride in his eyes at his accomplishment. "Oh,

Adam!" she exclaimed, wrapping her arm around his shoulders and giving him a hard squeeze. "Nice going!"

"Yeah!" he answered. "And you know, Miss Avery, this was the first test I actually didn't dread. It was almost like I wanted to take it, to prove I could do it."

"I knew you could!"

"My hands got real sweaty, though." He laughed, and she felt her spirits lift at the sound.

"That happens. But you did well. I'm proud of you."

"I couldn't have done it without your help."

"Well, I enjoyed teaching you." She patted his arm and stepped back, holding out his test paper.

Adam stuffed it in his coat pocket. "I want to get a perfect score the next time, though. I want to get an A, Miss Avery."

"You can. You're no dummy, Adam Makinna."

He gazed at her, his eyes glistening, and she saw his shoulders straighten and his chin raise ever so slightly. Her heart swelled with happiness at the change in him.

"Will you still help me, Miss Avery? For as long as you're here?"

"Of course I will. Anytime, Adam."

"Thanks!" He turned and loped across the yard a few paces and then whirled back around to face her. "Thanks a lot, Miss Avery!"

"Good night, Adam." She raised her hand to wave good-bye. "And thank you for the flowers!"

He waved and ran to the edge of the bluff, disappearing down the trail to the beach.

Her reaction to Adam's happiness soon wore off, much to Camille's dismay. By early evening she was emotionally and physically exhausted and fell into bed without bothering to build a fire or take off her clothes.

Sometime in the night a noise woke her. At first she thought Mak-ee-nah had come to visit, then remembered that he couldn't come into the cabin. She touched the amulet and found it was not at all warm, a sure sign that he wasn't in the vicinity. Camille squinted into the darkness, wondering what she had heard but unwilling to get out of bed. Then she saw the back door open and the figure of a man slip into the kitchen. Someone had picked the lock and broken in.

Camille froze, feigning sleep and watching through slitted lids as the man crept across the floor toward her. In the darkness she could see only a silhouette of a tall, thin man with slightly stooped posture. His hands were empty of weapons, but that didn't mean he was unarmed. Camille's heart hammered in her breast as the man minced closer, all the while looking about him as if searching for something.

When the intruder came within fifteen feet, Camille closed her eyes and forced her breathing into the drawn-out pattern of deep sleep. She could feel every hair on her scalp stand on end as the man loomed over her bed and stared at her. Who was he? Was he going to hurt her? She had nothing with which to defend herself, so she continued with her charade of slumber, hoping whoever he was he would be fooled enough to leave her alone.

She could hear the intruder's breathing, a harsh intake and exhalation of breath as he stood above her. Then his soft tread moved to the fireplace and continued around the cabin. He was looking for something. But what?

Camille opened her eyes slightly and watched him move about the room, quietly pulling out drawers and bending to spy under chairs and tables. Once or twice he sighed as if in disappointment or frustration. Try as she might, however, she could not make out his features in the darkness.

Suddenly a vehicle drove up outside. The intruder jerked to attention and listened as the engine was shut off and a door slammed. Then he hurried to the back entry and slipped out as quietly as he had come.

Camille bolted out of bed and ran to the front door, yanking it open before Kit had even had time to knock. He stood on the porch, holding a grocery bag.

"Camille!"

"Kit, someone broke into the cabin and he just ran out the back!"

Kit stared at her for a moment as the sense of her words sank in. Then he shoved the bag in her arms and dashed around the side of the cabin, leaving Camille standing on the porch. She returned to the cabin and flipped on the lights. She set the bag on the table without looking at its contents and hurried to the back door to look outside, just in case the intruder was hiding in the shadows at the back of the house. She saw nothing, however, and could hear Kit tromping around in the woods at the rear of the yard.

Camille returned to the house and went to the bathroom. Not until she had brushed her teeth and splashed water on her face did she realize her hands were shaking uncontrollably.

Kit came in a few minutes later, and Camille looked at him expectantly.

"Whoever it was got away."

Her shoulders slumped in disappointment.

"Didn't you get a good look at him?" Kit asked, striding into the cabin.

"No. It was too dark. All the lights were off."

"What did he do?"

"He just looked around, as if trying to find something."

Kit rubbed his jaw and paced the perimeter of the room as if to discover clues relating to the intruder, but he could see nothing to identify the man who had broken in. When he got to the back door, he made certain it was locked. Camille watched him, warming to the way he took care of her. Kit pulled the curtains closed above the sink and then walked over to her.

"That does it. You're not staying here."

"What?"

"I'm taking you back where I can keep an eye on you."

"You mean to the lodge?"

"Yeah. And don't give me that noise about Lydia not wanting you. I want you there and that's where you're going to be."

"But, Kit—"

"But, Kit, nothing. Throw some of your things in a bag, Camille."

"Whoever it was didn't hurt me."

"No, but what about the next time?"

"I'd rather stay here."

"You shouldn't be alone, and with the Japanese at the lodge I just can't stay here with you. So I want you to come back with me."

"Lydia will be furious."

"Lydia can go take a hike. Now are you coming or do I have to throw you over my shoulder and force you to come?"

Camille liked the image of being thrown over his shoulder. The thought of being at his mercy was not at all repugnant. But it was no time to play games with Kit, and to tell the truth, she was a bit frightened by the ease with which the intruder had broken into the cabin.

"All right. I'll come."

"Good." He followed her to the closet near the bathroom.

"Do you have something fancy?" he asked.

"Why?"

"We're having a salmon dinner tomorrow night in honor of the Japanese."

Camille glanced over her shoulder at him. "Do you want me to go?"

"Yeah."

"You mean with you—as your date?"

"Yeah." He looked down his nose at her, the color high on his cheekbones, almost as if he expected her to refuse. "If you feel up to it."

"I'll be all right." Camille pulled another outfit from the rack and transferred it to her left hand. She looked up at him. "And I'd be honored to go with you."

18

At the lodge, Kit ushered Camille upstairs. All was dark and quiet, except for the jingle of Sandy's dog tags as she came to the door to greet them. He turned on the light in the hallway upstairs and led her to a room at the end of the hall.

Camille stepped into the chamber, a suite much like the one she had stayed in when she'd first come to the reservation, only this room was lived in. She recognized the gray-and-brown sweater hanging on a peg by the door and Kit's black boots on the floor nearby. File folders and books were stacked on the small table by the window, along with the daily newspaper and a coffee cup.

A thrill of anticipation coursed down her back as Kit came into the room behind her. Did he expect her to sleep in his room? Surely there must be ample space in the lodge for an unexpected guest. She knew she should feel uncomfortable being in Kit's quarters, with the obvious implication that she share his bed for the night, but oddly enough she felt calm and safe. Kit strode to the table and deposited the brown paper sack.

"What's in there, anyway?" she asked, drifting toward him.

"I thought you might like a glass of wine and a snack. I bet you didn't eat today, did you?"

"Not exactly. I didn't feel like it."

"That's what I thought."

He pulled out the bottle of wine, a bag of grapes, some cheese, and a box of wheat crackers while Camille approached the table. The sight of the food made her stomach grumble, and Kit smiled at her. "You are hungry—just as I suspected."

"I guess I am."

"Wait here, and I'll get some dishes."

He turned and left the room while Camille went past the connecting fireplace and poked her head around the corner into the bedroom. His bed was made, the spread neatly folded beneath the two pillows. A pair of worn suede slippers was lined up in front of the nightstand and a black terry velour robe was draped over the chair by the fire. For a man's room, it was neat and tidy, a fact not lost on her.

At the sound of Kit's footsteps in the hall, she ducked back into the main room and made a pretext of inspecting the dead coals in the fireplace.

"If you take care of the food, I'll make a fire," Kit remarked, handing her a plate, knife, napkins, and two wine-glasses.

"Okay."

She cut slices of the cheddar cheese and pulled the grapes apart, arranging the clusters on the plate, along with the crackers and cheese. While Kit lit kindling she pulled the cork on the wine, a chilled Chardonnay from an island winery in nearby Puget Sound, and filled the goblets. By the time she had disposed of the empty wrappers and put the remaining food back in the bag, she turned to find Kit replacing the fire screen at the hearth. He brushed his palms together.

"There. In a few minutes we might even get warm."

Camille smiled. She hadn't noticed the chill in the room. In Kit's presence she forgot to think about how cold or hot she felt. She was usually preoccupied with other sensations, such as how he made her pulse race, how his dark good looks enchanted her, and how wonderful it felt when his hands and lips touched her skin. Even now the thought of his touch made a flush rise in her cheeks. She grabbed the plate of food and a glass of wine.

"Where would you like to eat?" she asked.

"How about here, in front of the fire?" He patted the small couch that was drawn up near the hearth and then reached for the wine. He remained standing while she retrieved the second glass. Not until she sat down did he lower to the cushion at the other end.

"I thought you might want some privacy. That's why I brought you up here instead of sitting in the lobby. There's no telling who might happen by down there."

"I appreciate it. Thank you." She sipped the wine. The cool smooth taste of the Chardonnay was like a welcome caress. She sat back. "Did you ever find Old Man last night?"

"No. I looked everywhere. I meant to tell you that's why I never made it back to the cabin. I spent more time on the road than I anticipated."

"Do you think anything has happened to your grandfather?"

"No. He's tougher than he looks, Camille. Don't

worry." He drank his wine and gazed at her over the top of the glass. "How about you? Are you feeling any better since this morning?"

"A little." She glanced at the fire and fought the lump that immediately formed in her throat at the mention of Barbara. "I thought I was ready to face the possibility that something had happened to Barbara, but I guess a person can't prepare for such an awful finality."

"I know what it's like. I lost both of my parents when I was five."

She looked up in surprise. "What happened to them?"

"They died in a plane crash. They were going to Washington, D.C., to join a march for civil rights. They made it only as far as Chicago."

"I'm sorry, Kit."

"It's okay now. I know my life would have been different had they been here, but the world keeps turning, and you learn to go on."

"I know. But I'm going to miss Barbara so much." She turned away and shielded her eyes with her hand so he couldn't see her tears. After a moment of silence, she felt him rise from the couch and heard him step in front of her.

"Come here," he said softly, reaching down for her wrist. With his other hand he took her wineglass and put it on the table next to his. Then he drew her to her feet.

Slowly she rose and let herself be enfolded in his arms, held as she had longed to be held all day. Burying her face in the soft fabric of his black chamois shirt, she let the tears come, releasing her grief to him. He stroked her back and ran his hand over her hair and with his touch assured her that she could cry as long as she needed to. His patient, silent support eventually helped her tears to subside, but she remained in his embrace, too shattered to break the link of comfort.

Camille turned her head, and the button on his pocket flap pressed into the corner of her lip, but she was too numb to care. She clung to him, shutting her eyes against the vision of Barbara wrapped in her shroud of kelp.

"Are you all right now?" Kit inquired, stroking her hair.

"I keep seeing her on the beach—" She broke off, unable to keep her voice from cracking.

"You should have gone back when I told you to."

"I know." A week ago she would have bristled at Kit's statement. Now, however, she knew that such a phrase was not a criticism of her behavior but part of Kit's way of showing his concern. She sighed. "It was inevitable that I find out, anyway."

"You didn't have to see her like that, though."

"I can handle it." As if to prove her emotional strength, she stepped out of his embrace, wiping her eyes with her fingertips. "I'll get over it." She pressed her lips together and blearily stared at the fireplace, well aware that Kit studied her face.

He reached for her wineglass and gave it to her. "Here, Camille. Why don't you take it easy and sit down?"

"Thanks." She sank onto the couch cushion, still numb. "What bothers me most is the thought that she might have suffered, that she might have been afraid when she died. I can't stop thinking about it."

"Don't do that to yourself. It won't help Barbara, and it certainly won't help you."

"But she might have been murdered."

"I know. The possibility has crossed my mind." He pulled a grape off a cluster. "And another thing that bothers me is that Two Hand asked me to keep quiet about finding her until the Japanese leave."

"Why?"

"So it won't sour a deal they've hatched to sell the Island of the Dead to the Japanese."

"But what if she was murdered? The longer we wait, the easier it will be for her killers to escape."

"Exactly. That's why I don't intend to keep this hushed up."

"Two Hand wants everything hushed up. Even the artifact theft." Camille finished her wine. "I'm starting to wonder if he pursues criminals at all."

"That thought has crossed my mind, too." Kit put his empty wineglass on the small end table near his elbow. "Aren't you going to eat something?"

Camille looked at the plate of food. At first she had been hungry, but their talk about Barbara had put a knot in her stomach and a lump in her throat. Her appetite had vanished. To appease Kit, however, she took a cracker and munched on the corner.

"What about going to the island and looking around?" she ventured. "Would you take me there, Kit?"

"I could. But not tomorrow. We're just too busy. That trip could take the whole day, once we go out, look around, and come back."

Camille sighed again, twirling the stem of her empty glass between her fingertips.

"Do you want some more wine?" he asked, leaning toward her.

"No thanks. I'm feeling groggy already."

Kit took her glass and set it near his. Then he turned back to her, stretching his arm out on the back of the couch. "What are you planning to do?" he asked. "Have you thought about it at all?"

"No." She shook her head and looked at her hands. "I haven't got that far."

"Will you go back to your girls' school and forget the book?"

"That would be like abandoning Barbara altogether. This book was her pet project, her shining star. I just can't leave it unfinished, stuck away somewhere in her parents' attic."

"How about finishing it yourself?"

"You mean writing it?"

"Isn't it nearly completed?"

"Yes, but—" She stared at him in wonder. The thought hadn't occurred to her that she could work at the editing of the book and get it ready for publication.

"What you don't have in the way of editorial content, I'm sure my grandfather would supply. He loves to tell old stories. And he likes you. From what I hear, I think he'd tell you much more than he told Barbara."

Camille's flagging spirits rose at the idea. She could make the book a legacy of Barbara's. Working on it would keep her close, as if Barbara were still a vital part of her life.

"That's a great idea, Kit. I'll probably have to extend my leave of absence, though."

"You're welcome to stay here as long as you like."

She glanced at him. "So you haven't rented the cabin to anyone else for the summer?"

"No, but I'm talking about you staying here at the lodge. I don't think it's a good idea for you to be at the cabin alone. Maybe sometime tomorrow or the day after, we can drive over and get the rest of your things."

"But living here with your family? I don't know. . . ." At her hesitation, she noticed his hand clench into a ball.

"No strings attached, Avery," he put in. "I just want you to be safe."

She nodded, confused again about where she stood with him on an emotional level. One time he was intimate and loving and calling her Camille, and the next he was removed and brusque, using her last name as if to distance himself from her. She didn't know what to think of him.

"It's a good offer, Kit, but what happens when you leave? Lydia will still be here and she'll want to get rid of me."

"I might not be leaving as soon as I expected." Kit shifted on the couch and turned his gaze to the fire. "There are things here that need to be looked after before I go back."

"But isn't your time here limited? Aren't you on vacation?"

"Yeah, but I'm considering extending it."

She glanced at him, wondering what it was about the reservation that compelled each of them to linger. Was it the reservation, or was it the growing bond between them that urged them to stay in each other's spheres—at least temporarily? Yet was she reading more into it than was real? She might feel drawn to Kit, but his reasons for staying might be a hundred and eighty degrees from hers, involving duty to his family and tribal matters that had nothing to do with her.

Though she longed to tell him how she felt about him, she bit back the words, unwilling to suffer the same rejection he had shown Lydia on the deck the other night. She could stay at the lodge and deal with her attraction to him, but she could never remain in the lodge if she revealed her love for him and he turned her down. It would be too humiliating, too heartbreaking. She couldn't jeopardize the opportunity to complete Barbara's book by allowing her emotions to run away with her. For now, she must remain silent and hope that Kit would give her some inkling of how he felt about her.

She studied his sharp profile and the lines at the corner

of his eyes where his dark lashes shadowed his cheek. More than anything she wanted to reach out to him and kiss his face, but she remained sitting in her own corner of the couch. Feeling her regard, he turned.

"You're awfully quiet," he remarked. "What are you thinking about?"

"Nothing. I'm just tired. It's been quite a day."

"Yeah." He stood up. "Tomorrow's going to be a long one, too. We should go to bed."

"Yes, we should."

His words raised gooseflesh on her arms. *We should go to bed.* He said it so casually. But going to bed with Kit would be the farthest thing from casual that she could imagine. Their brief encounter on the beach had been hurried and clumsy because of the cold weather and their clothing. She wondered what it would be like to lie with Kit in a bed, when they had all the time in the world to explore and enjoy each other's bodies. Flustered at the thought, she rose and crossed her arms over her chest.

Kit noticed the gesture and smiled. "I hope you don't mind sleeping here."

"No, but I don't want to inconvenience you. Isn't there an unoccupied room I could stay in?"

"The finished rooms are being used by the Japanese. The rest are in a shambles of paint buckets and dropcloths. I don't want you in any of them right now."

He carried the wineglasses and plate to the table. "I'll take these downstairs and put the food away. There are clean towels in the bathroom over there." He nodded toward a door on the other side of the fireplace.

"Okay."

"Feel free to put your clothes in the closet and make yourself at home."

Camille swallowed, wondering if he intended to make

himself at home with her. Would he come back and climb into bed with her? Would he let her fall asleep while he puttered around and then slip under the covers, touching her in the darkness when they could both pretend they were in a dream state and not in full control of themselves? A thrill passed over her at the thought.

"Are you all right, Avery?"

She heard the name he used and blinked back to reality. *Avery.* He was into his cool and removed state. He probably wouldn't even spend the night in the same room with her, much less offer himself to her in bed. He had given his support and comfort and had been thoughtful enough to worry about her sustenance. But he had chosen to leave her alone. Perhaps it was better that way.

"Yes." She breathed in and glanced up at him. "I'm fine."

He walked across the floor, carrying the brown bag and the dirty dishes, and she hurried to his side to open the door for him.

He paused in the doorway. "I'm really sorry about your friend."

"Thanks."

"We'll find out what happened, I promise."

She nodded, crushed that he was leaving her.

"Well, good night, Avery," he said.

"Good night."

She closed the door and turned to face the room. The fire crackled merrily on the grate, shadows played over the cedar log walls, and the furniture was worn and homey. The serenity of the room should have given her comfort. But without Kit in it, the room seemed dark and empty.

Disappointed, she trudged across the floor to the bedroom. She stripped off her jeans and sweater, left on her T-shirt, and put her discarded clothes in a pile on the chair beside Kit's robe. Then she bent and pulled down the bed-covers, slipping under the heavy blankets and cotton flannel sheets. Camille's head sank into the pillow while she breathed deeply, savoring the scent of Kit's body, which lingered in his bed, even though the sheets were clean. She stretched out her legs, wondering which side he slept on, wondering what it would feel like to reach out and touch him. The few times she had spent the night with her boyfriend in college, she had felt trapped and uncomfortable if he insisted upon embracing her during the night. But she longed for such an embrace from Kit.

Camille flopped onto her stomach and pushed her nose into her pillow, squeezing it, delirious with want for him. She was in his room, in his bed, but to be here without him was the cruelest form of torture, a sweet agony more painful than any she had ever known.

Long after midnight, a strange noise awoke Camille. Something had hit her bedroom window. Groggy and dizzy, she glanced at the alarm clock on the nightstand. Three o'clock in the morning? Perhaps she had just dreamed the noise. She laid her head back down and decided to ignore it, but the sharp pinging sound repeated. Could someone be throwing gravel at her window? Tired and fumbling in the dark, she stumbled to the window and drew back the curtain to look outside. There on the bluff stood Mak-ee-nah. He motioned with an impatient gesture for her to come down.

Camille instantly snapped wide awake. Whatever he wanted of her seemed important. She threw on her discarded clothes, pushed her feet into her boots, laced them up with hurried jerks, and draped the amulet around her neck, hiding it between her shirt and sweater as always.

Then she slipped out of Kit's room and crept down the stairs, careful not to make any noise. She grabbed her parka from the peg by the lobby door and threw it on as she let herself out to the deck. Mak-ee-nah and his wolves were waiting for her just beyond the railing.

"Where have you been, Mak-ee-nah?" she asked.

"I have been following the man with the truck."

"Oscar Duarte?"

He nodded.

Camille wrapped her coat around her, wishing she had brought gloves with her. The wind off the strait was bitter cold. Yet Mak-ee-nah, in his sea otter robe and pale yellow cloak covered with black designs of the sun and moon, didn't appear to be cold at all, even though his feet were bare.

He motioned for her to sit, and she lowered herself to the stairs leading to the bluff. Mak-ee-nah stood in front of her, while the wolves sat in a semicircle around them.

"When I came to see you last night, I saw Oss-car come out of your house."

"The intruder was Oscar?"

"Yes. I ran after him. He is an old man and could not run very fast. I could have caught him if I had had the amulet." He crossed his arms and gave her a sidelong glance full of meaning.

She ignored the look. "So what happened?"

"He got in his car and went away."

"Too bad. We need to catch him in a criminal act, so we can press charges against him."

"Press charges?"

"You know, accuse him of doing something wrong so that he can be stopped."

"Did he hurt you, Ca-meel?"

"No, he was looking for something. He thought I was asleep."

"Do you know what he seeks?"

"No. But it must be something important, something linking him to the artifact theft. That's all I can figure."

"I saw you leave with the man who makes you cry."

"Kit." She wondered whether Mak-ee-nah purposely chose not to remember Kit's name or if he simply didn't want to say it.

He nodded. "Did you not say you would forget this man?"

"I don't think I'll ever be able to forget Kit."

"But the man who makes you cry is no good for you, Ca-meel. A good man makes a woman smile, as I do." He touched his mouth and waved his hand, as if throwing a smile in the same manner a person would throw a kiss.

At the gesture, she grinned. She couldn't help herself. "Yes, you make me smile. But so will Kit someday, once he realizes that I am not like all the other women he's known. He doesn't trust many people. When he learns to trust me, then he'll make me smile."

"I trust you now." He swaggered closer, his bare feet splayed in the sand.

"You, Mak-ee-nah, are a big flirt."

He tilted his head. "Flirt?"

"Yes. You like to tease me."

"Tease?"

"To say things so I will choose you over Kit."

Mak-ee-nah paused in thought, his index finger curled over his lips. Then he leaned toward her. "Yes, I am a big flirt, *klootz-mah*. And I will tease you many times. You have no father or brother to tell you how to be wise about men. So I will tease you many, many times until you learn."

Camille shook her head in amused exasperation, realizing that an explanation of the intricacies of the English language would take time, and she was too tired to cope with such a task at the moment. With a sigh, she got to her feet.

"I'm tired, Mak-ee-nah. Perhaps we can talk more tomorrow night."

"Do you not wish to hear what I found about Oss-car?"

"Of course. What?"

"All night I trailed the tracks of his car. He lives in a big lodge the color of the sky not far from the tribal land."

"You found out where he lives?"

"Yes. Until the sun began its journey, I stood among the bushes, watching his house. Afterward, I had to change into my animal spirit form. It was then that I saw Oss-car come out of his lodge and leave in his red car."

"Did you follow him?"

"Yes. It was easier to follow as a bird. He drove to an old lodge in a big field. In the lodge I saw many boxes hidden under dried grasses."

"Dried grasses?"

"Yes. Some of the grass was tied in shapes like boxes."

"Hay!" Camille exclaimed. "Oscar has hidden the artifacts in a barn!"

"A man came in a big truck and took the boxes."

"Oh, great. Now those will be lost to the Nakalt."

"I looked at the crest on the truck, as you looked at Oss-car's crest."

"You did?" She glanced at him in surprise, realizing that nothing much escaped Mak-ee-nah. What would he be like when in possession of the amulet and able to fully affect his physical surrounds? A thrill shot down her back.

"I will make the design for you." He turned to find a stick. Then he carefully drew the letters and numbers in the sand, forming them as seen through the eyes of a man more accustomed to dealing with animal shapes than man-made abstractions. But his letters—however far from their original patterns—were constructed of flowing curves of varying thicknesses, done by a man who knew the beauty of lines and curves. When he was finished, he tossed the stick away.

"There. That is what I saw."

Camille said the letters and numbers out loud and then smiled up at him. "Good job, Mak-ee-nah. Maybe we can recover the items if I get this to the police right away."

"You are good for my people," he replied. "Someday they will know this."

She flushed at his praise and hugged her arms. "Was that you on the beach this morning, Mak-ee-nah, in your raven form?"

"Yes. I follow the amber, *klootz-mah*."

"When you are a raven, can you understand what people say?"

He shook his head. "My ears, when I am a raven, are not human ears. I hear your voice, but it sounds like running water. I hear the sound, but there is no meaning to it."

"But you know who I am."

"Yes. I will always know who you are, *klootz-mah*. It is the rest of the world and you, who do not know."

"Who am I?"

"You are *queece klootz-mah*."

"And what does that mean?"

"You are the Snow Woman, daughter of the North Wind."

Camille fumbled backward, going up a step. "But the Snow Maiden is just a legend. If she ever really existed, it was long, long ago."

"I have thought very much about this, Ca-meel. And I have decided that the spirits must return just as the *so-har* come back to us. It is yet another circle. Always spinning, always coming back to where it first began. We are part of that circle. And now you have come back to the Nakalt to give the amulet to my people."

"But what about the rest of the prophecy? There is supposed to be a chief involved."

"*Tyee?* I am *tyee.*"

"Everyone thinks Kit is the *tyee.*"

"I am *tyee.*" He thumped his chest impatiently. "I am the one who has died and come back to my people. You, *queece klootz-mah,* have brought me back to life. And when the amulet is given to our son, then we will go to the Land Above together."

"Our son?" Camille retreated another step. "Wait a minute. No one told me about having a son."

"You do not know the story of the Snow Woman?"

"Just bits of it."

"Then sit, Ca-meel, and I will tell you of the daughter of the North Wind who fell in love with a great *tyee.* That is me." He threw her a sidelong glance and a smile.

"I know that much," she retorted, sinking onto the stairs once more. She clasped her arms around her legs and looked up at him. When he was satisfied that she was settled and willing to listen, he began his tale.

"Once long ago, the Nakalt were a powerful and happy people. Their *tyee* was strong and good, empowered by an amulet with amazing powers which brought many fish and much fortune to the village. The *tyee*'s younger brother was jealous, however, and wanted to be the first *tyee.* So he set upon the *tyee* while he prayed in the forest, killed him, and stole his amulet.

"The older brother had been a handsome man and a great whaler. He was much admired by the Snow Maiden, daughter of the North Wind. When she saw the great *tyee* lying dead, she asked her father to blow breath back into him so that he could live in the sky with her and be her husband. Her father did so. And the older brother married the Snow Maiden.

"From his home in the sky, the older brother could look down upon his village and see his people starving. His wicked younger brother misused the power of the amulet, bringing misfortune to the Nakalt. While his people suffered, the older brother could not be happy living in the clouds with the Snow Maiden. He longed to return to his home and could not see the beauty of his wife. This broke the Snow Maiden's heart, for she loved the older brother very much.

"Once again she asked her father for help. She begged him to transform the older brother into a man again, so that he might walk among his people for three moons, enough time to help the village. The North Wind did as his daughter asked, and knowing how her heart would pine for her handsome husband, he changed her into a woman so that she could accompany him on his journey. The Snow Maiden went to earth as a beautiful white-haired woman."

Mak-ee-nah paused and reached out to touch her hair. "You are this woman, Ca-meel."

Camille hugged her knees more tightly but made no response.

Mak-ee-nah continued. "The Snow Maiden's father warned her that if she and her husband failed to return in three moons, she would melt away and be no more.

"At first the villagers were frightened to see their former *tyee*, certain he must be a *memelose*, a dead person walking the earth. But he assured his people that he was there to help. He used his spirit power to call the fish-people, and soon the villagers had plenty of food to eat again. They began to doubt the power of the younger brother. This angered the young *tyee,* and he challenged his older brother, setting aside the amulet so that it would not get damaged during the fight. Of course the older brother, being a strong man and great warrior, was victorious. He did not kill his brother, however, but banished him forever, which everyone knows is worse than death."

"So that was it?" Camille asked, thinking the story was over.

"No, *klootz-mah.* Unfortunately for the people, Raven flew by during the battle and stole the shining amulet.

"This was a terrible blow, Camille. Without the amulet, the older brother could never restore health and happiness to his people in the time allotted by the North Wind. If he asked the Snow Maiden to stay on earth, she would melt and be no more. Yet if he went to the Land Above with her, he would be leaving his people to die. The *tyee* knew he must choose between his people and his beautiful Snow Maiden, whom he had come to love with all his heart. This dilemma distressed the *tyee* very much, until the Snow Maiden became deeply concerned for him. She asked her father to cause a storm that would blow Raven from the sky. Her father did so, and Raven tumbled through the air, dropping the amulet into the hands of the Snow Maiden.

"She placed the amulet around the neck of her husband while the people cheered and prepared for a big feast. But the *tyee* told them that his time on earth had run out and he must return to the Land Above with his wife. The people were frightened, unsure of their future. They would have no *tyee.* The Snow Maiden reassured them by giving birth to a son, who grew to manhood in one day and became the new *tyee.*"

"In one day?" Camille asked, incredulous.

"Magical things happened in the old times," Mak-ee-nah replied. "Things we cannot explain now. But let me finish the story."

"Okay."

"To this son was given the amulet and the promise that the *tyee* and the Snow Maiden would come back to the earth again to make certain all was well with the people. Then the Snow Maiden and her spirit husband walked into the mist and were never seen again.

"Yet when snow falls on the lodges of the Nakalt, the people know that the Snow Maiden is with them once more, watching over them."

19

"So," *Mak-ee-nah said,* obliterating the license plate number by running his foot through the sand. "That is the story."

"And you think I am the Snow Maiden."

"Yes."

"And if I give the amulet to you, then we will have a son and eventually go to the Land Above. It sounds preposterous!"

"This frightens you, *klootz-mah?*"

"Yes, I—" She scrambled to her feet. "Well, first of all, I haven't even lived most of my life yet. I'm only twenty-nine years old. I don't want to go up to the Land Above or heaven or whatever it is. That means I have to die, doesn't it?"

"Perhaps."

"And how am I supposed to have a son who grows to be a man in just one day?"

"Why do you question it? It will happen. It is part of the cycle."

She glared at him and then walked across the deck to the door that led into the dining room. "No offense, Mak-ee-nah, but I don't wish to be your wife. And I have no desire to be the Snow Maiden."

"Why?"

"I came here to help write a book and that's all."

"You came here to bring the amulet to the Nakalt people, to fulfill a prophecy."

"I've got other plans."

"Plans for the man who makes you cry?"

"Yes. You don't seem to understand. I love him."

"He is like me, Ca-meel. You can choose me and still be happy."

"He is of my time, Mak-ee-nah. He understands the world as I understand it."

"But I can make you smile. And I will be good for you. We were together once"—he indicated the sky—"up in the clouds with the North Wind. You were my wife. I was your husband. Do you not remember me, *queece klootz-mah*?"

"No, I don't."

"Then why have you fallen in love with a man you have known for a handful of days? What makes your heart leap out to him?"

"His concern. His beauty."

"His face is my face, *klootz-mah*. When you met the man who makes you cry, you saw me again and you fell in love."

Camille blinked and put her hand on the doorknob, slightly confused by his argument. She had to admit that she was amazed at how quickly she had accepted the fact that she was in love with Kit. She had never fallen head over heels in love before and until coming to the reservation had never believed in love at first sight. But she had loved Kit the moment she saw him—when he had called her name to awaken her from sleep, and she had looked up to see him in the light. But had she fallen for him because his appearance matched the image stamped on her heart by a man she loved already in another lifetime?

"You are silent, Ca-meel. You know I speak the truth?"

"I'm not sure. I'll have to think about it."

"Give me the amulet so that I may prove my worth."

"Soon. I'll give it to you soon, Mak-ee-nah." She pulled open the door. "I'll go to the authorities in the morning and tell them about the truck and the barn. But you must show me where the barn is. Will you come to me tomorrow morning?"

"Yes. But I will not wait forever for the amber."

"Just one more day, Mak-ee-nah. Please."

"One, *klootz-mah.*"

She hesitated at the door and looked back at him. He stood watching her, his head thrown back, his feet wide apart in a proud stance, his hand on the head of the wolf with the notched ear. Had she been the wife of such a man? Or had he invented a tall tale to trick her? Somehow she didn't think Mak-ee-nah would stoop that low. But where did Kit figure in the story? Did he count for nothing? She couldn't accept the idea that he was a useless accessory.

"Good night, Mak-ee-nah."

"Good night." He raised his hand in farewell.

Quietly she slipped into the house and up the stairs, trying not to think of Mak-ee-nah's tale. Now she knew how Kit felt, being labeled as a player in a prophecy and having all of life's choices stripped from him. No wonder he had rebelled and fled the reservation. The concept of being a pivotal character for an entire people was a huge responsibility, one that a young man would naturally fear and resent.

She undressed and crawled back into bed. As she laid her head upon the pillow, the thought occurred to her that her life hadn't been all that exciting, and that she hadn't made much of her choices in life, other than to go to college and teach. She tucked her hands under her pillow. What worthwhile things had she done with her choices? Until now, her existence had been a common, everyday kind of life. If she were the Snow Maiden, her life would change drastically and end sooner than she had planned. Did she want that? Did she want Mak-ee-nah?

She turned over and pulled the covers up to her ears. Why was she wasting her time thinking about such nonsense? Surely none of it could be true. She was not a Nakalt. She was a white woman. And as Kit had said, she didn't belong in the Nakalt legend.

In the morning, Camille woke up to the sound of a shower running. She sat up with a start, thinking at first that she was in her apartment at Lewis Academy, then that she was in the cabin on the bluff, and finally she remembered she was in Kit's bedroom. He was probably around the corner taking a shower, where it would be more convenient for him.

Camille slipped out of bed, rubbing her eyes and wondering what she should do—let Kit get dressed while she feigned sleep the whole time? That would be easier than trying to pretend they were total strangers to one another's bodies. While she considered the other alternative—that of a more honest interaction and one she favored—her glance fell on Kit's robe still draped across the chair. She picked it up, intending to leave it in a conspicuous spot near the bathroom so he would have something more appropriate than a towel to wear back to the room where he had spent the night.

She rounded the corner of the fireplace, mincing in her bare feet upon the cold wood floor. To her surprise, she found the bathroom door ajar and caught a distorted glimpse of Kit's tan figure and dark head behind the textured glass of the shower door. She quickly looked away, feeling like a voyeur again, and tried not to make a sound as she put his robe on the counter by the sink.

"Is that you, Camille?" he called out.

"Yes. I thought you might like your robe."

"Thanks."

She turned and glanced at the shower door again and saw his arm reach for the shower knob. The water shut off abruptly. Camille hurried out of the room and heard the grating of the shower door as Kit opened it. With her back to the bathroom, she stood in the parlor, wondering what to say. She wasn't accustomed to greeting a man after his morning shower.

"I'm sorry if I woke you," he remarked.

"That's all right. I should be up anyway."

He came up behind her, and she pivoted, not sure what she'd see. His black hair was wet and tousled, standing in shining points on his head. His chest was bare and sleek, and his hips were wrapped with a blindingly white towel. "If you need to use the bathroom, I can wait."

"N-no, go ahead," she stuttered, glancing from the towel to his face. The sight of his clean, nearly naked body wreaked havoc with her sense of propriety.

"My things were here, so I thought I'd just sneak in before you got up."

"That's all right. Really, Kit, you should be sleeping

here in your own room and I should be somewhere else."

He gazed down at her, his black eyes sparkling. "I don't mind you being here, if you don't mind me."

"I don't mind."

"Good." He returned to the bathroom and grabbed a comb. "Did you sleep well?"

"I slept like a rock." She ventured toward the doorway, watching him straighten his hair.

"Good." He leaned over the counter and surveyed his face in the mirror, running his fingers over his jaw. "Think I need to shave?"

She stepped closer to get a better look. What little beard Kit had didn't show enough to require shaving. "It doesn't look like it."

"Good. I hate shaving."

"I thought Native American men didn't have to shave."

"Sure they do, especially the northwest coast Indians. Some of the men in my tribe wore beards and mustaches in the old days, which surprised the explorers, I've been told."

"I've never heard of that."

"It's true. In the old days, my ancestors used to pluck out their facial hair with mussel shells."

Camille grimaced at the thought, and he grinned.

"I favor the convenience of electricity myself." He pulled out a drawer and uncapped a container of deodorant.

Camille marveled at the conversation she was having with him in the bathroom, as if it were not out of the ordinary that she should be there to watch him prepare for the day. She had never known such intimacy with a man and found herself enjoying the experience. She watched him roll the deodorant over his underarms. At the movement, his back muscles rippled and the skin stretched tightly over his rib cage. She caught herself staring at his gorgeous physique and flushed when she found him regarding her in the mirror.

"You look pretty in the morning," he said.

"I do?"

"Yeah. I like the way your hair's all messy. You usually look so neat and prim, never a hair out of place."

She laughed softly. "You make me sound like the old schoolmarm that I am."

"You're no schoolmarm," he retorted. "Not with eyes like yours."

"Really?" She felt another blush spread across her cheeks. She had never discussed her appearance with anyone but Barbara, afraid she would be teased about her pale hair and dark brows. But she knew Kit wasn't the type of man who enjoyed teasing, so for the second time in her life she let herself open up. "I've never liked my eyes."

"Why not?"

"They're a strange color. And my eyebrows are too dark."

"No they're not." He turned and leaned on the counter. "You have beautiful hazel eyes, and your eyebrows heighten their color. I think you look distinctive."

Camille had never thought of herself as distinctive. She rather liked the term.

"And why do you wear sweaters all the time? Don't you know what a beautiful little shape you have?"

"I'm short and chunky."

"You're not!" He laughed. "Whoever told you that?"

"Tons of people when I was a kid."

"You're no kid now, Camille, believe me. You shouldn't be hiding behind those bulky outfits you wear."

She stepped backward, amazed at his comments.

"That T-shirt you're wearing is the best outfit I've seen you in yet."

"This old thing?" She looked down at herself, trying to ignore the pleasure she felt at his praise, and noticed that her breasts had responded to his words as well. Her nipples were growing hard and erect, easily seen beneath the light cotton shirt.

"And those breasts of yours are like lie detectors." Kit reached out and grasped her wrists, pulling her up to him. She dragged her feet, resisting—but only slightly—while her heart beat so wildly, she was sure he could see it hammering beneath the shirt. "You're trying to stay cool and collected, Camille, but I know you're feeling something totally different inside. Look at your breasts perking up."

"Kit—"

He drew her against the angle of his body, still leaning against the counter, still wrapped in a towel. The terry cloth brushed her bare legs, and his warm hands slipped under the T-shirt.

"Will you take it off?" he asked hoarsely. "So I can see you?"

Camille swallowed as her body flared into full arousal. Yes, she would let him see her. She longed to bare herself to him in more ways than one, but for now she had to restrict herself to the physical. Quickly she made a silent vow not to say anything rash to Kit about her feelings for him and then let herself succumb to her need for him. She reached down for the hem of the shirt, and he helped her slip it over her head. He gazed down at her and dropped the shirt in a puddle of cloth at their feet, completely oblivious of everything but the sight of her.

She gazed up at his flushed face, her breath coming in heavy gasps as her breasts seemed to swell toward him, aching for the touch of his mouth. If he didn't bend down to her in a moment, they would shatter from pure desire.

"You're beautiful," he whispered, running his hands over the hard points of her breasts. She moaned in answer. "You have the most beautifully formed breasts I've ever seen. Your skin is like snow, your nipples are like wild strawberries."

"Kit, please—" She stepped against him, pressing into his towel.

His hands moved downward to frame her rib cage, and then he bent to take the tip of her left breast into his mouth. Gasping, she clutched his head and held him there, closing her eyes against the shafts of ecstasy and longing that shot through her.

She writhed against him as he suckled her, first one breast and then the other, and twisted in his embrace until she was the one pressed against the counter. Camille let her head roll back as she felt herself soar into the private world she shared only with Kit.

He kissed the slight valley between her breasts where the amulet hung against her skin and continued the path up her chest to her neck. Then he pressed a hard kiss beneath her jaw and placed his forehead on her shoulder.

"I don't know what's happening between us," he said. "I can't stay away from you. It's crazy."

"It is," she answered, running her hands through his thick damp hair. "But I want you so much, Kit."

He raised his head and looked into her eyes. "Even if it's just sex?"

"One of us may be making love. And that's enough for me."

He gazed at her while two patches of crimson shadowed the ridges of his cheekbones. She returned the stare, unabashed and unafraid of her honesty.

"Then let's get out of this damn bathroom," he said, sweeping her into his arms. "And do it right."

He lifted her effortlessly and walked across the parlor toward the bedroom, nuzzling her and squeezing her until she squealed in delight.

"I'm amazed my towel is still on," he said. "I can't hardly walk with wanting you."

Camille's entire body flushed at his words. She reached up to encircle his neck just as someone pounded on the door and called his name.

"Damn," Kit exclaimed, pausing in front of the bedroom. "It's Lydia."

Without waiting for a reply, Lydia burst into the room.

"I knew it!" Lydia shouted.

Kit felt Camille twist in his arms as if to get down, but he held her tightly and refused to release her. All she had on was her underwear, and he wasn't about to let Lydia catch a glimpse of her nakedness. He hoped the reassuring squeeze he gave Camille was enough to give her courage to face Lydia after being caught in such an indelicate situation with him. But much to his surprise and satisfaction, he looked down and saw not a hint of shame in Camille's eyes.

"I knew she was in here with you!"

"And now that you know, you can leave," Kit replied, trying to control the anger in his voice. He walked through the doorway to the bedroom.

Lydia followed, her bracelets jingling. "I won't have you bedding that slut in my house! I won't have it!"

"Leave us, Lydia."

"How can you have her here like this? Have you lost your mind?"

"Have you lost your pride," Kit retorted, shielding Camille's nakedness as he put her down, "that you can barge into my room and violate my privacy?"

"I'm trying to save you from the clutches of that slut."

"If you call Camille a slut again, I'll turn you out."

"You wouldn't dare!"

"Try me. I'd be happy to oblige." He strode to the door and flung it open. "Leave, Lydia. And don't ever come in unannounced again, do you hear me?"

She stomped past him, holding her head up high. "Wait until the elders hear about this."

"Tell everyone. I'm not ashamed of my actions."

She paused as if in surprise and stared at him.

"In fact, it might help clear up the misconception around here that you and I are meant for each other."

"Bastard!" She reached out to slap him, but Kit caught her wrist in midair.

He glared down at her. "Camille is staying on at the lodge. She will be treated with respect. And if I hear one complaint about you, Lydia, you're going back to your father."

"Listen to yourself," Lydia retorted, her lip curling in disdain. "She's poisoned you against me."

"You've done that yourself. No one's to blame but you."

"You're mistaken. And you're making an even bigger mistake by bringing her here."

"I'll decide that." Without a hint of his usual gentleness, he grasped her forearm and pulled her to the hall. There he released her. "I shall not speak to you again," he said. "I shall never say your name again. From this day on, you are invisible to me."

"You can't be serious!" She gaped at him in astonishment. "You can't mean that! Kit!"

He turned his back and strode into his room, slamming the door behind him. His towel was in no danger of coming off now, and he could walk perfectly well, thanks to Lydia's intrusion. As his stomach churned with anger, he stalked to the bedroom, where he found Camille making the bed. He stopped on the threshold and watched her, his rage rolling off him as he filled his vision with the sight of her hands fluffing his pillows.

"Sorry about that," he began, knowing no words could convey the disappointment he felt in missing the chance to take her to bed.

She turned and smiled sadly. "It's okay, Kit."

He tightened his towel. "It seems we are destined to be interrupted."

"I've heard the third time is the charm, haven't you?"

"That's what they say." He was surprised at how good a sport she was. Her poise, good sense, and honesty continued to amaze him. But now was not the time to try again with her. The air was still heavy with Lydia's venom, and he knew his heart would not be in his embraces. Above all, Camille deserved his full attention. Perhaps after the Japanese left, he'd make arrangements to take her away for the weekend so they could have as much time together as they wanted, without the threat of interruption.

And maybe by then he'd know for certain which one of them was making love.

Oscar punched in Two Hand's office phone number and waited impatiently for him to answer, all the while playing with a gold coin in his right hand.

"Donald Two Hand," came a gruff voice on the other end.

"Where in the devil have you been?" Oscar demanded without preface.

"I've been busy, Doc. In case you haven't heard, Barbara Stanton's body washed ashore yesterday."

"I heard. I heard."

"Well, I had to take care of that. And by the way—Kit Makinna thinks she might have been murdered."

"He does, does he?"

"I asked him to keep quiet, but he wasn't too keen on the idea."

"Shades of his brother."

"Yeah. And I don't like it. This isn't going as you planned, Doc."

"Yes, it is, Two Hand, and that's why I'm calling." He held the gold coin up to the light and smiled. "I've got a doubloon in my hand."

"A what?"

"A doubloon. An old Spanish coin."

"You serious?" Two Hand sputtered.

"I've never been more serious in my life. And I've got ten more gold pieces on my kitchen table."

"Where'd you find them?"

"Near the clay bank by the beach."

"The clay bank?"

"Yes. The storm must have dislodged them. I went out yesterday by myself to see what I could find on the other side of the island. And lo and behold, there they were, lying on the ground!"

"Who-ee!" Two Hand yelped so loudly that Oscar had to hold the receiver away from his ear. "I'll be damned, Doc. Here I am, finding bodies, and you're finding Spanish doubloons!"

"The fort has to be there somewhere. And once we find

that, we'll find the rest of the treasure. It's only a matter of time."

"Yeah, time."

"What about the Japanese visitors? Can you get away to the island today?"

"Not hardly. We're having a big feast and some ceremonial dances. I'm participating, so I have to hang around today and tonight."

"What about tomorrow?"

"Tomorrow the Japanese'll be going out to the island. You'll have to keep clear of the place, Doc, it being sacred and all."

"Fine. I'll just go out today by myself."

"By the way, that Avery woman does have Barbara Stanton's journal. Makinna mentioned that he might be able to get it for me."

"Good. I broke into the cabin last night, thinking she would be at the lodge, and Makinna showed up and just about caught me."

"I take it you didn't get the journal?"

"I didn't even see it. And I looked everywhere. Who knows where she hides it."

"What happens if she and Makinna start asking questions, though, Doc? What happens if the FBI gets in on this?"

"By the time anyone makes a move we'll be long gone, Two Hand, long gone."

"That's what you say."

"And you better believe it." He smiled again, feeling ten years drop from his tired muscles. "I'm taking these gold pieces out to the barn for safekeeping. Then I'm going to the island."

"If you find anything, let me know."

"I'll call you."

Oscar hung up and did a little jig around the kitchen table. He hadn't felt this happy in eons.

At the breakfast table, Camille took a bite of one of Hattie's delicious huckleberry muffins, still warm from the oven, and looked over the table at Kit. "What time is the dinner this evening?" she asked.

"Seven o'clock, with dancing afterward. We're leaving about six forty-five to get over to the community house. Why?"

She shrugged, wondering if she should tell Kit about her plans to investigate Oscar's barn. She knew Kit would object to her going alone, but she didn't want to wait around for his help. He was due to take the Japanese on a tour in an hour and would be gone most of the day. Afterward he would be busy preparing for the salmon feast and wouldn't have time to help her. Besides, in the back of her mind Camille could hear Lydia accusing Kit of baby-sitting her. *Baby-sitting.* The phrase made her angry. She was a grown woman and didn't need anyone to hold her hand, not even Kit.

"I have to run some errands."

"Do you need wheels?"

"Well"—she sipped her coffee—"that would make it easier."

Kit reached into the pocket of his jeans and pulled out a cluster of keys. He slid off a silver key and held it out. "Take my Jeep."

"Don't you need it?"

"I'll be driving the van all day."

"Are you certain?"

"Sure." He smiled and dropped it in her hand. "Just don't run off to Canada with it, okay?"

"Okay." She accepted the key and looked into his eyes. "Thanks, Kit. You're always helping me."

His left eyelid fluttered almost imperceptibly as he gazed at her. Then he broke off and looked out the window. "Just being a good neighbor, Avery, that's all."

20

After breakfast, Camille grabbed her parka and went out on the deck, looking for Mak-ee-nah in his raven form. Almost as soon as she stepped outside, she spied a black bird gliding out of a nearby madrona tree. He landed on the rail, just inches from her hand.

"Mak-ee-nah?" Camille said softly, not wanting to make a fool of herself if anyone happened to be watching.

The bird cocked its head and peered up at her, his shoe-button eye ringed by short black feathers that looked like eyelashes.

"Ready to go?"

The bird clacked its beak together.

"You fly, I'll follow." She showed him the car keys, hoping he would realize she would have to go by road and not in a straight direction. Then she walked to the Jeep and got in, making sure the raven was still on the railing. The bird swooped down and perched on the hood of the vehicle, proving to Camille that he understood.

Camille put the key in the ignition and glanced at the dashboard controls. Kit's truck was clean and uncluttered and smelled faintly of his scent. She sat back and breathed in, glad that he had loaned her his vehicle. Then she started up the engine, turned on the heater, and rolled backward out of the parking space. Mak-ee-nah took off, flying down the lane to the main road.

Driving through the small town of Crescent Bay, Camille realized how long it had been since she had seen civilization. But the fact didn't bother her. She was accustomed to being cut off from the city. The Lewis Academy was located in a rural area outside Charleston, and she rarely left the grounds for most of the school year.

The only other time she had seen Crescent Bay was in the dark, which had concealed the run-down appearance of the town. Most of the houses were weather-beaten and unlandscaped, yet they fit in somehow with the windblown bluffs and huge stands of cedar that ringed the wide gray bay from which the town took its name. With one eye on the raven up ahead and one eye on the scenery, Camille drove past Crescent Bay High—home of the unbeaten Bears, according to the sign near the road.

Just after the school, the road turned to a gravel lane that headed inland. Camille slowed down and bumped her way deeper and deeper into the forest until she came over a rise and saw an old homestead in a valley. Sitting in the middle of the valley near a meandering river was an ancient gray barn. Oscar Duarte's warehouse? As if in answer, the raven soared across the meadow toward the building and alighted on top of the crooked weather vane shaped in the form of a running horse.

Camille pulled behind a copse of trees to conceal the Jeep and then walked down the hill to the back of the barn. She could see no sign of anyone, except for a faint pattern of tire treads in the mud of the dirt lane. The barn looked deserted, as did the house a few hundred yards down the drive. The windows of both buildings were broken, and the moss-covered roofs sagged on their rotting timbers. The homestead probably hadn't been lived in for fifty years. What better place to hide stolen artifacts?

Still, Camille couldn't be sure she was the only one around. She moved cautiously, keeping low until she came to a door in the side of the barn. She pushed it open and walked down a narrow hall bordered on both sides by small storerooms and the remains of a crude bunkhouse. The barn was dark and musty and smelled of moldering wood—the comforting scent of horses and cattle having dissipated long ago. At the end of the hall, she came upon the main floor of the barn, which was lined with stalls and had a hayloft on one end. Remembering Mak-ee-nah's mention of bales of hay, Camille walked to the loft area to look for evidence of the stolen artifacts.

She found a rusted pitchfork leaning against a wood support and used it to sift through the loose hay. Perhaps Oscar had missed something, left one clue with which she could link him to this barn and the theft, and possibly the death of Barbara. As she was rooting around in the hay, she heard a vehicle approaching.

Camille froze. Who would be coming out here? Oscar? She glanced around, searching wildly for a place to conceal herself. She caught sight of a wooden ladder reaching to the loft above. While the vehicle stopped outside the barn, Camille climbed up and scrambled onto the rickety floor above, easing back from the edge so that she could not be seen.

The main door of the barn opened on ancient hinges with a drawn-out screech. She saw the silhouette of a tall, stooped man, the same silhouette as that of the intruder who had broken into the cabin. Oscar Duarte walked across the floor of the barn, limping slightly. He went straight to the old pile of hay and out of her view. Frustrated that she couldn't watch what he was doing, Camille inched her way forward, far enough to peer over the edge. The old hay was full of dust and cobwebs, which tickled her nose and made her eyes water, but she forced back a sneeze and held her breath for as long as possible while she fought the urge to cough.

Oscar took a small bag out of his coat pocket, grinned at it, and then knelt on the floor. He brushed away the hay and felt along the plank floor. To Camille's amazement, he lifted one of the planks, put it aside, and dropped the bag in a hole in the floor. In her eagerness to see what was in the hiding place, she hunched forward, pulling herself by grabbing on to a nearby beam. The movement, coupled with her weight shift upon the edge of the loft, cracked a rotting beam beneath the loft floor. The floor tilted with a lurch, nearly tossing her to the ground, and she would have fallen but for her tenacious grasp of the beam above her head. Another crack and the loft floor plunged downward, knocking Oscar off his feet. Camille hung in midair, her feet flailing helplessly as Oscar glared up at her in anger and surprise.

Then, in a final calamitous touch, the beam she held on to pulled free of its moorings and gave way. Camille dropped through the air and hit the flagstones with a thud. Hay filtered down upon her, covering her with a fine coating of dust. She scrambled to her hands and knees, coughing and sneezing, hoping to recover before Oscar Duarte could catch her. But for a few moments all she could do was crouch on the floor and wait for her eyes to quit watering.

"You!" Oscar shouted, panting as he gained his feet.

Camille squinted up at him. His slight body wavered before her as she sneezed and wiped at her eyes.

"Get up!" Oscar demanded.

Camille's vision cleared enough to see that he had produced a small pistol, which he pointed at her. She glanced around, wondering whether he would shoot her if she tried to run for the side door, and decided against bolting, unsure of Oscar's character.

Coughing, she struggled to her feet and brushed the hay from her hair and off her shoulders.

"What do you think you're doing here?" Oscar said, taking a step closer.

"I was looking for stolen items taken from the Nakalt burial grounds."

"How'd you find out about this place?"

"A little bird told me."

"Funny, Miss Avery. But I'm not amused."

"Neither am I, Duarte. You're stealing sacred objects, and I intend to stop you."

"And how, pray tell?"

Camille glanced at his pistol and back to his face.

A sneer curled his lips into an ugly, crooked line. "You see, I have a gun and you don't, Miss Avery. So just who is going to stop whom?"

"You wouldn't shoot me," Camille began, her words more certain than the way she felt inside. "You wouldn't kill me over Nakalt artifacts."

"Perhaps not. But I can't have you going to the authorities. That would make me very unhappy."

"Unhappy? How do you think the Nakalt feel about having their graves robbed?"

"What they don't know won't hurt them one bit." He brushed a strand of hay from his thin brown hair. "Besides, a golf course is going to be built on the island. They can't care too much about the dead out there."

"It depends on whom you talk to."

"What would you know? I've spent the last six years living near the reservation. I know these people for what they are. And believe me, Miss Avery, they don't give a damn about artifacts. All they care about is whether they have enough money to buy booze and cigarettes."

Camille lunged at him, unmindful of the gun. Oscar skittered backward and fired the pistol to scare her. She stopped in her tracks, enraged and glowering, her anger intensified by her helplessness.

"I can see you won't cooperate, Miss Avery."

"With a man like you? Never."

"Too bad. Because you aren't going to leave this place alive."

"You wouldn't dare kill me!"

"You suffer under a misconception. Either you are more stupid than you look, or you don't realize how serious I am."

He waved the gun toward the side door.

"What are you going to do with me?"

"For now, lock you away where you can't get into any more trouble."

"And then what?"

"Keep you here until you tell me where Barbara Stanton's journal is."

"I don't know where it is."

"You're lying." He jabbed the pistol in the small of her back. "Now get moving."

Too angry to be afraid, Camille stumbled toward the side door until Oscar told her to stop in front of one of the storerooms. Then he flung open the door and pushed her inside. Camille staggered headlong into the dark cubicle, dimly lit by a small window far above her head.

"There," he exclaimed. "You can stay here until your memory improves."

Camille rushed back toward the door and flung herself against it even as she heard a bolt slide in place on the other side.

"Don't bother to scream," Oscar said from the other side of the thick wood door. "It won't do you any good. There's no one around for miles."

"Go to hell, Duarte!"

"Oh, I probably shall. But I intend to enjoy my retirement first. Good day, Miss Avery."

She stood close to the door and listened as he walked out of the barn and drove away. As the sound of his Volvo disappeared, Camille sighed and turned to survey her surroundings.

The storeroom was about twenty by fifteen feet, with a door on the short side and a window opposite. From what she could see, the window was so dirty that it barely allowed light to pass through it. And she knew without trying that she would never be able to reach high enough to use the window as a way of escape. Above the window ran a huge log beam, one of the main supports of the roof. Camille studied it with a deepening frown, wondering if it was as rotten as the beam in the loft.

Sighing again, she glanced around. The room was bare except for some cardboard boxes stacked against the wall. She walked over and opened the flaps of one. It contained a jumble of canning jars, home to a variety of spiders, and metal jar rings spotted with age. The second box was full of castoff clothing and a pair of cowboy boots. The third box, newer than the others, was taped shut. Camille used her thumb nail to break the seal. Then she pulled back the flaps and peered into the box. Her heart dropped to her feet.

There in the box was the gray chassis of Barbara's laptop computer.

Her first instinct was to grab the computer out of the box. On second thought, however, she realized the chassis might be marked with Duarte's fingerprints, which would be valuable evidence in court. She shouldn't disturb it. Camille frowned down at the box. If the computer was here in the barn, did that mean that Oscar had locked Barbara in the barn as well? What had he done with her after that?

Camille clenched her teeth and forced her thoughts to a different subject. She had to get out of the storeroom and stop Oscar Duarte once and for all, but how? She pulled on the door handle with all her strength and rattled the door, but the bolt held fast. She couldn't get out that way. Once again she turned and looked up at the small grimy window. Another impossible exit. She was stuck.

Disheartened, Camille sank to the floor and hugged her knees, wondering how long it would be before anyone missed her. Kit would be busy most of the day. Hattie planned to spend the entire day baking fresh bread and pies. Adam had probably been roped in by Lydia to work around the lodge for the entire weekend. No one would think about her. No one would miss her. Not until seven that evening would anyone know she was missing.

Camille leaned her chin on her kneecap while her gaze roved each corner of her prison cell. She looked up, thinking how Barbara had hidden her journal on the beam in the cabin. Her gaze ran along the foot-thick log, as silvery with age as the totem poles on North Beach. The beam met the wall of the barn a few feet above the window. Too bad she wasn't a rat and could scamper her way up the wall, across the beam, and over to the windowsill. Too bad she wasn't a spider like the ones in the canning jars and could spin a silken bridge to the window.

A silken bridge to the window. Camille looked at the beam again, then the window, and then at the second box, while an inkling of a plan blossomed in her thoughts.

She scrambled to her feet and emptied the contents of the second box. The articles of clothing mounded around her feet. She picked up a man's white shirt and tugged at it with both hands. Though old, the fabric was still tough. She threw the shirt in a separate pile and then rummaged through the rest of the garments for the largest pieces and those in the best condition. Then, with her heart calm and steady, she sat on the floor and knotted the clothing together to form a fabric rope. Using only the best pieces, she created a rope about fifteen feet long, which when flung over the beam would hang about six feet on either side, not nearly long enough.

Camille added the remaining garments to the chain— ending with a gray woolen sock with a hole in the toe—and spent a good half hour trying to get it up and over the beam. But the weight of the cloth wasn't heavy enough to drag the rope over the beam and down to the ground. She'd need something to weigh down one end.

Glancing around the room proved once again to Camille that the place was barren, except for the three cardboard boxes. She couldn't see a single board or rock on the flagstone floor. She'd have to make do with the contents of the boxes. She eliminated the box full of jars and rings, knowing it would be too dangerous to throw glass through the air. The second box was empty. That left the third. Though she was reluctant to disturb the laptop computer, Camille reached down and moved it aside, using the end of the cloth rope. Beneath the computer was a manual and the power adapter. Camille picked up the adapter by its cable and held it in the air near her nose. The adapter itself was smaller than most radios used by joggers. But it was as heavy as a piece of lead and would slip easily into the old gray sock. Camille nodded in satisfaction and put it down so that she could untie the sock from the chain and insert the adapter.

The adapter did the trick. With one well-aimed toss, Camille sent the cloth chain up and over the beam and caught the other end as it swung back toward her. She slid the rope into position near the wall, tied it into a knot to keep it in place, and then tested the strength of the cloth by hanging on it, her feet still on the ground. The rope stretched but held together. Next she yanked on it, pulling her weight off the floor. The rope held.

Camille wiped her palms on her jeans and grimaced at the wall. She wasn't accustomed to gymnastics or mountain climbing and prayed that her arms would support her as she tried to walk up the wall. She clenched her teeth and reminded herself it wasn't a matter of trying to walk up the wall. She *had* to walk up the wall, or she'd never get out of this barn.

Taking a deep, resolute breath, Camille reached for the rope and put her right foot on the log wall of the barn. Then, grasping the knotted rope, she pulled herself up, gasping and groaning, until she got near the window. There she found she could wedge her foot on the tiny sill as she leaned against the huge beam, which was in good enough condition to support her weight. She remained wedged between beam and window, catching her breath as she planned her next move. She'd have to break the window and somehow climb through it without slashing herself. And who knew how far she'd have to drop from the window to the ground.

After a minute or so she knew she'd have to make a move. She couldn't remain wedged in the rafters forever. Besides, her foot near the window, which supported most of her weight, was already cramping from the strain. Camille braced her hips on the beam and used the heel of her free foot to smash the glass of the window. Icy wind blew in through the gash. Camille continued to kick out as much of the glass as she could. She straightened, wondering how badly she'd cut herself if she went through the window, for a few pointed tips still clung to the glazing.

Camille pulled up the end of the rope and took the adapter out of the wool sock. Then, after some careful shifting of her position, and holding on to the rope for safety with one hand, she leaned forward and used the back of the adapter to scrape the window frame free of glass. From her new position she could see down to the ground, which was covered with tall green plants whose saw-toothed leaves seemed vaguely familiar. Camille stared down at them.

"Ducky," she muttered. "Nettles again."

For a moment she glared at the stinging plants in dismay, but she decided she wouldn't get stung much this time, since she was dressed in jeans, boots, and a coat. Only her hands were exposed. She'd just make sure to hightail it out of the nettles once she hit the ground. In fact, as she pulled away from the window, she realized she could use her rope chain and crawl down the side of the barn just as she had crawled up. She wouldn't even have to jump in the nettles.

Heartened by the prospect, Camille tied the rope in a slipknot around the beam and tossed the free end out of the window. Then, with a tricky bit of maneuvering, she managed to back through the window. Her hands and arms burned with the strain as she crawled down the side of the barn. A stiff wind blew her hair into her eyes, which made the job even more difficult. But she gradually lowered herself to the ground and, once on solid footing, scampered out of the nettles to a patch of grass near the corner of the barn.

Camille stood on the grass, shaking out her cramped shoulders and trembling hands. Her palms burned, her arms ached, and her whole body was covered with a sheen of sweat. But she had made it. She was out of the barn. And now she had evidence that Oscar Duarte had something to do with Barbara's disappearance and possibly her death.

Not wasting another minute, Camille skittered around to the front of the barn and ran back to the storeroom to retrieve the box that still held the laptop computer. She pulled the adapter out of the pocket of her parka and dropped it into the box as well. Who knew what she might find on the computer once she had the chance to view its files, and she'd need the adapter if the computer's battery was dead.

She also took time to retrieve the mysterious pouch left under the floorboards by Oscar Duarte. She pulled out the bag, which was unusually heavy. Curious, Camille opened the bag and reached in to find a cache of old coins. She held one up to the light and was amazed to see a gold doubloon. Had Oscar found buried treasure? Camille stashed the pouch in the box with the computer and stood up, not about to waste precious time staring at the gold pieces.

As she came out of the side door of the barn, she was startled by the large black raven as it swooped down at her head.

"A lot of help you were," she called out, carrying the cardboard box up the hill to the Jeep.

The raven cawed loudly and swooped past her head again, so close that Camille had to duck.

"Hey!" she exclaimed. "Mak-ee-nah!"

She opened the back of the Jeep and hoisted the box into the truck. When she closed the hatch, she saw the bird headed directly toward her again. What was wrong with him? He seemed more agitated than ever. Was Oscar coming back? Was she in danger?

"What is it?" she demanded, avoiding the tips of his wings as he glided past and landed on the hood of the vehicle. She walked to the driver's side and opened the door.

"What? Do you want me to follow you again?"

The raven tilted its head.

"Okay. I'll follow. You lead."

She got into the Jeep and started the engine. The raven flapped into the air and rose up, following the lane farther into the valley.

Soon, however, the dirt road angled upward, winding around on switchbacks until they reached the summit of a small mountain that faced the Pacific Ocean. Here the trees were sculpted by the wind off the sea, twisted into wraiths by the harsh weather, stunted by their continual battle against the elements. The bluff seemed other-worldly, spooky and darker than the rest of the landscape, and she was suddenly reluctant to continue.

Mak-ee-nah alighted in a snag of sea pine and cawed. Camille stopped the Jeep and climbed out.

"What is it?" she asked. "Why have we come all the way up here?"

The raven bobbed its head between its shoulders and soared to a bush nearby, waiting for Camille to follow. Zipping up her coat, she ambled forward, unsure if she was correctly interpreting the actions of the bird. As soon as she got to the bush, the raven soared to another pine twenty feet away. Camille walked to him, and he flew off again. The pattern continued for about a half hour, down a faint trail in the rocky landscape. Camille was beginning to think she was being led on a wild goose chase and that she should turn back. She had more important things to do than follow a raven into the Olympic wilderness. Besides, she didn't like the looks of this dark, rock-strewn expanse.

She was just about ready to turn back when the trail jutted around a corner and angled between a jumble of huge rocks that had rolled down the mountain eons ago. The raven cawed and clacked and paced the top of a huge black boulder covered with lichen. Camille frowned and stomped around it, cold and impatient, wondering what the fuss was all about.

When she got to the other side of the rock, she sucked in her breath.

There was Old Man, lying on the ground, his frail, withered body surrounded by wolves.

21

"Old Man!" she exclaimed in horror.

The wolves gazed at her but didn't move. They seemed to be giving their body heat to the old man by lying close to his body. The notch-eared wolf cocked his head and panted as Camille appoached.

"It's all right," she crooned to the wolves. "I'll help him."

As if on cue, the wolves rose to their feet and padded a few yards away to sit.

Camille knelt by Old Man and touched his shoulder.

"Old Man," she called, hoping he could hear her.

His parchment-lidded eyes fluttered at the sound of her voice. Camille caressed the side of his face with her hand. His skin was warm, thanks to the wolves. She wondered how long he had been lying there.

"Old Man, it's me—Camille."

His lids fluttered again, and this time they opened, revealing black eyes dull with pain.

"I fell," he mumbled. "My leg—"

Camille glanced down at his legs but couldn't see any apparent injury.

"Which one?"

"My left. Below the knee. Broken."

"All right, Old Man. I'll get you out of here. Don't you worry."

His eyes closed and he seemed to relax, as if he trusted her to help him.

Camille tried not to panic. She had never set a bone or even splinted one, for that matter. As a teacher she had taken first-aid training and knew the theories, but she'd never actually had to employ them. Now it was up to her to help Old Man. And since he was so old, her care might mean life or death to him. She sat on her heels and looked around.

She could use a stick to splint his leg, but how would she get him to the truck? He was probably too weak to hobble on his good leg, and she wouldn't be able to offer him much support, being short and small herself. There was no way to carry him out. Even a makeshift stretcher would require two people to walk him back to the Jeep. If she drove to town for help, she would waste valuable time and endanger him even further. She couldn't bear the thought of leaving him alone on this forbidding hilltop, much less leaving him to die.

She couldn't leave. But she knew she wasn't capable of carrying Old Man to safety. She couldn't do it herself. Biting back a flood of frustrated tears, Camille glanced up. The raven sat on a branch above her, staring at her.

Only one recourse remained to her—the amber necklace. If she gave it to Mak-ee-nah, he would turn into a man. He could save Old Man's life. Though she was uncertain of the consequences of giving the necklace to Mak-ee-nah and relinquishing such power to him, she decided it was her only choice. She prayed for the legend to be true, that Mak-ee-nah was a just and kind man, and that once in possession of the amulet he would not abuse his power.

With a trembling hand she reached into the neckline of her sweater and drew out the amber disk. Carefully she pulled the thong over her head and held out the necklace. It swung in the wind. The raven cocked his head.

"This is yours, Mak-ee-nah. Take it and help me save Old Man."

She raised up the necklace as the raven dropped to the ground. His eyes were bright and piercing as she gently draped the thong around his feathered neck.

A thunderclap rumbled overhead and startled her. Rain pelted her as she watched the raven flap upward. A momentary wave of terror passed over her as she wondered if she had given the necklace to an ordinary bird who would take away the amber forever. Yet this bird had led her to Old Man. This bird had to be Mak-ee-nah.

Even as she doubted her actions, she saw a blur of black as the raven ascended and then hung in the air, becoming in another clap of thunder the magnificent creature she knew as Mak-ee-nah, powerful *tyee* of the Nakalt.

"So!" he bellowed triumphantly, turning to face her. His face was alight with joy. The amulet hung on his sculpted body, between the planes of his powerful chest, as if it had been tailor-made to fit his form. The rest of his body was naked, except for a loincloth fashioned of black feathers.

Camille scrambled to her feet, wondering what he was going to do.

"So!" he exclaimed again. "The amber is mine!"

"Yes," she answered, stepping backward.

"I am a man! I am human!"

"Yes."

"You will not be sorry, *klootz-mah*. Do not worry."

She nodded, still wondering what would happen. Her idea of what she might regret probably differed greatly from his.

"And now we will take this ancient one back to his lodge."

Camille sighed in relief. She shouldn't have doubted Mak-ee-nah. She wiped her rain-soaked bangs off her forehead and turned to Old Man.

Camille found two branches with which to immobilize Old Man's leg and tied them around his shin with her T-shirt, which she had ripped in two. Then, as if Old Man were as light as a scarecrow or a rag doll, Mak-ee-nah lifted him into his arms and gently carried him to the Jeep.

Camille opened the back door and unlatched the rear seat, easing it down to form a flat area on which to lay Old Man. She moved aside the box she had taken from the storeroom and then got into the back of the Jeep while Mak-ee-nah stood holding Kit's grandfather in his arms. Between the two of them they managed to ease Old Man into the hatch and settle him with Camille's parka draped over him for warmth. Then she turned to Mak-ee-nah.

"I have to take him to a doctor. Let's go."

"In this vehicle?"

"Yes. Hop in."

He glanced at the Jeep, cocking his eyebrow in distrust.

She smiled at him. "It's okay. I'm a good driver. Just go around to the other side, push the button on the door, and get in!"

She climbed in the Jeep and waited. Mak-ee-nah turned to the wolves, who had followed them to the road, and said something to them in his native language. Notch Ear turned and trotted away, leading the rest of the wolves through a stand of sea pine and down the mountain.

For a moment Mak-ee-nah struggled with the button on the door and then got in, settling himself on the seat while he looked all around the cab.

"Close the door, Mak-ee-nah."

"So!" He slammed the door with much more force than necessary and then settled back, his arms crossed.

"Ready?" she asked, grinning at him.

"Yes. Go, *klootz-mah*. I am not afraid."

The heck he wasn't. She hid another grin as she shifted into drive and barreled down the mountain, headed for Makinna Lodge. Mak-ee-nah braced his hands on the dashboard and held on for dear life.

They pulled into the parking lot at the back of the lodge just as Adam walked across the deck with an armful of firewood.

Camille rolled down her window. "Adam!" she yelled.

He looked back at the sound of his name. When she motioned for him to come to the truck, he put down his load of wood and jogged up to the window.

"Adam, you've got to show me where the hospital is. Old Man's been hurt."

"Old Man?" Adam exclaimed. "Is he bad?"

"Broke his leg," she answered. "Can you come with me?"

"Sure. I'll tell Hattie where I'm going. Be right back!"

He flew across the deck, darted into the back entry, and reappeared an instant later, his coat in his hand. Then he got in the Jeep. Mak-ee-nah stood off to the side in the shadow of the madrona trees. He had decided to stay to look for Oscar while Camille took Old Man to the hospital.

Adam glanced at Mak-ee-nah. "Uncle Kit, I thought you were with the Japanese."

Mak-ee-nah shut the door while Adam stared at him. Adam's jaw dropped as he apparently realized the man with the tattooed face and ring in his nose was not his uncle at all. In fact, he was like no Nakalt man he had ever seen.

"Who are you?" he said, gasping.

"I am Mak-ee-nah. *Tyee.*"

"*Tyee?*" Adam croaked, leaning forward so he could see Camille.

"It's a long story, Adam. I'll tell you all about it when we get to the hospital. Now where do we have to go?"

"Port Angeles. About fifty miles."

Camille's grip tightened on the wheel. She raced through Crescent Bay, unmindful of police who might be lying in wait for speeders, her mind focused on the old man stretched out in the back of the Jeep, suffering.

That night at six-fifteen, Camille rolled into the parking lot of Makinna Lodge and set the brake. She was dead tired. The day had been long and grueling, but at least Old Man was out of danger. She wasn't sure she'd have enough energy to attend the salmon feast. She unlatched her door, grateful that Mak-ee-nah was not with her. She had no desire to explain his presence to everyone she met, at least not until she'd had a cup of strong black coffee and a bath.

Kit burst from the house as she slipped out of the truck.

"How is Old Man?" he asked, trotting up to the passenger side.

Adam got out. "He's fine, Uncle Kit. He wouldn't stay overnight at the hospital, so we brought him home."

Kit opened the back door and helped his grandfather

out, supporting most of the old man's weight but still allowing him the dignity of keeping to his feet. Adam joined his uncle and wrapped Old Man's arm around his neck to bolster his other side. Camille slid the cardboard box out of the back and followed the men to the steps of the lodge and into the warm, dry house.

She was so cold, wet, and tired she thought she'd never feel warm again.

Hattie bustled around the registration desk. "Old Man! God be praised! We were so worried about you!"

He looked at her over the tops of his glasses. "The wolves kept me warm."

"Wolves?" Hattie looked from Old Man to Kit and then to Camille.

Camille swept past her. "We'll explain later. We have to get Old Man to bed."

"Nonsense!" Old Man sputtered. "I'm going to the feast. I have much to tell my people."

"For crying out loud, Old Man," Kit protested. "You nearly lost your life out there. You can't go to the feast tonight."

"I can and I will. You will not stop me, Kitsap. This is a very important night. And I will be there."

Kit sighed, exasperated. "You're going to bed."

"Kitsap." Old Man clutched the sleeve of his grandson's shirt. "I am an old man. I will not live to see many more feasts. This is important to me. Very important."

"You're talking nonsense—"

"I will rest, and then you and Adam and Miss Avery will take me there."

Kit turned. "Is he on some kind of painkiller, Camille?"

"No. He wouldn't take any of the prescribed medicine."

"Worthless powder," Old Man muttered. "Medical science, bah!"

Camille smiled. If Old Man could grouse about doctors, he was going to be all right. She put her hand on the stair rail. "We'll take you, Old Man, if you promise to go right to bed afterward."

He pushed up his glasses and looked at her. "I promise, Miss Avery."

"Good. I'm going up to change, then, Kit."

"Make it fast, Camille. We only have about a half hour."

She hurried up to his room and turned on the water in the shower to warm it while she stripped off her clothes. It felt odd not to have the amulet against her skin as she disrobed. She wondered what the Nakalt people would think when Mak-ee-nah showed up at the celebration. And what would Kit think when he saw his double in the flesh? Camille stepped into the hot shower and closed her eyes, trying to draw strength from the steaming water.

The shower did make her feel much better. She combed her hair, smoothed on body lotion, and slipped into her outfit, a simple black skirt and a white angora sweater with pearls sewn in a circular design around the neck. Then she applied her makeup, wishing she didn't look so wan, and hoped her rose-colored lipstick would brighten her appearance.

After she'd finished with her makeup, she fluffed her platinum hair, which was nearly dry already, and slicked it back behind her left ear.

Just as she was about finished, she heard someone knock on the door. "Come in," she called.

Kit entered the room, carrying a steaming mug. "Hi," he said. "Hattie made some fresh coffee for you. Would you like some?"

"I'd love some!" She stepped out of the bathroom.

Kit glanced at her, and his gaze went down and up and back down again, as a slow smile of approval melted the usual bitterness at the corners of his mouth. Camille felt as if she had stepped back into the warm shower.

"You look wonderful," he murmured, walking up to her.

"Thanks."

She took the mug from his hands, and he reached out and cupped the tops of her arms, admiring the fine drape and softness of her elegant sweater. He caressed her shoulders, squeezing the tops of her arms, and then bent down to kiss her ear.

"You smell good enough to eat," he whispered.

His words and lips sent a thrill down her back, and she nearly spilled the coffee.

"Kit—"

"Okay, okay." He smiled and backed away. "I don't want to muss you."

Camille took a sip of the coffee and gazed up at him, her eyes warm with love. He also looked great. He was dressed in black, with a white shirt and a burgundy-and-black tie. The dark color set off his hair and eyes and accentuated the whiteness of his teeth. He was clean-shaven and newly scrubbed, laced with the seductive yet feather-light cedar scent he favored. Camille breathed in and smiled. He had never seemed so handsome to her.

"You look great yourself, Mr. Makinna."

"Not magnificent?" he asked, mocking her. "Like that Mak-ee-nah character?"

"Okay, stupendous. You could make a woman swoon at a hundred paces."

"Why aren't you swooning, then?"

"I would, but I have more important things to do."

"Like what?"

"Like putting on my earrings."

She turned on her heel and went back to the bathroom. The coffee and Kit's appearance had given her the jolt she needed to change her mood. She felt happy, almost light. As she selected a pair of pearl studs, she heard Kit come up behind her. She concentrated on her task, pushing the earring through her lobe and sliding on the back, ignoring the fact that Kit was watching her every move. After she put in the other earring, she let her gaze wander up to his in the mirror, and a tight feeling wrapped around her heart.

He stood behind her, his black suit matching her black skirt, his white shirt a twin of her white sweater. For all the world they looked like a matched pair, as if they belonged together, as if they could pose for figures on a wedding cake. Kit met her glance, and she saw the familiar patches of crimson paint his cheekbones as he flushed—perhaps from the realization that they looked so good together. Slowly he raised his hands and grasped her shoulders, while they stared at each other's reflections. In that moment Camille thought she saw love flash in Kit's eyes.

"Who are you?" he said softly, his voice hoarse.

"I don't know anymore," she replied. "I'm losing myself here."

"Losing?" His thumbs caressed the base of her neck. "Or finding?"

"That's a fine line to draw sometimes, Kit, don't you think?"

"Yeah. It is." His hands stopped stroking her, and he broke eye contact. "Are you ready to go, Avery?"

She nodded and felt him draw away. How she hated it when he drew away—and he could do it so quickly, at the slightest provocation. She followed him out the door, which he held open for her.

"Camille," he began as she passed into the doorway.

She turned, expecting him to continue. "Yes?"

"You saved my grandfather's life today. For that I am truly grateful."

"It was nothing."

"It was a lot. He might have died out there."

"He's got a will of iron, Kit. He would have survived somehow."

"I still don't know how you managed to find him."

Camille didn't want to explain how Mak-ee-nah helped her or that he now possessed the amulet. She wanted Kit to find that out for himself at the feast. "Kit, we should go. It's six forty-five."

"Yeah." He shut the bedroom door behind him. "Let's see if Old Man is still awake."

Kit had imagined walking into the community house with Camille on his arm, well aware that the sight would cause a stir, not only because his people thought he was meant for Lydia, but because Camille Avery was such a striking woman and not of the Nakalt tribe. He would have been proud to walk in with her—and was anxious to show her off, actually—and yet tonight he entered the hall with his ancient grandfather on his arm. Had the doorway been wider, he could have been lucky enough to come in with Camille at his side, if not on his arm. Yet due to the crowds already assembled, he was forced to walk with his grandfather and Adam while Hattie and Camille brought up the rear.

Even so, he enjoyed the silence that fell when Camille came through the door, capturing everyone's attention. Kit looked back and saw her moving through the crowd, unaware of the effect she created, her hazel eyes darting around with interest at the cedar planks, painted screens, and the row of alder fires over which slabs of salmon cooked. Kit smiled to himself and helped his grandfather toward the main dais while he heard the name *Lydia* whispered by more than one of the people around him. He didn't know where Lydia was. He hadn't seen her all day, as a matter of fact. But he didn't care, either. Lydia was not his concern anymore.

At the dais, Kit introduced his grandfather to the Japanese entourage, who bowed and spoke of their honor in meeting him. Then Kit introduced Camille as his friend, explaining her work at the reservation. She was settled at the table, as was Adam. Then Kit sat down beside her and pulled in his chair. He was highly conscious of his thigh against hers at the crowded table. Yet she did not move away. Feeling like a schoolboy at a movie theater, Kit slipped his hand under the tablecloth and found hers, wrapping his fingers around hers. He held on to her while he made conversation with the Japanese man at his right. In the back of his mind, however, he thought of nothing but Camille's hand in his and the way she let her fingers relax, as if the position were natural.

Kit hardly tasted dinner, even though it was a bountiful feast of salmon, corn bread with blackberry jam, green salad, and fresh fruit. He was too busy thinking of the way he could convince the elders that a golf course wasn't the answer to the problems of the tribe. He had to come up with a way to change their minds about selling the property but wasn't sure they would listen to a man who'd been off the reservation for six years.

The salmon went down his throat and stuck in a lump. The corn bread, though moist and chewy, seemed like sand in his mouth. He washed down his dinner with coffee and ached for the meal to be over so he could hold Camille's hand once again and think of the night to come.

Surely she would spend the night with him. He couldn't face another night without her.

Kit glanced at her and found her talking to a Japanese woman on her left, carrying on a conversation about how Japanese prints influenced the French Impressionist artists in the late nineteenth century. Kit's glance traveled down the flowing lines of Camille's ivory profile while a flush of pure love washed over him. He could no longer deny that he was in love with her. And when this endless dinner was over, he was going to duck out of the crowd, take her somewhere quiet, and tell her how he felt about her.

Kit's hand shook as he reached for his water glass. If he were honest about it, he would admit to himself that what he really wanted to do was take her to the waterfall and ask her to be his wife. *His wife.* His heart raced at the thought. What would she say? She wouldn't say no. She couldn't say no. It would destroy him. He took a gulp of water. Perhaps he should wait and ask her after everything had settled down and he was more certain of his future and her feelings for him.

At that moment Camille turned and glanced at him, her hazel eyes soft and luminous. Her hand reached for his leg under the table and spread across his thigh, which sent a bolt of desire through him. He covered her fingers with his hand and returned the smile, while the noise of the crowd buzzed unheeded around his head.

After the dinner dishes were cleared, the door in the screen opened and four drummers filed out to the stage area. They set up their drums of hollow planks and arranged their collection of rattles, which were in all kinds of carved animal shapes from birds to bears.

Then they began to drum, a simple beat at first, played just with their rattles. The rhythm slowly gained in intensity and complexity, adding deep tones of the cedar drums. Camille watched, fascinated by the feathered costumes of the drummers and the paint that glittered in stripes and dots on their faces. They had painted their eyebrows in black crescent shapes that lent a surprised or menacing expression, depending upon the way they used their facial muscles. Camille could imagine how fierce they'd look thundering down a beach, waving their battle clubs and yelling a war cry. Their appearance brought Mak-ee-nah to mind, and Camille wondered why he hadn't shown up yet. Knowing Mak-ee-nah, however, he was probably waiting for the right moment so he could make a grand entrance and strike awe in the hearts of the Nakalt. She smiled to herself, recalling the image of Mak-ee-nah's cocky expression and sparkling eyes. No matter when or how he appeared to his people, he would look impressive—it was simply inherent in his bearing and nature.

Once the drummers established a cadence, they were joined by dancers, dressed in the costumes and wooden masks of a bird and a whale, portraying the legend of the huge thunderbird that lived in the mountains and was so large that it could pluck a whale out of the sea. The beak of the thunderbird could be opened to reveal the mask of a scowling human face by pulling strings hidden inside the mask. The dancers hypnotized and delighted Camille, and she found herself swaying backward and forward to the pounding drums and chants.

The next dance featured a man in a bear costume who stalked out in a lively pantomime of the animal. The bear mask was carved in ferocious lines painted red and green, with tufts of fur glued around the edge and bones for teeth. Kit leaned close, using the moment as an excuse to press against her upper arm. "This dance is about a daughter of a chief who went to the mountains to pick berries. She ridiculed bears in front of her friends. The bears, upon hearing the insults, set upon the women and killed all but the chief's daughter. The daughter was given to the king of the bears as a wife. She bore a son, half man and half bear, and by all accounts both the childbirth and suckling of her child were incredibly uncomfortable. But she became the progenitor of all who have the bear as their crest."

"And the moral of the story?" Camille asked.

"Never insult a bear," Kit replied, squeezing her hand. "This dance is usually done by taking a 'victim' out of the audience. So lie low, Avery."

He winked at her. Camille gazed at him, her heart bubbling over with happiness at the warmth she had enjoyed in his company this evening.

She was still looking at him when she heard the crowd hush. Even the drums had died, with only the shake of a single rattle counting out the time. Camille glanced up and saw the huge bear stomping toward her in exaggerated steps.

"Am I it?" she muttered in an aside to Kit.

"It appears so." He released her hand as the crowd began to chant and the ladies to clap. The man in the bear costume dragged Camille out of her chair, pulling her onto the dance floor. Camille smiled, trying to play along, but the man was rough. He yanked her by the arm and dragged her to the stage in front of the drums, posturing and weaving around her. Then he pushed her through the door in the screen.

Camille tumbled forward into darkness. Before she could regain her balance, she was grabbed from behind. Then someone slapped a piece of tape over her mouth.

22

Camille writhed and dragged her feet, but she was pulled out of the back of the community house by the man in the bear costume. Rain beat down on her as the man yanked her across the grass to the parking lot, where another man waited. Camille peered up, working her jaw against the tape in a futile attempt to cry for help. But all she could make were muffled grunts that no one could hear, especially over the drums pounding behind her. In the parking lot was the same pickup she and Mak-ee-nah had seen parked in the forest. Oscar Duarte climbed out of it and hurried toward them.

"You're a resourceful young lady," he said, grabbing her arm. "But you made it worse for yourself, getting out of that storeroom."

She yanked her arm out of his grip and glared at him, but he only chuckled, well aware of his advantage. He pulled a piece of twine out of his jacket pocket.

"Since you aren't cooperating, Miss Avery and you apparently are something of an escape artist"—he continued to talk while he moved behind her—"I'm going to have to tie your hands."

She struggled again, but the man in the bear costume crushed her against his torso and forced her arms back, trapping her in a steel grip that overpowered her petite frame. She wondered who the man behind her was and why he would help Oscar Duarte if he knew how Oscar disdained the Nakalt. Frightened and enraged, Camille turned her face to the side while Oscar lashed her wrists together, pulling the twine so tightly that she was certain the bonds would cut off the circulation to her hands.

"That ought to do it," Oscar said. "Take her to the truck."

The man in the bear costume pushed her forward, and she stumbled in the muddy grass, falling upon one knee.

"Get up!" Oscar demanded.

Camille ignored him. She wasn't about to do anything to aid their cause, not when they intended to abduct her.

"Get up!" Oscar repeated tersely.

She shook her head.

"Difficult little bitch," Oscar swore between clenched teeth. "Get her up, Two Hand."

Two Hand? Camille jerked around in surprise, trying to see the eyes through the holes in the bear mask. Two Hand was helping Oscar Duarte? The chief of police was in on the artifact theft? She couldn't believe it. And yet, after a moment's consideration, it all made sense. His complicity in the crime was the reason Two Hand had wanted her to keep quiet about Barbara's disappearance, about the artifacts, about Barbara's death. Could he have helped Oscar kill Barbara? Camille nearly gagged at the thought.

Then she felt true fear course through her. These men

might mean her real harm—not just abduction and imprisonment, but death. Would Kit realize something had happened to her when she didn't reappear in the community house—or was her detainment part of the dance? How long would it be until someone noticed her absence?

The man in the bear costume reached down and grabbed her left arm, yanked her to her feet, and pulled her toward the truck. His hand squeezed unmercifully. She thought her arm might come out of its socket.

Tears welled up as he dragged her to the passenger side of the truck. Oscar opened the door, and Two Hand reached down to pick her up when he was suddenly thrown to the side, taking Camille with him.

Unable to break her fall with her hands, she hit the gravel parking lot, landing on her shoulder and rolling onto her back. She looked up, blinking the rain and tears out of her eyes, and saw Mak-ee-nah pick up Donald Two Hand and throw him against a car.

"My God!" Oscar gasped in horror. "Who is that?" He backed away from the pickup door, watching Mak-ee-nah wrestle Donald Two Hand to the ground.

Then Oscar seemed to regain his faculties and glared at Camille, who had managed to scramble to her knees.

"Get up!" Oscar shouted over the grunts and crashes of the two men fighting. *"Now,* Miss Avery!"

She looked up at him and saw the deadly gleam in his eye. Before she had time to obey, however, he clutched a handful of her hair and forced her to stand. Camille edged to the door of the truck, her head bent at an angle so he wouldn't pull her hair out by the roots.

"Get in there!" he exclaimed, shoving her onto the bench seat. She fell across the seat and he pushed her legs in and slammed the door. Then he ran around the front of the truck, jumped in, and drove out of the parking lot.

Camille craned her neck to see out of the truck, hoping Mak-ee-nah would be victorious. The last thing she saw before they turned the corner was Two Hand staggering backward in the grass and a line of dark shapes loping along the road behind the truck. Mak-ee-nah must have sent the wolves after her.

"Now you're going to show me where that journal is," Oscar commented, wiping the rain off his face. "Once and for all."

Camille stared at him, realizing that Oscar's voice held the same deadly tone as the look he had given her moments before. She struggled with her bonds, trying in vain to loosen them enough to slip out one hand. But the twine was tight and held fast. Already her fingers tingled with numbness.

Kit glanced again at the community house door, wondering when Camille would come back. Surely she should have returned by now. He wanted to get up and leave but knew it would be rude to interrupt Lydia's dance. Worried and distracted, he returned his gaze to Lydia, who danced upon the stage as the Snow Maiden. She wore a beautiful costume made of mountain goat fur and white leather heavily decorated with dentalium shells and copper medallions. She had braided her long black hair and wrapped the braids with white fabric hung with feathers. Her neck and arms were draped with bangles of copper, shell, and wood. As he watched her, she stepped toward him, dancing only for him. Her hands reached out to caress his face while Kit sat rigid, his eyes hard and unseeing as she demonstrated her love for him in front of hundreds of Na-kalt tribal members. Her behavior was shocking, especially since she had just lost her husband. Many of the elders whispered among themselves, and when Kit glanced at his grandfather, he saw Old Man's mouth pulled tight with disapproval.

Just as Lydia danced backward toward the stage, Kit saw the community door burst open. A man dressed in the bear costume stumbled forward, pushed by another man who strode into the lodge. Kit jumped to his feet in astonishment. He couldn't believe his eyes. There stood the most magnificent man he'd ever seen, proud and fierce, his powerful chest heaving and his hair blowing behind him as he shoved the other man toward the dais.

"It's Mak-ee-nah!" Adam exclaimed.

Kit staggered backward, knocking over his chair while everyone looked from Mak-ee-nah to Kit and back again. The resemblance was overwhelming. If Camille hadn't mentioned how much they looked alike, he would have passed out from sheer shock. Yet even with the forewarning, he was still amazed by Mak-ee-nah's physical presence. All around him people began to chatter—in English, in Nakalt, in Japanese—and the jumbled words tumbled him into another world, as if he were separating from his surrounds.

Incredulous, Kit gaped at Mak-ee-nah, his world shattering around him. All the things his grandfather had told him—the prophecies, the stories, the traditions—all suddenly rang true at the appearance of the legendary chief. In a single instant Kit knew the glory of being a Nakalt and embraced the past without question, as if a burning fireball had been hurled at him and struck him in the heart. His hand splayed across his chest in an involuntary gesture to keep the fireball inside.

"Mak-ee-nah!" he gasped.

All eyes turned to him, including those of Old Man, who nodded sagely.

Mak-ee-nah flung the man in the bear costume to the floor in front of the dais and put his foot on Two Hand's back to hold him down.

"This man has stolen from the dead." Mak-ee-nah addressed Kit, his deep voice carrying to the farthest corners of the hall. "And he has delivered the Snow Maiden to the Spanish one, Oss-car."

"The Snow Maiden?" Lydia repeated in disbelief, stomping forward with her hands on her hips. "*I* am the Snow Maiden!"

Mak-ee-nah turned to Lydia, glanced at her costume and her face, and looked away in disdain. "You are not the Snow Maiden, *klootz-mah.*"

"Yes, I am! I am the Snow Maiden!"

"The Snow Maiden has been taken away by Oss-car. You"—he turned back to her—"are wasting much time."

Lydia stumbled backward, her face blanching, while the crowd went wild.

Mak-ee-nah held up his hand, and instantly the people quieted, anxious to hear what he had to say. "This man has betrayed us." Mak-ee-nah reached down and tore off the bear mask to reveal Donald Two Hand, who crouched on his hands and knees, his head hanging in shame, while the Japanese exchanged expressions of shock and dismay at the dishonorable appearance of their business associate.

Kit observed their reaction and wondered if Two Hand's shame would be enough to sour the deal regarding the Island of the Dead. He knew the Japanese were sticklers about honor. But now was not the time to worry about Nakalt real estate problems or Japanese ethics. Where in the hell was Camille? And what was Oscar Duarte planning to do with her? He held up his hand just as Mak-ee-nah had done, and the crowd hushed.

"Where has Oscar taken Camille?" he asked.

"In his truck. To the river road. I have sent my brothers, the wolf-spirits, to track him."

"Will you go with me?" Kit asked, striding around the table.

Mak-ee-nah nodded. "I will go."

"Me too!" Adam chimed in.

"And me," Old Man called out, his voice cracking.

Mak-ee-nah smiled at the grandfather and scooped him up in his arms. "You will go, old one. Come."

Frank Hall raced up, puffing from the exertion. "Kit, I'll follow you in my truck."

"So will I!" another Nakalt man shouted.

Kit's heart swelled with gratitude as a dozen more men offered their services. He and Mak-ee-nah led the way outside, where they jumped into the Jeep and raced out of the parking lot.

"She gave you the amulet," Kit said, turning the wheel.

"Yes. It is mine."

Kit glanced at Mak-ee-nah, wishing he had time to study the man up close. It felt strange to look at someone who was so similar in appearance to himself and yet came from such a different time. Camille had every right to be impressed with Mak-ee-nah and call him magnificent. He was an impressive man, every inch a *tyee*.

"Mak-ee-nah helped her save Old Man," Adam put in, leaning forward on his seat.

"So that's how she got him off the mountain," Kit replied. "I wondered how she did it."

"Now we must save Ca-meel." Mak-ee-nah crossed his arms. "She is the Snow Maiden and must not die before the prophecy is fulfilled."

Kit squinted. "Damn!" he said, flipping on the windshield wipers. "It's starting to snow. I can't see a thing."

"It is no matter. My brothers will tell me where Oss-car goes."

Kit fishtailed around a corner, then headed down the river road, praying they would be in time to save Camille. No matter how diligently the wolves followed Oscar, they could not compete with the technology of man, be it motor vehicle or automatic weapon. Oscar could very well have outdistanced Mak-ee-nah's wolves. And if Oscar had a gun, he could have shot Camille by now. To purge his mind of fear and concentrate on the dangerous driving conditions, he forced himself to think of something else. *Two is one, one is two, two is three.* In his mind he repeated the puzzle again, filling his thoughts with the chant as he sped through the blinding snow with a caravan of pickups and cars behind him.

They drove in silence for twenty minutes until they rounded a curve near the bay, where the Quincille River emptied into the strait. Old Man sat up in surprise.

"My dream," he declared. "There is the bridge, Kitsap. She must be here."

"She is here, Old Man," Mak-ee-nah agreed. "My brothers are close by."

"Stop the Jeep, Uncle Kit," Adam screeched. "There's a guardrail busted. They must have gone over the edge!"

Kit skidded to a stop in the snow, sliding dangerously close to the drop-off near the bank of the river. All three men got out, leaving Old Man standing by the truck, while the rest of the vehicles pulled up along the road.

Kit's heart pounded in his ears as he half ran, half slipped down the bank, following the tire tracks. Oscar must have lost control of the truck coming around the bend and plunged over the side of the road. In the darkness and driving snow, however, he could see no farther than ten feet ahead of him. In what condition would he find Camille? If she were dead, he wouldn't be able to bear it. Not dead. Not dead. The phrase became a new chant as he hurried toward the river.

He plunged through the underbrush, dreading the moment of discovery, praying the truck hadn't rolled into the Quincille River. It was a deep river, full of strange currents and murky pools. He could hear the clumps of many footfalls behind him, could hear Mak-ee-nah's breath at his shoulder. But he had to be first. He had to be the one to find her.

Two is one, one is two, two is three. Not dead. Not dead.

Then he saw the truck, piled into a huge fallen cedar, the hood smashed and shortened by a good four feet. On impact, the rear of the truck had swung around and was now teetering on the edge of the riverbank. Ten feet below him Kit could see the swirling black water of the Quincille. His heart lurched in his chest as he dashed for the passenger door. He could see a dark shape sprawled across the dash behind a shattered windshield.

"She's here!" Kit yelled, hardly recognizing his own voice. He pried open the door and it dropped on broken hinges, tipping the truck even more out of balance.

"Take care," Mak-ee-nah warned behind him.

Kit ignored him and leaned into the truck, reaching for Camille. He could see dark smears on her forehead and knew she was hurt but couldn't tell if her injuries were serious. He couldn't even tell if she was dead.

Slowly he drew her out, her legs lifeless and dragging like those of a dummy. He cursed when he saw her arms were bound but knew he had to get her away from the truck before he could assess her condition. Mak-ee-nah grasped her under her arms while Kit bent to lift her by her legs.

Suddenly the ground gave way. Kit felt the earth drop

out from under him and was aware of the truck tipping behind him. He grabbed for Camille's legs, instantly thought better of it, and with a yell of terrified helplessness plunged backward into the river. As if in slow motion he sailed through the air. He looked up and caught a glimpse of Mak-ee-nah with Camille in his arms, her shoes dangling over the jagged edge of the bank. Less than a second later he broke the surface of the frigid water. Something hit his head, a blow so powerful he saw stars. Then all was black.

Mak-ee-nah watched Kit slip under the water and then hoisted Camille into his arms. Adam stood at his elbow, pointing and yelling to Frank Hall about Kit's possible location in the river. Five men rushed down the bank with Frank, who was already taking off his shoes as he ran.

"Adam, take Ca-meel to the Jeep."

"But my uncle Kit!"

"We will find him. But you must see that Ca-meel gets warm. Now go!"

Gently he transferred Camille's limp body to Adam's waiting arms. Then he slid down the riverbank, knowing he had to save Kitsap Makinna. If he didn't save the man who made her cry, he would never see Camille smile again. For the first time since his "death" so long ago and his imprisonment as a raven-spirit, he wished he were a bird again and could fly across the water to look for Kit. Now he was limited to the powers of a human and must use his hands and his head.

The men were quarreling when he arrived at the water's edge.

"He must be trapped under the truck!" somebody yelled.

"No, I think I saw him down that way!" another retorted, pointing farther down the river. Mak-ee-nah followed the gesture, knowing the river widened downstream and was dotted with small islands in its delta. It might take hours to find Kit should his body be swept into one of the many channels of the river.

Frank Hall climbed out of the water, dripping and sputtering. "I couldn't see nothin'," he said, wiping the water from his face. "And Jesus, it's cold!"

Someone offered his jacket to Frank, but he waved him off. "I'm going in again. If we don't find Kit soon, he's a goner."

Frank waded out and plunged back into the river while the rest of the men combed the bank. In the distance Mak-ee-nah heard a wolf howl and knew his warriors were close by. He felt no rush to find Oscar Duarte, whose tracks had led from the truck down a trail that paralleled the river. Oscar wouldn't get far, not with the wolves in close pursuit. Mak-ee-nah climbed up the bank and scanned the surface of the river, willing his vision to embrace the night and see through the snow. He touched the amber on his chest and prayed to *Ah-welth* for guidance.

Camille woke up with an intense headache. She touched her forehead and was surprised to feel something warm and gooey on her fingers. Blood? Then she remembered how she had crashed into the windshield of the truck. Moaning, she opened her eyes and saw a blurred face come gradually into focus.

"Miss Avery!" Adam cried, leaning over her. "Thank God!"

"Adam?" She blinked. How had Adam got to the truck?

She struggled to sit up and realized her wrists were no longer tied.

"I don't think you should move around too much, Miss Avery. You've been in a bad accident."

"How'd you get here?" She looked around at the Jeep, at the cars parked all over the road, at Old Man, who stood on the bridge ahead of them. The movement made her head roar in protest. "What's happening?"

"Oscar lost control of his truck. You guys crashed into a tree."

"Yes," she replied, her thoughts sluggish. "I remember now."

"Everyone drove out to rescue you, Miss Avery. We found you in the truck, but it fell into the river with Uncle Kit."

"With Kit?" She sat up straight, her vagueness dropping away. "Is he all right?"

"I don't know. They can't seem to find him."

"What?" She stared at him, aghast. "Adam, what?"

"They can't find him!" Adam glared at her, his eyes dark with worry. "He pulled you out of the truck and then fell in the river!"

Camille struggled to grasp the door handle, her hands stiff and uncooperative. "No!" she wailed. She pushed open the door and nearly fell out of the Jeep.

"Miss Avery! Come back!" Adam dashed around the Jeep, but she scrambled toward the bridge, slipping in the snow with every step.

"Come back, Miss Avery!" Adam yelled.

Dizzy and heartsick, Camille ran to Old Man, who stood at the railing of the bridge, watching the commotion down below.

"Have they found him?" she cried.

"No," Old Man replied, shaking his head sadly. "It is too dark, Miss Avery."

"Oh, God!" She clutched the rail and hunched over it, weeping uncontrollably. Though she felt Old Man's arm slide around her, she knew no comfort in his touch. "Kit!" she whispered in anguish. "Ah, God!"

"Miss Avery, you must return to the truck. Adam will take you home."

"No. No!"

"You are hurt. It is too cold for you to stay out here without a coat."

"I can't leave. Not when Kit is out there somewhere."

"You will not help them by your weeping, my daughter." He patted her back. "You must take care of yourself. And do not worry. Mak-ee-nah is there. He will find Kit-sap."

"No, I won't leave." She brushed the snow off her arms, as if to prove she wouldn't get too cold. Old Man gave her a funny look over the tops of his glasses.

"Adam!" Old Man called, turning aside. "Come and take Miss Avery home."

Adam trotted up. "Come on, Miss Avery."

"No, I can't leave until Kit has been found."

Old Man faced her. "You must leave. It will do you no good to endanger yourself or the child you carry."

Camille slid her hands from the rail. "The child?"

"Yes." Old Man glanced at her belly and then looked her in the eyes. "You are the Snow Maiden. I have guessed as much. My vision on the mountain reinforced my belief. And Mak-ee-nah knows you are the Snow Maiden as well. I need no more proof."

"But how can I—" She broke off, knowing very well how she could have gotten pregnant. "But the prophecy says I will be the wife of the great *tyee*. Mak-ee-nah. I can't be carrying his child."

"You do carry a child, then?"

"I don't know. I was just referring to the legend—"

Her thoughts swirled, her head pounded, and she felt as if her knees were going to buckle. Could she be pregnant? What about Kit? If she were pregnant, the child would be his, not Mak-ee-nah's. The legend seemed to be getting mixed up, and she couldn't make sense of it when her thoughts kept going round and round in a dizzying circle.

"You gave the amulet to Mak-ee-nah," Old Man mused. "So he is the *tyee* of the legend. You are the Snow Maiden. So you belong with him."

"But what about Kit?"

"Perhaps I was wrong about him."

"No! It can't be true, Old Man!"

He sighed and gazed down at the river. "Perhaps that is why Kit is gone from us now, my daughter. Perhaps he has gone to the Land Above in place of Mak-ee-nah, so that the great *tyee* can stay here on earth with us."

"No!"

Camille whirled around, unable to consider such an idea. Life without Kit was something she couldn't bear to think about. He couldn't die. Not like this. Not without knowing how she felt about him, that she loved him.

"Adam, take Miss Avery home," Old Man said behind her. "I will stay and watch."

"Come on, Miss Avery," Adam said in a monotone, his voice flattened by grief and shock.

At the sound, Camille realized with a stab of guilt that he was suffering more than she was. He had just lost his father, and now it appeared he had lost his uncle. Yet he was expected to look after her, even though he probably wanted to stay and help search for Kit. Camille wiped away a tear that had slipped down her cheek and turned to face him.

"All right, Adam. Let's go."

23

"Is she awake?"

Camille heard the hushed voice of Hattie Johnson near the bedroom door. She opened her eyes, surprised to find she had slept through the night. Then the whole nightmare of what had happened came back to her in a flood of despair, and she wished she could turn over and go back to sleep so she could avoid the inevitable facing of reality.

"Miss Avery?" Hattie asked, stepping closer.

Camille turned toward her voice and saw Adam and Hattie standing near the bed. By the shadowed look on Adam's face, she knew the outcome of the search for Kit. Her heart fell, and she put her hand over her eyes.

"We found him," Adam ventured. "I thought you might like to know."

She swallowed and nodded, too distraught to speak.

"Mak-ee-nah did it, actually. He swam across the river and back. It was a miracle that he even found him at all."

Camille pressed her lips together, fighting a wave of grief. She heard Hattie sigh and felt her hand stroke her hair.

"They did all they could, Miss Avery. All they could."

Camille sniffed, wishing they'd just leave her alone.

"We're going to take him to the funeral home, Camille," Adam said. "I thought you might want to see him first. You know, maybe be alone with him."

"If you want to, that is," Hattie put in.

Camille sat up. She brushed back her hair and glanced at Adam and then Hattie. Her eyes felt scratchy. Her head was on fire. She felt as if she were a hundred years old.

"I do," she finally replied, easing her feet over the edge of the bed. "I want to see him."

"He's downstairs, in the unheated storeroom. Hattie can show you."

"All right." She swallowed and stared at the wall, too traumatized to move.

"Miss Avery?" Hattie asked, leaning over to look at her face. "Are you going to be okay?"

"Yes. I'll be fine." She tried to smile. "Um . . . thanks. Just give me a few minutes."

"If you want anything, I'll be right downstairs," Hattie added.

"Thanks."

"I've got coffee on the stove, breakfast, anything—you just say the word."

"Thanks, Hattie."

"I'll be down there, too," Adam said, placing his hand on her shoulder in a gesture that was too familiar to bear. Camille stood up.

"Thank you. I'll be down in a minute to see"—she pressed her lips together until she could regain control of her voice—"to see Kit."

◆ ◆ ◆

A few minutes later, Camille opened the door to the storeroom, where Kit lay stretched out on a wooden bench. She left the door ajar and ventured forward, almost afraid to look at him. Even from the door she could see the unnatural pallor of his skin. She wasn't sure she wanted to imprint the image of his death upon her memory, but she couldn't deny herself one last look at him. Quietly, without breathing, she slipped around the bench and knelt at his side.

In death his beauty was stark and rigid, carved in alabaster. She had never seen him asleep, and the sight of him with his eyes closed, with his lids covering the fierceness of his gaze, was a startling change for her. A hot tear slid down her cheek as she regarded his ashen profile.

"Kit," she whispered in anguish, brushing a strand of hair off his forehead. His skin was cold, so unlike him, that she drew away in shock.

To think that hours ago he had smiled at her, held her hand, winked at her, and now lay here like this . . .

Trembling, Camille took his hand in hers and brought it up to her cheek. "Kit!" she said, her heart breaking. "Oh, Kit—"

He was gone from her. The only man she had ever truly loved was gone forever. Heavily, Camille rose and sat on the edge of the bench. She reached out and touched his hair—the last time she would ever feel the silken strands slip through her fingers. She ran her fingers over the sharp contours of his face, realizing she would never see his cheeks flush again. She traced the outline of his mouth, knowing she would spend the rest of her life starving for his kiss, his voice, his touch.

"I love you, Kit," she whispered. "I can tell you now because you can't laugh at me or walk away. I love you."

She gazed at his face while tears dropped unheeded on his neck. "If only you had trusted me enough to believe it."

Then she drew down the sheet, wanting a final look at his beautiful body. Just as she was about to lower the sheet farther, she heard a noise at the door and looked up. Mak-ee-nah stood in the doorway, filling up the space with his larger-than-life presence. Camille sat up straight, still holding the edge of the sheet, and wondered how long Mak-ee-nah had been standing there.

"He was a brave man," Mak-ee-nah said, walking toward her.

"Kitsap," Camille replied, nodding.

"Yes. *Kitsap,"* Mak-ee-nah repeated. He stood above Camille and gazed down upon her.

She wished he hadn't come. Knowing her time alone with Kit was over, she smoothed down the sheet and rose.

"I heard you were the one who found him."

"Yes. I am sorry I was too late, Ca-meel. I know you loved this man."

She nodded again.

"Now the man who makes you cry will make you cry forever, won't he, *queece klootz-mah?"*

"Yes."

"Come to me, Ca-meel." Mak-ee-nah drew her to him. For some reason, she let herself be pulled into his chest. She felt the amulet on her cheek but didn't draw away. Mak-ee-nah's arms came around her in a gentle embrace.

"I will never make you cry, will I, *klootz-mah?"*

"I don't know."

"I do. I know." He kissed the top of her head. "You will never cry for me because I will never be in your heart."

Camille clung to him, knowing he was right. No man would ever be in her heart but Kit.

"Something is wrong with the legend, *queece klootz-*

mah. The prophecy is not going as planned. You were destined to love me, not the man who makes you cry."

"I can't help how I feel."

"I know that, *queece klootz-mah.* I know." For a long moment he held her and ran his hands up and down her back. "I look like him, but I am not him."

"No. You're not." She pulled back. "It isn't that you aren't special to me, Mak-ee-nah. You are. It's just that I"—she looked down at Kit and drew away—"I loved this man."

"In time this feeling may pass."

She walked away. "I only wish it would. I wish I could fall in love with you and complete the Nakalt prophecy. Your people need a leader like you. But right now, I can't say that anything will come to pass. My heart has died with Kit. Do you understand?"

"So." He crossed his arms and gazed at her. But this time the sparkle in his eye was replaced by a somber glint. "I understand."

She put her hand on the doorknob and turned. "Who knows? Perhaps we flatter ourselves, Mak-ee-nah, by thinking we are part of a grand scheme. Perhaps our lives mean nothing."

"A terrible thought," Mak-ee-nah replied.

"Yes. But a possibility."

Camille slipped out of the lodge without eating breakfast or talking to anyone. For a few minutes she stood on the deck overlooking the strait and gazed with unseeing eyes at Vancouver Island. Sandy sat at her feet, whining every once in a while as if she, too, were lost in grief. Camille heard the commotion of the Japanese loading their belongings into their rental cars and caught snatches of the musical voices of the Japanese women as they took photographs of the lodge grounds. Not wanting to talk to a single soul, Camille left the deck and walked across the bluff with Sandy at her heels. She descended the stairs to the beach and spent hours walking in the wind and mist, trying to make herself believe she could go on with her life.

Later that morning she drove into Crescent Bay to talk with the new acting chief of police, a young man whom she had seen at the dinner the previous night. He had left a message with Hattie that he wanted to see Camille as soon as possible.

He showed her into Two Hand's messy office and asked her to sit down. He seemed anxious to please her, fumbling and bumping into the desk—a far cry from Two Hand's reluctant assistance.

Camille sank onto a chair, hating the smell of old cigarettes and musty paper that permeated the office and that had clung to Two Hand even in the bear costume. She brushed the tip of her nose and did her best to ignore the odor.

"Thanks for coming, Miss Avery."

"My pleasure," she replied, crossing her hands in her lap. "I want to file charges against Oscar Duarte and Donald Two Hand."

"Charges have been filed against Two Hand. But we can't do anything about Duarte."

"Why? Because he is white? Will I have to go to the county sheriff?"

"No, Miss Avery. Because he is dead."

"Dead?"

He nodded and studied her face as he leaned forward. "I'm sorry. I thought you must have heard."

"No." She moistened her lips. "I haven't talked to anyone."

"Would you like a cup of coffee?" He rose and steepled his hands on the desk.

She licked her lips again. Was he avoiding the prospect of disclosure? He seemed so young and nervous that she felt sorry for him and nodded her head in assent, even though she didn't care if she ever ate or drank again.

He took his time preparing the coffee and then came back into the office, putting a steaming mug on the desk in front of her. He sat down on his chair and picked up a pencil to keep his hands occupied. Camille watched his every movement, her eyes feeling dry and dull.

"How did Oscar Duarte die?" she asked, wrapping her fingers around the warmth of the mug.

"We're not sure. We found his body near the beach where the Quincille River empties into the strait. He'd been"—the officer paused, looked at the pencil, and then glanced back at Camille—"well, it looked like he'd been mauled by a dog."

"A dog?"

"A very large dog. The tracks around his body were huge, the size of a wolf. But there aren't any wolves around here anymore, so it must have been somebody's dog."

A chill raced down Camille's back. "You say he was mauled?"

"Yeah. His throat was torn."

Camille sat in silence for a moment, considering the horrible death Oscar must have suffered. Her hand shook as she raised the coffee cup to her lips and took a sip.

"Two Hand has confessed everything. He claims that Oscar Duarte killed your friend, Barbara Stanton, and David Makinna when they discovered his smuggling operation."

"Just as I suspected," Camille put in.

"There's supposed to be a barn where Oscar hid the artifacts."

"I know where that is. Oscar trapped me there yesterday."

"You'll have to show me where it is, Miss Avery, once you're up to it. We're still looking for the truck bearing the plates you reported, and have some good leads on it."

"That's good."

"We also got a call from Barbara Stanton's parents. They have made arrangements to have the body sent to San Francisco and asked me to try to find you, since you weren't answering your phone."

Camille hadn't been to the cabin for what seemed like days.

"They're having Miss Stanton's service on Monday."

"That's tomorrow."

"Yes, I know." The young officer reached into a desk drawer and drew out an envelope, which he slid across the desk toward her. "I took the liberty of making arrangements, Miss Avery. Some of us—well, we used to be Kit's friends in the old days—and we felt we owed it to you."

Surprised, Camille opened the yellow envelope and drew out a book of airline vouchers. She glanced at the itinerary and then looked up. "Round trip?" she asked.

"You want to come back, don't you, Miss Avery? Old Man Makinna said you were working on a project with him."

"Well, yes, I—" She broke off, unsure of what she had intended to do once she got back on her feet. "I do have a book to finish."

"Kit's funeral will be on Thursday. Will that give you enough time?"

She nodded, trying to block out the image of Kit being buried in the snow-covered ground. Afraid that she would break down in tears, she got to her feet and held out her hand.

"Thank you," she said, shaking his hand. "You've been more than kind. And buying a plane ticket—"

"You have saved part of the Nakalt heritage, Miss Avery, which is much more valuable than a trip to San Francisco, believe me."

He smiled, and she ducked out of the police station, hoping she could make it to the Jeep before she broke down altogether.

Camille returned to the lodge to pack for a late afternoon flight, going through the motions numbed with grief. Adam drove her to Port Angeles, where she took a small plane to Seattle and then changed planes for San Francisco. The trip was like a dream to her, as if she were watching a movie with the sound turned off. And it took every ounce of her strength to move one foot in front of the other.

Mak-ee-nah waited until dusk to slip into the storeroom, thankful that Adam had left unexpectedly to take Ca-meel to Port Angeles instead of transporting Kit's body to the funeral home. Had Kit been taken off the reservation that afternoon, there would have been no chance to carry out his plans. He drew the sheet off the face of the man who made Ca-meel cry and gazed at him for a moment, trying not to think of the dream that had died with this man. Yet perhaps a flicker of hope remained. Perhaps there was a way to salvage life from the ashes.

With a grunt, Mak-ee-nah hoisted Kit into his arms and pushed open the door that led to the parking lot in back. He looked right and left and, seeing that no one was about, stepped into the frosty night, his feet leaving prints in the fragile layer of snow on the ground. Soon he was joined by his ten loyal warriors, who loped ahead, knowing instinctively where the path would take them.

Mak-ee-nah walked deep into the forest until he came to the waterfall, the site of Kit's vision quest. There he stopped and gently laid Kit upon the slab of stone at the base of the falls. The wolves sat in a semicircle around the stone while snow fell lightly upon Kit's shroud and wind rustled through the cedars above, keening softly. Mak-ee-nah knelt down and drew away the sheet, exposing Kit's pale body to the night and snow. Flakes of white stuck to his lashes and hair. Slowly, Mak-ee-nah rose and raised his arms to the sky.

"*Ah-welth,*" he cried, tipping his face to the heavens. "Hear my prayer, Great Father."

He closed his eyes and prayed, knowing that to fail his people again would be worse than anything he could imagine, worse than spending two more centuries as a raven. To save his people, he would do anything. Anything that *Ah-welth* demanded. And to save his people, he knew that life must be restored to Kitsap Makinna.

Old Man scowled as Hattie helped him into bed, gently lifting the heavy cast as he sank to the mattress. When he was settled, he watched her tuck the blankets around him and make sure the pillow was adjusted the way he liked it. As she straightened from her task, an eerie howl broke the stillness of the night.

"What's that?" Hattie asked, looking toward the window.

"Wolves," Old Man replied.

"In Crescent Bay? What are wolves doing here?"

Old Man pursed his lips and then nodded his head. "They are here for Kitsap. They are singing for him."

"It sounds strange." Hattie returned her gaze to Old Man while she rubbed the backs of her pudgy arms. "I've never heard anything like it."

Old Man nodded.

"Don't you think it sounds kind of scary?"

"No." Old Man smiled, closing his eyes. "It is a wonderful song. Listen—they sing for his spirit."

Camille stayed the night with Barbara's parents in San Francisco, went to the funeral in the morning, saw a doctor about her head injury, and then repacked her clothes, feeling more and more as if she were dissociating with real life. Barbara's mother was concerned about her silence and begged her to stay on with them until she felt more like herself. But Camille insisted upon returning to the Northwest, to the reservation, using the book deadline as her excuse to leave. But in her heart she knew she wanted go back, that she was lonesome and heartsick and couldn't wait to see Makinna Lodge again.

She had much to do there—finish the book, tutor Adam, and tell the tribe about the Spanish doublloons which lay forgotten in the cardboard box in Kit's room.

On the plane she looked out of the window at the gray-blue water of the Pacific Ocean and thought of the way the water had called to her so long ago.

Home, home, home.

Camille leaned back and closed her eyes. She was going home. In six hours she'd be home.

♦ ♦ ♦

Kit moaned and sat up. His spine was stiff and his ribs hurt with every breath he took. He rubbed the backs of his chilled arms, wondering where he was and why he had been sleeping stark naked out in the middle of nowhere—in the snow, no less. His hand bumped something hanging on his chest. He looked down in surprise, astonished to find he was wearing the amber amulet. How did that get there? And how had he managed to swim out of the river? He couldn't remember a thing after the bump on his head.

"For crying out loud!" he exclaimed, chafing his hands together as his breath puffed in a frost plume. He stood up. Where in the hell was he, anyway? He turned around, toward the sound of cascading water, and realized he was in the forest at the place of his vision quest.

On the ground lay a rumpled sheet. Kit grabbed it and wrapped it around his freezing body. Then he noticed a dark lump on the ground. He stepped closer, discovering Mak-ee-nah's sea otter robe and the rest of his garments lying in the snow.

"Mak-ee-nah!" Kit shouted. He glanced around for a sign of the chief but saw no one in the gray light of dawn. "Mak-ee-nah!" The roar of the water swallowed up the sound of his voice. Kit looked down and could see no tracks in the snow, as if the garments had been left there hours ago. Why? Where was the great *tyee?*

He was reluctant to touch Mak-ee-nah's belongings, knowing the garments belonged to a great warrior. But his respect for Mak-ee-nah lasted only a few more minutes before he realized that he would freeze to death if he didn't get some clothes on. Grimacing, he bent over and snatched up the soft pelt. Something fluttered onto the snow as he raised the robe. Raven feathers. Kit stared at the knifelike shapes of the slender black plumes, wondering how they had gotten there. Mak-ee-nah must have been collecting them.

Too cold and stiff to think any further, Kit hurriedly pulled on the robe and then searched for the colorful belt with which to cinch it. He found a pair of doeskin moccasins beneath Mak-ee-nah's yellow cloak, along with a jumble of the *tyee*'s jewelry. Though his fingers were unusually stiff and his joints unwilling to cooperate with the demands of fine motor function, Kit managed to scoop up the baubles, intending to return everything once he got back to the lodge and located Mak-ee-nah.

He settled the cloak around his shoulders and felt his body heat immediately warming the layer of air beneath. Relief flooded over him and he sighed, knowing he had a chance at survival now that he had protection against the elements. But he also had a long walk ahead of him. He squinted at the trail before him, just now emerging from the shadows of the forest.

He hoped Camille was all right. The last he had seen of her was her feet hanging over the disintegrating bank of the Quincille River. He had to get back as soon as he could, had to find out what had happened to her.

"Please, Lord, let me find her alive," he murmured. "Let her be alive." He set off down the trail, his stiff knees and ankles protesting every step of the way.

Later he burst into the lodge, only to find it deserted. Where was everybody? He tramped up the stairs to his room and flung open the door. Camille's belongings were gone. He strode to the bathroom. Her cosmetic bag was nowhere to be found. Her clothes were missing. All that remained of her was the faint scent of her cold cream wafting from the hand towel.

Kit's heart dropped in his chest. At least that's the way

it felt. He staggered out of the bathroom, crushed and desperate.

"Hattie!" he shouted. "Where are you? Old Man!"

Silence hung over the vacant lodge. Kit had never felt more alone, more abandoned. More *frightened*.

Still wearing the clothes of the *tyee*, he scrambled down the stairs and dashed into the family room. No one was there. Not even the smell of breakfast lingered as a reassurance that someone had been in the lodge in the past few hours. Had they all gone to the hospital? Could Camille be in real trouble? Or worse?

His hand shook as he dialed the number of the aquaculture center, hoping Frank Hall might know where everyone was. The phone rang and rang. Exasperated, Kit dialed the police station.

"Nakalt Tribal Police," a woman dispatcher answered.

"Hi, this is Kit Makinna," he began.

Dead silence hung on the other end.

"Hello?"

The dispatcher hung up the phone without saying another word. Kit stared at the receiver as if it were broken, wondering at the woman's reaction. Maybe there had just been trouble with the line. He dialed again.

"Nakalt Tribal Police," the woman answered, her voice wary.

"Ah, you're there." Kit adjusted the phone closer to his mouth. "This is Kit Makinna, and I need to—"

"Is this some kind of joke?"

"No. Can you tell me—"

"I don't have time for prank calls, mister. These lines need to be open. So whoever you are, don't call back."

"Wait—"

She slammed down the receiver.

Kit tried the number two more times, but she wouldn't

answer the phone. He sighed and leaned on the counter, realizing he wouldn't be able to get hold of anyone. He'd have to wait until the rest of the Makinnas got back or else walk into town. Too worried about Camille to hang around doing nothing, he decided to take a quick shower, change into some clothes, and hike to Crescent Bay.

Just as he was about to climb the stairs, he heard the front door open. Hattie stepped into the lodge.

"Mak-ee-nah?" she called.

Kit turned fully, and when he did so he saw Hattie's jaw drop.

"Hattie!"

"Kitsap?" She took a step backward, reaching behind her as if to catch hold of the doorknob. Her eyes were as round as pennies.

"Hattie, what's the matter?"

Staring at him, she mouthed words with her lips, but no sound came out.

"Hattie, for crying out loud! What's wrong?" He walked toward her, alarmed by the fear he saw in her face.

"Kitsap!" she gasped. "How—what—"

"You look like you've just seen a ghost."

For a moment she stared at him with such stark terror in her eyes that Kit reached out to her, afraid that she would faint. Screeching, she ducked his hand and whirled around to yank open the door.

"Wait!" Kit exclaimed, lunging for her. He grabbed her upper arm and pulled her back into the lodge, while she blubbered in protest, which quickly turned into horrified tears once she realized he wasn't going to let her escape. Why in the world would she react this way?

"Please, please don't hurt me!" she cried.

"Hattie, what's gotten into you?" Kit held her at arm's length and stared at her. "It's me, Kit."

"You're dead!" she gasped, her glance darting over his face and then away as if she were afraid to look at him for any length of time.

"I'm what?"

"Dead!"

"Hattie, you're talking nonsense."

Adamantly, she shook her head and pulled at his grip, refusing to meet his gaze.

He sighed. What in the hell was going on? Was she crazy? He wasn't dead. Anyone could see that. Hattie must be in some kind of shock.

"Hattie, come here. Sit down." He urged her to sit on a nearby chair. She sat down and crossed her arms over her chest but kept her eyes trained on the cedar planks of the floor.

Kit rubbed his chin, wondering how to approach her. Then he knelt down beside her.

"Hattie, there's no reason to be afraid of me. I don't know what's going on. But I do know that I'm not dead." He paused, realizing that he hadn't felt so energized in years, even after his long trek out of the mountains. Was it because he was wearing the amulet?

"They took you from the river," she whispered in a voice so low he could hardly hear her words. "You were dead—"

"I must not have been."

"You were cold. Lifeless. We put you in the storeroom out back."

"You did?"

"You had drowned. Your heart wasn't beating."

Kit stared at her. "There's been some kind of mistake—"

"Then someone stole your body yesterday. We've been

looking everywhere. Everywhere." She looked up at him, her eyes still round with fear.

"This is too much!" Kit sputtered. "I don't remember drowning. All I remember is falling in the river and being hit on the head. And then I woke up to find myself out in the woods, naked as a jaybird. I came back as soon as I could, but everybody was gone."

She blinked as if trying to take in all that he said.

"Just tell me one thing, Hattie. Is Camille okay?" He studied her, holding his breath and dreading the worst.

The question seemed to reassure her somewhat. Her expression softened. "Yes. She just got a nasty bump on her head."

"Thank God. I was afraid she was—" He broke off, unable to voice his fears. "But where is she, then?"

"She went to California."

"California?" His voice cracked as he rose to his feet.

"She said she'd be back."

Kit stomped to the fire. Sure she'd be back. Camille probably hightailed it off the reservation as soon as she could. He couldn't blame her. The time she had spent here had been full of trauma—one crisis after another. And he hadn't been man enough to tell her that he cared about her—the only reason she might have stayed.

He glared at the fire, fighting the way his heart had plummeted at the news of Camille's absence. He ached to see her, and the need to hold her was so intense that he thought he'd break apart out of sheer disappointment. How could he endure the days until she returned, *if* she returned?

"Where is she?" he asked.

"San Francisco," Hattie replied, her manner considerably more at ease. "At Barbara Stanton's memorial service."

"Oh. Barbara Stanton."

"Yes. Kit, she'll be back. I know she will."

"How can you be so sure?" He sighed. "Who in their right mind would come back here?"

"She said she'd be back. And Miss Avery will stick by her word." She stood up and tilted her head, taking a step toward him, "It really *is* you, isn't it, Kitsap?"

"Yes." He tried to smile at her but knew his effort was less than satisfactory. "It's really me."

Hesitantly she reached out to touch his arm, as if testing the truth of his words. He stood stiffly while she squeezed his forearm and his bicep. Then she touched his face. Her dark eyes bore into his own as if to read deep into his thoughts.

"It's a miracle," she murmured. "That's what it is. A miracle!"

24

Kit trotted up the stairs, feeling unusually fit and vigorous. There was no denying he was alive and loved. Every person who had learned of his miraculous recovery in the past few hours had whooped for joy—even Old Man. The doctor who had been summoned to examine him had tried to explain the miracle in scientific terms, saying that the frigid water of the Quincille River had probably slowed down the metabolism of his body, enough to save his life. His body processes had been so repressed, it had only appeared that he no longer breathed. The time spent in the cold storeroom had maintained his unconscious state. But how he'd gotten out of the storeroom and into the forest was anybody's guess.

The only down side of the afternoon was his inability to get in touch with Camille in San Francisco. The Stanton phone had gone unanswered for hours.

Even so, Kit felt a wonderful sense of well-being. The

amulet bounced against his chest as he strode down the hall to his room, intending to take a shower at last.

He'd been mistaken for dead. How had his "death" affected Camille Avery? Was she all right? He was dying to see her. Kit opened the door to his room, smiling at his own choice of words. He'd had his fill of dying. He was ready to live now. He grinned and crossed the floor. He felt happy. In fact, he was so happy, he felt as if his heart would explode.

Kit strode into the bathroom and flipped on the light. He took off his clothes and hung them behind the door. When he turned, he caught sight of his reflection in the mirror above the sink. For a moment he gazed at his torso, knowing something had changed but unsure what was different. There seemed to be a large bruise beneath the amulet. He drew off the amulet, wondering if the sight of the amber made his reflection seem foreign to him. Carefully he set the necklace on the counter and then raised his glance to the glass again. The bruise was long and narrow, tilted slightly, bearing a great similarity to the shape of a raven feather. He touched the mark, expecting his skin to be tender, but the mark was not sore. Was it a stain? Kit tried rubbing it off, but the spot remained on his skin. Strange.

He breathed in and exhaled, watching the rise and fall of his chest, knowing something infinitesimal had changed. He ran his palms over the planes of his breasts. Even the feeling of his skin and flesh was different, a shade of difference so minute that he doubted his own perception. But he couldn't deny the change he felt inside, as if some dark cloud had lifted from his heart. Perhaps that was what happened when a person was given a second chance at life. Whatever it was, he felt great.

Kit turned on the shower. How long would it be until

he'd see Camille? He couldn't wait to show her that miracles could happen, that he was alive. He couldn't wait to see her face.

After taking a shower and donning a clean set of clothes, Kit returned to the main floor, hoping Hattie would fix him something to eat. He was ravenous. When he breezed into the kitchen, he saw Hattie pause at the sink and look at him the way everyone had been looking at him all day, as if he were untouchable, not really himself. Old Man had arranged a special council meeting for that evening just so he could relate Kit's incredible story to the rest of the tribe. Perhaps after the meeting, when everyone had heard the tale, they would be more inclined to accept him.

"What about Mak-ee-nah?" Kit asked. "Where's the great *tyee?*"

"No one knows. He seems to have disappeared."

"I hear he was the one who found me."

Hattie nodded. "He was a special man, just like we've always been told. To see him was one of the greatest moments of my life."

Kit turned to her. "And mine."

Hattie wiped her hands on a dry towel. "Would you like a snack, Kitsap? It's still a few hours before dinner, and I bet you're hungry."

"As a matter of fact, I'm starving," Kit replied, opening the refrigerator. "By the way, where's Adam and Lydia?"

"Adam is still at school. Lydia is gone."

"What do you mean?"

"She has left the reservation."

"Why?"

Hattie shook her head as she opened a tin canister. "Her shame was too great. She couldn't face anyone after the feast Saturday night when she claimed to be the Snow Maiden and Mak-ee-nah told her she was wrong."

Kit pulled out a carton of milk and set it on the counter. Hattie paused, holding the tin.

"All her life she's believed that she was the Snow Maiden. All her life."

He nodded silently.

"And to find out that her entire life was lived for nothing—and to dance so blatantly for you, Kit—well, she ran off. I can't say I blame her. But I can't say I pity her, either. She brought much of this on herself."

Kit poured two glasses of milk while Hattie stacked oatmeal cookies on a plate. She picked up the plate of cookies and faced Kit. "Do you believe what Mak-ee-nah said, that Camille Avery is the Snow Maiden?"

"Yes." Kit lifted a glass. For the first time in his life he didn't doubt his beliefs, and the relief he felt nearly dropped him to his knees.

"How can you be so certain?" she added.

"I just am." He pinched her cheek, and Hattie blushed with pleasure at the familiar gesture and gave him a genuine smile full of her old warmth.

The taxi pulled up at Makinna Lodge. Camille knew the fare would be astronomical, but she didn't care. She had wanted to get back to Crescent Bay as soon as possible, without waiting for Adam to pick her up in Port Angeles. She had even paid extra to change her ticket so she could leave San Francisco a day earlier.

She counted out money for the driver and picked up her bag, gazing at the orange-barked forest of madrona trees and the familiar welcoming sight of the lodge. Camille breathed in and sighed sadly, happy to be back but knowing it would never be the same without Kit. She'd simply have to learn to cope.

The door was unlocked, but the house was empty. Camille looked around, poking her head into the kitchen and family room, wondering where everyone could be. Then she shrugged and took her suitcase upstairs to Kit's old room. She set it on the floor and slipped out of her coat while she glanced idly around the room. No one had packed Kit's belongings. Maybe it was a Nakalt custom to leave a person's earthly possessions in his living quarters for an interval of time after his death. Maybe they thought she'd like to pack them away. She'd gotten the distinct impression from everyone since Kit's death that they recognized her as his woman. Camille smiled at the thought, and her heart twisted. She had believed her heart couldn't break any more, that it was beyond hurting, but another chunk felt as if it had just fallen away.

Tiredly, Camille hung up her trench coat next to Kit's gray-and-brown sweater. The events of the last few days had drained her. Barbara's funeral had been particularly rough, and a tougher funeral was still to come. Kit's. Camille covered her eyes and stumbled to the bathroom for a cool washcloth. She had to stop crying. There was no point in sobbing again.

When she reached the bathroom she noticed Kit's toiletries were still on the counter. In fact, she could still smell his cedar cologne on the air. She closed her eyes and breathed in, imagining that he was still with her, that he would walk up behind her and caress her shoulders. Why hadn't someone disposed of his brush, his toothbrush, his razor? Such intimate objects, so common and unobtrusive, were the most powerful reminders of his death.

Camille took a quick shower, turned off the lights, and slipped into bed, snuggling into Kit's sheets, well aware that someday the scent of him would fade and she would no longer be able to imagine him there with her. That would be the day she would stop weeping. That would be the day her heart would stop aching. She promised.

Kit opened the door to his room and paused on the threshold. Something was different. He glanced around the room, half expecting Mak-ee-nah to show up and demand his amulet. Kit's glance landed on the beige trenchcoat hanging on the peg next to his sweater, and his heart flopped over. Didn't that trench coat belong to Camille?

He hurried to the bathroom and looked in, but all was dark. Then he strode around the fireplace and opened the door of his bedroom. Someone lay in his bed, curled up in his covers, her blond hair tousled against the pillow.

Camille had come back. She had returned to the reservation. His heart leaped with joy. For a moment Kit stood watching her sleep, studying the peaceful profile of her delicate porcelain face. Then she stirred, as if subconsciously aware of his surveillance, and turned onto her back, flinging her arm over her head. Kit stepped into the room and was about to pull off his sweater when he considered the effect his sudden appearance in bed might have on her. His return from the dead had shocked his friends and neighbors. No telling what reaction Camille might have should she be awakened by a dead man.

Yet he couldn't just stand there and let her continue sleeping, not when his hunger for her was so great, not when he needed desperately to hear the sound of her voice and see the light in her hazel eyes. More than anything he wanted to tell her that he loved her.

Silently he moved to the side of the bed and sat down next to her hip. He reached out and gently brushed the platinum hair from her brow. She wrinkled her nose at his touch but did not awaken.

"Camille," he said softly, slipping his hand over hers. "Camille."

She stirred and mumbled something in her sleep.

"Wake up, my heart," he said.

She sighed and opened her eyes. For an instant she stared at him, blinked, and then scrambled backward to the head of the bed, her eyes full of alarm and confusion while she tried to yank her hand from his grip.

"Camille," he exclaimed, squeezing her fingers.

"Kit!" she screeched.

"Don't be afraid," he urged.

"You're dead!"

"No, I'm not. I'm alive, Camille."

"You can't be. I saw you. You can't be!" She pulled at his hand.

"Wait, Camille, listen to—"

"No!" She shook her head and glared at him out of the corner of her eye, as if she were ready to bolt. Her fear of him twisted his heart, yet he didn't know what to do to convince her not to be frightened. He knew that keeping her by force would only make her struggle more, so he released her, and she skittered away and jumped off the bed. She rushed for the door, but paused near the threshold when she realized he wasn't in pursuit. She pushed a hand through her hair.

"I'm dreaming," she ventured.

"No. You're awake."

"This is some kind of trick."

"No. I'm real." He stood up. "I don't know how, and I don't know why, but I've been given another chance at life."

For a long moment she stared at him as if trying to decide whether or not he was speaking the truth. He could almost see the wheels turning in her head.

"Why didn't anyone tell me?"

"No one knew. I just woke up today."

"Woke up?"

"Yeah. Seems it was just a problem with my metabolism. The cold water slowed it down. But when I tried to call you at the Stantons—to tell you that I was still alive—no one answered."

Camille took a step backward. "I can't believe this. It can't be true. I'm going to wake up and you'll be gone."

"I'm going to be right here, Camille." He opened his arms. "I'm alive, believe me. I feel more alive than I've ever felt in my whole life."

She tilted her head to one side and studied him. Something had changed about Kit, but she couldn't put her finger on it. His eyes were still black and fierce, his hair was still thick and glossy, but something was different. Was it his mouth? His usual bitterness, accentuated by the lines at the corners of his mouth, seemed to be gone. For an instant she was reminded of Mak-ee-nah's carefree smile and his lack of sarcasm.

But the change in Kit made her even more suspicious. "This has got to be some kind of trick—"

"No." He held out his hands. "Why don't you believe me?"

She looked at his hands and then at his face but didn't budge from the doorway. "You're different. You're a *memelose*, aren't you? You're one of the walking dead."

"Who told you about the *memelose*?"

"Mak-ee-nah did when he told me the legend of the Snow Maiden."

"I am not of the walking dead. I'm just me. Kit." He sighed and gazed at her, his arms sinking to his sides, knowing if he took a step toward her, she'd probably run out of the room. That was the last thing he wanted.

She raised her chin and studied him again. Kit thought he saw tears glistening in the corners of her eyes. He ached to enfold her to his chest, ached to kiss away her sorrow, but he held himself back until she made the first move.

"I saw you dead," she whispered.

"I know it seems impossible—"

"You were cold, lifeless."

"I can't explain—"

"I thought I'd never see you again."

"Nor I you."

"Oh, Kit!" She ran to him and flung herself into his arms, nearly knocking him backward. "Kit!" she cried, burrowing against his chest and locking her arms around him in a grip so fierce, he thought she'd break his neck.

He clutched her hard against him, his heart bursting with happiness as he embraced her. "My heart," he whispered. "I've come back to you."

"I can't believe this is happening," she replied.

"Just kiss me."

She pulled back and looked up at him, her eyes swimming with tears. Her small hands slipped up the column of his neck as she gazed at him. Then she ran her hands up the sides of his face, tracing the edges of his lips with her thumbs, as if to smooth away something she saw there. Her fingertips eased along his jawline and curved at the flare of bone near his ear. She turned her palms outward and covered his cheeks, touching him as a blind person might inspect another's face. He didn't move, didn't breathe, as she felt her way across his features, and he closed his eyes as her fingers passed over his brows and then caressed the hair at his temples.

"It *is* you, Kit," she murmured. "It is. Tell me I'm not dreaming this."

He gazed into her hazel eyes and felt himself melt inside at the look of almost childlike anxiety he saw there. "It's no dream, Camille."

He closed his eyes and bent toward her lips, touching his mouth to hers. At first she hesitated, as if still not convinced he was real. Then he combed his fingers through her platinum hair and pressed her against his mouth. She made a slight moaning sound and then reached up to draw his head down while she stood on tiptoe. Her body arched against him at the movement, her breasts and pelvis tipped into his, and he responded in a flush of need so great that he sucked in a breath as if he'd been struck.

He kissed her desperately, his mouth slanting over hers, their lips fused by joy and pain, melded in utter disbelief at the miracle that had brought him back to life. And now that he was alive, he would show her how much he needed her, tell her how much he loved her, and never again hold back because of his doubts about women. Camille was like no other woman. She had proved it over and over again, and he hadn't let himself believe in her until too late. He hadn't let himself believe in anything.

But it was not too late now, and his days of doubting were over. Kit kissed her throat and looked down at her. She rolled her head back, eyes closed, lips parted, as she succumbed to his touch. She trusted him, bared herself to him as if he would never hurt her again. And he wouldn't. Never again would he turn away from this woman or vent his bitterness upon her. Kit squeezed her shoulders and cradled her head in his hand, urging her to look at him, and she opened her eyes, which glistened at him like quiet pools in the rain forest.

"I love you so much," he whispered, feeling his cheeks flush. "Do you know that, Camille?"

"You never let on—"

"I was afraid to. I was sure you'd leave."

"Why?"

"Nothing in my life has been permanent. I never thought you'd be permanent, either. And for the longest time I fought every feeling I had for you."

"Because I would leave you?"

"Yes. And leave the reservation. I thought you'd come to your senses and realize what you were getting into. Being involved with a man like me is more than most women care to handle."

"Because you're an Indian?"

He swallowed. "Yes."

"Do you think that matters to me, the color of your skin?"

"It did for most women. I was all right to take to bed. But that's as far as they wanted to go."

"I'm not like those others."

"I didn't know. Not to sound conceited, but I thought you were after me simply because you liked the way I looked."

"At first I was. When I met you, Kit, I couldn't believe how handsome you were. I kept telling myself to be logical, not to succumb to the physical. But I couldn't help myself. I couldn't help the way I felt. For the first time in my life, I had a full-blown crush on a man."

"A crush?"

"That's what I thought it was. I wasn't the type who believed in love at first sight. Not until now. But there was so much more about you than your looks. Your concern— the way you care about other people made me love you even more."

Kit flushed again and looked down, amazed at the things she was saying.

"But I couldn't tell you. How could I justify the way I felt without sounding as if I were infatuated with you, with your looks? That night when I got stung by the nettles and you kissed me—and you thought I didn't care for you? Kit, I was so crazy about you at that point, I couldn't trust myself to speak."

He stared at her, truly surprised. "I thought I had offended you."

"No." She caressed the hair above his temple. "I longed to open up to you. I just didn't trust my own feelings. But Sunday morning when I saw you lying there, drowned and lost to me forever, I knew I should have told you long ago what my heart had been dying to tell you."

"And what is that?"

"That I love you, with all my heart, with all my soul. That somehow we were put on this earth to be together— call it fate, call it prophecy, or call it just blind luck—and we've managed to find each other."

"We have. By some miracle, we have." Kit brushed her bangs off her forehead and gazed into her eyes. "Are you staying for a while, then, here on the reservation?"

"I'd like to. Will you?"

"Yes. There's much I have to do here."

"I'd like to help, Kit."

He drew his thumb over her lips while his entire body hummed with desire. Yet before he could let himself touch her further, he had to ask her one more question, the most important question of all.

"Then will you stay," he began, his voice husky, "and be my wife?"

"Yes." She reached up and kissed him. "Oh, Kit, you know I will."

His heart exploded in joy, and he swept her off her feet, carrying her to the bed. Gently he set her down, half falling on top of her when she wouldn't let go of his neck. She was still kissing him and running her hands through his hair while he struggled to take off his sweater. For a moment he eased back, just long enough to pull the garment over his head. At that instant he heard Camille gasp.

"Kit—you've got the amulet."

"I know. I woke up with it on."

He leaned back down to kiss her, and the amber swung between them. Camille reached up to stop the motion and clutched the golden gem. She stared at it in shock, then glanced up at Kit, her eyes sharp with surprise.

"What's the matter?" he asked, preferring the soft, hazel pools of desire he had seen in her eyes only moments before.

"Kit, the amber is getting warm."

"So?"

"That means that Mak-ee-nah is coming."

"Does it?"

"It did when I wore it." She released the amber.

"Maybe not when I have it. I'll tell you, since I've been wearing the necklace, I feel like a different man." He unbuttoned his shirt and peeled it off. "I feel extraordinarily good. Did that happen to you?"

"No." Camille sank back on the comforter and stared at him, her expression dark and questioning.

He bent to kiss her, but she drew away.

"For crying out loud, Camille, what's the matter?"

"Kit, there's a bruise on your chest."

"I know. I must have gotten it during the accident."

"It wasn't there before." She stared at the spot between his breasts where the mark in the shape of a feather shadowed his skin.

Kit looked down at himself, wishing he had never worn the amulet into the bedroom. He wanted to make love with Camille, not discuss Mak-ee-nah and the amber.

"It looks like a raven feather, just like the one in the amber."

"It doesn't hurt. It's more like a tattoo, if you ask me."

"Yes. . . ." She reached up and gingerly traced the spot with her fingertip. "How did you get it, though?"

"I don't know. And I don't care." He ran his hands down her torso. "All I know is that I'm dying to make love to you."

"Kit, wait." She struggled up on her elbows. "Where is Mak-ee-nah?"

"I don't know. No one's seen him."

"No one?"

"Not since yesterday. Why? Are you worried?"

"Is the amber getting warmer?"

"Yeah." He touched it. "It is."

Camille looked wildly about the room. "He's coming."

"Does that frighten you, *klootz-mah?*"

Camille jerked around to face Kit. "What did you just say?" she gasped.

"*Klootz-mah.*" He shrugged and smiled at her. "It's a Nakalt word for—"

"For woman. I know. Why did you call me that?"

"I don't know. It just slipped out."

He was confused by the way she was staring at him. To reassure her, he reached out to caress her cheek. "What's the matter?"

"You've changed somehow. At first I thought I was seeing things, but now I'm not so sure."

"What do you mean?" He studied her, anxious to hear her assessment, for he had thought he had changed, too.

"There's something in your face, your smile, that reminds me of Mak-ee-nah."

His pulse quickened. "Anything else?"

"Nothing concrete. It's just a feeling. . . ."

"But what could it mean?"

She blinked, looked at the amulet, and then glanced at his face, her brows knitted together. "Could it be the prophecy after all?" she whispered.

"What are you getting at?"

"Don't you see—the legend of the Snow Maiden could be coming true after all."

"I don't follow you."

She sat up straight. "All along, Mak-ee-nah thought he was the *tyee* destined to be the husband of the Snow Maiden. But all along, it was you!"

"What are you talking about?"

"I'm talking about your puzzle, Kit. *Two is one. One is two. Two is three.*"

He ran a hand over his hair. "What does that have to do with anything?"

"It works out! It all works out! I should have seen it before!"

"For crying out loud, Avery—what works out?"

She smiled a radiant smile at him and tucked her feet under her hips. "I, the supposed Snow Maiden, fell in love with a mortal. You."

"So far, so good."

"But that mortal died."

"Me again."

"Yes. And when you came back to life through a miracle, all the people were afraid, thinking you were a *meme-lose.*"

"That happened all right."

"And just like in the legend, you have come back to help your people by using the power of the amulet."

"But what about the brother in the legend, who stole the amulet?"

"Perhaps he is allegorical, and your struggle with Donald Two Hand over the Island of the Dead is symbolic of that."

Kit shrugged, only half-convinced.

"But what about the raven who took the amulet to the sky?"

"That was Mak-ee-nah."

Kit stared at her. "Mak-ee-nah?"

"Yes. He wanted so badly to be a mortal again, to be the *tyee* who could redeem his people. But he gave it up for you, Kit. And perhaps, by giving his life force to you, he saved himself as well."

"Why would he do such a thing? Why do it for me?"

"Because." She paused and looked at the dying fire.

Kit watched a sad expression touch her features, and he studied her closely. "Why?"

"I think because he knew I loved you."

"So he gave himself up for me? That's an incredibly unselfish move on his part."

"Not entirely."

"What do you mean?"

She raised her head and gazed at him, her eyes bright with glistening tears. "I think he is with you, Kit, inside of you."

"What!"

"I think he still lives within you. That is how you came to have the amulet. That is how you came back from the dead. And that is why you seem different to me now."

Kit stood up. He couldn't believe what she was saying. And yet, crazy as it sounded, it explained a lot of things for which he had no answers, including the empty set of clothes by the waterfall.

"And the puzzle?" he asked, his voice cracking.

"Two is one." She held up two fingers. "At first both you and Mak-ee-nah existed, two versions of the same man."

She got to her feet. *"One is two."* She closed the space between her fingers until they touched. "Now that you have the amulet, you and Mak-ee-nah have merged and are one being."

"But that doesn't explain the entire legend. If I am the *tyee* of the prophecy and you are the Snow Maiden, we are supposed to have a son together who becomes a chief, and who grows to manhood in a single day. Explain that."

Camille nodded. "Perhaps time is also allegorical. What is one day to the spirit world, to the age of the universe? One day or one lifetime—there's very little difference when compared to eons of years."

"What about the rest of the puzzle? *Two is three?*"

"You two men, Kit—you and Mak-ee-nah—will produce a third great *tyee*." She held up another finger. "Our son."

Kit felt goose pimples blossom on the backs of his arms. She had answered the riddle. Her reasoning even explained the vision he had experienced during his spirit quest—that of a raven diving into his chest. Mak-ee-nah had plunged into him, had become part of him, just as the raven had, and the act had branded him with the strange mark on his chest. It defied all logic, all rational explanation, but he knew in his heart that Mak-ee-nah was with him. And that explained the sudden disappearance of the great *tyee* and the pile of raven feathers at the waterfall. "You're right," he whispered. "You're absolutely right."

She nodded, and her hand drifted down her torso to rest on her abdomen. Kit's gaze followed the movement. He had seen other women make such a gesture, as if cradling something when they had a life growing within them. Another wave of goose pimples sped across his skin. He glanced at her face and saw a small smile raise the corners of her mouth. Camille was pregnant? The possibility made his heart soar.

"You have something else to add?" he asked, trying not to get his hopes up.

"Old Man's charm worked"—she smiled and shrugged—"well, just like a charm."

He laughed. "You're pregnant?"

She nodded. "I found out yesterday when I went to a doctor in San Francisco."

Kit beamed. For a moment he stood there and gawked at her, too flabbergasted to move. Then he walked around the bed, his legs so shaky he thought he'd fall. "Really?"

She nodded. "*Klushish?*" she asked, grinning.

"You don't know how *klushish!*" he replied. "I feel so blessed, Camille, like I'm a brand-new man."

"You are, Kit," she murmured, embracing him. "You are."

"Because of you." He hugged her and put his nose in her hair. "You've changed my life so much." He kissed her. "I love you, my beautiful Snow Maiden."

"And I love you, *tyee.*"

AUTHOR'S NOTE

The Nakalt Indians portrayed in this book are a purely fictional tribe whose traditions and history are based on the coastal people who live on the northwestern tip of the Olympic Peninsula of Washington State (the Makah) and the lower portion of Vancouver Island, Canada (the Nootka). The legend of the Snow Maiden is fictional but retains the flavor of many of the stories told by coastal Indians.

The Native American language used in this book is based on a diary kept by John Jewitt, who was a captive of the Nootka Indians and who spent two years living among them. He wrote of his experiences in *The Jewitt Narrative*.

The Spanish fort mentioned in the story was an actual site. In 1792 Spaniards established the colony of Núñez Gaona to spy on British movements across the Strait of Juan de Fuca. Conflicts with the Makah forced Commander Salvador Fidalgo to abandon the place.

In 1806 there were an estimated 2,000 Makahs living in northwestern Washington. In 1853 smallpox decimated their number to five hundred. Today there are approximately 1900 Makahs enrolled as tribal members.

AVAILABLE NOW

RAIN LILY by Candace Camp

Maggie Whitcomb's life changed when her shell-shocked husband returned from the Civil War. She nursed him back to physical health, but his mind was shattered. Maggie's marriage vows were forever, but then she met Reid Prescott, a drifter who took refuge on her farm and captured her heart. A heartwarming story of impossible love from bestselling author Candace Camp.

CASTLES IN THE AIR by Christina Dodd

The long-awaited, powerful sequel to the award-winning *Candle in the Window*. Lady Juliana of Moncestus swore that she would never again be forced under a man's power. So when the king promised her in marriage to Raymond of Avrache, Juliana was determined to resist. But had she met her match?

RAVEN IN AMBER by Patricia Simpson

A haunting contemporary love story by the author of *Whisper of Midnight*. Camille Avery arrives at the Nakalt Indian Reservation to visit a friend, only to find her missing. With the aid of handsome Kit Makinna, Camille becomes immersed in Nakalt life and discovers the shocking secret behind her friend's disappearance.

RETURNING by Susan Bowden

A provocative story of love and lies. From the Bohemian '60s to the staid '90s, *Returning* is an emotional roller-coaster ride of a story about a woman whose past comes back to haunt her when she must confront the daughter she gave up for adoption.

JOURNEY HOME by Susan Kay Law

Winner of the 1992 Golden Heart Award. Feisty Jessamyn Johnston was the only woman on the 1853 California wagon train who didn't respond to the charms of Tony Winchester. But as they battled the dangers of their journey, they learned how to trust each other and how to love.

KENTUCKY THUNDER by Clara Wimberly

Amidst the tumult of the Civil War and the rigid confines of a Shaker village, a Southern belle fought her own battle against a dashing Yankee—and against herself as she fell in love with him.

COMING NEXT MONTH

COMING UP ROSES by Catherine Anderson
From the bestselling author of the Comanche trilogy, comes a sensual historical romance. When Zach McGovern was injured in rescuing her daughter from an abandoned well, Kate Blakely nursed him back to health. Kate feared men, but Zach was different, and only buried secrets could prevent their future from coming up roses.

HOMEBODY by Louise Titchener
Bestselling author Louise Titchener pens a romantic thriller about a young woman who must battle the demons of her past, as well as the dangers she finds in her new apartment.

BAND OF GOLD by Zita Christian
The rush for gold in turn-of-the-century Alaska was nothing compared to the rush Aurelia Breighton felt when she met the man of her dreams. But then Aurelia discovered that it was not her he was after but her missing sister.

DANCING IN THE DARK by Susan P. Teklits
A tender and touching tale of two people who were thrown together by treachery and found unexpected love. A historical romance in the tradition of Constance O'Banyon.

CHANCE McCALL by Sharon Sala
Chance McCall knows that he has no right to love Jenny Tyler, the boss's daughter. With only his monthly paycheck and checkered past, he's no good for her, even though she thinks otherwise. But when an accident leaves Chance with no memory, he has no choice but to return to his past and find out why he dare not claim the woman he loves.

SWEET REVENGE by Jean Stribling
There was nothing better than sweet revenge when ex-union captain Adam McCormick unexpectedly captured his enemy's stepdaughter, Letitia Ramsey. But when Adam found himself falling in love with her, he had to decide if revenge is worth the sacrifice of love.

HIGHLAND LOVE SONG by Constance O'Banyon
Available in trade paperback! From the bestselling author of *Forever My Love*, a sweeping and mesmerizing story continues the DeWinter Legacy begun in *Song of the Nightingale*.

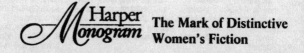

Harper Monogram   **The Mark of Distinctive Women's Fiction**